The Last Weekend

Hannah Begbie studied Art History at Cambridge University before working as a talent agent representing award-winning writers and comedians for more than a decade.

While developing her debut novel, *Mother*, she won the City University's Novel Studio Prize for New Writing. Published by HarperCollins in 2018, *Mother* went on to win the Romantic Novelists' Association Joan Hessayon Award for New Writing. It was Book of the Month on Mumsnet and a pick for Fern Britton's inaugural Book Club for Tesco. Hannah's second novel, *Blurred Lines*, was published in July 2020. It was a Clare Mackintosh Book Club pick and won *Woman & Home*'s prize for Best Psychological Drama of 2020.

Hannah is currently adapting *Mother* with Tom Edge and Clerkenwell Films as a television drama for the BBC and developing several comedy dramas with leading TV producers. She lives in London with her husband and their two sons.

The Last Weekend is Hannah's third novel.

www.hannahbegbie.com

@hannahbegbie
@hannahbegbie
/HannahBegbieAuthor

T0372166

ALSO BY HANNAH BEGBIE

Mother
Blurred Lines

The Last Weekend

Hannah Begbie

HarperCollins*Publishers*

HarperCollins*Publishers* Ltd
1 London Bridge Street
London SE1 9GF

www.harpercollins.co.uk

HarperCollins*Publishers*
Macken House, 39/40 Mayor Street Upper
Dublin 1, D01 C9W8, Ireland

First published by HarperCollins*Publishers* Ltd 2025
1

A catalogue record for this book is available from the British Library.

ISBN: 978-0-00-849902-0

Set in Sabon LT Std by HarperCollins*Publishers* India

Printed and bound in Great Britain by Clays Ltd, Elcograf S.p.A.

For my parents, Nigel and Jenifer,
with love and gratitude

You cannot swim for new horizons until you have courage to lose sight of the shore.

William Faulkner

Prologue

4.45 a.m. Bank Holiday Monday, 31 August
The water between Blue Bracken Island and Sandpiper Cottage

This is it, then. This is how I'm going to die.

She had hoped that an inelegant mess of breaststroke and doggy-paddle would keep her moving forward, at least enough to keep her head above the sulphurous estuary water. But the tide had turned on her and then she was going sideways. She was no longer timing her breaths against the chopping waves and everything tasted of salt. Briefly the swimmer trod water, wondering if there was time to turn back, but found that she was halfway between everywhere and so, to pass the time before she drowned, she swam forward again.

How long would the end of her life take? Seconds? Minutes? Once it was done, would she sink and be carried by the currents, her body trundling across the estuary mud out towards the open sea, or would she float face down on the surface like a bloated, dead whale? She hoped that she would float, like a message-in-a-bottle, because then her friends would have a chance of being saved.

Teenage drone enthusiast interviewed by the local news: 'I was flying my kit trying to get some footage of the cliffs and

1

then I saw something in the water and flew it closer to get a better look. Then I called the police, and that's how they found the other women.'

Would they know that she had thought that scenario through? Or would that annoying imaginary teenager get all the credit? That didn't seem at all fair, but it's not like she'd brought a waterproof pen and paper with her to lay out the multifaceted nature of her act of heroism, for the benefit of interested journalists.

Most likely she'd be a cautionary tale in the papers: *Stupid Woman Does Something Stupid and Dies Stupidly*. A yardstick of misery, spurring readers to reflect on how their too-tight jeans and five-week-long colds weren't so bad after all. Far worse than fearing you *look* like a crinkly plastic bag was being zipped into an actual one by the coastguards.

Did the coastguards do the zipping up, or did they leave that for the police? Did the police have their own boats? What if an amateur fisherman found her and never really got over it despite years of therapy spent elucidating why it wasn't his fault that he went fishing for mackerel but caught a dead woman instead, his hook snagging on her comfortable underwear?

None of this was fair.

Their Airbnb was highly rated and owned by a Superhost. It had cost a small fortune to rent. Surely you shouldn't be allowed to drown after paying all that money? On the website it had looked like the perfect backdrop for the perfect weekend: highlighter blue sky, tall violet flowers, Dorset's signature gorse and pine, sand dunes and seclusion and water that looked like it had absconded from the Med. Water to splash around in and admire over fancy Aperol-based drinks, not water to slap you around, flood your nose and eventually run away with your whole life.

How many others had managed to go on a short weekend holiday with good friends and survive, unscathed but for fried skin and a parched set of organs after four days drinking? Perhaps having shed some tears from the delicious catharsis of sharing all the stuff they'd been saving up for months to talk about? All the promotions, demotions, heartaches, plans, disappointments, hopes and new physical aches. How many others had managed to return home feeling the warm after-glow of time spent happy and laughing in the company of people they loved, yet also relieved to be back in their own space because a day longer might have been overkill?

Not them, it seemed.

It was unfair enough to make her want to survive the water. To cheat the local news of her humiliation. To spare the amateur fisherman those hours and hours of counselling.

So she kicked harder, and she moved, mostly sideways but also forwards, just a little, and that wasn't nothing, even though the distance was still impossible and any warmth in her body was disappearing, and everything else that was left in her was ebbing faster and faster, ebbing with the tide set on taking her.

Chapter 1

Annie

8 a.m. Tuesday, 30 April
London

On the first day of trying to get her best friends together, Annie had opted for an Easter egg as her job-done reward, made possible by her corner-shop holding a stock clearance sale that had also included luxury mince pies from the previous Christmas. Annie had chosen something huge and wrapped in red and gold foil, perfectly designed both for losing her temper and recovering it again. The smashing happened at eight, the egg was eaten by 8.30, and by nine, spiralling into a full-body sugar-crash, Annie needed a mince pie to even herself out, realizing that she might be about to become the world's first person to develop diabetes because of how rubbish her friends were at replying to messages.

It never used to be this hard. There had been a time when they couldn't meet quickly enough, holed up in the pub with pints and crisps within minutes of any one of them sending out the bat-signal. Now it was normal to wait days for a response and any number of further days to agree on a day they could all meet, and even then, that day would need to be changed at least twice because of work, children, house leakages, cars breaking, partners, partners leaking, children breaking and allegedly requiring A&E. Now, a whole year had gone by without the four of them being in the same room at the same time. That should have been impossible.

Annie understood, of course she did. Sometimes it had been her things that got in the way. But there was a difference between it being nice to see each other and it being *important*. The difficulty here was that while she knew it was important, they didn't, and it sort of had to stay that way if her plan was going to work.

Today she needed some urgent decisions on a date and a budget so she could make stuff happen.

She glanced up at her round-faced daughter, Em, who at only two years of age, had the same appraising and calm glance that her own mother used to have before telling Annie, *better get on with it then*. Em slammed a breadstick with her fist, sending shards of it shooting across the tray table of her highchair and onto the kitchen floor, reminding Annie of the time her mum had thrown a small frying pan at the wall and shouted *it's all too bloody much!* Would Em turn out to be endlessly calm, endlessly irate or the kind of person who occasionally threw pans and smashed Easter eggs with a bunched fist?

Annie shook off the thought and picked up her phone, dialling while she collected up pieces of breadstick.

'Wait, wait, wait, hold on,' said the bright voice on the other end of the line. 'Let me put you on FaceTime. I've cut all my hair off. Literally just now. You need to see this.'

Although looking at Suze's hair hadn't been on Annie's to-do list, Annie did immediately need to see it. Suze's long blonde tresses had been her trademark, along with her height, since they'd first met at university. In her head Annie bumped Em's morning schedule by three minutes and prepared herself.

'I'm not going to put my camera on,' Annie said, 'because I've got my hands full. But you go ahead, let's see the damage.' The truth was that Annie didn't want Suze to see her face, which was somehow managing to look both storm-cloud grey and sheet white through a combined lack of sleep and crying for four hours, none of which was relevant to Suze's haircut.

The haircut was a big change.

'It's great, though,' said Annie. 'Interesting.'

'I just realized it was going to keep on growing unless I stepped in.'

'An intervention.'

'I didn't even use a mirror.'

'You can't really tell.'

'I sort of want people to be able to tell I did it myself?' Suze looked away from the screen and tipped her head to the side like she was looking in a mirror beyond.

'No, sure, right. Maybe just tell them if they ask? You've done a great job. Now, did you get my email?'

Annie had thought that an email would allow everyone the chance to read and reply at their own pace, given their busy, leaky, work-heavy, children-riddled lives. The fact that she was now chasing it up less than twenty-four hours later was not lost on her. She'd laboured over almost every word, whittling it down to a pithy three-sentence missive that nobody, not even Claire, could claim was too long to read in one go.

She'd thought about what to call them, which she had

never thought about before. Hey, Girls? Hi, Guys? Yo, Babes? How's My Bitches? Dear Friends? My Loves? You Twats? None of them quite right, some too light, some too breezy, some too heavy. After serious analysis it turned out there wasn't a one-size-fits-all term of endearment suited to both the circumstances and the four women, so in the end she hadn't used one. They could always look at their name in the email address bit and decide for themselves what they were: mates, a pack of bitches, best beloveds – it didn't really matter. What possibly did matter, meaning that Annie left it in the email she'd eventually sent, was the way she'd signed off.

I love you, I miss you.

'It might have gone to your junk mail?' said Annie. 'Maybe it's gone to everyone's junk mail? The email, Suze? I sent it on Monday.'

'Monday, as in yesterday?'

Suze's face disappeared from the screen and Annie was treated to a twisting helter-skelter of whatever room Suze was in: a square cabinet, a rectangle of light, until the image came to a crashing halt on a Pantene shampoo bottle. Annie seemed to have been parked on the side of the bath.

'Yes. Yesterday.'

'That's not very long ago.' Suze's face appeared abruptly on screen again before she lifted the phone onto something near so she could both talk and do something with her hair. The result was that Annie felt like Suze's mirror. And therefore, like she only had a fraction of the attention she really needed.

'I know,' said Annie. 'But I was really hoping you'd reply.'

'Well, I probably will, but I'm not psychic. I can't just instinctively know when someone's emailed me.'

'Don't you get notifications?'

'I turned them off. They make me feel like I'm being nagged all the time.'

'But if you don't have notifications on then you need to check your inbox?'

'Jesus Christ, Annie, it's only Tuesday! You're sounding exactly like my mum whose entire week is built round when she walks down the road for a Terry's Chocolate Orange. Can you please turn your camera on so I can see you?'

'No. The point is that people have expectations.'

'I don't. I don't care if someone doesn't reply to me, or at least I don't lose sleep over it if they don't.'

'Could you read it now?'

'With you on the phone? How do I do that?'

'You can be on the phone and do other stuff at the same time.'

'Can you?'

'Yes. You're doing it now! You're styling your hair and giving me a tour of your bathroom.'

'How do I get email while I'm talking to you?'

'Now who's sounding like your mother?'

Em gave Annie a look that made very clear her feelings about further delays to her food being served.

'I have to give Em her breakfast,' said Annie. 'Maybe read it and call me back?'

'No, I think I've worked it out. Hang on. Oh my God!'

'What?'

'There are fifteen emails from Martin on how to prepare Walt for going to school. He's given each one a different subject line. There's *Making Friends* and *First Day Tears*. And wait, what's this: *Snacks and Props*? What is he on about, props? Oh, his toy monkey, Minky. For God's sake, don't we all have better things to do?'

'Suze, I do have to go now. Can you read it and call me back?'

'He's included statistics for how many kids cry on their first day.'

'How many is it?'

'Forty per cent during the school day, rising to seventy-three per cent by bedtime.'

'That sounds like a lot.'

'I can forward it to you if you like?'

'Em's only two, it can probably wait.'

'Yes, but you're going to need that info at some point and Martin would say you'd better get preparing now!'

'No, there's no . . .' Annie took a long, deep breath and swallowed the rest of her sentence. 'Look, the email basically says: can we all go away together? A week in Paris or Amsterdam. Cheap flights and an Airbnb, maybe in the next few weeks? Don't overthink it, just do it? I'll organize the whole thing, I just need everyone to say yes to a date.'

There was a silence. 'Cool! Sure. I'm into it.'

'OK, so I'll get on with it then?'

'I'm definitely into it, seriously I am, but does it have to be a whole week? It's just that I've got one month left to hand in my PhD and then I have to apply for more funding.'

'Four days?'

'I can't really afford anything, either.'

'Nor can I, but doing this matters. It could be a once-in-a-lifetime kind of thing. And if you spread the cost out over your whole lifetime it'll be, like, less than ten pence a day.'

'If the airline lets me send them seventy pence a week, then great, let's go for it.'

'Come on, Suze. You, me, Maura and Claire drinking sangria in a low-rent bar somewhere that's hard to say when you're pissed? We never do that anymore. You and me haven't even been to see Claire's new place yet. We've been rubbish. Even Maura's made more effort than us.'

There was another silence before Suze spoke. 'OK, OK. Look, if we can do four days or less, and it's not somewhere that forces me to sell a body part to pay for it, then I'm in.'

'Sell your hair?'

'Great idea. That'll kickstart things with a few quid. OK, OK, maybe Zagreb? Zagreb looks cool.'

'I'll look it up.'

'Great, thanks, love you, see you, gotta go.'

Annie slumped back.

Spring sunshine poured in through the windows, casting fingers of gold across the small dining table. Outside her front window the rush hour raged. That was the downside of having a sweet cottage painted in blue and white with a small balcony perfect for the summer months but positioned on the edge of the Westway, one of London's main arterial roads, its fumes forever leaking through her kitchen window.

She'd need to get herself and Em ready for the day, soon. Ready for a world she just wanted to hide from.

She collected up a small clothbound book from the dresser and scribbled some notes inside. *Suze. Deadline. Upcoming trip. Broke.* Then she secured it with a hairband one way, and then another the other way, so that the words wouldn't fall out.

When she dialled Claire, it rang out. But she knew it would.

In the last year she could count on one hand the number of actual phone calls they'd managed, but, in fairness, Claire had the youngest child of all of them, a one-year-old, and Annie understood all too well how little time you ended up having to yourself in that situation: that the days were too hectic to pick up the phone for a conversation and by the time the baby was down for the night the only thing you wanted to do was flop into bed with chocolate Mini Rolls and a sitcom. Annie suspected that Claire managed to fit in some additional sex too, but that was less relatable given that Em's father had left the country a few weeks after Em arrived in the world.

The point was that Annie understood the bone-deep exhaustion of meeting a small person's needs, and if Annie actually wanted to speak to Claire, she'd have to mimic their behaviour with the equivalent of a non-stop baby meltdown. That meant ringing her mobile and her house until Claire thought it was an emergency, which was a dick move, undoubtedly, and also what needed to happen. Annie dialled again. On the fourth try, Claire picked up, sounding gratifyingly worried about her.

'Everything OK?' Claire was slightly breathless, as if she'd just got in from running a 5K. Annie could hear the baby crying in the background.

'Yes, great,' said Annie. 'I was just calling about my email so that I can, you know, get on with it.'

'Graham's still not sleeping,' said Claire.

Annie blinked, because every time Claire said her baby's name Annie pictured a middle-aged man in a suit demanding to be breastfed, and that wasn't fair to baby Graham.

'You know I'm still breastfeeding?' Claire said pointedly.

Annie couldn't remember whether she knew this or not.

'And he's just not sleeping. Did I say that already? Karl won't cope if I go away at the moment. He's not taking the bottle.' This time Annie had visions of Karl mewling for Claire's milk. 'Every minute of the day he feeds. He doesn't like normal food. I should try and wean him, but I can't get round to working it out I'm . . . I'm so tired.'

'So just bring the baby.'

'Graham.'

'Graham, yes, and we'll all help. We'll help you and Graham.' Annie held her breath.

'I can't drag Graham around Paris. He's like a dog, so sensitive to smells; it would be so unsettling for him and then his sleep will get even worse. And besides, you don't want me getting my breasts out at the Louvre.'

'It's France. They'd *love* that.'

'I wouldn't.'

'Anyway, Suze can't afford Paris, so that's out. She was thinking Zagreb. I don't know where that is.'

'It's in Croatia. It's the capital.'

'Sounds fun.'

'It's just not a good time for me to be going away, Annie.'

Annie felt all her tightly held strings of control spin and tighten into a knot. 'Oh, come on, Claire, there's never a good time for anything!'

There was a heavy silence during which Claire would have been absorbing then deciding to ignore this outburst. Claire instinctively understood when someone wasn't their best self, never took it personally and was superb at letting it go. Annie had always loved her for it, but she loved her even more for it in that moment.

'What if . . .' Annie breathed in so hard her diaphragm ached. She knew she was going to regret what she was about to say. 'What if I found somewhere to accommodate us all? All the partners? And the kids?'

The husbands and partners were fine. There were even times when they could be more than fine, times that Annie almost warmed to their individual characteristics, but they were not people she had chosen. She'd chosen Suze. Claire. Maura. These were her best girlfriends, the godmothers to her only child. Two of their names were written into the back page of her new passport as her Emergency Contacts. Once upon a time it would have been her mother's name there, but her dementia had become so severe that she could no longer talk, which isn't much use if you're a foreign official trying to get help for the hapless foreigner they've been lumbered with.

'Come on!' Annie said. 'It'll be a chance for me to meet the baby.' She paused. 'I'm sorry I haven't been up to see him yet. You know what it's like.'

'It's still like that for me . . . And you know, I get it. Car seats are so tricky to fix.'

'Yeah, but I'm genuinely sorry.'

'It's my fault for moving outside the M25. And the renovations are making things extra hard.' Claire paused. 'Suze and Martin came for lunch the other day and Walt ended up standing on a beam in the loft conversion. I nearly died of the stress. Had to get him down by laying a trail of M&M's like he was a rabbit.'

'Do rabbits eat M&Ms?'

Annie continued chatting on autopilot, all the while wondering if Claire had invited Suze or Suze had just turned up. If Claire had invited her, why had Annie become second on the list? Why didn't Suze mention her visit when they spoke just now? And why hadn't they put anything on the WhatsApp group about it? The four of them always WhatsApped when they saw each other in smaller groups so that no one felt excluded. It wasn't a rule, but it might as well have been. Some things you were just supposed to know.

But then it's not like they'd ever been equal friends. Annie and Maura were the first to meet at university and they were *best friends* with each other. It wasn't a label that needed to be spoken aloud, nor was it a secret or a problem, it just *was*, an acknowledged baseline fact like the roundness of the world or the coldness of snow. And that was fine, because the group was dotted with known asymmetries. Claire also called Annie her *best friend*, all the while knowing that Annie and Maura were true best friends. And everyone knew that of the others it was Suze who was closest to Maura in spirit because Suze would never pine after the label *best friend*, which enabled her to be Maura's second-best friend without it being a problem. Even if they didn't all like each other precisely the same amount, they liked each other way more than they liked other people, and that was the point.

So why were Suze and Claire contravening the rules of engagement by meeting and not telling the rest of them about it? Was there some weird professional reason why Suze's current academic subject of interest was relevant to Karl's healthy fast-food business? Maybe Suze thought that sharing proof of Claire's *better life for our child in the clean air of the countryside* might stick in Annie's craw, given the Westway was currently suffering roadworks and an epidemic of related horn-tooting.

Maura, in an uncharacteristic display of energy, had

voluntarily popped down to see Claire but had been open about it, setting up a sub-WhatsApp group afterwards for just her, Annie and Suze called *Karl Chose Those Curtains* and dedicating it to detailing the story she'd been given for each of the pale pink sofas, white carpets, shiny beige curtains and the many scattered *objets*: tin flower-pots, blackboards and embroidered cushions with messages etched and stitched into them like *If gin isn't the answer, you've asked the wrong question* and *If my cat doesn't like you I probably won't either*. Surely Karl had been responsible for the cat cushion in the same way he'd been responsible for the decision to move Claire so far away from them? When did they even get a cat? Claire liked boho blankets, books and richly coloured threadbare kilims. Where had she *gone*?

We are arseholes, Suze had typed.

We only notice cos we love her, replied Annie.

No, im just an arshole, replied Maura, who had disabled auto-correct on principle, often typed with one thumb and seemed to take perverse pride in not correcting herself, ever. *Shes a rerm*, Maura had added, and neither Suze nor Annie had asked for a clarification, perhaps fearing that whatever it meant was going too far now.

Karl had a predilection for hosting 'kitchen suppers'. Karl once told Maura he had manifested a business plan for delivering protein-packed boiled eggs to your dog. If anything was wrong with Claire, it was Karl's fault and it was temporary.

'I have to go, Annie, Graham's fussing.'

'OK, but please, Claire. It would be really good for us all to spend some time together. It's been too long. And anyway, I think Maura needs to talk.'

15

'Maura always needs to talk. She's incapable of *not* talking.'

'Look,' said Annie, thinking quickly and speaking quietly so that Claire would have to press the receiver closer to her ear to hear. 'I need to tell you something. This is more than just a weekend away, Claire. The thing is . . . Maura is in trouble.'

'With the police?'

'She'd be thrilled if it was that. But no, I think it's her and Dex.'

'What? God. Really?' There was a pause. 'How bad is it?'

Annie should have stopped there, but she didn't. Lying about Maura and Dex wasn't great, especially given how plausible the lie was, but Claire would definitely understand why she'd done it, if the lie ever came out – so Annie decided it could use a small shove in the desired direction. 'I'd say it was bad.'

There was a rustle on the end of the line. 'So Dex won't be there, obviously. For this weekend thing. Even if the rest of us bring our partners?'

'No, he'll be there. And you can't say anything. But I thought you should know why you have to come, even if Graham's being difficult.'

'He's not difficult. He's a baby.'

'You know what I mean. The point is, we'll all be there so yes, please bring Karl. It'll be nice to see him. And the baby. Graham.'

'Fine,' said Claire. 'Fine. But it'll have to be next month.'

'Next month, OK, I'll make it work,' said Annie, before hanging up.

One to go. She was really pushing it now, approaching

a hard stop on her window to have these conversations. If she couldn't get Maura now it might be Day Four before Annie got this thing tied down, by which point Suze would probably be booked into a hairdresser in Mexico and Claire would have signed Graham up to an unmoveable schedule of academic studies and hobbies.

Getting Maura at the right time was a fine art. Her first window for premium communication was 7 a.m.–9 a.m., fuelled by coffee and the second window was 7 p.m.–9 p.m., fuelled by wine and a desire to burn it all to the ground. The hours in between were characterized by exhaustion, stress, raised voices and a stated need to be almost anywhere other than the kitchen, supermarket, bathroom, outside the school gates, on the way to the school gates, child's doctor or dental appointment, in the headmaster's office (and not for sexy reasons) or any extended period at the kitchen table where she undertook her day-job designing decals for nurseries. And especially not anywhere near or worshipping at the doors of a bloody fucking dishwasher.

Maura was essential. Essential to the trip. Essential to Annie's life.

Maura spent an amazing amount of time on WhatsApp, deeming it a good way of remaining in contact with the people who actually understood her, rather than her twins Alfie and Freddy and *Ego-Dex*, who all seemed to treat her like a walking hotel and vending machine. She didn't require a response to most of her messages, mostly sending observations, links to new shoes she wanted but could never afford, complaints about Dex, links to dresses she wanted but could never afford but amazingly could afford when she was much younger in a fucked-up twist she hadn't seen coming.

She also sent beautiful snapshots of things like a rubber glove on the tablecloth, or soap suds subsiding in a roasting tin – in other words, the aftermath of something she had either cooked or cleaned and that no one had praised her for.

Annie waited for Maura to be online and then sent a WhatsApp. *Can we chat about our weekend away?*

Maura went offline. Then she was recording a voice message.

Sending a voice message by way of a reply to a WhatsApp was an infuriating habit of Maura's, especially when Annie was overwhelmed with other things and just needed to talk in the old-fashioned way, with two people taking turns to speak in real time. Maura's voice notes had become longer and longer, becoming like mini podcasts, which was fine if you wanted something amusing to listen to while you unloaded a dishwasher but otherwise showed a complete disregard for the concept that the recipient might simply need to hear the point she would eventually get to.

The truth was, Annie saved almost all of Maura's voice notes, because she loved her.

Still waiting for Maura to finish, Annie wrote: *Did you get my email?* All the while wondering how, of all the incredibly difficult things Annie had been through in the last few weeks, it was triangulating her friends that was proving to be hardest of all.

After a few moments, Maura wrote: *Just sending a voms nit.*

Can we just talk instead?
Stp interuping.

Annie fed Em her breakfast and waited. Eventually she was able to press play on a completed voice note.

'Hi Spannie my gorge, my love, I was saving your email for a good time aka sitting on the sofa with two bottles of wine. No glass. Laugh emoji. But there hasn't been a single good time since you sent it for the usual reasons and so I'll read it in a second, after I send this to you, because by then I'll have called Dex a massive wanker – MASSIVE, just fucking ENORMOUS – and that feels so much better already. No, of course I love him, he just drives me crazy. Sorry, that was Alfie looking at me like I'm confessing to hiring a hitman to take his dad out which I haven't done yet but isn't the worst idea Alfie's had. Alfie, I'm teasing you, just do your bloody phonics and stop listening to my phone calls.'

Maura was recording another voice note as Annie listened to the first.

The fact Maura was furious with Dex was not unusual. Before she had the twins, Maura had been at her happiest with messy nights and new people, right boys and wrong things said, wrong boys and right things said, sticky situations and too much booze. She thrived on conflict and complications and in her teens and twenties had channelled all of it into her paintings which sold fairly well for a few years and got her a few *One to Watch Under 30 in the Art World* features. Since having the twins and giving up her own art in favour of something that paid the bills reliably, every frustration with family, with the art dealer that fired her, the state of the planet, the government, her mother and her fear of developing bingo wings had flowed through one vein only: Dex.

Recently, when Maura said she'd thrown a mug at Dex but hadn't hit him, Annie had voiced relief. But Maura's response had been simply that she worried her reflexes and aim were failing her.

Maura sent a follow-up WhatsApp: *I'll read your email now.*

In the meantime, Annie skipped through the second voice note, picking up the key points. Maura still seemed to be sparking with rage with the events from the previous week. Her mother had written a panicked email to the entire family professing her love and pride in them all when she thought she was about to die in an earthquake that struck her five-star hotel in Grenada and that turned out only to be a tremor. Her mother had then addressed the email to the entire family (including its most tedious member, *Fucking Beige Paul*) but left Maura off it by mistake. A few days later Dex had landed another exhibition and a magazine called *?Someday?* had profiled him as the most exciting artist working in acrylic under fifty.

Under 50?! Maura had written on their group WhatsApp. *Is that even a thing now? I thaght Under 30 was the bar? I though the fucker had missed all tht stuff and the bastead snakes in with an Under Soething article.*

At the end of that week Dex made a point of being unable to find his socks without Maura, which according to Maura was either his way of indicating he needed her, or him wishing he had a butler but only being able to afford a wife.

Annie recalled that during the same week, Maura had breezily mentioned that Dex was dealing with his artist's block on work for the current exhibition by making frequent trips to a local expensive nick-nack shop that sold slim pens he didn't need, returning with tales of the pretty shop assistant's smacked-up cat and yet another candle smelling of pointless things like woodsmoke and chocolate. When Maura said anything breezily, it usually meant it was anything but.

Annie's phone pinged again.

Paris for a week? YEES. And how are you? Is cleing fixed yet?

The ceiling was not yet fixed, but Annie was touched that Maura had remembered it. Maura's capacity to switch so violently from self-involvement to self-awareness, from narcissism to real empathy, was remarkable, like a broken lighthouse whose beam did not rotate fully and instead always swung fifteen degrees in one direction, and then back in the other. You never knew when and for how long it would get stuck on each setting, but the secret was to let it run until the beam switched, knowing that it would, eventually. All that was fine if you knew and understood this, and were patient enough to wait – which not everyone was – and provided you weren't the equivalent of a boat being tossed about by a storm in the middle of the night, which Annie was this week.

Annie thought about opening up her little blue book and noting down these nuances in her friends, all these shards of light and shade. She didn't want to forget all the good bits. But now Maura was ringing her.

'I'm in,' she said. 'Get me those sweet, sweet cocktails and slabs of pâté at sundown.'

'Mild change of plan. A few days in a cheaper European city. Like, um, like . . . Zagreb. With partners and children.'

There was a pause. 'Are you kidding me? My whole family mini-breaking together in Yugoslavia?'

'Yugoslavia doesn't exist anymore. Zagreb is in Croatia.'

'I don't do Geography any more than I do Crocs or batch-cooking. You know that. So don't even—'

'I didn't know where it was either till Claire told me.'

'Is this Claire's idea?'

'Suze wants to go to Zagreb. Claire is still breastfeeding Graham hence why we have to bring all the families.'

'I'm sorry but I'll fucking kill them all. The kids will be a nightmare and Yugoslavia's been through enough shit already, hasn't it?'

'I can get us a big place . . .'

'Like a stadium?' She paused. 'Are we honestly bringing partners? Martin and . . . and . . . Thingy?'

'Karl.'

Maura groaned. 'Dex will shoot himself.'

'Isn't that what you want?'

'It'll be a murder-suicide pact thing. He'll murder me for making him do it and *then* he'll kill himself.'

'He'll deal with it. We were thinking end of the month. In three weeks' time or something like that?'

'I can't. We can't. Dex has his *The Bitch* show coming up in August and only one of us gets to sit around wanking, drinking beer and calling themselves the public's answer to Monet in neon. Don't get me started. Apparently, he's working so hard at the moment he doesn't even have time to buy loo paper. And yet he has time to sit on the loo for nearly an hour using the paper some other fucker with a less interesting job, aka me, bought. Really, why did you get me started on this? Can you believe I used to be more successful than him? I could have *been* someone and—'

'What do you mean? You were . . . I mean you are someone. By which I mean you still could be.'

'Yeah, cheers, thanks a lot but can you name a single giraffe designed specifically for a nursery wall that has recently been under the hammer for ten grand? Or made the news? Or that's wanted by anyone over the age of five? No.

I didn't bloody think so. Make my own art? That's not going to happen until Dex does more to help around the house. I haven't even got time to watch TV.'

'No TV at all?' Maura usually knew everything there was to know about everything on television.

'All I'm saying is can we do it this summer instead? We'll come straight after the exhibition.'

'Can you come sooner and just . . . leave him?'

'I don't think we're there yet. And getting a divorce lawyer would be—'

'No, I mean, just leave him at home for the weekend.'

'But that would mean me bringing the kids and then I'd just spend the whole time breaking up fights and making snacks when I'd want to be getting blasted with you on Vodka Martinis. I'm sorry, but it's summer or bust for us.'

Was it too early in the morning to scream? Annie didn't want to frighten the motorists who were already stressed about the roadworks. And Em wouldn't like it either.

'Are you still there?' said Maura. 'Sorry, babe. At least if it's summer, Claire might have got round to weaning Gray-Gray so we can go clubbing for the night and find some TA's to flirt with?'

'Teaching assistants?'

'Territorial Army, Annie? Hot army personnel?'

'OK, OK,' said Annie. 'I'll talk to the others and we'll find a date and then I'll get booking. No problem. No problem at all.'

Annie spent the entire day at work playing catch-up after her series of frustrating morning phone calls. Late to drop Em at nursery, late for every meeting, late to collect Em from nursery. And just as she'd arrived home and was unzipping Em from her pram and dreaming of wine and TV, her phone rang with an unknown number on the display. She'd never have answered it normally but in the last few weeks, unknown numbers had taken on an importance, as if their anonymity gave them a special power to bear information that could change the course of her day, her week or more.

'Annie. Martin calling.'

Annie's heart sank. She'd need to find a way of curtailing this call quickly.

'Martin Bingham. Suze's boyfriend?' The voice went on.

'Yes, hello,' she said, trying to sound upbeat. Of course she knew who it was, she'd known from the moment she'd heard his ever so slightly nasal tones, even though she'd not had a phone call from him in two years. She didn't have his number stored because there'd never been a need to call him and any arrangement, like the one strained dinner party they'd all had together and never reprised, had been made through Suze. The man had the charisma of an accountant without a single hobby but perhaps that was because, of all the partners in her friends' lives, Annie knew him least. Suze complained less about Martin than Maura complained about Dex and praised him less than Claire praised Karl. There were times Annie wondered whether Suze spoke so little about Martin simply to make sure she, Annie, didn't feel like the only one without a partner. In any event, Annie had never understood the logic of Suze – the kind of person who inveigled her way backstage without a pass, over borders without a passport, onto white water rivers without a lifejacket and onto first class without having paid – having ended up with a man like Martin.

'I was just calling to say I think your idea for a weekend away is perfect. Suze just messaged to tell me.'

'Oh,' said Annie, her soul brightening. 'Thank you.'

She hadn't realized how much she'd needed this positive cheerleading after the uphill struggle that was getting them all on the same page, albeit a page that none of them knowingly knew they'd been put on.

'It's exactly what Suze needs. And I'm calling to offer my services.'

'Services?'

'Yes. Research. Booking. Cooking. You lot are so important to each other I want to do everything I can to help you spend a special time together. You keep me posted on your plans and I'll be sitting by the phone at the ready.'

The irony of Martin, being about as well known to her as a distant cousin, being the only one to actively call her about this important weekend, was not lost on her.

'Thanks, Martin, I really appreciate it.'

'By the way, my friend was stuck for an idea for his god-daughter's birthday and I recommended Big Family Fun dot com and he said it went down brilliantly.'

'Well, actually they're one of our competitors. Our site is Big Fun For Families dot com.'

'Oh God! I'm so sorry!'

'It's not your fault. My boss should have picked a better name.'

'Big Fun For Families. I'll get it right next time. You know what? I'm going to write it in the back of my diary. No more mistakes, Martin!'

'Honestly, it's a miracle anyone books packages with us. If you google "family" and "fun day" we're the 91st result you get on Google.'

'But you've still got a job! So you must be doing something right.'

'I have to go now, Martin.'

'Send me to-do lists for the big weekend. Anything and everything. Consider Martin on board.'

'I will. Thanks for calling.'

Annie hung up, leant down to kiss Em's warm cheek and was batted softly in the face with a ragged grey bunny.

'This is going to be fine,' Annie said, blinking back the sting of tears. So the four of them weren't going to toast the sun as it set behind the Eiffel Tower, or work things out over steak frites and wine until the bistro closed for the night. So she wasn't going to get the answer to her question in the next few weeks. Instead, she would have a few days somewhere on the English coast with her friends, their partners and children in a few months' time. The question of how to get her three best friends together – and alone for long enough to have a serious conversation – remained. But the point was that as long as she got them, it would be fine. It had to be fine. There was no other alternative other than for it all to be absolutely fine.

Chapter 2

Martin

6 p.m. Friday, 28 August
Sandpiper Cottage, Jurassic Coast, Dorset, UK

By early evening all the guests, apart from Annie, had arrived at Sandpiper Cottage on Dorset's Jurassic Coast. The temperature in the small kitchen-diner was absolutely tropical and the volume of chatter and children exceptionally intense on account of no one being able to locate the keys to the sliding deck doors and windows. Martin's neck tickled with the downward movement of fine sweat trails, and when he found his jaw aching with the effort of smiling (how else to participate in jokes about a history he did not share?) he decided to step outside for a breather.

But standing in the main arterial corridor, listening to the stuttering sounds of laughter about where the bloody-plastic-folder-guide-book thing could possibly be, Martin realized that no one had told him where he was going to sleep. Not inclined to assume anything, he plopped his large khaki stuff-sack outside the smallest room. Then, glancing back into the living room to check that Walt was happily ensconced with the twins (at four he was only a year younger, though he shadowed them like the fanboy of two teenage rock stars)

27

Martin stepped out of the front door into the direct glare of the evening sun.

Being the first to arrive, Martin and Walt had already taken two turns around the grounds and the place really was a looker: simple, sure, but the combination of moss-green roof and beige breeze-block walls co-ordinated perfectly with the creamy sand beaches, chalk cliffs and lush green surrounds of woodland (comprising a range of deciduous and coniferous trees). There were not one but two private beaches: one bordered by a chalky shallow cliff that could only be reached through the woodland and another at the front of the house looking out onto a wide expanse of estuary. The lodgings were unfussy but perfectly pleasant. With all bedrooms lined up dormitory-style along a corridor, polycotton linens, linoleum floors and bathrooms that had seen better days, it was a place designed for its guests to be having fun in the outdoors. And the nearby shed was chock-full of potential ways for having that fun from buckets and spades to paddleboards, kayak and a sweet little yellow rowboat. With opportunities to spot puffins and, more thrillingly perhaps, to find an old coin or something from the waterlogged remains of a 2000-year-old Iron Age log-boat that had been dredged off the bottom of the water next to neighbouring Blue Bracken Island in the Sixties, they certainly weren't going to be starved of things to do.

There was a village shop selling pies and a range of both normal and sourdough bread just twenty minutes down a long road that wiggled through the woodland. They really were marvellously cut off from other people, so cut off they apparently had their own microclimate so that the sun could be blasting away above them one minute while rain hammered down across the water the next. Or vice versa, he supposed. But fingers crossed, it had been a glorious summer thus far.

When he caught sight of Annie walking slowly up the drive toward him, he muttered the words, 'what a blessed relief,' realizing that of all the weekend's guests, she was the one he would feel most comfortable sharing a puffin-spotting kayak trip with – perhaps because, aside from Suze, she was the one he knew best, which was still to say *not very well at all*. He was under no illusion that she was the head of the octopus, the driving force behind this important bonding weekend, and he wanted to do everything he could to help her make it one to remember. He'd be lying if he said he didn't want to impress her . . . nevertheless he felt that she was most like him, by virtue of being a stoic and a misfit who'd had a tough time in the last few years. No doubt she referred to him as 'her friend's boyfriend', though he'd had a small but important role when the going got tough in Annie's life.

By 'tough' he meant the 'aftermath' of Annie having been abandoned by Canadian love-rat Ted mere weeks after a C-section, constant night feeding, mastitis and gastroenteritis. With the prospect of single parenthood looming over her like the Grim Reaper's scythe, and both her body and finances struggling, Martin had often envisaged himself as 'the outer skin of an onion' – his job, to make sure the home fires were burning so that Suze, the next layer of onion, could support Annie, the centre of the onion. All those friends, those brilliant friends, had done what they could to help Annie in the midst of such chaos: sitting with her, making endless tea and sandwiches and stews, sleeping over and taking the baby at dawn while she caught up on sleep and cried and bled and fed and wondered what she'd been thinking having a child with a man she'd been with less than a year whose name was, of all things, *Ted*.

On one occasion Martin had carried an almost box-fresh Em around the block in a baby carrier, hushing her to sleep while Suze had counselled a distraught Annie. On another occasion he'd even helped out 'at source', bringing Annie brownies and rearranging the beans and pulses in her kitchen cupboards as she sat and tried to feed Em while saying that her boobs felt like they were on fire. He'd left, feeling like his efforts were better than a poke in the eye, but nowhere near as good as if he'd been Suze who'd sadly had to work that afternoon.

'Hola!' he called out to Annie, trying to proffer a piece of cake but finding his arm constrained by the button-down shirt that was too tight around his throat and across his back. He'd stood nervously in the shade of the wardrobe's open doors that morning for around fifteen minutes as he cogitated over whether to camouflage himself or to stand out amidst a gang of exceptional people. Clearly he'd failed on both fronts because now he found himself sporting a neither-here-nor-there mix of office and caravan holiday style without having provided for the blistering airlessness of a heatwave.

Despite the fact that Annie was a hundred yards or so down the drive, bent over in a soft curve with the weight of several ginormous totes and her absolutely gorgeous pudding of a daughter, he could see her brow crinkle in confusion. He suddenly felt painfully aware of the place where the rolled-up bottoms of his denim cut-offs dug into the wider parts of his thighs like nauseatingly tight elastic bands.

'There you are!' He stepped out of the direct sunlight

and walked to meet her down the tree-lined shale driveway, wanting to help ease the weight she carried. 'Let me take Em, and then you can tuck into the Bakewell?'

Despite Annie's brand of comforting normality writ large in her wild, vertiginous hair, cheap 'n' cheerful flowery mum dress and exhausted demeanour, the lack of a warm and welcoming smile created a grind of nerves in Martin's abdomen. Was she annoyed that his list of holiday offerings, as outlined on the WhatsApp group some weeks back, wasn't enough? He wanted to tell her that he'd added more to the list since his last update, though he wouldn't tell her how much he'd struggled to carry the pre-scorched aubergines, pavlova and several sauces and joints that could be used as the basis for a meal, along with Walt and the bags, through Paddington Station. Suze had followed a few hours behind, coming straight from the British Library, so he'd borne it all single-handed, but with gladness.

Annie was a nice person, but she did seem irked. Was he radiating some sort of fundamental tedium? It made him glad that he'd asked Suze to keep schtum about the fact he'd recently lost his job, a fact that was certain to make him even less interesting than he already felt. She'd said people wouldn't mind but he wasn't so sure – and anyway, he would. He didn't want to be the only one without a purpose in a group of people who radiated *purpose*. Whether it was Dex with his paintings, Karl with his fast-health-food business, or Maura with her glamorous painter's past and Suze with her ground-breaking research, these people were visionaries, the kind who left legacies Martin could only dream of. Martin had nothing to offer them: no contacts, no especially good stories, not even a decisively coloured head of hair they could admire. He was clear-eyed about that much. He would have forgiven Suze's friends for questioning why on earth such a mousy, neutral *backdrop of a man* was in a relationship with a woman like Suze who was all elfin-cropped hair, widely spaced eyes, curious brain and height. And they'd be right to pose the question, but if there was one thing that he and Suze agreed on it was that her friends would never, ever know the answer.

'You don't need to take her,' said Annie, her brow glossed with sweat as she lowered Em to the ground and took hold of her hand to make the last few hundred yards on foot. Though they were shaded by trees, the sun seemed to pierce through every available gap, beaming both heat and bright light to make Martin squint and sweat. Perhaps Annie was just hot and irritable? Nervous, too – surely the price she paid for having the kind of popularity that enabled her to both instigate and confidently count on all her friends turning up for the weekend. She was probably wondering whether it would all go to plan.

'You mustn't worry about anything. Everyone's here,' he said brightly.

He was surprised to see such emotion in her eyes when she looked up at him, as though she might cry with surprise.

'Please let me help with your bags?' he said. 'I'm free as a bird.'

Then, without warning her, he reached for a bag only for Annie's arm to quiver, loosen and straighten so that everything she'd been holding slid off her like rings on a rail: bags, totes and blankets, a shopper that spilt apples and Tupperware and a leaking water bottle onto the drive. But it was the set of clear plastic folders and stapled sheets that she'd been holding

clamped under her arm that made her gasp when they came
fluttering down to land on the dusty shale. She dived for the
papers, collecting them up and grabbing them out of Martin's
hands as he tried to do the same.

'Oh, I am . . . so sorry . . . here,' he said, handing them over
to her and noticing that several had Em's full name written
on them in Sharpie.

She looked on the verge of tears again as she crammed
something that looked like a small blue prayer book into one
tote, folding all the papers in after it.

Martin was taken aback by her response, even more so
when she bashfully met his eye, wiped hair off her damp
brow and said, 'Sorry, Martin. Let's start again? I'm just . . .
it's been a long drive. The sat nav gave up down the long
country lanes, never thought I'd get here. Anyway, boring,
sorry. How are you?'

'God no, I . . . I'm good.'

'Do you know the code for the gate down there? I need to
open it so I can drive the car in.'

'Sure. It's 1234. If you give me the car keys, I can . . . Are
you OK?'

Her arm was shaking slightly as if it still held the weight of
several bags that were all now piled up on the path.

'Tired, just tired. Doing too much, you know?'

This time she allowed Martin to gather up all her stuff.

'Slight change to the schedule,' she said. 'Did Suze tell you
that I wrote to everyone last night saying I'd booked us into
a spa? Only for twenty-four hours. Tomorrow morning to
Sunday morning. My treat.'

'How amazingly generous! That's going to be one noisy
spa though! We're a big tribe, that's for sure.'

'God, no, I mean, no . . . It's just for me, Suze, Claire and Maura. Can you imagine how much it would cost if we all went? And even worse, for *Dex* at a spa? He'd be so bored and so vain and so weird. And the kids would trap themselves in a sauna. No way. Chaos. No. I'm afraid it's just the four of us.'

Martin tried to think of something to say in response but the words got stuck and jumbled at the back of his throat. 'God, no, great, quality time, good.'

'So,' said Annie. 'It will be an opportunity for you men to really . . . you know . . . talk. Get to, um . . . know each other.'

'God, no, great,' he said again, a bright smile plastered to his face, though his stomach and soul were on the floor. What on earth would he say and do with Karl and Dex during those twenty-four hours, other than sit and listen to them like they were a talk radio station, feeling both awkward and awful?

'Actually, Suze didn't mention it at all,' he said. 'But she's been so busy. It sounds like another stroke of Annie-genius, though. Maybe I could make a roast for the Sunday? Really make a full day of it before we head home on the Monday morning? Schedule a game of pétanque together in the afternoon? Kick off proceedings on your return with my brownies and a coffee? Elevenses, let's say?'

'Or thereabouts,' said Annie. 'Sure though. Sounds lovely. But Martin? Please make sure everyone chips in with the chores? I've not had time to update the meals and cleaning rota so the three of you will have to sort out who does what while we're away.'

'Roger that,' said Martin. 'Absolutely wonderful,' he said, with even more vigour, keen to avoid any sense that he was disappointed and full of dread about this last-minute change.

'Suze needs time with you all more than anything, just chilling, just relaxing and recovering. She's been broadening her research on psychotropic drugs . . . you'll know more than I do.'

'No, I . . .'

'Well, having an application accepted for a fully funded research trip to Peru doesn't just fall into anyone's lap, does it? She put months of work into it.'

'Yes, wow. I'm sure . . . Peru? Six months? I didn't . . . When is she going?'

'Soon,' Martin said, registering the blunt shock on Annie's face. Was she shocked because it was news or shocked that it was so soon and for so long?

'OK . . . good. We'll have to catch up very thoroughly at the spa, then. Obviously Claire's worried about the mattresses being crap, and Maura hates the fact they don't serve alcohol and Suze doesn't like being told to relax by anyone, but the point isn't the beds or lack of alcohol—'

'No,' he said. 'It's time spent together, isn't it?'

She looked at him. 'Yes. Yes it is. Actually, Martin. I wonder . . . could you?'

'Could I look after . . .'

'Em? No. Karl's doing that . . .'

Martin tried to hide his disappointment: looking after Em would have given him something to do that was useful, so he didn't have to sit like a lemon between Karl and Dex.

'What I was going to say is: would you mind giving Karl a hand? Claire says he's much more engaged with toddlers than babies but . . .'

'No, sure, of course. I'll be his assistant? Of course!'

Martin suddenly felt very tired. It might well have been

the long journey with all the buses and trains and broken air conditioning followed by Walt puking into Martin's baseball cap while he balanced the pavlova in the other hand as the taxi ran rodeo over the rocky path to the house. But mostly it was the prospect of being in the company of those two illustrious men without Suze to temper it.

Annie stumbled and righted herself quickly. 'I obviously need a good night's sleep . . . Beautiful round here,' she said, as they reached the house. 'Quite cut off, though.' She nodded toward the house. 'I bet Maura hates it.'

'But there's so much to do vis à vis water sports, though it's worth noting there have always been terrible tidal pathways here,' he said, 'that cause boats to sink if you don't know your stuff and the very literal remains of a . . . Annie?'

But Annie had come to a halt and was staring at the cars parked on the shale.

'They really are all here,' she said, as if to herself. 'Now for the hard part.'

Chapter 3

Annie

6 p.m. Friday, 28 August
Sandpiper Cottage

'Oh sodding shit.'

Annie's first reaction, muttered under her breath, when she'd seen Martin ambling toward her wearing a kooky combination of office and ill-fitting beachwear, was uncharitable. Arriving at the bottom of the driveway and being unable to get the car through the gate had triggered in her a fresh wave of nerves about the weekend. She'd needed a few moments to get a handle on her sticky and repetitive thoughts, not least the tiring journey which had been hot due to the car's ill-functioning air-con, and stressful due to a huge tailback from a horrific accident she refused to look at and could only hear the aftermath of in the disembodied form of sirens.

But, as she stepped past Martin to stand at the threshold to the kitchen, her sandals kicked off, hot feet cooling on the tiles, watching the circus of adults and children navigate the tight space, she breathed deeply, allowing herself a moment of believing things would work out. Here she was, and here they were. Her favourite women in the world.

'Annie!' Maura shouted at the top of her voice, barrelling towards her at speed. She pressed her own glass of bright orange cocktail into Annie's hand, gathering her into such a strong embrace against her soft, summer-warm body, that Annie had to catch her breath.

'I am so fucking relieved you're here,' Maura slurred into her ear, breath sweet with Aperol and the Mango vape she had recently started sucking on to wean herself off the ten-a-day habit that had started out as the occasional single secret stress-cigarette habit.

'Spannie!' sang Suze, bounding across the kitchen, not waiting for Maura's hug to end before she threw herself around them both, all long bones and linen, spiced perfume and day-long heatwave sweat. In the background someone shouted that they'd finally found the bloody key to the sliding doors so they wouldn't all boil to death in there.

Annie stepped back and gave Maura and Suze a smile, feeling the prickle of happy tears in her eyes. She glanced into the room to see Dex skulking by the glass sliding doors, absorbed in a phone call. He glanced up briefly, perhaps in greeting though it was always hard to tell exactly what Dex's cool, unmoving yet beautiful features were communicating. Karl and Claire hovered nearby, passing their baby back and forth between them like a hot potato, looking absolutely exhausted. Claire gave Annie a weak smile and held up a hand to indicate she'd be over in a minute. Martin hovered behind Annie, holding her bags like a loyal assistant and chatting about where to put everything so no one tripped and ended up in Accident and Emergency on the first night.

The noise was deafening as boxes and bags were explained, unpacked and manoeuvred into different cupboards, drinks were poured and spilled and refilled, and four children and a baby who'd recently been set free from hours trapped in a hot car or train wailed and ran laps round the kitchen and through the open doors onto the deck and back again. The air smelt of the sea, someone's awful soapy aftershave and the low, queasy rot of an unclean fridge. Maura's guttural, deep-throated laugh rippled through the room, punctuated only by her shouting 'Get off the phone!' in the direction of Dex and a series of 'heys!' and 'ois!' at Freddy and Alfie: her five-year-old, mostly identical, twins who now seemed to be stripping down to their pants and doing what they could to create jeopardy with a couple of bamboo canes.

Maura sucked on her vape. 'I think Karl's about to invite Dex down to see his meat get made in the artificial meat plant because apparently the shapes and the colours are unlike anything you've seen before and might inspire a new idea for a painting.'

'Please let Dex not be a dick about it!' laughed Suze sarcastically and Maura thumped her on the arm.

'Fuuuck, that's loud,' said Suze, at the sound of a series of repetitive snaps as one of the twins – Annie suspected Alfie because of two energetic twins Maura said he was the more energetic – repeatedly slammed at the tiled floor with his bamboo cane. This seemed to be one stimulus too much for baby Graham, who sent his cries higher and louder, which in turn seemed to encourage Em and Walt to start shouting something indecipherable at the tops of their voices, too.

Annie was about to suggest the kids go outside and be really noisy when Martin joined the three women, smiling broadly, taking Suze gently by her arm and handing her a beer.

'Isn't this fabulous?' he said. 'It's like a merry bunch of

cats out on the rooftops for a right royal knees-up. They're getting on like an absolute *palace* on fire.'

For a few moments they all watched Walt following Alfie and Freddy with intense and adoring eyes.

Suze looked at Martin with a dilute smile and swigged her beer. 'Yeah, it's sweet.'

'They're going to grow up in one big network of support and love if they keep on seeing each other like this. How precious. Like cousins. One of life's great adventures.'

'One of them, sure,' said Suze, an iron edge to her voice that made Annie's spine tingle. 'I might try and calm Walt down now so I can put him to bed soon. Can I borrow your iPad, Maura?'

'Good idea,' said Martin.

'I'll grab it for you,' said Maura. 'I'm going to do the same with mine. Get them to bed so I can drink with abandon. I'll just finish this,' she said, shaking a full glass from side to side and draining half of it. 'Hey, Dex,' she shouted over the noise. 'Can you bloody help me with these kids? You're on holiday. Family time. Remember? Let's get some Weetabix into them and get them stashed.'

But Dex hadn't heard, or pretended not to hear, so instead Maura rifled through an enormous tote the size of a binbag to search for an iPad, all the while telling them that feeding and putting the two kids to bed was a military operation requiring as many hands on deck as possible so was it any wonder her life was a shitshow when Dex couldn't be bothered to help. Karl, managing to look fresh and pressed in pink chino shorts and white short-sleeved shirt despite what must also have been a hot and long journey, had been distracted by the children and was following them around with the baby in one arm and a box of Trivial Pursuit, adult version, in the other, insisting that it was about time to mellow-down.

Claire still hadn't said hello to Annie and yet she was now talking to Dex by the sliding doors, her tired paleness now pixelated with patches of pink flush. She crossed her arms and glanced coyly down at her feet, laughing, as Dex, his face now more dynamic with smiles than Annie had ever seen, seemed to be doing the same.

'Oi! You two!' said Maura, calling over, causing them to look up in tandem and violently pulling them out of a shared moment.

They wandered over together, Claire collecting Karl on the way, holding on tight to his hand.

'Hi, Annie,' Claire said quietly, her face back to its pallid stillness, eyes wide with a hunted expression. She looked thinner than when Annie had last seen her and less strong, though her hug wasn't so much weak as non-committal.

Alfie arrived in the circle of adults, craning his neck up to look at Karl and shouldering his bamboo cane perilously close to Claire's face. 'Are you Dull Karl?' he said.

Maura scattered hard machine-gun laughter into the air. 'Gah! Bloody hell! Kids!' she spat hysterically. 'The things they say! Where did you get that from, soldier?'

'If dull means "lives in the suburbs", then that's me!' said Karl gamely, a tense smile playing at his lips.

'I'm sure it's not quite that!' said Maura, looking gratefully in Karl's direction. '*Superb Karl* is what we call you in our house. *Brilliant Karl of the ground-breaking broccoli burger!*'

Everyone knew Maura had over-egged the pudding, including Maura herself, and tension hung heavy in the air.

Annie scratched at her hairline and glanced at Claire whose eyebrows were raised in shocked disbelief.

'You know what?' Claire said. 'I need to get Graham down to sleep.' As if it was the break she'd been looking for. 'Where are our bedrooms?'

'Yeah, of course. We should talk about rooms.' Annie hadn't thought about sleeping arrangements because time asleep hadn't felt as pressing as time spent awake with these people. 'Er, Martin? You were the first here, did you see anywhere you'd like to sleep?'

'Don't worry about me,' said Martin, piling Tupperware into a tower. 'I'll honestly sleep anywhere because I sleep like the dead. I'll take a camp bed, a roll mat, the floor of the shed.'

'You won't need to do that. There are plenty of beds.' Annie glanced over at Suze. 'Why don't you and Suze go in the double at the end?'

Another crack sounded out – hollower, louder and cleaner than before – turning all eyes to the centre of the room. A large, grass-green ceramic vase that had been standing proudly on a low coffee table now lay sideways in three separate pieces in the pale shadow of Freddy and a raised bamboo cane. Annie closed her eyes in disbelief and at the sheer inevitability of something or someone getting broken.

'Shitting hell, Freddy!' hissed Maura, grabbing not one but both of her children under her arms like a tigress with her cubs.

'Fuck sake,' snapped Dex. 'I thought you said we were getting these kids to bed, Maura?'

'I bloody asked you to help,' hissed Maura under her breath.

Martin winked at a shocked Freddy and said, 'It's all right, happens to the best of us.' And Annie found herself catching Martin's eye in a blink-and-you'd-miss-it moment of recognition from her bag-collapse earlier, remembering how assiduous and kind he'd been when she'd been feeling anything but.

'I'm sorry, mate,' said Dex, glaring at Martin. 'But it bloody doesn't happen to the best of us. It happens to those of us who weren't looking at what they were doing with their bamboo canes.'

'I'm sorry, Spans,' said Maura, sweating under the weight of her children.

Martin walked over and put a calming hand on Maura's shoulder. 'It's all right. Bit of superglue will fix that. And a dash of gold paint for good measure. They call it the Japanese art of kintsugi.'

'What's that?' said Annie quickly, because it sounded like the kind of thing Maura would refer to as bullshit that she didn't have time for, and she was already looking stressed.

'It's when you fit the pieces of a broken object back together and highlight the cracks with gold paint. It reminds you that breakages are part of the history of things, symbolizing acceptance, healing and resilience in the face of adversity.' Martin's eyes positively shone with pleasure at his own explanation.

'It symbolizes a sodding bill,' snapped Dex, glaring at his sons. 'And kids that are completely out of control.'

A shiver ran through Annie. She wondered if Dex had any idea of how his brittle behaviour played and if Maura had become immune to the effects of their bickering on other people. She wondered whether it was just the booze that blunted Maura's responses, whether any of it bothered the kids. She made a mental note to write it all down in her notebook later. She wasn't judging. Except that she was. Because it was important.

Suze sidled up to her. 'About Martin and I sleeping at the end of the corridor. Can you just . . . change that? I don't want to sleep in the same room as him. I'm exhausted and he's up and down all night needing the loo.'

Up and down? Martin had told them all that he slept like the dead.

'Really? Does it matter for a few—?'

'Yes, it matters,' said Suze.

'Fine,' said Annie quietly. 'Change of plan, everyone! Because the taxi is coming early I think us women should all sleep in the two twin rooms tonight? Me, Em and Claire in one. Suze and Maura in the other. Martin can take the box room at the end with Walt, while Karl and Dex can take the two doubles with their respective children.'

'I don't know,' said Claire. 'I'm weaning Graham. Our last planned night feed is tonight so—'

'Won't it do both of you some good if you're in a different room from each other?' said Annie. 'He won't smell the milk that way. You can probably just pop in when he cries?'

'Come on, Claire. It'll be like a sleepover,' enthused Suze. 'And when did we last do that?'

'And you can sleep where you want on Sunday night,' said Annie, wanting both of them to be happy and because by then none of this would matter.

Claire looked doubtful.

'The cab's coming at six in the morning,' said Annie. 'This way we won't wake everyone else up.'

Suze mouthed, 'Thank you,' to Annie.

'You bloody what?' shouted Maura. 'Why *that* early?'

'Because it was a last-minute booking and the massages are early doors,' said Annie. It was the lesser of two evils at the cheapest spa she could find, the first evil being the lack of alcohol. She hadn't been able to bring herself to tell Maura about the early morning, too. Maura was a demon without enough sleep and they all knew it.

'You can sleep in and come later,' said Suze.

'Fine,' said Maura.

'No,' said Annie, stridently. 'We are going together and staying together and coming back together.'

'Ah, sounds so cute,' said Karl. *Cute?* 'Go on, Claire-Bear, me and Gray will be fine. If there's a problem, I'll come and get you. It'll be good practice for tomorrow night when you're away.'

Claire didn't say anything, because Claire wasn't one to make a fuss about anything much, least of all when she was outnumbered.

'Personally, I won't be going to bed at all tonight,' declared Maura. 'I'll be drinking all the whisky sours I won't get to drink at the organ-harvesting spa. So honestly, those that don't want to bunk can join me in getting wasted on the beach.'

'You need to sleep,' said Annie. 'Please get some sleep?'

'All right, Mum,' said Maura.

'I'm going to lie down now,' said Claire. 'It will settle Graham. It's a new place and he hasn't been sleeping and he didn't sleep in the car, or much last night, or much the night before that actually and he probably senses that tonight is our last night.' Claire's voice cracked a little and she shielded her face with her hand, scratching her hairline.

Maura's beam snapped quickly onto Claire. 'Sit down, Claire, and have another drink. You cannot go to bed like one of the five-year-olds. Karl can stash Graham in his cot, can't you, Karl?'

Claire glanced at Karl, raising her eyebrows. 'It's OK, actually I—'

Karl lifted his arms in a quasi-yawn to reveal the under-sleeves of his chalk white T-shirt and himself to be the perpetrator of the overpoweringly soapy aftershave that was making Annie's stomach turn and her head ache.

'Fine with me,' he yawned. 'I just do what I'm told.'

'You what?' said Maura, splashing a few fingers of gin into a glass the size of a cantaloupe melon and passing it to Claire like she might bloody need it. 'You just do *what*?'

Oh God. Annie knew where this was going. 'Where's all that novelty gin you said you were bringing?' she said to Maura, taking her by the arm and leading her in the opposite direction.

'I didn't just double up on the Hendrick's – cucumber and juniper – I tripled up and only bloody brought *moutard* flavour. That is mustard flavour to you and I,' she said, giving a wicked smile, now thoroughly distracted from the Karl line of questioning.

'Come on,' said Dex to Maura and the twins. 'We really have to get these clowns settled before they firebomb the place.' Then, Dex gave Annie a knowing glance. Perhaps he too had picked up on the incipient spark in Maura's eyes.

Annie stood by as Claire gave instructions to Karl about Graham, wanting her to get on with it so there was less chance of Maura returning and questioning Karl.

'His bunny's in the red bag,' Claire said. 'And there's a clean milk bottle in the straw bag which you'll need to fill with milk.'

'Aye, aye, Captain,' said Karl, glancing around the room to find Maura, presumably to show his eager compliance before she snapped his arms off. He awkwardly prised a tearful Graham from Claire's arms and, after a minor struggle, opted to hold Graham under his soapy underarm as if he was a strapless man-bag. Graham collapsed into tears, probably out of discomfort, and Karl turned back. 'Sorry, which bottle in which bag? Oh, babes, I think he misses Mummy and might need a Mummy kiss. And while I've got you, maybe you should just check out the set-up in the room re: the blackout blinds?' Annie couldn't fault the man for being thorough.

Claire looked resigned.

'It's OK,' said Martin, jumping in. 'Karl, mate, why don't I grab that stuff from the car, then you can change the nappy plus the milk, etcetera, while I put up the cot and check the blinds?'

'Thanks,' said Karl, looking grateful. 'I would appreciate that. I'm not match-fit re: . . . You know. Babies.'

As they all got themselves together, gathering up bags and bottles a new soundtrack played in the background: Maura and Dex screaming at each other down the end of the corridor. The sound sent waves of pain through Annie. She wanted to tear out the pages of her blue notebook and cry.

Chapter 4

Annie

8 p.m. Friday, 28 August
Sandpiper Cottage

Em had fallen asleep in Annie's single bed without a problem, so while the rest of them got their children to bed and their stuff unpacked, Annie took herself off to the deck at the front of the house. She sat at a wrought iron table, surrounded by wide-brimmed plants, looking out onto Blue Bracken Island in the far distance and the silvered trails of speed boats enjoying the last rays of a setting sun.

In a parallel universe this piece of time would have been a carefree loose end when she might have helped her friends put their kids to bed by reading them a story, hanging out with Maura at the hob while they mixed cocktails or walking up the driveway with Claire, admiring the view and just chatting about stuff, normal stuff, in the moments before everyone gathered together again. But all that felt a world away from how she felt. Hollowed out with exhaustion, and distanced from the people she loved most.

She'd approached the peripheries of a conversation between the three men, wondering if talking with people she didn't know as well might force her into a different frame of mind, but she'd reversed quickly and quietly, leaving them to discuss where the barbecue ought ideally to be stationed: by the sea for the simultaneous enjoyment of the view, near the kitchen fire extinguisher for health and safety, on the actual deck though the smoke might sting their eyes and impede their enjoyment of the view or, by far the most sensible plan in Annie's opinion, they ditch the barbecue and cook everything in the oven so no one lost their mind with hunger.

She couldn't spend the whole weekend recovering from bursts of normality by removing herself. She needed to talk to her friends sooner rather than later but would it feel better or worse? Would it be like ripping off a plaster or just covering her wound in salt? Besides, there didn't seem to be a natural space for what she needed to tell them: the air was thick with tension and errant energy, not least Claire's downright *ghostliness*. She realized she'd been naïve to expect them not to pack up their worries in their suitcases, like rocks amongst their sun cream and shorts. She was guilty of packing a boulder in amidst her own pants and T-shirts.

She could hear Maura, Claire and Suze gathering at the back of the house, just a few feet away, so she stood up decisively, her stomach knotting, and set out to find the space to talk to them.

Annie couldn't help but smile when she arrived at the back of the house, interrupting Maura mid-flow.

'You look like the front cover of the Boden summer catalogue,' Annie laughed.

Showered and changed into bright whites and a host of rainbow colours, without kids and husbands in tow, her friends had taken on a new lightness. They sat perched on and around the dry-stone wall under a bamboo arch twined with shell pink roses against a backdrop of thick pine trees. The air smelt of honey and moss and salt.

'Boden? I'd rather advertise a hip, independent New York based clothing label,' said Maura.

Despite the claggy heat of the early evening Annie caught Claire covering her beige T-shirt with her cardigan, a T-shirt Annie knew was from Boden because she had the same one.

'You're such a fashion snob, Maura,' said Annie, smiling good-humouredly and winking at Claire.

Maura climbed onto the wall, gathering up Lucozade-coloured swags of silk from her skirt at the same time as trying to hold two glasses of something in one hand, the contents of which were splashing down her front in long, dark streaks as she spoke. Her hair tipped down in tangled tangerine trails alongside the neon pink flash of a bra strap and over a washed-out old Ramones T-shirt that slouched off one shoulder. Her eyes were smudged and her cheeks flushed. She looked gloriously, messily, beautifully herself.

Claire moved along the wall in elegant and brisk movements, like a starling, plucking up glasses and towels and kids toys. She wore frayed pale denim shorts and her light brown hair was pulled back into a loose ponytail tied with a neon yellow scrunchie. Annie had never seen Claire wear colour in her hair before, least of all neon.

Suze was lying on her back with her legs resting against the pebble dash wall of the house, wearing an oversized primary green T-shirt, black cigarette pants rucked up to show a chain round her ankle lined with white shells, spikes of blonde hair sticking up like the Statue of Liberty's crown.

'As I was saying,' continued Maura, 'we're all in the King's Arms and one of the school mums, Carlotta, says *So, Maura, are we going back to yours again?* She's a TV producer. Works in arts docs? Wants to go out like *all the time.* And then Si gives me one of those *looks* because the last time they all came back to mine after the pub it got a bit, you know, *dirty-flirty*, between me and Si when Sade came on the Alexa.'

'How are you even having these soirees?' said Annie. 'I thought you didn't have time to watch TV?'

'A girl needs to let off steam once in a while! As I was saying, Carlotta is like . . .'

Even when she was at her worst, in a fearsome tear-stained fury, Maura was fancied by a lot of the men, and also women, who met her. On first meeting they would experience the force of her: a woman who had everything a little bit more than, or a little bit less than, other people. A voice that was slightly lower than normal, breasts and lips and hips that were just that bit bigger, an outright laugh that was a little louder, a chuckle that was a little more joyful, comments and views that were a few degrees left of what anyone else would ever dream of saying. Her constitution was stronger: she needed less sleep and more chocolate. On Maura, badly applied make-up made her look better, not worse.

Annie smiled her best smile. 'Can I just take this opportunity to interrupt you and say—'

Suze jumped to her feet and threw her arms round Annie. 'Oh, I have missed you and your speeches!' She held on to Annie so tight that Annie had to swallow and close her eyes to push back the tears.

Annie was the last to let go and when she finally did, she said 'It's not a speech, it's just really to say—'

'That you've made more cocktails!' shouted Maura. 'And that you were right, that this was a lovely thing to do and that we're all difficult, lazy bastards, apart from Claire who has the most legit excuse not to travel, but that it was worth the ten and a half thousand WhatsApps in the last few months, because you fucking love us?'

Annie smiled and turned to Claire who seemed more absorbed in tidying up around them, collecting toys and towels, than what was being said. Annie wanted Claire to know that she'd been grateful for the suggestion that Karl look after Em while they go to the spa. She'd agreed to it because she'd wanted Claire to feel invested in the weekend. But she would never tell Claire that she'd brought Martin in as back-up and assistant because Karl didn't seem to have that much common sense when it came to kids, a hunch that had been corroborated when Annie had seen him proffer a box of adult Trivial Pursuit as a way of calming down five-year-olds.

'Claire? Will you come and sit down?' said Annie. 'Can I get you anything? I know you're tired.'

Claire stopped what she was doing and looked at Annie, eyes wide. 'I just want to, you know, finish this tidying? Then I should get to bed soon as we've eaten.' She spoke quietly, as though she didn't quite have the energy to get the words out. Annie watched her as she collected up a full glass of cocktail, holding it close to her chest, a bright pink sippy cup hanging loosely off the finger of her other hand, a sad gaze resolutely fixed on toenails painted a standard holiday red.

'So,' said Annie, girding herself to speak, goose bumps on her arm despite the warm summer heat, hairline prickling with sweat.

'Martin wants to do this again next year,' said Suze.

'Already?' said Claire, looking up. 'But we haven't even got through this one yet!'

'Maybe try harder to make it all sound less like a chore?' said Maura. 'What else were you going to do this weekend? Play cricket on the village green?'

'Ha ha!' said Claire, though her eyes strained. 'It's not big enough for a game of cricket.'

'I'm up for another one of these weekends next year. Anything for a holiday. Next spring?' asked Maura.

'I don't know,' said Annie.

'I'll probably be travelling,' said Suze.

'Good to see you all brought the party spirit,' said Maura. 'What we need is to get back to my story and that *look* that Si gave me. You can tell, can't you,' she said in the warm and conspiratorial tone she adopted when it was just them, the friends, when she sensed that rumples needed to be ironed, 'when someone looks at you. In that way, I mean? You can tell if there's a spark, it's like a firework going off in your—'

'Yes,' said Claire quickly, picking up a bowl of crisps at Maura's feet and pushing the two glasses Maura was drinking from close to the wall so nothing got knocked over. Maura had a tendency to gesticulate.

Maura pulled something invisible off her painted mouth and then positioned an unlit cigarette between her lips. 'Just a matter of time with Si.'

'Keep it down,' said Suze. 'All the windows are open to the house. Dex'll hear?'

'Let him,' said Maura belligerently.

'You wouldn't do anything, would you?' said Suze.

'I might,' said Maura.

'She wouldn't,' said Annie, looking reproachfully at Suze. 'So don't encourage her.'

Annie noted that Claire was pushing a leaf around with her big toe. Something more than exhaustion was bothering Claire. Tired Claire always laughed along at a joke, always had something to add, even if it was occasionally to repeat what someone had just said.

'I don't get it,' said Suze. 'You and Dex have so much sex. I don't get why you'd chase a middle-aged school dad?'

'Well, for a start, more people have affairs than you think. Parents anchored down by the early years of childcare probably wanting to break free a bit.'

'And?'

'And also, Si looks about twenty-four.'

'And?'

'He's chasing me.'

'There's my answer!' said Suze.

'It's nothing to do with my ego,' said Maura defensively.

'Never said it was.' Suze winked at Annie in a *here-we-go* kind of way.

'Not everything is to do with me.'

'Nope, definitely not,' said Suze. 'In fact, I'd say almost nothing is.'

A shadow passed over Maura's face. 'I suppose I want to know that I still have value. Off the shelf . . . if you know what I mean?'

'What, like a can of baked beans?' asked Suze.

'Like a quality box of truffles,' retorted Maura. 'Anyway, Dex saw the way I was dancing with Si.'

'What did he do?'

'Nothing. He just made sure that I heard him flirt loudly

with his gallery assistant on the phone the next day. The same gallery assistant he always flirts with. So you see, he's doing it, too. Checking his value.'

'It's like price wars between you,' said Suze.

The sippy cup slipped off Claire's finger, the rounded lid falling open, liquid pooling over the paving stones and around her scarlet painted toes.

Maura rifled chaotically around in her huge bubble-gum pink quilted tote bag, gold chain swinging off its edges, and pulled out a sherbet pink table napkin. 'There, babe,' she said, handing it to Claire.

'Can I just . . . I need to tell you . . .' said Annie.

'There's my bloody lighter!' Maura said enthusiastically, head still partly submerged in her handbag.

'I thought you'd ditched the fags,' said Annie.

'Desperate times call for desperate measures. My handbag used to smell of Marlboro Lights and Chanel Number 5, now it stinks of Haribo.'

'Could be worse,' said Claire. 'Could smell like the inside of someone else's lunchbox.'

'Not yours,' said Maura. 'Seriously, when exactly did you last eat? Is that why you're so quiet? Because you're only just surviving on fresh country air?' Her tone wasn't unfriendly but it wasn't friendly either. 'Did you have lunch?'

'I don't know, I can't remember.'

'How anyone could forget when they last ate is beyond me. Food is how I measure what time of day it is and how long it is until I get to have a little drinky.'

'Everyone loses a bit running around after kids . . .'

'Not everyone,' said Maura good-naturedly, pulling up her Ramones T-shirt and rolling her belly like a belly dancer.

'You know what?' Then she pulled down her skirt in front of Claire, kicked it to the side and wobbled her thighs. 'Check out these bad boys.'

'Jesus,' said Claire, smiling, and Annie allowed herself to breathe out a little, 'I can see your bush fighting its way out of your pants.'

'Good luck to it. This pant elastic is tight as a drum nowadays. Nothing is escaping that,' she said, pinging it against her skin. 'You know what I think, Claire?' Maura paused as she lit her cigarette. 'I think you're thin because you live in the Home Counties.'

Claire gave a tight smile. 'What do you mean by that?'

Maura was travelling faster than originally thought to one of her *unique places*. She looked up at Claire. 'Just all that walking the dog in a field, or whatever.'

'I don't have a dog, Maura,' said Claire calmly. 'I have two Siamese cats.'

'I wonder what the Peruvian air will do to me?' said Suze quickly.

'I wonder,' said Maura, knocking back her drink. 'Presumably get you high. Which is what always happens when you travel into international airspace. Just me and Annie in the fatty-city air then, fattying about amidst the pollution, eh, Spannie?'

'Not strictly true!' said Suze. 'Don't forget Si the School Dad.'

Annie really needed to talk to them but not like this. It was time for the secret weapon intended to unite them all with the power of the past.

'Hey, look at this!' said Annie, pulling a battered printed hardback from her bag and opening its pages. Their graduation yearbook. The four of them huddled together in a photograph on page 7: Maura, all black eyeliner and white bleached hair, Claire in a woollen V-neck, hair scraped into a ponytail, Suze in a short kaftan and Annie, more puffed round the face than she was now, in tartan trousers and an oversized T-shirt. They'd been into indie rock and cider and laughter and boys and cigarettes, preferably all at the same time.

They laughed and gasped in delight. Claire seemed especially animated to be transported back to the past. 'I snogged that bloke Dev Whatshisname that night. That was all I'd ever hoped for. Where was I supposed to go after that? That was my biggest dream.'

'Look at you, Spannie! Don't you still wear tartan trousers?' laughed Maura.

'Only at cocktail parties,' laughed Annie. 'Anyway Maura, do you remember you nearly ended up at A&E that night? You were very close to needing your stomach pumped after all that cider.'

'And Suze missed the train to her grandma's funeral the next day, trying to break into Downing Street,' said Claire.

'Wow,' said Maura sadly. 'I look so, so different.'

'We all do!' said Annie. 'Suze wouldn't wear a kaftan now, I'm much fatter there, you don't have blonde hair and Claire looks like an adult now.'

'That's not it,' said Maura slowly. 'I looked so full of *hope* and *vitality* then.'

'Vitality?' sneered Suze, playfully pinching her. 'What are you, ninety?'

'About four years after that picture was taken, I conquered the British art scene for about ten minutes,' said Maura ruefully.

'Come on, Maudlin Maura, you need another drink,' said Suze.

'You still look nice,' said Claire. 'You had nice clothes then and you have nice clothes now. Look at me. I was chubby and seemed to think I should scrape my hair back until I looked bald.'

'Don't be silly. We were eighteen and drinking loads. We didn't have the good judgement we have now,' Annie said, trying to make Claire feel better. 'I showed Karl this picture earlier and he said *there's my girl*. And Dex looked over our shoulders and said: *Claire's got better with age. She's much prettier now.*'

As soon as Annie said it, she regretted it because Maura's face dropped.

'He said that?' Maura shifted uncomfortably, Ramones T-shirt still hitched up.

There was a loud clatter as the metal crisp bowl that Claire had assiduously lined up against the wall went flying across the paving, coming to land next to Maura's discarded skirt. If it had been an accident, Maura would have picked up the bowl, but she didn't and instead no one did anything except breathe in, like they always did when Maura was coiling up like a spring.

Chapter 5

Martin

8 p.m. Friday, 28 August
Sandpiper Cottage

After the kids had been fed, bathed and put to bed, the women declared they were *going for an explore*, in a tone that strongly indicated they did not want to be followed. Martin and the men found themselves hovering about the kitchen island, scavenging for conversation and snacks. As Martin wove in and out of Dex and Karl's meaty frames to gather olives and hummus from the fridge – he had suggested he barbecue the dinner but Annie was keen that the rota be followed to a T – he noticed anew the extent to which he was on the backfoot physically speaking.

Martin was, so far as men were both short and tall, on the shorter side of short. Dex, while being mid-height, was both dense and broad while Karl was taller and narrower, like the leg of a drainpipe jean. The two of them would probably displace the same amount of water in a science experiment while Martin would displace roughly half. Dex and Karl's colouring and physical looks, however, had minimal overlap. Dex was all hazel eyes and white blond hair – attractive in the way the sibling of an A-list movie-star might be – and

Karl, despite his ink-black hair, glassy blue eyes and café crème skin, hailing from a country Martin felt keenly he should know yet wondering whether he had ever been told and simultaneously feeling guilty that he had never asked, was a few hottie-points behind that.

Martin found himself involuntarily smoothing down his shirt, rucking up his shorts and flattening the mousy-coloured, wispy pieces of hair around his crown that didn't play ball at the best of times, least of all in claggy humidity – as if all that might raise him half a percentage point in the direction of Dex and Karl's benchmark. And yet he didn't want to get too mentally caught up in aesthetic issues because on balance, things were going reasonably well with no humiliations to speak of, only some terse words from the Dex and Maura camp about the fine Japanese art of *kintsugi* which Martin felt fairly sure was borne of the stress, heat and familial noise.

As he wiped down surfaces and laid out a smorgasbord of deli-goods, Martin decided that he would unofficially make the kitchen his domain as it was a good way of contributing positively to the weekend while keeping an essentially low profile. He'd been delighted when the gang had decided to use yet another set of fresh glasses for another type of cocktail because at this rate the dishwasher would be at full tilt without a break all weekend, meaning there would always be somewhere to escape to.

'Do you do much weightlifting, mate?' asked Karl, his gaze landing on Martin's skinny forearms as he slid a tray of hot, pastry-based canapés out of the oven.

'I bench-press Walt from bed to bath which must be a few kilos!' he replied.

But his riposte fell flat.

'You'd be surprised at how lifting weights can change your life,' Karl continued. 'I suppose I feel that physical and mental and professional health go hand in hand. Wouldn't you say, Dex, mate?'

But Dex was communing with his phone, vape and Bluetooth headset all at once and didn't reply. Martin's body tensed like a plank on Karl's behalf.

'Should I take the ladies a plate of sausage rolls?' asked Martin, looking for an excuse to step out of the kitchen.

'I wouldn't,' said Karl. 'Not unless you want to interrupt a conversation they'll be having about you. Or us. I'd leave them to it.'

Dex took his headphones out, sat down at the kitchen table and leant forward on his shapely forearms. 'Anyone else get completely duped about this weekend?' His tone was resonant and considered, like treacle falling slowly from the lips of its tin. He buffed his iPhone screen with the edge of his nice T-shirt. 'Is a Friday to a Monday actually a long weekend? She'd have been more honest if she'd said we were going away for half a week. Or a quarter of a month. Or 1/48th of an entire bloody year, whatever the bloody maths is.'

By *she*, Martin presumed he meant his wife, Maura.

'No, the maths are mostly right I think, give or take some decimals,' said Martin, and Dex glanced back at him with an unreadable expression which made his stomach twinge.

'It's not so bad, is it, mate!' said Karl, in a way that didn't expect an answer, his voice a tone higher, but still imbued with a rich depth of manliness and authority Martin could never hope to reach. 'Setting the world to rights with Mr Martin and I,' added Karl, sliding children's toys around the table like he was in *The Matrix*. Karl had changed outfits since he'd arrived and was wearing tight cycling shorts under a pair of looser, shorter, shorts, and a pink polo shirt with the collar popped. There was talk he'd already been for a run and used some hand weights.

Dex looked more interested in watching Karl line up crayons on the table in no particular order.

'Actually, Dex,' said Karl abruptly, 'I think you'll have something to say about this topic, being of the stature that you are. Martin was asking me earlier how it was I found my purpose in life and I was saying that it's to do with how effectively you can tap into the collective human psyche. So if Martin wants to think big—'

'Yeah, what work are you doing at the moment, mate?' said Dex, turning to Martin. 'Don't think I've heard Maura mention what you do for a living.'

Martin swallowed. 'Oops, hold on.' He swallowed a second time. 'Sorry, I've a bolus of olives and snacks stuck in my—' He swallowed a third time, still hoping the short interlude would be enough to distract Dex from his line of questioning. But no. Dex was still looking at him with his icy, beautiful eyes.

'Just university admin stuff. Nothing glam!' said Martin, in the shortest and sweetest manner he could summon.

'So what I was saying to Marty,' said Karl, still looking at Dex. 'Is if he really wants to get excited by his work, aka use his work to change the world, then he should start from a place of thinking about what people *need*. For example, if people are going to insist on bloody dying all the time, what do they, and their poor families, *need*? How do you make money from the death industry? Indulge me here because this is the important bit . . . Now, you don't want to be the coffin bearer because that's being a company man – and whoever hit the big time being that? So what you do, is *think big*. Isn't that right, Dex? Open up an old folks' home. Or even better, an undertakers! An embalming business. A place that makes coffins. Or even just the brass handles. I'm spit-balling here. In summary: identify a universal *need*, marry it with your passion, then boom! A rich and healthy business is born.'

'Sure,' said Martin. 'I can see how that would work if you're passionate about death.'

'Hmm,' said Dex, as if he was still digesting what Karl had said. 'No one *needs* my paintings. They just *want* them.'

Karl looked at him quizzically, then laughed and said, 'No, sure, mate, of course: that's why you're in art and I'm in business.'

'Art *is* business,' said Dex baldly.

A silence fell and Martin supposed that one of the upsides to a lack of success was that you didn't get your head cut off in a clash of the Titans.

Alfie wandered into the kitchen, hair ruffled, head bowed. 'I can't sleep. I'm too hungry.'

'Get back to bed, Alfie, mate,' said Dex, his spine straightening, jaw tightening. 'Everyone else's kids have managed it.'

'Can't sleep,' the boy said.

'So you said. Christ, get to bed!' Dex hooked his hands into his belt so his thumbs fell in a V, neatly pointing to his willy. Martin hated the fact that he knew Dex's willy hung at a forty-five degree angle but Maura had told Suze and Suze had told him and sometimes it was hard to concentrate on what Dex was saying given what he knew about his odd biological secret which, on the upside, could sometimes take the edge off how nervous Martin felt in his presence.

'I'm not tired and my bed's not comfortable and I didn't have enough dinner,' said Alfie.

'It's a new place, maybe he's a bit unsettled?' said Martin.

A shadow passed over Dex's face as he got up and grasped Alfie's hand to usher him back down the corridor toward bed.

Karl was rearranging the crayons into a rainbow when they both heard Dex shouting down the corridor. Martin plucked a banana from the fruit bowl and followed the noise.

Halfway down the corridor, outside the bathroom, Dex loomed over his son, a handful of the boy's pyjama sleeve bunched in his hand. 'Don't ever fucking talk to me like that again! Apologize.'

Martin hadn't heard what Alfie had said or done to merit how frightening Dex looked. He just saw the pale fear on the child's face. It was late, everyone was tired and hungry. Martin could see that. And so he cleared his throat, loud enough to be heard.

Dex spun round. 'What do *you* want?'

Though Martin was a little shocked by Dex's vehemence, he walked tentatively down the corridor to where the two were standing. He was not looking at Dex when he spoke, but at the boy, who in that moment was his priority.

'Come with me, Alfs,' he said, leaning past Dex to offer his hand to the boy.

Alfie took his hand and Martin led him back to the kitchen, Dex following behind like a storm cloud.

Once they were standing by the kitchen island, Martin said to the boy, 'Watch this.'

Martin had all their attention as he theatrically dropped pieces of bread, one by one, into an enormous, seemingly endless *eight-slot* toaster.

'Watch this,' Martin said again, as if they hadn't all heard the first time. They sat transfixed, waiting, until around forty-seven seconds later, Martin clicked his fingers in the air with a flourish at the very moment the bread popped up, toasty brown.

Alfie cheered, all the cheekiness of the evening's cane-escapades, all the pale exhaustion and fear suddenly replaced with sunshine and awe.

Martin felt chemical sparks of delight dance through his body.

'Are you magic?' said Alfie.

'Ha ha! No, no, just regular old Martin!'

'There you are, mate!' Karl laughed. 'You don't need to open up a funeral home! Just get yourself a caravan and a funny hat and you'll be the area's top travelling kids' entertainer in no time! Amazing!'

Martin's heart swelled. Perhaps there'd be room to expand his remit from the kitchen if things carried on going so well? He buttered up the magic slice of toast for Alfie, swiftly peeled and chopped the banana over the top and presented it to the boy on a plate. 'There you go, sailor, magic sleep food.'

The men watched in silence as Alfie scoffed the toast in record time. It was only when the child had skipped off to bed that Martin broke into a warm smile, pure satisfaction bubbling up from a deep sense of having *nailed it*.

But when Martin looked up, he saw that Dex had an odd spark in his eyes, as if he were stuck between settings. There was a flash of something deep and emotional and rich, like he was close to tears, and a narrowing of the eyes that managed to make him seem both hot with rage and stony cold with something else Martin could not put his finger on.

It sent a chill through him.

'It's all right—' Martin started.

'Happens to the best of us?' snapped Dex. 'Is that what you were going to say?'

'No, look, I understand. Every parent loses their rag. I'm not judging, Dex. Alfie's happy, pressure's off you, I get to be a magician for a minute. Everyone's a winner?'

But Dex just stared at him, hand wrapped around his wrist, knuckles glinting white, as Martin felt the fragile structure of his confidence in the weekend shake. Martin stepped back and caught his ankle sharply on a skirting board before turning round and walking quickly back down the corridor, a shaming foolhardiness racing through his blood for thinking he could promote himself so quickly and readily from kitchen duties.

Chapter 6

Annie

Annie shoved the yearbook back into her bag and swore never to bring it out again. Maura's clenched and uneasy response to Dex's praise of Claire had sent a thick and thunderous storm cloud over all of them.

'Mau?' said Annie, looking down at where Maura's skirt lay miserably like a deflated life-ring. 'Are you going to get dressed?'

Maura was fidgeting with the hem of her T-shirt and looking appraisingly at Claire's smooth and elegantly crossed legs. 'We're all baring our best bits so maybe I will, too.' She then proceeded to tear her Ramones T-shirt over her head in one swift move to reveal her cream-white carafe-shaped torso.

The whole exchange sent further jolts of concern through Annie's bones. Maura was no stranger to stripping off: she had never tried to hide any part of herself behind a towel as she changed in a shared dorm or hotel room, or danced in a field. She was completely at ease with her body and its imperfections, which made them all feel the same about their own when they were in each other's company. It's just that this display wasn't *that* kind of nakedness. It wasn't collective nakedness born of ease and solidarity. Maura's current nakedness was symptomatic, oppositional and, Annie feared, weaponized. Nevertheless, Maura walking around naked and unpredictable with booze, while everyone else including the men was fully clothed, would be humiliating for her in the cold light of a sober tomorrow.

'Get dressed, we need to eat,' said Annie.

Maura ignored her. 'In fact, I don't need this either,' she said, stopping suddenly and unhooking her bra – allowing her pendulous breasts with their characterful giant areolas, which they all knew Dex and Maura had named Samson and Delilah, to tip out. She brought to mind any number of pre-Raphaelite paintings Annie had seen on her mother's old fridge magnets.

'Maura,' Annie tried again, walking toward her slowly, holding out a big beach towel in both hands, like she was a bullfighter.

'Listen, Sister Annie, I'll take my bloody pants off too if you keep trying to hide me away.'

Then Maura was swiping for something on her phone and batting Annie away. 'A little bit of dubstep,' she said, starting to dance on the deck in her pants, one arm in the air, head leaning against it as if it was a pole, feet fixed to the ground, gently bouncing on her knees in time to the beat.

Claire glanced urgently over at Annie to *please do something*.

'Looking good!' whooped Suze.

Suze didn't possess a radar for consequence in the way that Annie or Claire did. She was hashtag blessed with the advantage of living in the present: joyful and unexpected and deeply unhelpful during moments like this.

'Stop encouraging her,' Claire hissed. But neither Maura nor Suze heard.

'Join me?' sang Maura.

'I can't,' said Suze. 'Gotta think about dinner. I'm on the rota.'

Think about it? 'Yeah, come on,' said Annie, gritting her teeth, 'let's get inside and help Suze make dinner else we'll die of starvation and alcohol poisoning.'

'Nope,' said Maura.

'I'll do the dins,' said Martin, stepping out of the sliding patio doors. But no sooner had he clocked Maura than he shielded his eyes. 'Oops, sorry.'

'Come on, Marty, dance with me!' said Maura.

Martin gave a game and blushing wiggle on the spot, before walking backwards into the house, palm over his eyes, saying things about last-minute hot hors d'oeuvres.

Moments later, Dex and Karl came out of the house. Annie wanted to shield her eyes in the way she had when she'd driven past a car crash on the way up there.

Karl had his head turned to Dex, mid-conversation. 'When you really boil down the meat of it to the chicken bones underneath, what I was trying to communicate to Martin was the notion of *find something you love and you'll never work a day in your life.*'

Maura let out a raucous laugh. 'That's so true. And in your case, Dex, I would just add that you'll never cook or vacuum or raise your children, either.'

Dex's face was impossible to read but Annie saw a mix of admiration and shame, the slow absorption and assessment of Maura's nakedness and wild eyes.

Claire looked pleadingly at Annie again but Annie felt as though every impulse in her was slowing down. Shock, overwhelm, exhaustion, something else . . . She didn't know anymore.

'What you doing, Mau?' said Dex, with a still-jawed calm.

'About to go for a swim,' she replied, wiggling her hips and saluting him. 'Karl, you'll come for a swim, won't you?'

'Oooh, I'll definitely come for a swim,' said Karl, tearing off his pop-collared shirt. '*Skinny-dippy evening swimmy* doesn't happen in our parts!'

'Do I look better than I did when we were nineteen, Dex?' said Maura, tipping her head to one side.

'What?' said Dex.

'Maura . . .' started Annie. But she stopped, realizing that to say something to Maura now would be like trying to catch a firework halfway to the clouds.

'Do you think you should put your baps away?' said Dex. 'I mean they sort of . . . it's a bit of fun . . . but they're for private viewing. Karl, mate, can you pick your jaw up off the floor? Maura, you've had too much to drink.'

'Don't tell me what I've had too much of! Where's Annie?' said Maura.

'I'm right here,' Annie said, emerging slowly from her position at the edges of the pampas grass.

'Come for a swim with me, babe?'

'Yeah, come on, Annie!' said Karl.

'You know I don't,' said Annie, tensing a little at Maura's insensitivity and the ensuing silence.

'You should learn,' said Dex, addressing Annie, his gaze still fixed on Maura. 'It's an essential skill to have.'

'Annie used to swim for her county,' said Suze defensively. 'So she can swim.'

'I just don't,' said Annie.

'She's got trauma, Dex,' said Maura, gaze fixed on her husband. 'A bit like being married to you.'

'Can you just . . . not?' Annie resented her history being used in their psychodrama. She'd never told her friends the truth about why she was afraid of the water. And it was too late now. She'd lied instead, saying that when she was nine a baby shark had bitten her toes as she swam in the French Mediterranean. Nothing too bad, but enough to leave a shoelace of blood trailing in the water behind her, and to have a few people on the beach come to her aid. Annie had made the story small enough with big enough details that her friends had believed it.

'Dex, you're my *trauma*,' Maura said. 'Come on, Trauma, come for a swim! Karl's game.'

After a long and tortuous pause, and while still holding her gaze, Dex dropped his shorts. All Annie could think was *Oh for God's sake, please stop there*, relieved he had remembered to put underwear on that morning. She did not need to see his forty-five degree circus trick.

'Come on then, darlin',' he said, in a tone that was challenging and flirtatious, that managed to be both icy and warm.

Maura looked at Dex, then took Karl by the hand.

Claire stepped forward quickly and spoke breathlessly. 'Karl, actually, can you just pop and check we brought all the baby porridge and snacks in from the car so you know where things are tomorrow morning? You have to hit the ground running with breakfast else Graham will kick off, and—'

Karl pulled his hands away from Maura, putting his palms up as if weighing both options.

'No, come for a swim!' insisted Maura.

'Oops,' Karl said, leaning backwards, like he was dodging the crossfire. 'I just do as I'm told.'

A shadow passed over Maura's face. Annie wanted the ground to open up and swallow her. Or maybe Karl. To protect him from what he had unwittingly walked into for a second time.

'Here we go again,' said Maura. 'The man runs his own business and yet he has to be told what to do when it comes to the kids. Like he's some kind of ape.'

'Maura, stop,' hissed Annie.

'It's not rocket science, Karl. Kids aren't magically operated by women alone. You can chime in.'

'Of course he can chime in,' said Claire, her mouth moving, but her face frozen. 'He doesn't have to because he works all day and I'm at home with Graham.'

'Totally,' said Karl. 'Graham is much happier with Claire. He cries when he's with me. He's like *who is this clown?* Probably because up until now Claire has been giving him the breast and to be honest if someone was doing that for me, they'd probably be my number one.'

'I didn't need that image in my head,' groaned Suze quietly.

'Well that's very nice,' said Maura through gritted teeth. 'A clean arrangement,' she said primly. 'Ours is messier than that, isn't it, Dex?' But she didn't wait for his reply. 'Ours is chaos. Kids. The neighbours' kids. Snacks, dinner, more snacks. A minute after I've finished clearing up the neighbours' snacks, it's time for Dex to come down from his white-painted studio to declare that he's here to eat, but that he'll be returning there to do more work. Only then he decides to ask a mate round without telling me what he's doing. So the vodka comes out of the freezer and the mate turns up and they sit round the kitchen table, which also happens to be my only space to work. So they drink vodka and eat Doritos while I try and put the kids to bed upstairs. When I come back down to the kitchen there's drum and bass playing too loudly for Mrs Johnson next door and there's hummus in my work-computer keyboard: so that's my work ended for the night. It's no wonder I'm still working on the jungle animal range. Too much hummus in my keyboard to move on to the zoo. I'm dying to design a fucking gorilla for a nursery wall.'

'Not enough space, not enough tables, not enough time and too much hummus for Maura ever to have been a *player*,' said Dex tiredly.

'Mainly not enough support from you,' said Maura, scowling blackly back at him and looking like she might say something deal-breaking and awful, but stopping herself at the last minute.

'It sounds very lively *round your yard*!' said Karl in a faux Cockney accent which Annie assumed was sweetly designed to dispel the tension.

'Sure. I guess it is lively,' said Maura, turning her gaze to Karl again. 'I'm definitely not filling up the Volvo with coolant every Sunday night, mowing the lawn at 10 a.m. on a Saturday and snapping the lights off at 9 p.m. after a detective drama.'

'My God!' said Karl. 'That is, like, *exactly* our life!'

Claire glowered at Maura.

'We could totally do with shaking things up, babe,' Karl said, turning to Claire. 'Have a few more friends round once in a while. People definitely don't put vodka in the freezer round our way. It's a standard old boring wooden cupboard for my voddy.'

73

'Maura, shall we call it a night?' said Dex.

'Let's go to bed, Karl,' said Claire, looking at her husband with pain in her eyes.

'No!' shouted Annie, so loud that everyone turned to look at her. 'No one is going to bed. Maura, stop being a dick. Apologize to Karl.'

Maura looked up suddenly, like Annie's words had snapped her out of a reverie. Then she looked at Karl, her eyes softening, contrite. 'I'm sorry, Karl. I've had a lot to drink—'

'Claire, why don't you come swimming with us, too? Double date?' said Dex.

'Claire is good at many things but swimming isn't one of them,' said Karl.

'Claire hates swimming,' said Maura.

'I don't mind it, actually . . .' said Claire, sounding annoyed.

'Go on, Claire!' insisted Dex.

'Lay off!' said Maura sharply. 'She doesn't bloody want to.'

Annie observed Karl wedged between Dex and Maura, now wearing nothing but his smalls and socks and, inexplicably, still his leather deck shoes. Annie felt her brow knit in confusion. What possessed Karl to continue standing there? Surely he should have stepped away several minutes ago?

'You know what? Sod it,' said Claire, as she started to undress.

Maura stopped swaying her hips and then Annie saw it all: the despair in Maura as she watched her husband glance hungrily at Claire peeling off her clothes to reveal a concave stomach, the smooth lines of her bra and the waistband of her denim shorts sitting on neat hips. Nothing dug or spilled over or bulged. Claire looked so slim and Annie could not deny it: amazing. Annie hoped Karl had been distracted enough by untangling the knot in his leather deck shoes to miss the way Dex had looked at his wife.

'On second thoughts, I'm going for a swim, but not here. And not like this,' said Claire, resolute, perhaps even a little angry.

'I'll come with you,' said Dex.

'Stay where you are,' said Maura. 'You can't go swimming. You should check on the boys. They'll still be awake, they always are. They never bloody sleep when they should, probably because they're waiting for the day you'll actually spend some time with them.'

Suze whistled through her teeth.

Dex looked over at Maura, a cloud passing over his eyes. 'What the fuck, Maura?'

Then he turned on his heel and followed Claire off the beach.

At that very moment the dubstep track came to a halt and Annie wanted to scream 'stop' at them all.

Both the light and temperature seemed to have dropped at speed, and with it Maura's transformation from sexy siren to hunched, naked mum standing on the deck in her pants. She looked stricken, ashamed and full of rage, her arms wrapped round herself, standing next to her friend's husband doing the same in his tartan boxers and socks, looking to her for guidance on whether they were going to go for an awkward swim à deux, or not.

Then Maura leant down and picked up an empty French beer bottle left there by Dex or Karl, and hurled it at a tree. It bounced off but shattered and splintered like a firework on the crazy-paving path below, exploding into the surrounding bushes. Annie took off her own cardigan and walked quickly toward Maura, wrapping it round her quivering shoulders. Maura clung onto Annie.

Martin appeared a few moments after the sound of breaking glass.

'Nobody move!' he said, clapping his hands. 'I'll sort it! I know *exactly* where the dustpan is.'

But it was going to take more than Martin's Japanese art of kintsugi to fix the hairline fractures that were creeping out toward the edges.

Chapter 7

Annie

9.30 p.m. Friday, 28 August
Sandpiper Cottage

On a dry-stone wall facing the water, Maura sat with Annie on one side, and Suze on the other. No one said anything as the last of the light disappeared.

Maura, dressed again in her skirt and T-shirt, with Annie's cardigan loosely draped over her shoulders, bowed her head as if contemplating bad news. Her left wrist was bound loosely with sky-blue thread bracelets and chains, each of her fingers and thumbs decorated with a ring, specks of black nail polish making each fingernail look like a tiny map of the world.

'Maura?' Annie said eventually, squeezing Maura's hand then letting go to stretch and un-stretch her calf muscle on the shale. 'Are you ready to . . .'

'Swim?' said Suze mischievously, jumping up to refill their glasses from a fresh jug of neon-orange cocktail and ice cubes.

Annie raised her eyebrows at Suze. 'I was going to say *talk*. Maura, are you ready to talk?'

But Maura held up her hand and said nothing.

'Is Claire OK?' said Annie, because she wanted to shift

the beam in Maura's mind and because she wanted to know whether it was just her who was experiencing Claire's pale and preoccupied ghostliness. Claire had barely looked at her since they'd arrived and the only time she'd seen Claire smile was when she'd been talking to Dex in the kitchen earlier that day.

'I think she's fine,' said Suze idly. 'Tired, probably. The baby.'

'She's more beautiful than ever,' said Maura, looking up. 'She lives in the countryside with a couple of cats and doesn't have to work. She's obviously fine. But my *God*, the way Dex looked at her? It's one thing flirting with a gallery assistant, but another to ogle one of my best friends. He's never done *that* before. Designed as the ultimate punishment. Good thing I know how his filthy brain works.'

'I think you two get off on it,' said Suze.

'Maybe,' said Maura thoughtfully. 'Probably,' she smiled, though her smile faded quickly. 'It's got worse this year. That shopgirl who sold him a Ferrero Rocher-smelling candle, school dads, school mums. A lollipop lady, even. They've all been chess pieces in the husband and wife game of price wars. It's like . . . we can feel each other pulling away and . . . Well, anyway, at least I know what he's up to. Claire won't know *what* to make of it all.'

'She's not the competing kind – especially not when it comes to her friends. Look,' Annie said decisively, 'Dex can be an absolute twat.'

There was no point in denying that much and yet Maura's eyes flashed with a warning. Annie was straying too close to the line of an unwritten rule that stated the only one who was allowed to trash a husband or partner was the one joined to them contractually or emotionally.

'Maybe the resentment issues between you can be resolved by sitting down and working it out?' said Annie, trying to be more constructive. 'Getting a rota and working out who does what and when with bed, bath, whatever, so that you get time to make your own work again. What about the weekends? Surely you can—'

'Rotas are irrelevant, Annie. You cannot rota an ego as fat as Dex's. He doesn't want to make time for me. Why would he do something as mundane as empty a dishwasher and cook fishfingers when he could be building his kingdom? There's only space for one king! What with that and the fact that we have endless bills to pay, I won't be able to make my own work again until the kids leave home.'

'OK, fine, I'm just saying that I get it! He's not supportive!' said Annie. 'He doesn't do anything to help. Exactly like that complete chopper, The Canadian. At least you don't have a partner who promised to be around and then couldn't hack five minutes of being a dad.'

'OK,' said Suze. 'You have to stop calling him *The Canadian*. It just sounds like you're blaming all Canadian men for the fact you're a single mum.'

'Maybe I do? Maybe I'm fed up with men. Maybe I'm a man-blamer?'

Annie's cheeks flushed with belligerence. She could hear herself. It wasn't that she thought all men were crap and all women weren't. It was simply that she was galvanized when her friends' partners were useless or arrogant or crap because for a moment it made her feel as though they were coming back to her, narrowing the gap that had been made when she became a single mum, when her challenge, to raise a life on her own without the support of another adult, became so very different to anything they were going through. The loneliness of her task was bottomless, so sometimes it was too tempting not to try to narrow the gap further, however clumsy and crass her efforts.

'I dunno,' said Suze, kicking at the shale. 'Maybe The Canadian leaving when he did was a good thing for you both – he might have saved you lots of pain in the future . . .' She coughed. 'After all, people do sometimes change their minds about relationships when circumstances change.'

But it wasn't OK that he'd left. If Ted had been nicer and more loving and more resilient and stronger and better then she wouldn't have to be here now, feeling such a knot of pain in her stomach where joy should be instead. She felt hot tears rise in her throat and sting her nose.

'Gah, can we stop talking about relationships!' spat Maura. 'And problematic people. Whose bloody idea was it to bring these men – and all the human beings we made with them! – along on our rare weekend together?'

'It was mine!' snapped Annie. 'Because it was the only way of getting you all together!' She couldn't hold back her tears. 'It was impossible otherwise with your children and husbands and cars and . . . Yes, The Canadian left me, Suze, and I have a small child, no siblings, a father I haven't seen since I was ten, and a mother who doesn't recognize me anymore, so quite a lot of the time I feel alone. And scared. But *you* . . .' She caught her breath. 'You three are *my* family. The only one I've got. It's a wonderful thing to know that, despite what's happening in your life, you can always seek refuge in your best friends. And this weekend was my way of reminding us all of that.'

'All right, all right,' said Maura, cowed, quiet.

But Annie didn't want to hang around for any more of their responses.

'I'm going to get Claire now,' she said instead, gathering up the glasses and dishes as she went. She needed to deal with this now. 'So that we can hang out like we used to.'

Back inside the house, Annie checked the empty bedrooms and the kitchen for Claire and found nothing and no one until she came to the closed bathroom door in the corridor. She knocked gently. 'Hey, you OK? Please come out? It's all OK out here. Please can we talk? I need to talk to you.' She whispered Claire's name again but when the lock slid in the door it was Martin who answered through the crack, releasing a foul-smelling cloud.

'She's not in here!' he said. 'Unless she's fallen down the bog. Seriously though, I feel like everyone needs to eat so shall I just throw something together?'

Annie couldn't think about food anymore. Her stomach felt both numb and achingly painful. 'I really think we should stick to the rota? Would you mind? Otherwise no one will know what they're supposed to be doing and we'll fall into a complete mess. Maybe just prise the drink out of Suze's hand and give her a shove in the direction of the kitchen which is, after all, where she belongs?'

Martin's face fell in shock.

'It was a joke, Martin,' said Annie. Maura and Suze and even Claire would have got that. 'I think we both know she's the complete opposite of that?' she said, just to make sure Martin didn't think she was anti-feminist.

'Yes,' said Martin, glancing down at his feet thoughtfully. 'I suppose she is. The complete opposite of that.'

Annie made her way to the back of the house, passing the

unpacked wellies and anoraks in giant supermarket totes, to the driveway and a shed that bordered the edge of the pine woodland. She pushed open the door out of curiosity: it was possible she might find a brooding Claire there, sitting on the floor, knees drawn up. But instead she found a wooden rowboat which was painted such a lovely lemon yellow its image belonged on a teacloth. There was also a kayak, two paddleboards, and a bag of charcoal – none of it a surprise because she was the one who had booked the property knowing that it could provide activities like barbecues and sailing, in other words, ways to both integrate and break off the partners and children into different silos of organized fun for the outdoors, just like the cleaning and cooking rota and Tupperware did for the indoors.

With such careful thought and systems in place, why was everyone insisting on making such a bloody mess of things?

With no one in the shed she stepped back outside and it was then that she heard it: Claire's glittering, tinkling laughter deep into the woodland and beyond. The sound of Claire at her happiest. Was she on the phone? Had Karl gone out to meet her so they could enjoy the romantic moonlight together? She swallowed down a gritty, throat-scratching envy. So what if he had? She should be pleased for them!

But then she heard something that made her want to strain every part of herself to hear properly: Dex. His low-pitched tones and laughter. A silence. More of Claire's best laughter. Silence. Water splashing. A joyful scream. And another fucking silence! What exactly was happening in those dripping, evil silences? On the next shot of laughter, Annie, all her senses heightened, found herself running through an opening in the woodland, driven by the urgent need to break the silence and tear apart whatever it held in its sticky web before it suffocated them all.

She stepped out onto the edge of the beach, the very 'private' second beach, and stood in the shadow of the pines. She saw Dex and Claire in the water – facing each other, hair slicked back, shoulders glistening – before she saw the clothes that had been tossed messily onto the sand around her. Claire's Boden T-shirt. His stupid slides. She waited for a few moments, to watch them, the life frozen in her throat, as if she was about to witness a car crashing into a wall, hoping it wouldn't happen, hoping that her instinct that they were about to touch one another, kiss one another, was wrong.

What she saw was two people bending toward each other like flowers to the sun, radiating a raw attraction for each other. It was so thick and overpowering she thought she could even smell it amidst the salt and pines. Were they about to kiss? Or had they just kissed? They were saying something, though she couldn't hear what. She was curious and she was horrified as she watched them draw almost imperceptibly closer again.

Then she was stumbling onto the beach, her ankles rolling over into the sand.

'What exactly is going on here?' she called out, cringing at the headmistress-bossiness she'd never before heard in herself.

Claire was the first to turn toward her and the first to wade back through the water to the shore wearing only her pants. It did not escape Annie that this was exactly how Maura had been dressed less than an hour ago: almost like Claire was emulating Maura, or that Dex was gravitating to the blueprint of Maura, only one that was smaller, thinner, less gobby and therefore easier to manage. Annie's mind smoked with the possibilities.

'Well?' Annie snapped.

'Keep your baggy cotton pants on, Annie,' said Dex calmly. 'We were just swimming in a place where the current's less strong.'

'It's not what you think,' insisted Claire, standing back on the sand. 'We were going to swim round to the front and surprise you,' she said, rapidly drying down her legs with her shorts before pulling them back on.

'Right, good, makes sense,' said Annie abruptly. 'So the plan was going great guns until it was *me* that surprised you doing absolutely nothing other than discuss the shipping forecast? Good God, but I wasn't born yesterday! Whatever's going on: Claire, you need to go – now, back to the beach at the front of the house and I'll meet you there. Go on, go.'

Claire gave Annie a look she couldn't quite decipher. Anger, perhaps, as though she was about to say something but which quickly gave way to a childish obeisance, bowing her head and leaving the beach as instructed.

Dex took his time stepping out of the water, as if challenging her to hurry him up, else to look directly at his penis. When he reached the sand he looked at her, eyes shining in the moonlight. 'Water's too cold to swim, anyway,' he said, as if *that* was the problem.

'What exactly do you think you're doing, seducing Claire?' Annie put her hands on her hips.

'Why? Are you jealous?' Dex smirked with an eyes half-closed smile, like that might convince her off the fence. Like he actually *believed* she, Annie, had always fancied him. What messed-up Twat-Planet of the Absolute *Twats* did he live on? She didn't think it was possible to hate him more.

'Oh, fuck right off and put your bloody pants back on,' she said. 'No one wants to see that angular monstrosity glinting in the moonlight.' It was the only thing she could think of to say to this man she wanted to push out of her orbit like the pain in her stomach. 'Bang your assistant or your chocolate-smelling nick-nack girl or whoever else it is you've got on the go—'

'You what?' he said, pulling on his boxers.

'—but don't you dare go near our friends. My *God*,' she said, as it all started to form an uncomfortable shape in her mind. 'Have you ever considered the fallout of you being with Claire? How many families you'd break up? Or were you just thinking of yourself, as usual? Just take-take-taking what you want. Getting a bit of extra on the side with Claire. My God, Claire! Did you choose her because she was impressionable? What about *her* marriage?'

'Impressionable? That's so patronizing. An Annie classic.'

'Are you using her? To make Maura jealous? You won't have a family if you carry on with this stupid behaviour. Sticking your dick where it doesn't belong. Making your wife put aside her own life and career to care for the family *you* wanted. Honestly, you're leaving her with so much, you might as well just leave her. You and The Canadian should go bowling some time.' She felt pieces of her past crash up against her present like storm waves over a beach walkway. Smashing themselves onto the concrete, with nowhere to go but back out to sea.

'I don't know what you're talking about. Maura will do whatever Maura—'

'You always come first!'

Dex's brow rumpled and he smiled, his words stuttering with a mocking laugh. 'Are you not getting enough attention?'

'That's not what I mean.' Annie felt flustered and hot. 'I mean she comes second to *you*: to your life and *your* career. She told me she can't take any time off to do her work at night or during the weekends because while you're splashing your bloody paint all over the country, someone has to look after the kids.'

'Right,' he said. 'First of all, do you have any idea of how mental she is at the moment? She's fucking unhinged. A *damaging* person. A person who causes actual damage.'

'I know she threw a mug at your . . .' Annie shifted uncomfortably and folded her arms. What kind of damage was Dex talking about?

'And secondly,' said Dex, his face flushing with anger, 'what the fuck are you talking about when you say she can't take any time off? I've looked after the kids every weekend for the past four months just so Maura can take some time to rest, and God forbid, maybe even do a bit of work. You of all people should know that because she seems to spend most of it in coastal Airbnbs with you. I'd suspect you two of having an affair with each other if the idea wasn't so disgusting.'

'*What?* I—'

'And if you want evidence of what I've done with those children when I should have been working . . .' He yanked a leather wallet out of the shorts still lying on the sand. 'Here you go.' He pulled out scraps of paper and threw them into the sky like ticker tape. 'Tickets and receipts. To the Science Museum and fucking Legoland, just a few of the things I did with my children, or at least *tried* to do with my crazy children, while she was *looking after you*. So tell me, Annie, what exactly do you both do while "putting yourselves first"? Drink an entire distillery of gin while listing my failures on one of your tight-arsed whiteboards? Because you sure as fuck weren't standing under the diplodocus in the main hall of the Natural History Museum fielding the fortieth fucking question about where the next snack was coming from!'

Annie didn't say anything. She had not been sitting on her arse drinking gin. She had not seen Maura at the weekend, or for anything more than coffee, in over a year.

Chapter 8

Annie

10.25 p.m. Friday, 28 August
Sandpiper Cottage

The conversation with Dex made Annie want to break something. Instead, she gave her best trapped-squeal of a scream: designed to release some of her frustration, but not attract unwanted attention. As it was, any sound was masked by an almighty crack of thunder across the sky. Annie looked up in anticipation, but the rain didn't come.

What a piece of work that man was with his smirking cheekbones and fashionable T-shirts. But worse than such outright vanity, Annie had been left with nagging questions about Maura. What kind of damage had Maura caused? Why had she used Annie as an excuse to go away for the weekend? Where had she gone? And why was Maura lying to her best friend?

Dex was fundamentally untrustworthy. That much she knew. He exaggerated and played down, speaking the same way he painted: a little bit here, a little bit there until he'd put his neon farmyard view of the world to you as though it was the only one in existence. Despite littering the beach with bits of paper he claimed as evidence in the form of museum tickets, Annie wasn't sure she believed what Dex said any more than she believed he didn't go to the gym to achieve his shapely arms. The man was cresting forty. Arms like that didn't just *happen*.

As Annie walked back to the beach at the front of the house to find Claire, she mulled on what and who were the unstable parts of the chemical bond that had otherwise been completely stable. Any un-sound bonds needed fixing or strengthening or changing – but God, if there wasn't a worse time to do it. It was clear the evening had run out of calm possibilities to say what she needed to say to all of them, and so she would need to talk to them at the spa. The spa was a guaranteed period of time where they could shine a beam on all the positives and get back to the way they'd always been. No ire, no irks. Just the simple and happy refuge of old, rock-solid friendship.

Back on the main beach, Annie was relieved to see Claire waiting for her, and yet the sight of her, head bowed and kicking the sand, was a fresh and painful reminder that Claire's bond might need re-adjustment.

'What were you thinking, pissing around naked with Dex like that? Do you have any idea of how *bad* that looked?' said Annie, trying and failing to sound calm with a statement that sounded like a question but wasn't at all, because she didn't really want to know the answer. Had they already kissed? Were they about to kiss? Had Annie managed to snuff out the start of something bigger by interrupting at the crucial moment? She thought this was most likely. Absolutely. In which case the whole thing could be written off as a moment of madness, a *what happens on the Jurassic Coast, stays on the Jurassic Coast* moment.

'Where are Maura and Suze?' asked Annie, when it became clear that Claire wasn't going to answer her anyway.

'I don't know,' she said quietly.

'It's like herding cats,' said Annie exhaustedly. 'This was supposed to be a nice weekend, Claire. Nothing but a *straightforward* set of conversational transactions and a sharing of information.'

Claire looked up and gave Annie a searching, sad look. 'If that's what you wanted then you should have booked us tickets for an accountancy conference.' She sighed. 'Things aren't as straightforward as you . . . they haven't been *straightforward* between us for while.'

Annie rode over the statement, like the wheel of a cart over a bag of bones. She had no idea what Claire was talking about and, more to the point, didn't want to know. It probably wasn't relevant anyway.

'Things are only complicated if you make them complicated, Claire. Otherwise they are extremely straightforward. For example, there is no need to complicate things by moving out of London or getting into the water *naked* with the husband of one of our best friends.'

Annie didn't understand it. Claire was sensible. One of those sensible people who was always on time. She was least likely of them all to get demoted, exiled or have her stomach pumped. She wasn't given to putting anything on the line, in fact she was a way-behind-the-line person. She ate almonds and drank enough water, and though she wasn't currently working for a FTSE 100 company, she mostly dressed like she was, wearing the same palette of colours from oatmeal to black with the occasional pop of tweed or beige.

'So I shouldn't have moved out of London because it

complicated things for *you*?' said Claire, tipping her head to the side.

'Look,' said Annie ignoring her question. 'Is your exhaustion and stress throwing you into some kind of crisis where you entirely lose your judgement? Couldn't you have dealt with your stress by eating an entire cake, like Maura?'

'I'm not like her.'

'Or change your hair, like Suze?'

'I'm not like her, either. Or you. Or any of you.'

'Claire. You need to sleep. And you need to talk.'

'Is that your panicked way of saying I've got post-natal depression?'

Annie paused. 'Have you?'

'No. I don't think so.'

'Well then, maybe it's my way of asking whether you're planning on further complicating things by giving Dex a woodland-based blow job at dawn?'

'My God! Of course not.'

'Good. So from now on, just make sure you stay where I can see you.'

'I'm not doing that, Annie. I'm not a child.'

'And you're not behaving like a middle-aged woman, either. Which is where friends like me come into their own.' Annie inhaled deeply. 'I see your exhaustion. I see you're acting a bit skew-whiff, and I'm here to steer you through dark waters like a cruise ship guides a dinghy.'

'You mean like a dinghy guides a cruise ship?'

'Fine, sure, if that's what you want.'

'Yeah, well that's how it works on the actual sea. Small boats like dinghies have purpose, too.' Claire's look flickered from steadfast to resigned in a second. 'I have to get back to the house. Graham still has one final night feed and . . .' Her words stuttered. 'I can't believe I used this weekend as a focus to wean him. And now, with Maura being so . . . and you being so . . . to be honest I'm not sure I want to go away with you all now.'

'Please don't say that.'

Annie hadn't meant to sound so desperate but she couldn't tolerate hearing Claire's words. They made her feel so sad and so panicked because Claire . . . Claire was fundamental to her plan.

'There's definitely a lot to talk about,' Annie said calmly. 'But please don't leave on a bad note. We can sort it all out. Just stay with me a bit longer?' Annie wouldn't need much time to adjust the bond, find out if Claire was OK, show some empathy, work out why she seemed so preoccupied and then offer some solutions. A half hour would do it, she thought. A half-hour bond-adjustment job.

'No. I'm tired and I want to see my baby. If you want to talk to me, you'll have to do it while I feed Graham.'

Annie wouldn't have Claire's attention if she did that. And after she'd fed Graham and they'd finished having a half-talk, who knew where Claire would wander off to and what else she'd get up to with Dex roaming around like a panther in heat. She needed to find somewhere Claire couldn't escape from, somewhere Claire was captive without feeling like one.

'You're right!' said Annie, having a brilliant idea. 'Dinghies may be small, but they can be powerful. In fact, I'll row you in one now. There's one in the shed. A rowboat thing.'

'A rowboat *thing*? God, no. Are you joking? Anyway, you hate the water.'

She did. But her only job now was to shore up Claire's

support and to put other people's needs before her own fears. 'We'll just sort of bob up and down in the shallows. Safe from everything. Away from everything. Just for a bit. While we have a talk.'

'You have no idea how onerous that sounds. I don't want a lecture on a boat when the only way out is to swim back to dry land.'

'I promise I won't lecture you. And I'll make a midnight feast.'

'Still no.'

'I'll include a carrot.' She paused. 'And an apple. Come on, Claire. We'll sort everything out, then I promise we'll go to bed and you can feed Graham and sleep in a single bed next to me and tomorrow we can go away on a nice spa break and have a mud wrap and you'll be really happy. Isn't that better than walking out on an argument?'

Claire looked at the moon and then back at Annie. 'Ten minutes.'

'Great! The boat's yellow. Like daffodil yellow? Like it's been freshly painted for us. This is going to be lovely! And the oars look like they've been professionally distressed.'

'Like me,' said Claire quietly.

'What? No,' Annie said, as she grasped Claire by the hand and led her back in the direction of the shed. 'Distressed as in: stripped, bleached. Made to look authentic?'

Inside the thick creosote and damp-smelling darkness they took their positions either end of the rowboat to slide it off its wide shelf, making sure two oars were safely stowed inside.

Claire picked up her side easily and waited for Annie to do the same.

'This thing looks as light as a coconut shell, so why isn't

it moving like a coconut shell? It's not moving,' said Annie, her heart fluttering with panic as she tried and failed to lift her side, arms shaking with the effort. Her panic rose further, coming to rest in a smouldering heap at the bottom of her throat.

Not now, please not now, just give me a bit more time.

'It's OK,' said Claire calmly. 'Shift the boat round a bit? It's just stuck on the side of the shelf there.'

Claire didn't wait for an answer and instead walked round and gave the boat a tug. They looked at each other for a moment and both smiled gently. This was the calm and practical Claire who Annie knew and loved.

They lifted the boat onto their shoulders but Annie had only taken a few steps when her legs wobbled, as though their inside marrows were made of jelly and the bone of rubber. Overwhelmed, suddenly, by the sense that they were two pallbearers carrying a coffin and not a boat, Annie's legs buckled and she fell to her knees on the gritty concrete floor of the shed, the sharp and heavy lip of the boat landing hard on her shoulder. Claire caught her end of the boat quickly, to stop the whole weight from landing on Annie, and used her strength to tip it on its side and onto the concrete floor.

Claire sat down next to Annie on the floor, taking hold of both her hands.

'Hey,' she said. 'Are you OK?'

Annie looked up at her, eyes full of tears. 'Actually, no,' she said. 'I've been struggling . . .'

'I'm sorry,' said Claire, squeezing Annie's hands gently. 'Do you want to talk about it?'

'I don't know, I just . . . I'm just really stressed out with everything and I can't think straight.'

'It's hard,' said Claire. 'I know exactly what you mean. Young children, old parents, paying the bills, trying to get your body back to where it was before pregnancy.'

'Yes, that's all tiring, not so much the snapping back into shape, but the rest, I—'

'Well, it's *exhausting*. The other day I'd been up all night with a teething Graham and Mum called me, worrying that her emails had escaped through the wall when she'd unplugged her computer. And then Karl was like, *babe, I've got people coming round from the office can you make one of your lasagnes*. And I'd been trying to get the final boxes unpacked from the move and I was feeling tired and hormonal and I just wanted to cry.'

'Yes,' said Annie. But she didn't say anything else because what was there to say when the only thing she had in common with her friend in that moment was the urge to fucking cry.

Annie left Claire to push the rowboat over the sand and down to the water, and walked to the kitchen to fill a tote with snacks, her separate conversations with both Dex and Claire repeating on her like a bad curry.

She swept supplies off kitchen surfaces as quickly as she was able: the ridged glass bottle of tequila without a worm that Maura had brought, a crumpled red baby blanket, a pink paper bag of doughnuts she'd bought at the service station earlier that day, a half-empty bottle of mineral water with condensation from the day's heat and a full packet of Maura's cigarettes. Annie had never smoked but if she was ever going to start it would be then. And usually she loved doughnuts but she hadn't touched the packet of three: more signs, if they were needed, that her world was upside down.

It was OK, she reassured herself: her friends would heft it back onto its axis.

Back on the beach, Annie hurled the tote into the rowboat and the women hefted its daffodil yellow weight into the shallows. Annie shuddered as the cold water crept over the tops of her feet, stepping through it quickly as if it were molten lava and into the gritty-bottomed boat.

Taking an oar each, Claire sat on the front bench and Annie squeezed in next to her. With no direct eye contact, that formation would mean Claire could say the unsayable. Should it be needed. Which Annie was confident it wouldn't be.

'We won't go too far, and just the shallows,' said Annie for her own assurances as much as anything, driving her oar into the mulch beneath to push them a little further out. She intoned the words 'safe, safe, safe,' to herself, quietly enough for Claire not to hear, the very same words a swimming instructor had given her on the edge of a swimming pool one Saturday afternoon a year ago.

Until that Saturday Annie hadn't put her head under a body of water that wasn't a bath, shower or rain, since she was nine. And she certainly wouldn't have gone within spitting distance of a swimming pool had she not become a mother, and known that of the many survival skills her child would need in the world, swimming was the most important. Swimming might save Em's life one day. Might save Em years of pain and shame. Might, might . . .

And so, Annie was faced with a choice. Take some of her own swimming lessons again to remember the skills, so that she could do what was required of her and get in the water with Em to learn. Or don't take the swimming lessons, don't take Em into the water, don't feel the discomfort, and put

Em off anything to do with swimming and the water in the future . . . yet bear the consequences should one day Em find herself in dangerous waters and be unable to save her own life because Annie had never taken her for swimming lessons.

That Saturday afternoon, and on the many Saturdays that followed, a nice man in his late twenties called Dylan had crouched at the edge of the pool in his flip-flops and encouraged her to breathe slowly through the panic until she was strong enough to lift her feet off the bottom and take some strokes again. She cried for most the time she was in the water, for the loneliness of facing that challenge of motherhood without a partner or friends, and for what had really happened to her and her friend when they were nine. All she'd needed to bridge the gap between the two sadnesses was to ask for help. And yet, she hadn't.

Despite conquering some of its shallower territories, her loathing and fear of the water remained: its quiet and unknowable depths still held boundless possibilities for destruction and for that alone, she would never forgive it.

Calmer now, Annie glanced up and looked around.

'How beautiful!' she exclaimed before the rowboat tipped to one side and then the next, leaving her smothering a sharp gasp.

'Should we use our oars? Have you done this before?' said Claire.

'What? No? Have you?'

'No! You sounded so confident I thought you did it every summer or something?'

'It can't be that hard,' replied Annie calmly. 'Think of those people in the movies who just sit in a rowboat and chat, miles from nowhere with a beer and fishing rod. I think you've just got to put your thing, your oar, in the water and pull, you know? Like this?' Annie dipped her oar in deep and pulled, but the oar jumped out of its rowlock and she had to lunge to keep it in the boat.

Annie tried again. 'There we go!' she said brightly. 'Your turn, Claire.'

Claire dipped the oar, shallower that time, and pulled, turning the boat in a half circle.

'Excellent,' said Annie, glancing to the side to see Claire's almost indecipherable eye roll to the sky. 'Now, let's try together.'

Annie waited for Claire to raise her oar so she could co-ordinate her own movement, but the boat tipped again and Annie's stomach lurched into her throat.

'Come on!' said Annie. Hadn't Martin said there were riptides? And dead sailors? 'Let's move it along! We have to try and move our oars at the same time!' She tried not to dwell on how many skeletons had decomposed beneath them. And the fact they might be at the centrifugal centre of Dorset's very own Bermuda Triangle.

'One and two, and one and two,' Annie intoned.

The movements were unstable and uncomfortable but after a bit, they hit an uneasy, clunky and slow beat backwards, like an amateur drumming group, moving parallel to the shoreline.

Shallow enough for Annie not to be sick in her lap and deep enough for the boat to gain momentum, Annie began to feel herself on the edges of enjoyment.

Around them, the summer night's sky hummed grey, fringed at its lower edges with the orange and silver beacons of Poole holiday homes. They might have been a thousand miles across the globe given the warmth of the night air. There was no more thunder and Annie was sure, no rain on its way.

Instead, the skies were clear and a silver glow of moonlight picked out the long inky slab of Blue Bracken Island ahead with its thick group of trees jutting up like a mongrel collection of bottle cleaners. Why was it easier to breathe in the countryside? Was this why Claire had decided to raise her kids away from the city? Did she know something they didn't about fields and extramarital affairs? For someone who was so calm and straightforward, was it possible that, despite all the years they'd known each other, Claire possessed a depth of knowledge that Annie wasn't aware of yet?

'Come on then, you wanted to talk,' said Claire.

But it was so beautiful and calm out there, the furthest Annie had felt from her own tumultuous reality in a long time, that she found herself wanting a little more of it. She didn't want to be arguing with anyone or facing anything hard. She just wanted more of this peace.

'Annie?'

The rowboat tipped to and fro again as their oars fell out of synch, and with her stomach's next lurch, Annie felt vulnerable once again.

'Can you not dig into the water so much please, Claire? Do what I do and stay further to the surface. Scoop less?'

Claire did as she was told.

'I just want to say,' said Annie, 'that I'm really glad nothing else happened between you and Dex on the beach, because it doesn't bear thinking about. We're all blood sisters, Claire . . . We pricked our fingers and shared our blood in a London pub, pledging emotional allegiance for the rest of our lives. That's not nothing.'

Claire still didn't say anything in response and Annie was frustrated at not being able to see the look on her face.

When Claire eventually spoke, her tone was cold. 'You have to stop doing that.'

'What, saving you from yourself, or the jaws of Dex?'

'No, sending me off like that. The way you did? Back to the beach, like I was a kid.'

Annie couldn't understand why she was focusing on that and not the reminder of how important these friendships were. Probably because the guilt of betraying Maura was too white-hot to focus on. 'We all make mistakes, Claire. God knows I have. Never get into bed with a Canadian, for a start.'

'What if it wasn't a mis—'

A sound like a siren, an alarm or a bird rang through the night air.

'What was that?' said Annie, her heart leaping, limbs tensing up and aching with fear.

The sound rang out again, this time more tunefully. 'Is that Maura? Singing? And Suze?'

They both twisted round. In the near distance ahead, Maura and Suze were on the edge of a wooden jetty, Suze sitting with her feet dangling over the water and Maura standing, silhouetted against the moon, hair tipping over her shoulders, skirt tucked into her knickers, swaying a bottle in the air like a lighter at a concert as she sang 'Total Eclipse of the Heart' throatily and almost tunefully.

'Can we turn back?' said Claire. 'I want to go back. I don't think I want to see Maura . . . I told you, I just want to go to bed and feed Graham.'

But her words overlapped with Maura swinging into the opening verses of 'Fairytale of New York' and hurling her bottle into the air in an enormous arc.

'Maura!' laughed Suze, as the bottle landed with a splash. 'You're polluting the waterways!'

'Never mind that,' said Maura. 'I seem to have lost my whisky.' Then Maura was singing less loudly and bending over the side of the jetty, peering into the water into a space nowhere near where her whisky had landed. She stood up abruptly, swung her long-chained handbag over her head like a lasso, and they all watched in horror as that, too, took flight, in the same direction as the bottle.

'Wait!' shouted Annie. 'We'll get it!'

She drove her oar into the water and moved heavy chunks as best she could. 'Come on, Claire, put your back into it!'

Annie looked up just in time to see Maura raise one arm into the air in greeting. Maura then said something no one could understand at the same time as tipping to one side, as though the words had been the weight to unbalance her, before falling head-first into the water.

'Maura!' shouted Suze, when Maura's head emerged. 'Stay there! Head above the water, babe. So we can see you!'

Maura was spluttering and laughing.

'Take my hand,' said Annie, pulling the rowboat up beside her.

'No!' shouted Maura with the force of someone who was fuelled on whisky alone. 'My handbag. I have to save it. My phone's in there.'

'Why did you throw it in the water?'

'I was using it as a lasso to get the whisky bottle.'

'Of course you were.' Annie rolled her eyes. 'Maura, get out of the water. The bag is long gone, down there with the dead sailors.'

'Great,' she shouted. 'If I go after it I might get laid.'

Annie hated Maura being in the water and wanted her to get out before something terrible happened. 'Come on, get in the boat now,' she shouted, panic rising in her throat.

'She can't get in here,' hissed Claire under her breath.

'Put your issues away, Claire,' chided Annie impatiently.

'No, I mean she won't be able to get in without capsizing us.'

Maura grabbed onto the side with both sodden hands and fixed them with a glare. 'Challenge accepted, fuckers.' And then proceeded to bear down on the side of the boat with all her might.

'No, please, Maura,' said Claire, crying like Maura was twisting her arm. 'Can't you just climb up the jetty steps rather than get in here?'

'It'll be fine,' said Suze, 'just give her a hand. It's less fun if she just climbs back onto the jetty.'

'Come on, Claire, help her,' said Annie, taking hold of Maura's arm, wanting Claire back on board their friendship, and the plan to save Maura from the terrifying depths of the water.

But Claire leant backwards, away from where Annie was trying to haul Maura.

'Where are you going?' shouted Annie, dismayed at Claire's leaning away, rather than in, to the rescue efforts. 'Come and help.'

'Didn't you do science? Someone has to rebalance the weight in this boat.'

'Stop calling me fat,' laughed Maura.

'Come on fatty boom-boom!' shouted Suze. 'Try harder to haul your massive arse into the boat.'

Maura was laughing, Suze was laughing, Annie was split

between laughing and crying hot, anxious tears and Claire was in tears, looking stricken and pained and panicked as she tried to rebalance the rowboat.

Against all odds, and some loud heaves and shouts about scraped thigh-meat and the grief of losing her best friend – otherwise known as the whisky bottle – Maura's curvaceous, drunk and singing body ended up face down across the boat.

They were only a few feet from the jetty.

'I feel left out,' said Suze mournfully, as Maura shuffled and shifted into a seated position.

'Well, we're getting out now,' said Claire, taking hold of her oar. 'Going home.'

Annie didn't say anything, taking hold of her oar, too. But as they got to within a foot of the jetty, Suze took three swift steps down the rusted ladder and stepped right into the space next to Maura.

The whole boat tipped like it was in a gale force storm.

'Omigod!' shouted Maura, bursting into laughter again.

'Stop!' shouted Annie, as the boat tipped and righted. Her stomach churned and dropped, her blood ran cold, hairs jumping up on the back of her neck, palms stinging with how much she gripped the side of the boat as she said, 'That was a mad thing to do,' furious and shaking once the boat had settled.

'Fantastic!' shouted Maura. 'What a blast.'

'Can I get out please?' said Claire. 'I need to see my baby.'

'Come on, let's have an adventure!' protested Suze. 'This is important. What are you going to remember more? Sitting on the jetty discussing where your life's gone wrong, or getting out onto the open water in search of dead sailors on that island over there?' Suze pointed an accusing finger at Blue Bracken Island.

'I don't want to go into the open water,' said Annie.

'I really want to go home,' said Claire.

'I don't,' said Maura.

'What is *wrong* with you both?' said Suze. 'This, right here, is your life. You have to take these stupid little chances for adventure else they may never come round again.'

Annie looked at Suze, ready to dissent again, and yet pausing. 'Oh God, I don't know,' she said, balancing her oar on its side.

'She's right, you know,' said Maura. 'And the best fun we've ever had together is when we didn't plan it. Like that time we ended up in Paris when all we'd planned was a pint in King's Cross.'

'Guilty as charged for suggesting that one,' said Suze. 'Or at home with tea and cake when you should all have been at a party.'

Annie smiled because all of that was true. If she hadn't found Suze in a state of complete disrepair in one of the locker rooms in the university sports block, crying over some science graduate who'd broken her heart; if Annie hadn't taken her home and introduced her to Maura and Claire; if they'd decided to go to that house party instead of sitting up all night drinking tea and gin and playing Monopoly – then they might never be the friends they were now. Suze had been the last piece of the puzzle and it was all because of a changed plan.

'We'll sleep when we're dead!' said Maura, waving her arms in the air and making the boat rock violently.

'OK, fine,' said Annie, wondering whether this was supposed to be how they eventually found out. On the water. Or even the island. 'Let's do it. Claire? What do you say? Come on, blood sisters forever!'

Annie knew she'd agree. Much like when they chose the beds: a critical mass of votes was all they ever really needed for her to agree anything.

'Ten minutes there, ten minutes on the island, ten minutes sailing back,' said Claire. 'Any longer than that and I'm swimming back.'

'Good. Now, come on, Claire,' said Suze. 'You swap places with me so you're sitting next to Maura.'

'But . . .'

'Go on, and hand me your oar. Annie and I will get us there. Maura is way too drunk to be useful.'

'Yes but . . .' began Claire, as she handed over her oar and uneasily swapped places with Suze in a series of awkward and unbalanced moves.

'I've got Grade One water skills,' announced Suze.

'What is that? Pissing and water-boarding and cocktail making?' said Maura.

'No, you idiot. I learnt to row a boat in the Lake District.'

'Good,' said Maura. 'And how old were you when you did that?'

'Six,' said Suze.

'Oh, thank God,' said Maura. 'Because five would have been far too young for you to remember anything useful.'

Though the loose ends of the night were making her uneasy: the queasiness of what she'd seen on that beach, the pain of what Dex had said, the confusion of not knowing who to trust, Annie was sitting in a boat with her best friends. They'd have an adventure tonight, like the ones they used to have. And she'd tell them everything, which would put all loose ends into a nicely braided piece of perspective. For the meantime, they were pushing off the shores of their everyday lives and into the dark waters beyond.

Chapter 9

Martin

11 p.m. Friday, 28 August
Sandpiper Cottage

Martin stepped onto the shale and breathed in the hot and thick night air. He'd have put money on the arrival of rain after the exceptional thunder earlier, but perhaps they had been granted a reprieve. He hoped so. The next few days would almost certainly be easier to cope with if everyone was spaced out over the water, grounds and woodland, without the pressure to converse within the confines of the breeze-block walls.

He was hoping to locate Suze in the darkness, somewhere amidst the broad-leafed ferns and tall pines. They'd not had much chance to talk since arriving and he'd been beset with a niggling worry that his over-enthusiasm about the sleeping and cooking arrangements and the idea that the children might become as good friends as their parents one day, had been too much, too soon. Suze wasn't one to be pushed. He knew that. Ideas had to be hers to make them stick. But he so desperately wanted her to see how powerful a tonic it was when people came together. All the opportunities for shared information and collaboration and kindness. Sometimes he couldn't help but put a bow on it.

He saw her, then, wandering down the jetty toward the water, her arm interlinked with Maura's. She was laughing, in the way that Suze laughed when she felt most herself which is to say when she was with her friends or doing the things she loved. She never laughed like that at home which was exactly why she needed more of this kind of weekend. He should leave them to it.

Martin returned to the kitchen, deep in thought, with the express plan of making some Ovaltine, having a little tidy up and hitting the hay. He was bringing the milk to a good rolling boil when Dex entered the kitchen adjusting his shorts with one hand, pushing a wallet back into the pocket, and holding his phone with the other. He was flushed, preoccupied and gazing into the middle distance, and a little damp with sweat or water.

As Martin poured milk from the pan in a smooth, white, steaming line, he watched Dex put his phone away, retrieve a vape from his pocket, suck on said vape, attack a salami with a penknife, then chew each meat roundel vigorously before beginning the whole cycle again. How one person could be so engaged and yet look so disengaged was both intimidating and frustrating to Martin: like needing to solve a crossword puzzle on a subject he knew nothing about.

Martin said hello but he wasn't sure if Dex had heard, and he didn't try again. It was OK. It was the way the jungle worked. Men like Dex and Karl, who were confident and talented and reasonably good-looking weren't expected to communicate or emote or enthuse as much as everyone else. Things came to people like that. No need to fight for them, Martin noted things like these with the dull, passing ache of acceptance. It was no wonder these two men had their families firmly intact around them.

'Aw-right?' said Karl brightly, swaggering into the kitchen and making a beeline for Dex. 'Did you manage a swim? I have to say I went off the idea. Needed a bit of decompression time after the will-we-won't-we back and forth. Will they swim? Won't they swim? Kit on? Kit off? I felt like I needed a nap after all that. What are you watching there, Dex? A bit of CBeebies?'

'Eh?' Dex looked up. 'Oh, just checking the traffic. I'll be heading back to London in the morning with the kids. Everyone's tired and needs their own beds.'

'No!' said Karl, glancing briefly over at Martin, presumably horrified at the prospect of spending the next two days with him, which to be honest was a horror Martin shared in reverse. What would he talk about during the next lunch, dinner and breakfast, mano a mano, with Karl? Martin ran the numbers to see exactly how much time they would be spending together. Lunch on Saturday and breakfast on Sunday would be communal affairs so any attempts at conversations could be cut off at the knees with a child wanting this and needing that. But Saturday dinner? How would that work? A whole evening? What on earth would they talk about then? Geo-politics? Tempeh? Cottage cheese? He wouldn't know where to begin. And Martin could hardly expect a man as interesting as Karl to wax lyrical about his own favourite subjects: baked goods, dominoes and town planning. Martin was kicking himself for doing too much research into joint topics that might come up and not enough into individual specialities. He just hadn't been expecting this curve ball. He and Karl really were a weak link! Nothing in common. *Nothing.*

'Oh dear,' said Martin, 'I was going to spatchcock a chicken for tomorrow's lunch. You'll stay for that? Dex? Please?' He loathed the sound of desperation in his voice.

'Thanks, but I won't,' said Dex bluntly.

'Perhaps a little spliff, Dexy?' tried Karl.

Dex looked up while continuing to saw pieces off his roundel of meat, chewing, and then sucking the vape. He pushed the plate uninterestedly in Karl's direction. 'Perhaps, but not if you call me that.'

'There's a possible fly in the ointment,' said Martin, trying to come up with something to keep Dex there, his head crowding with problems and solutions that threatened to spill over the edges. 'I don't know if you heard that thunder earlier but it was a sign of things to come I'm afraid. A storm is a'comin'. Though you'll want to check its progress on the weather app because I'm no expert. On the upside, maybe if it's bad weather the women won't go to their spa in the morning? Then we can all be together as one big tribe? Perhaps some cricket? You'd like that, wouldn't you?'

'As you probably noticed, Maura's behaving appallingly,' said Dex, a flash of irritation marring his beautiful hazel eyes.

'She certainly looked like she was having fun hurling missiles!'

Martin had heard the crack of the bottle against the path but he'd had no idea what had happened in between that and the moment he'd found her stark naked around fifteen minutes before that.

'When she's like that she only tends to go in one direction,' said Dex. 'Which is the behavioural equivalent of the wrong way down a motorway at top speed. She'll come back from that spa thing all hungover and tired and riled up by everyone else in the echo chamber, aka Annie, who will tell her I'm an "insert-adjective-here bastard". Long story short: I'm going to leave before I get covered in shrapnel.'

Martin tapped at his phone hopefully. 'Here we are. As suspected, seventy-two per cent chance of a storm blowing through, creating poor visibility for driving.'

'Why did no one tell us this before driving hours for an outdoorsy weekend?' said Dex.

'To be honest, mate,' said Karl, 'maybe it was just a case of expecting that one long, hot summer would continue along the same old hot-summer lines? It probably didn't occur to the organizers to check the weather.'

'And we're in one of those areas,' said Martin. 'We have our own microclimate, so let's make the best of it while it rains!'

'Watch some sport?' suggested Karl. 'Put the kids to bed early? Say two-ish?'

'Lunchtime? Sport?' said Martin, perking up because he had done some research on sport as a potential shared topic of conversation for the weekend: especially because he wasn't a natural sportsman either on or off the pitch. 'Yes, indeed, sport. Did you see the West Ham game?'

'It was awesome,' said Karl, answering Martin's question but addressing his comment to Dex. 'We could watch the next instalment with a nice spliff? And when the sheen wears off that, spitball some ways to collaborate on business?'

'I'm the wrong person to involve in football,' Dex replied.

Martin looked down at Dex's feet, bedecked in mid-calf Persil-white sports socks and black-and-white striped slides. Martin would have loved the creativity and style to think of twinning such things, though he loved the rustic straw comfort of his espadrilles, impractical as they were in wet weather.

'The All-Blacks rugger tourno between NZ and Canada?' tried Martin.

'I don't know why you'd willingly attack another man with your head to retrieve something you could simply pick up in a shop, online, or later that night,' replied Dex.

'That's . . . that's sport, I guess . . .' said Karl. 'What about F1?'

'Nope,' said Dex bluntly. 'Anything to do with cars or a ball is not my bag.'

'Apart from your own ballbag, I do hope,' quipped Karl, and Martin laughed because he imagined Dex's angular appendage hanging out of his ballbag.

'Apart from rounders, actually,' said Dex, ignoring Karl's joke. 'Rounders I can tolerate because the bat reminds me of . . . of a truncheon.'

'In fact, anything to do with racing, coming first, second or third, balls, racquets, men and mud leaves me cold,' said Dex, adjusting himself inside his shorts.

Managing Dex was like rolling ten cannonballs up a hill without a single ballbag to hold them in place. The conversation was just an awkward mess of stilted attempts at trying to engage the one person in the room that didn't want to be engaged. So Martin allowed himself an ember of hope at the idea that any discord wasn't just about his failings or lack of conversational research.

'You know,' said Dex, scooping up his vape and penknife. 'I'll definitely be going home tomorrow. Too much going on at the moment to be in the holiday frame of mind.'

'Sure, no sure,' said Karl, looking crestfallen. 'No rest for the wicked.'

'I'm off to bed,' said Dex.

'As you wish,' said Martin.

But Martin felt sick to the stomach. To be left alone with two high-achievers he didn't know well was bad enough. But one? Terrible. The pressure was too immense and he wasn't convinced that the increased dose on his meds prescription could do the heavy-lifting that was needed. Besides, Dex's departure would fly in the face of Annie's plan to bring together this collective of individuals. However bad that storm was forecast to be, it was unlikely to stymie Dex's attempts. But Martin needed to do something. He needed time to think about how he would fit together the breaking pieces of the group with his own brand of kintsugi gold.

So he stepped outside onto the shale again, this time with the steak knife he'd used to open up the Ovaltine tin. He inhaled deeply and listened for conversation, relieved that he could no longer hear the laughter of the women. He made his way to Dex's large, dustbin-grey and obnoxious 4x4. An image of Dex gripping Alfie's arm came unbidden and Martin found himself gripping the steak knife hard, then raising his arm high and wide before plunging it into the car tyre with so much force his wrist felt like it might snap in two.

Chapter 10

Annie

11 p.m. Friday, 28 August
The water between Blue Bracken Island and Sandpiper Cottage

The moonlight picked out stippled white clouds in the far distance, but the sky above them was clear and inky, and the air, warm.

Annie and Suze sat side by side, plunging their oars into the water, having fallen perfectly and pleasingly into a rhythm while Claire, sitting opposite with her head bowed, had fallen into an uneasy silence.

Maura, on the other hand, was loud enough for them all, screaming with excitement at every bump over the low waves, singing the parts of 'Total Eclipse of the Heart' she could remember, occasionally using her hands as paddles and shouting 'Hoo-haa!'

Annie felt the cold grit of the boat's floor at the balls of her feet, the balmy air on her face and the gleeful yet terrifying sense that she'd unmoored from a part of her life. As they increased their speed, falling into the arms of an outgoing tide, she glanced up at the night sky, stars sparkling diamond bright, one as fat and large as a princess's engagement ring.

'The North Star!' said Annie, just because it was the biggest in the sky.

Suze guffawed. 'I'm sure you do, and it's fine if you don't, but: do you know where north is?'

Annie smiled. She'd never been lost enough to have to navigate exactly where she was going, so the answer was no. 'Of course I bloody know where north is! It's over there somewhere between east, west and south. Now, come on! One two, one two!'

Suze laughed and even Claire managed a quiet giggle.

Annie felt her wrists wobble, her forearms quiver and her hands threaten to let go of the oar. 'No, not yet,' she hissed quietly to herself, squeezing her eyes shut, feeling her legs shake with effort and fear. 'Not now,' she whispered more firmly, as if telling herself off.

'What did you say?' said Suze quietly. 'Annie?'

Ignoring her, Annie sang loudly, joining in with Maura. Soon, Suze and Claire had joined in too and maybe it was their singing, all the right words at the right time, together and in tune, that was propelling them along, or that the current was gathering pace beneath them – but the boat began lurching forward with an even greater speed.

Annie felt her stomach tip with nerves first, then excitement, followed by an incipient sense of safety on the water because she was with her friends. Because they shared the burden of speed and navigation. Because they were going to the same place. Because for the first time in many months she didn't feel alone. When she felt the rush of air across her neck she had to turn her head away from Suze to look out at the water, feeling her cheeks cooler where they were damp with tears. She didn't want to have to explain the messiness

115

of her heart both soaring in that moment and straining with sadness at the knowledge that there would never be another like it.

'Can we turn back now?' said Claire.

'But isn't this fun?' said Annie.

'Yes, but . . .'

Then Annie looked over her shoulder at the commanding trees of Blue Bracken Island ahead and its quiet, confident solitude. She knew then, deep in her bones, that even if it lay in the east, or the west, this place was her North Star. This was the place she would tell her friends everything.

It was impossible to tell how far they'd travelled by the time they reached Blue Bracken Island, more than an hour after leaving the mainland. The water was bone-achingly cold when they disembarked, but even the pain was part of the experience: different enough from concrete pavements and hot baths to laugh about, be glad of, even.

'Isn't it beautiful, Claire?' said Annie, gazing up at the navy night spattered with glittered star-flecks, up to her thighs in cold water, hands gripping tight to the side of the boat.

An expanse of white-sanded beach curved around a corner, lined with trees like candles on a cake, picked out in long slashes of neon white by the moonlight.

'We can be as loud as we want!' shouted Maura. 'Louder than any of our children.'

'Aren't you anyway? Never realized you were holding back,' laughed Suze.

Annie's feet sank into a slimy mud as they pulled the boat out of the water. She moved her feet quickly, instinctively, as though, if she didn't, it might hold on to her.

She turned to Claire as Suze and Maura stumbled up the beach. 'Hey, help me tie up the boat?'

'You don't need to eagle-eye me here, Annie. It'd be hard to give Dex a blow job at this distance.'

'I know. I just want to hang out with you, is all.'

Claire smiled.

Together they heaved the boat along the beach to a thickset tree trunk lying at the water's edge, a stubby branch sticking out of it. Annie pulled the towline out of the sandy bottom and lassoed it over the branch. She tried to loop it round the branch again and again but her hands wouldn't let her, her forearms stiffening. She tried again but it was no good: it was as if her arms refused to bend. 'Claire. Can you do this? Can you tie the boat up?'

'Er, sure . . .? I mean . . . why? Is it that hard?'

'I-I didn't eat enough earlier,' she said. 'Hungry. No energy.'

'OK?' said Claire, taking the rope from her and tying up the boat easily.

Annie felt a lot of things in that first hour on the island. A bit hungry, a bit cold, a bit tired. A stab of panic at being temporarily cut off from Em. What if Em woke in the dark of a strange place in the next few hours and was impossible to settle? Would Karl and Martin be able to calm her down? Had she planned it well enough to have two men her daughter didn't know look after her? What other choice did she have? Then she panicked even more, that she was cut off from anything *she* might need. Then followed by a breathless sense of liberation that she *was* cut off: if she couldn't be seen by the rest of the world, maybe all the difficult things would magically go away and leave her in peace?

'Let's play "It"!' shouted Suze, slapping Maura's arm and running off down the beach, Maura leaping into immediate and hot pursuit.

As Maura dived for Suze and missed, landing with a hollow flop in the sand they all laughed with every breath in their bodies. And then everyone joined in. Claire running in one direction and Annie in the other to escape Maura's surprisingly fast run.

'You won't bloody catch me, Maura! My legs are way longer than yours,' laughed Suze.

But Maura was determined and focused. 'Just you watch me, you lanky bimbo.' And she ran for Suze, throwing her onto the sand and pummelling her until she was breathless with laughter.

Then Suze was running after Annie and it was a chaotic mess of being caught and wrestled to the ground. For quite a long time, Annie was completely and utterly distracted by the joys of running and escaping and tripping and running again and escaping, then being caught and wrestled to the ground. On that beach, Annie forgot about being an adult. No serious conversation, no issues, no partners or worries. They were just like children, like the twins and Walt and Em in the kitchen earlier that day, running around with their bamboo canes and a delightful desire both to be caught, and not to be caught.

They were also themselves. A normal bunch of friends arsing around on the sand.

Annie couldn't remember the last time she'd laughed like that.

'I'm going to piss myself,' she said eventually.

'The entire island is your toilet. Don't hide your bush under a bushel,' said Maura. 'Just go anywhere!'

'And yet please be discreet and neat,' said Claire. 'I don't want to be standing in it when I need to go.'

'Just do it in the sea,' said Suze. 'Then you won't leave a trace.'

But Annie did none of those things.

She ambled off to the forest periphery, dropped her trousers and managed to urinate at the wrong angle all over her own feet. As she pulled up her trousers the blue clothbound notebook fell out of her back pocket, narrowly avoiding a patch of compressed, piss-soaked bracken. Annie stepped to the edge of the forest and, using the moonlight as a low lamp, bent the spine to open the book as fully as possible to the pages with the six columns: two columns per friend. A pro and con for each.

She scrawled the words *honesty: problems with* in both Maura and Claire's 'con' columns. Then in Maura's 'pro' column she wrote *fun, laughter, chase, good games, drama* (*drama pro: Interesting? Entertaining? Drama con: Self-absorbed? Exhausting?*). And Suze. *Unflappable. Mother. Career. Strong.* And also, though she didn't know why, the words: *Can I rely on her?* In a space of its own.

For Claire she wrote: *follower* and *good listener* and then *possible post-natal depression* in a space of its own.

Annie had sometimes wondered whether she'd had undiagnosed post-natal depression though she'd found it impossible to pull apart the impact of circumstances following Em's birth, from the hormones and the predisposition that was commonly said to cause it. There was physical pain from the feeding and mastitis, and mental pain from the rows with Ted and the uprooting of her life and independence. It had felt as if her internal scales were unbalanced: on the one hand there was the joy and beauty of her new child and on the other, the overbearing weight of emotional and physical pain that seemed mostly to cancel out all the good stuff. She'd felt grief that life had given her the stuff to tip the scales out of whack, and another kind of grief that she hadn't had it within her to rebalance them herself.

She had hoped that hope alone would drive her through the worst. She had been optimistic about her and Ted raising a family after just seven months knowing each other before she fell pregnant. What the hell! Let's ride the rollercoaster! You only live once! But then, after one terrible night, one that was worse than all the other bad ones combined, he left for good, telling her that he'd been thinking about it for weeks.

It was anathema to her then: to make a decision in advance and then wait, just to check it was the right one, while the other person remained ignorant and in the dark. Then to leave, so that the entire force of the shock was left with the person being left. It seemed so thoughtless and heartless: not to have a plan, not to take that person along for the ride and give them the chance to be ready for what was coming, or even to be given the chance to persuade them to stay.

Anathema, then. But now she knew different. Now she knew that people might have no control over when they left. And that you were lucky if you had time to come up with a plan at all. And that maybe it was hard to voice the plan because that would mean facing up to what was happening. And maybe you didn't want it to happen. Ever. In a million years, ever.

'We should play hide-and-seek,' said Maura, once Annie had returned to the beach.

'Yes! I'll hide!' said Claire, with an enthusiasm that

worried Annie. What if they couldn't find her on the island? What if she didn't want to be found?

'I don't want to lose you,' said Annie. 'Can we sit down in one space so we can talk?'

It had happened during pregnancy, this need to keep people close and, if not close, to know exactly where they were and when. Only on this particular occasion she needed to talk to them. This was the moment she'd been waiting for.

'Where is Claire going to get lost?' said Maura. 'Under a thin blanket of sand? Behind one of those incredibly thin trees? Come on. We have to stop worrying about every little thing and play hide-and-seek! I want to see what's on the rest of the island!'

'Just no,' said Annie abruptly. She felt the sparks of anger: mostly with herself for not being bolder and speaking up then, but also the situation: that even as joy presented itself to her, it was underscored with a grief and anxiety that stopped her from being able to fully enjoy it. 'We don't need to wander around. I really don't want people getting lost.'

'Or,' said Suze, gaze darting between Annie and Maura. 'Let's just finish the tequila Annie brought? Yes, let's just do that.'

'You're a genius for bringing the fags,' said Maura, looking through the tote bag. 'But an absolute clown for not bringing any fire to light them with.' Then she opened up the mineral water bottle and took a drink, proffering it to the rest of them.

When no one accepted the offer, she drank the rest.

They arranged themselves in a line on the sand, and swigged at the bottle of tequila, looking out onto the water in the direction they had come from. In the distance there were the very pale and blurred geometric shapes of the house and trees beyond, but nothing more. It felt neat. To Annie. They – the partners – were over there, while all her friends were here and entirely undisturbed. This was exactly what she had wanted.

So she cleared her throat and slid her arm into Maura's on one side and into Claire's on the other. She smelt Shalimar and sweat on Maura and florals and white wine on Claire.

Claire flinched and withdrew her arm. 'Sorry,' she said, 'I'm just feeling a bit sick.'

'So,' said Annie.

Everyone turned or craned in anticipation of what she was going to say, but with their collective beam on her she found the words freezing in her throat and windpipe, all the way down to the top of her gut. They'd had more fun in the last hour than they had done in the last two years of break-ups and babies and house moves. Wasn't this what she wanted, too? Her friends as she'd always loved and remembered them. And yet here she was, about to set fire to that.

'I—' she began, her eyes stinging.

'What the fuck is that?' interrupted Maura suddenly, looking out at the water. They all followed her gaze.

Annie saw it immediately and jumped to her feet, quickly followed by the rest of them.

'What, that?' said Claire.

'Yes, that!' shouted Maura.

'Oh, God,' said Claire, watching the dark shape of the rowboat floating away, tipping gently, several yards from shore.

'Someone go in and get it!' said Suze.

But the strong tide that had taken them there, the one that

in the past had caused boats to sink and sailors' lives to be taken, was now moving in the opposite direction, stealing the rowboat away from them. They all knew instinctively that to compete with the pace of the water was not a playground game. It would be pointless at best, dangerous at worst.

'Going, going . . .' said Maura wistfully, as they watched the boat blur at the edges, the further away it travelled.

They all joined hands, like a row of paper dolls set against the moonlight.

'Gone,' said Annie quietly.

Chapter 11

Martin

2 a.m. Saturday, 29 August
Sandpiper Cottage

Martin hadn't been asleep long when he heard Em call out for Annie followed by wailing, foghorn tears of distress. He poked his head round the door of Annie's bedroom, respectfully of course, just in case she was getting changed into her nightie, but she was nowhere to be seen. The women must still be out drinking and chatting under the moon.

Em was sitting upright, in the dim light of a tartan-covered side-lamp, the duvet scalloped around her waist, face flushed and damp. Outside, thunder rumbled in the distance.

'There, there, sweetpea, you're OK,' Martin soothed. 'What's that naughty thunder doing, hey? It's telling us that the rain is coming and Mummy will be back very soon. Did it wake you? Do you need your teddy?'

Em gasped in a sob and looked up at Martin as he scoped the room for anything to comfort her – a toy, a book or even Annie's nightdress, the smell of which might transport her back to a place of calm, like popping on a pair of ruby slippers.

Martin slid open the top drawer of an oak chest and

rifled through it quickly – heart hammering, fingers shaking, desperate not to be caught voyeuristically ogling Annie's pants (though they seemed to be cotton, large and nothing to get heated about). He could excuse it as much as he liked, but being caught with your head in a woman's clothes drawer looked nothing less than pervy.

He was losing hope of finding anything by the time he got to the bottom drawer when under a neat pile of colour block T-shirts, he recognized the cloth tote Annie had been carrying up the driveway earlier. Inside was a pile of chunky wooden-beaded necklaces and a grey toy rabbit. When Martin handed the rabbit over to Em, who hugged it like it was her own mother, he felt a surge of warmth at the sight, gold kintsugi joy rippling out everywhere at having improved a broken situation.

As he was about to stuff the tote back into the drawer he saw a pile of plastic wallets lying at the bottom, the very ones Annie had dropped on the driveway. The wallet at the top had Em's full name written in Sharpie pen so they were sure to be the notes Annie had written up as guidance for Karl and was no doubt planning on leaving on the kitchen table before departing for the spa. Martin would read them briefly, in case there was anything in there that might help now: that would be easy to explain away were someone to walk in. Annie had, after all, given him the honourable role of Karl's childcare assistant as they'd walked down the drive earlier that evening.

Martin perched on the edge of Em's bed and encouraged her to lie back down with her bunny. Then he pulled out the pages in the wallet, finding several little essays all stapled together under the headings: current likes and dislikes /

fashion / current toys / sleeping regime / downtime / how to talk about ballet. How utterly wonderful and comprehensive to include an essay on the gender politics of ballet! Karl was certainly more qualified to have these conversations so good on him, and good on her. And underneath all that, an essay on 'the teen years'. How extraordinary to go into that level of detail for a one-off weekend, but perhaps Annie subscribed to the notion that the seeds planted now were the giant redwood trees of the future.

He was returning Em's plastic wallet to the drawer when he saw another wallet marked up with Annie's full name. Essays on herself? Who for? The woman was so thorough, possessing such care and foresight and such capacity to *plan*! But maybe this attention to detail, this constant self-improvement and the tracking thereof was the secret to her great strength and unerring calm. Her ability to juggle all that she did.

Martin longed to look inside, in case there were any useful self-improvement tips he could use. He knew he shouldn't and yet he steeled himself, like he did when he peeked at the creams and treatments and lubricants and painkillers inside other people's medicine cabinets during a visit. He only ever looked because part of him thought a blue-bottled potion existed that only he didn't know about: something magic that made people feel good about themselves. Of course that magic didn't exist, but he still gained comfort from knowing what kinds of kintsugi gold other people used to fix their bodies and souls.

But inside that folder was not a shiny stack of leaflets and recipes and exercise routines and reading lists he could absorb to better himself, rather a sheaf of letters on dull

126

grey-brown paper bearing the NHS insignia. Patient number. NHS number. Both belonging to Annie. Hospital address. The first page, a letter of a few paragraphs. The word 'severe'. *Severe?* He read it over and over and then, with shaking hands, corroborated a few key terms by checking online. The terminology was medical. He didn't know what each word meant on its own, but he knew what it all meant in its totality.

He glanced at Em, her eyes closed, now settled back into a deep sleep. He took hold of her small hand, now flung over the duvet, and held it gently: scared to wake her but also needing to comfort, and be comforted, in that moment.

He blinked away tears; what was worse? The fact that her mother would be dead within a year, or that Em would be too young when it happened to remember anything about her?

Chapter 12

Annie

2 a.m. Saturday, 29 August
Blue Bracken Island

The sound of thunder made Annie's heart leap.

'Are you serious?' said Claire. 'I didn't bring a mac.'

'Just because there's thunder doesn't mean there'll be rain,' said Annie confidently. 'I think it'll pass us by.'

Claire looked at her doubtfully. 'In the same way we were just going to sit on that rowboat in the shallows? In the same way it was only going to take ten minutes to get here? I'm going to call Karl,' she said, turning away from everyone and stabbing at her phone. 'He'll bring some waterproofs in one of those other boats from the shed. Was there one with a motor? Karl can only drive an automatic so is a boat like driving a car? I suppose he could call a – a *boat-taxi*? Is there an app for a boat-taxi and are they likely to pick up people like us in the middle of the night?'

'They'll have an absolute laugh about us in the boat-taxi office if there is one,' said Maura. 'Won't take them a minute to work out that we're *Down From London*.'

'And the Home Counties,' said Claire briskly.

Maura took some slow steps forward until she was

standing with her toes in the water, gazing at a point in the distance where the rowboat had disappeared. 'Didn't think I'd die like this,' she sighed.

'Oh stop it,' said Annie. 'You sound almost relieved at the prospect.'

'On days when I've had no sleep and my kids are being dicks and Dex is being . . . Dex, I've sometimes dreamt of having my bones crunched up by a shark off the coast of a Caribbean island. On days like that I whack on some Kate Bush and put the finishing touches to my funeral plans.'

Suze smiled. 'Presume you haven't swung too far from the original blueprint?'

Everyone knew about Maura's funeral in the same way that no one knew about Claire's. It was one of the things Maura loved to talk about.

Maura swung her hair back like a cape. 'Springsteen tribute-band in a Working Men's Club for a winter death. Free leg-warmers, Espresso Martinis and bingo cards on arrival.'

'Still no Bach, church, lilies or poems about ticking clocks then?' said Suze.

'I'd rather die. Twice!' she said, sending a hoot into the night sky. 'Vodka-spiked ice cream and a DJ playing Nineties bangers in a tent, in the event of a summer death. Probably Claire's back garden.'

'*My* garden?' said Claire.

'Might as well make use of the fact you own some land.'

'It's only a slightly larger garden than the one we had, Maura. Market Crowbury wouldn't know what had hit it if a coachload of middle-aged Londoners turned up wearing sunglasses, clutching packets of Marlboro Lights.'

'Probably do it some good,' said Maura, and Claire rolled her eyes.

'Can we avoid planning too much in the wrong direction?' said Annie.

'Maybe we should stick to the possibility of mild scurvy?' said Suze, crossing her fingers sarcastically.

'Or being snogged to death by pirates,' roared Maura.

'I'm thinking more *how we're going to get off this island*?' said Annie.

'It's OK,' said Claire, catching Annie's eye. 'I just said I'd call Karl back at the house, but I'm having problems with the . . .' She tailed off.

'I always thought I'd go of an overdose,' said Suze.

'What, on your own research psychedelics?' said Annie, thinking of Suze at her desk in the British Library poring over anatomical diagrams of mushrooms as she researched all the novel ways psychedelics could change a person's life. She remembered what Martin had told her about Suze's impending research trip, and how little she'd known about Suze's plans.

'Taking something like fentanyl?' said Suze, head tipped to one side. 'A bit like Prince? I figured if we went the same way we might meet in the afterlife and then I could stand back to back with him and see how much taller I am. It'll be a lot more than he thinks.'

'We need to make a call to one of the men back in the house,' said Annie decisively.

'I said I wa—' Claire began.

'My phone's at the bottom of the ocean in the same watery grave as my knock-off Chanel handbag,' Maura interrupted, looking wistful. 'Anyway, I don't care. I'm happy to be lost with my favourite people. What's not to like?'

'In many ways, it's what you've always wanted to be,' said Suze.

'As successful as Picasso and hot as Madonna?'

'No. A *mum on the run*.'

Maura flew in her direction and pummelled Suze hard in the ribs until she couldn't stop laughing. 'Never, *ever* call me that again. I refuse to be labelled. Especially not as something printed on a fridge magnet.'

Annie glanced over at Claire to smile and eye roll at the sight of Suze and Maura play-fighting like cubs in a way that sometimes made it felt like she and Claire were the only adults in the room. But Claire was on the sand, gazing at the sky, both engaged and yet completely disengaged from what was happening – as if a feature film was playing behind her eyes with a soundtrack Annie couldn't hear.

'Good, excellent, glad you two are taking this all so seriously,' said Annie, still distracted by Claire. 'Suze, where's your phone then?'

'No idea. I'm on a digital detox pre-Peru.'

'Yeah, I heard about that research trip. Well done,' said Annie.

'Cool. Thanks,' said Suze, looking away.

'Is it just going to be Martin and Walt muddling along, while you're gone?' said Annie trying to sound casual.

But Suze must not have heard and was instead looking at something in the sand.

'So, phone-wise—' said Annie.

'Christ-All-Fucking-Mighty!' snapped Claire, which shocked Annie because Claire never swore, least of all using the church as a frame of reference. 'How many times do I have to say that I'm bloody calling bloody Karl?'

131

'Wow, sorry,' said Suze, as they all turned to face her. 'Didn't hear you.'

'OK, fine,' said Claire, her face softening, almost in tears. 'I said it like four times though . . . sorry, sorry for being so loud. I'm just, I'm just worried about Graham is all. You know that tonight was our last feed and I'm sad about missing it. I don't know if he'll get through the night without me. I've been there with him, every night since he was born . . . and now I'm here. This . . . this wasn't the plan. I had some things I wanted to say to him.'

'For God's sake. He's a bloody baby!' said Maura. 'He won't even remember your tits. Let alone,' Maura waggled her fingers in inverted commas, '"*the last feed*".'

Annie threw Maura a disapproving glance and rested her arm on Claire's shoulder. 'It's OK. This is fine. We'll get home tonight. I promise. You can chat to Gray then?'

Claire looked at her with hopeful eyes. 'Graham.'

'Graham,' said Annie.

Then Claire held up her phone and waved it around. 'I don't know how, though. There's almost no reception. One tiny bar keeps falling in and out.'

'I'll try, too,' said Annie. 'It might be the network provider. I've got a sliver of battery. I was saving it for emergencies but . . . we'll get through eventually. And if you get through first I'd like to speak to Karl. Ask how Em is.'

'Hey, Claire, just call Dex?' said Maura calmly. 'He's always glued to his phone. Have you got his new number?'

'What number? What new number? No. Why would I have his number?'

'Because he's a friend—'

'She doesn't need to call him,' said Annie urgently, eyes

132

flashing at Claire. 'What could he do? He was already looking swivel-eyed with booze and we all know he likes a spliff. What if he crashed the boat on the way here? That would be a whole other disaster.'

'You're making him sound like a reckless *addict*!' Maura looked at Annie, appalled. 'Is that why you asked Karl to look after Em? Because you thought Dex would fall asleep in an ashtray on the job?'

Annie waved her phone in the air and stabbed at it again. 'No. Of course not.' It was, in part. If never looking at, or chatting to, Em when they visited was the same as falling asleep in an ashtray. She moved on quickly. 'Shit, it's gone. The sliver's gone. The battery's gone. Claire? Are you still trying?' Annie was desperately trying to keep the panic out of her voice.

'There's nothing! Nothing at all! What are we going to do now? Seriously, what?' said Claire, eyes wild, voice rising, now mainlining both her own and Annie's white-hot panic. 'We have to try something else!' She began jumping up and down and waving her arms in the air, shouting, 'Help! Help!'

Suze folded her arms and watched Claire jumping about. 'Who tied up the boat?'

'Claire took over from me,' said Annie. 'Because I wasn't very good at it.'

'Yes, I did it,' said Claire, coming to a standstill.

'Cool, cool, cool. And *how* did you do it?'

'I dunno.' Claire kicked at the sand. 'With a knot. *Obviously* a knot.'

'What kind of knot, though?' said Maura. 'Like a reef knot, a hitch?'

'A what?' said Claire. 'I tied it up the best way I knew how. In a thing, like the kind I tie my trainers up with?'

'Oh, Claire!' said Maura, dismayed. 'You might as well have set fire to it and pushed it out to sea!'

'Actually,' said Suze, 'that would have been smarter because a burning boat floating across the water might have raised a few alarms on the coast. As it is we've no boat and no flare so—'

'Give her a break,' snapped Annie. 'Maybe if you two hadn't been arsing about on the sand pretending to be Wham! while we were securing the transport you could have helped and we wouldn't be in this position?'

'Yeah,' said Claire, her smile rigid, shoulders up round her ears. 'And besides, I didn't ever learn to knot a rope on Daddy's sailing boat in the Côte d'Azur like Maura.'

'Ouch,' said Maura. 'How many times do I have to tell you that we went to the Côte d'Azur once? We stayed in a simple farmhouse close to a boulangerie and several restaurants. We didn't sail. We hired bikes. I don't know why you always think that's so posh.'

'Because when you spend your childhood holidays in a camper van in Clacton-on-Sea whatever the weather, a French farmhouse is the bloody Ritz.'

'Anyway, it wasn't just a bow, was it?' said Annie quickly, trying to get them off the subject.

'No. It was a *double* bow,' Claire said proudly.

Maura and Suze both collapsed in the sand and groaned.

'Stop it, you two!' snapped Annie, seeing Claire's face fall in double-shame. 'And Claire? The best people tie bows. Thousands of accidents are avoided and lives saved each year with people tying bows in their shoelaces. You don't see people tying reef knots in trainers, do you?'

Claire looked at Annie. 'I'm going to see if I can get some reception further up the island.'

'Do you want some company?'

Claire shook her head sadly.

Time passed, though it was hard to know how much because Annie's phone battery had died and Claire had walked off with her phone, still convinced she could catch some particles of reception by waving it around in the air above her like a butterfly net. Annie's best guess was 3 a.m. when the drop in temperature and light signalled the lonely no man's land between day and night, the same time she had woken every night in the last few, feeling most afraid.

Maura and Suze lay on their backs chatting, watching the sky as though it was a TV show playing in the background. Annie sat upright, digging her hands into the sand, reaching through the layer that was still mildly warm from the day's sun and into the cold beneath, watching Claire pace the waterline.

Claire was so sensitive: so aware of her own, her child's and other people's feelings, which Annie knew would be nothing but a good thing in the years to come.

She had stopped at the water's edge and was gazing in the direction of where they'd come from with a disconsolate yearning in her eyes, arms wrapped tightly around her slim frame. Annie decided to join her, though she approached her with a new caution, like a newly born animal she didn't yet know how to treat.

'Nothing.' Claire handed Annie's phone back to her. 'We seem to be in a communication black-spot.'

'Hey,' Annie said. 'I know you're worried about Graham, but are you all right?'

Claire opened her mouth to speak and then seemed to think better of it.

'Claire? Are we OK?'

'Yeah,' she said, without looking at Annie. 'Do you remember that night when we were all at Maura's and I was about to give birth? Like, a year ago?'

Annie couldn't exactly, other than it being the last period of time they had seen so much of each other. Just as Annie was getting her feet back on the ground, just as Claire was about to move away and have a baby. Things seemed to get so busy. They seemed to need each other less.

'No, I—'

'Come on!' shouted Maura, sitting upright further down the beach. 'I'm freezing my tits off. We need to build a shelter for sleeping in.'

'Shelter?' said Claire, snapping back into the present, turning to Annie, her eyes filling with tears. 'That sounds like we might be here for longer than an hour?'

Annie took hold of her arm gently. 'There's not much we can do while the windsurfers – the people most likely to be first on the water – are asleep. We might as well sleep until they come.'

Claire turned her back and started walking toward Maura.

'Hey, wait,' said Annie. 'I'll come with you so we can keep chatting.'

But Claire didn't reply and kept on walking.

'Come on, you lot! Start by looking for appropriate shelter-materials,' said Maura, waving her arm in the air.

They all got to work, gathering up twigs, driftwood and ferns – anything they could find.

'Put it all in one pile?' Maura said. 'Get a move on, Suze! We want to gather it up before—'

Annie looked at her with a smile. 'Before we miss the tennis on BBC One?' Annie turned to look at the expanse of water beyond them. 'Would we be more protected if we slept in the foresty-woodland bit?'

Claire turned and looked at her. 'Protected from what, exactly? We're in the UK, not the *Amazonian Rainforest*. Right? Right, everybody, right?'

'Calm down,' said Maura. 'Yes, last time I checked we're in the UK, unless we've managed to sail to Ireland.'

'My God, your *geography*.' Suze rolled her eyes. 'This water isn't even the open sea, Maura.'

'Your point?'

'Well, Ireland . . . Oh, never mind. Look, it's not the predators we have to worry about. It's the *ghosts*? The hundreds of dead sailors Martin told us about don't just . . . disappear.'

'Er, yes they bloody do, Suze,' said Maura, winding dried grass around a twig. 'It's called *death*.'

'Can you two focus on the shelter?' said Annie.

'Suze,' persisted Maura.

'Don't test me on this, Maura,' said Suze firmly. 'Unearthly dimensions are my speciality.'

'Under the influence of psychedelics, sure,' said Maura.

'Illness, death, psychedelics, the middle of the night . . . They're all gateways into other dimensions and parallel lives that swim around us all the time. We have to be open to it to see it.'

'Not tonight we don't,' said Annie, before jumping out of her skin at the sound of a piercing shriek coming from the centre of the forest. 'What the fuck was that?'

'An owl,' said Claire calmly. 'You get them in the countryside.'

'Good. Right. Change of plan. We pitch our shelter closer to the water,' said Annie. 'Obviously not too close because I don't know what the tides or the waves do, like how far do they come up? Maybe what I'm saying is that we position ourselves halfway between the woodland and the water?'

'What, and split the risk of death equally between being attacked by an animal and drowning?' Claire's face twisted before she suddenly burst into tears. 'Ideally we'd be positioning ourselves in a double bed with Egyptian cotton sheets or anywhere other than this island!'

Annie reached for Claire so she could put her arms around her, but Claire seemed to nudge her away. Annie couldn't help but feel hurt, but consoled herself with the thought that the nudge could just as easily have been a bodily wrench caused by the emotion of crying, rather than something more distancing.

Annie ran her hand down her face as though she was trying to wipe a slate clean. There was so much that didn't feel right. Was she just feeling tired and hungry, cold and over-sensitive to everything? She rammed her quivering hands into her pockets, swallowed a lump in her throat and, just to stop herself from crying, focused her attention on Maura who was bending her decorative twigs into small curves.

'It's lovely, Mau,' said Suze. 'What is it? The doorbell?'

Maura looked dismayed. 'What do you mean *what is it?*' And they all looked blankly as she added the pretty twisted pieces to the stripped fir branches laid over a single piece of driftwood decorated with hanging trails of wild flowers. 'It's our bloody shelter is what it is.'

'It seems more of a . . . a sculpture?' said Suze.

'You are very bloody welcome to take a crack at it yourself,

138

Suze, and while you're at it, build a forcefield to keep the ghosts out?'

Maura was looking as belligerent as Annie had ever seen her, chin jutting out in challenge in exactly the same way Alfie and Freddy had, earlier.

Annie's response was to stem it all immediately by calling, 'Lights out!'

'Lights out!' shrieked Maura in glee. 'I love it! *Love* not being the one to have to say that.'

As Suze raked down the sand to create a good bed base under the thin and entirely pointless canopy of branches, she said 'I really need to be back on Monday to arrange my visa for Peru.'

'If you're not back on Monday you'll have more to worry about than a visa,' said Maura.

'If they don't discover we're missing tonight,' said Claire, her voice quivering, 'and they all wake up after we were due to leave at six, then no one's going to expect us back until Sunday. That means we'll be here for like . . . ever.'

'You're jumping ahead,' said Annie. 'It's like Oxford Street-on-Sea out there in the summer. Boats, floats, all sorts of stuff. We'll be fine.'

And with that they fell into a deep silence as they negotiated their positions on the sand for sleep.

'Maura, can you keep me warm?' asked Suze, as Maura lay down in the middle.

'What, because my belly fat acts like a duvet and your bony-ness acts like a sheet? Sure.'

And with that, Maura and Suze curled up like a couple on the sand, leaving Claire and Annie standing awkwardly either side of them.

'Where do you want to sleep?' Annie said to Claire, looking down at the raked sand.

'I don't mind,' said Claire, before stepping several feet away from Maura and Suze and lying down with her back to them both. Annie, wanting to honour her space, stepped into the large gap in between them all so that she was both surrounded by her friends and yet still cold with the empty space around her.

After a few moments she shuffled over to Claire's side and reached out to touch her arm. 'Hey,' she said.

'Sleeping now. Tired.' Claire curled into a tight, foetal ball, like a woodlouse under attack.

Annie decided then that she couldn't take Claire's brooding responses personally, or wait for them to peter out, else she'd lose both time and focus. Claire's tearful detachment was obviously a symptom of her anxiety and hunger, of her taking out her harder emotions on Annie: like a child with a mum. Annie decided it was nothing but a compliment, a searing testament to their closeness that Claire felt safe enough to be brooding with her. Whatever her issues with Karl, Dex, her weight, her mental health and the countryside, they could be dealt with.

The obvious solution was to 'hold space' for Claire's difficult emotions, so long as Claire metabolized them asap and got on with being her normal loyal self.

'Claire, I need to tell you something,' whispered Annie.

'About your shaky hands?' said Claire sleepily.

'Yeah. Thanks for not going into it with the others earlier. I really appreciated it, I wasn't ready . . .'

'It's OK, I get it . . . it's an old person's illness. Lots of people have it in our village. My nan had it, too.'

'Had what?'

'Arthritis? Makes your wrists weak. I get it. You don't want to bang on about it. You're not even forty. My nan only ate buns and chips so it didn't help her symptoms much. Scarborough in the Seventies, you know? There's a lot that can be done nowadays if you follow the principles of an anti-inflammatory diet. Broccoli. Nuts. Karl knows a lot about that stuff. You should talk to him.'

'No, sure, I'll keep that in mind.'

Annie rolled onto her back, blinked and stared up at the night sky, glossy and glutinous as tar. The sand that had moulded to fit her shape when she first lay down now felt like concrete and sent a deep chill into her hip bones. Her clothes hadn't dried properly from standing in the water to steady the boat, so her skin was rough and itchy with salt. She knew she wouldn't sleep easily. Vigilant by nature, her blood vibrated with cortisol at the best of times. She sighed. Would she ever feel safe again? Would she ever be able to trust nature or, for that matter, the human beings who told her things would work out in the end? How simple it would be just to have what Claire's nan had and solve it with a few pills and pumpkin seeds.

Annie reached into her back pocket for the notebook, wanting to capture some of her thoughts about Claire from earlier, but there wasn't enough light and she knew she was delaying the inevitable. The moment she told Claire the news, Claire would never see her as the same person again.

Annie plucked the single red baby blanket out of her tote and laid it over Claire's legs. Edging closer, to a few inches away from Claire's neck, Annie spoke, tears stinging her eyes.

'Hey, Claire, it's not arthritis.'

'Hmmm?'

Annie glanced back to check on Maura and the slow rise and fall of her soft curves, and at Suze's inert lightning-bolt zigzag of limbs in the sand. Once she was assured that the gentle yet guttural snoring pouring out of Maura was both clear evidence of a deep sleep, and enough of a sound shield for Suze in case she was awake, she turned to Claire again.

'First of all, I wanted to say please don't punish me for walking in on . . . that thing with Dex, whatever it was. I'm not judging.' She kept her voice low, ever conscious of the other two. 'It's just that life is short and I don't understand why you'd waste a single moment of it on a tosser like him. Maybe I *am* judging . . .' She stopped herself. 'I'm sorry. I'm just saying that you have to look at what matters. Which is this. Us four. Right? Family. I know you've got your mum and dad still. And a sister. And Maura's got her brother in Paris and whatever . . . but for me? It's you three.'

She adjusted the blanket again to cover Claire's ankles and wiped a tear away from her cheek. 'So I need to ask you something. Can you just, hold on?'

Annie tightened her fingers around the notebook for comfort, or guidance, like a set of non-religious rosary beads. She breathed in deeply. 'I need to offer one of you . . . A job?'

I need you . . . she said to herself, the sounds of the words failing to make it out into the dark night air.

'Fuck,' she spat, hoping the word would dislodge it all like a punch between the shoulder blades might dislodge a bit of food that was stuck at the back of her throat. 'And when I say one of you, I think I really mean you.'

She looked at the back of Claire. Nothing. Stillness and silence. Understandable. It was a big ask. And Claire was the kind of person who liked to assimilate. She wasn't the kind to jump in, like Maura, or to reframe it in a way that suited her, like Suze. She was considered and thoughtful and not remotely impulsive like the other two.

'What's the elevator pitch?' Annie said, because, as her boss always told her, if you couldn't sell your idea in a single sentence it likely wasn't compelling enough – and this was *The Sell* of Annie's life: 'I need you to be Em's mum.' She paused, nose sniffing with the tickled wet of tears. 'Claire? Please say something?'

Annie put her hand on Claire's shoulder gently and craned over to try to see her expression, only to find Claire's eyes shut. Then came the low rumble of a graceful yet definitive snore.

Annie sighed deeply and rolled onto her back, looking up at the sky, struck by every moment that would happen without her in the years to come. There were only a limited number of times she had left when she would be lost in the moment. This one, in the expanse of the sky and its stars above her, her skin clammy with both the pervasive heat of an unnatural summer and dead-of-night cold. The sand beneath her. Lying surrounded on all sides by the women she loved most in the world. She tried to hold on to it, but felt it slip away all too soon.

'Here goes,' she said quietly, addressing her words to the universe, like maybe it would change its mind if she said the right things in the right order.

'I'm asking you, Claire, because you're the calmest and most reliable and I think will deal with this situation the best out of all of us. I've written the job spec down, called it a *bible* if that isn't too lofty, more a set of guidelines which are back at the house in a plastic folder with Em's name on the front. When you suggested Karl look after Em it really made me think this would be a good chance to try it all out, don't you think?

'So what's important? Em needs to eat properly,' Annie continued, gaining traction, feeling the importance of speaking the words out loud for the first time. 'I like the fact you eat more vegetables than Maura or Suze. And look at Karl, he'll keep you all in chickpea burgers for a long time yet. You two are good, aren't you?'

Annie hesitated as she remembered Claire and Dex on the beach together. Then swept the thought away. Diet and food. That was easier to concentrate on. The downside of all that, with Claire, was that she didn't eat much herself. Annie could see the staircase ridges of her ribcage, thinner than she had ever been. Annie didn't want Em growing up to fear her body, like it was a beast needing to be tamed.

'It would be good actually,' Annie continued, 'if you could let Em eat everything? Trying different food is a metaphor, a training ground for life because if you don't try things, like experiences and people and countries, how do you ever know what's going to make you happy? For example, Em could love spinach and hate milk, or the other way round. It doesn't matter, it's just important that she have an opinion because opinions matter.'

But now she came to think of it, Claire's opinions weren't always strong, or forthright, or colourful. Not in the way that Suze's or Maura's were. Maura's were sometimes a rainbow rave in a fireworks factory.

Annie sat up to concentrate better. 'I'm actually worried, Claire, because if Em doesn't have an opinion on anything then she'll be swayed all over the place by the opinions of others. So what I'm saying is that you should definitely bring in Maura because, let's face it, Maura's made some shocking choices and what is the point in shocking choices if you can't pass on your wisdom to the younger generation? And if Em has a bad experience with sex or drugs? Use Suze. She'll help reframe the whole thing as a positive life experience.'

Annie felt nauseous to be saying these words and pinched herself to get on with it.

Money was an issue: raising a child was expensive. Claire, born to a postman and a dinner lady, hated talking about money and had especially hated it every time one of her friends had paid for something during their university days. Annie had never excavated it at the time, she'd never had to worry about money that much but she understood Claire's discomfort better now than she had then, as the bone-deep discombobulation of having a debt you could never repay.

Annie didn't have much money but what she did have she'd give to Claire. Karl was financially stable – though if Claire and Karl ever divorced, where would that leave Em and the bills that needed paying for in her life?

'But here's the dealbreaker,' Annie said, looking up at her shining North Star. 'It's a permanent position.' She swallowed. 'Very permanent, if I'm honest. And when do you start? There'll be a handover period when we get back that will last a few weeks, maybe a few months if I'm lucky. Then you'll hit the ground running.'

Annie put her hand on Claire's shoulder and felt it rise and fall gently with her breath.

'I'm dying, Claire.'

Annie had never said it out loud. Her heart hurt and her

tears felt so warm against her skin. 'I'm . . . dying. Can you believe I have to go so soon? Like leaving the party just as it's getting started? And then leaving my baby behind in the middle of a room full of people and streamers?' She swallowed, tears leaking from the corners of her eyes and slipping down her cheeks towards her ears. 'Except that I never get to come back and collect Em from the party. I never get to come back for her.'

Chapter 13

Martin

7 a.m. Saturday, 29 August
Sandpiper Cottage

Martin stood up close to the bi-fold doors and, opening them a crack to sniff the air's earthy chlorine tang – a sure sign that rain was on the way – he considered what a stroke of luck it was that the women had left early enough to avoid the worst of the weather to come. He could already see the bruised smudges of cloud gather over Blue Bracken Island and his chest tightened a little at the thought of those poor sailors shipwrecked there many years ago: their hearts must have broken at the prospect of never seeing friends or family again as their boat went down.

Martin's hands were wrapped around an oversized mug of hot coffee embossed with the words: *Keep Smiling, It Might Never Happen*. That morning, as the light rose, he'd lifted the mug out of the cupboard muttering, 'It bloody well did though, didn't it?' all the while curbing tears with the back of his hand.

He'd not slept a wink, at least not enough winks to change how bad and sad he'd felt when he'd gone to bed. He'd tossed and turned in his scratchy nylon single sheets that smelt of sherbet, but no amount of box-breathing, pacing, hot milk, or rereading his father's old holiday round-up mails would send him into the deep and long sleep he needed. He'd had half an ear out for Suze – she was the only person he wanted to discuss Annie's news with – but he must have fallen into some kind of sleep because he knew now that he'd missed her return and subsequent departure in the early-doors taxi.

When it came to sleep, he knew better than to cram his head with so much info before bed, though he'd leafed through Annie's notes several times, privacy be damned when faced with such colossal news. He'd already read the worst bit and the biggest favour he could surely do for her was to understand it all clearly, so that he could help explain it to others when she simply couldn't bear repeating it again. *Forewarned is forearmed. Knowledge is power.* He'd married up the notes and facts with some online research, a habit Suze usually warned against because it frequently led him down a rabbit hole where he concluded that a sore throat meant he had just months to live. But this time he had medical terminology and dates and tests results from which he could draw reasonable conclusions – albeit conclusions that made him sad and sick of soul. Her illness had been picked up late. The symptoms were currently being controlled with medication, though there was a time limit to how effective the pills would continue to be. Given her age, and when it was caught, it was hard to tell exactly how it would progress, but if she was here this time next year it would be a miracle.

He braced a hand on the glass doors and allowed his grief to overwhelm him for a moment. When it had passed, he slid the doors shut.

Martin just couldn't seem to put any distance between

himself and Annie's news. *Stop being so bloody sensitive, Martin!* his mother used to say, as if it was a character flaw. But what if, in this case, it was a superpower? Right from the start, his sensitive radar had picked up on Annie's insistence that this weekend happen, though, to be honest, it had come at a good time, just when Suze needed to be reminded that life was better when in the bosom of family and friends. And Martin had been nothing but a positive, supportive voice on Annie's *Hollibobble Me Up* WhatsApp thread as she laid out schedules and plans and shopping lists which were often met with Maura's gentle mocking that perhaps Uncle Annie Fun-Times was scheduling The Fun out of everything.

As Martin lay in bed that night he'd had a fantasy that involved Suze at the spa having fun with her friends – laughing, saying something about there being nothing worse than people wandering around in medical tabards as if they were about to harvest your organs. And then weeping at Annie's news. And then coming home to Martin's warm embrace as he said *Let's utilize the onion-skin scheme again, like we did last time there was a crisis in the group? We really helped people out and that felt good, didn't it? Nothing like the superstructure of community and friendship.*

First and foremost, Annie's news was a tragedy, but Martin would be lying if he didn't say it didn't dovetail nicely into his plans to try and make Suze stay.

Em cried out from her bedroom and Martin couldn't get there fast enough to comfort her.

'It's OK,' he said, stemming his own tears as he lifted her solid, warm and reassuring little body out of Annie's bed. Not wanting to infect her with his sadness, he balanced her on one hip, gave her the grey bunny and spoke in his best sing-song voice. 'Mummy must have given you a kiss last night because you slept like an absolute bunny in her den. And guess what? There'll be thunder again soon, and what does the thunder mean? That Mummy will be back before you know it. Now. Let's get some of your friends to play with.'

Holding Em on his hip, Martin sped on to gather up the other children as they began waking like dominoes. The twins, Alfie and Freddy, were next, hammering down the hallway toward the kitchen in their matching pyjamas, followed by Walt, who Martin fitted snugly onto his other hip. Moments later he heard Graham weeping and Karl groaning and shushing.

Martin knocked gently on Karl's door and opened it a crack, while trying to balance the children on both hips. 'Martin's morning creche is open for biz! You want me to take Graham?'

'Oh, mate!' said Karl, tearful with relief, covering the gape in his boxer shorts. 'You look like a child-candelabra with those kids hanging off you. If I have to read *Fireman Sam* again, I'll puke. He doesn't even understand it!' Karl drew a quick breath and wiped away something invisible from under his eyes. 'And I tried to give him a bottle but, but . . . he punched it out of my hand so hard it flew across the floor. What am I going to do if the little guy doesn't eat? He'll waste away.'

'He'll eat when he's hungry, don't you worry,' said Martin. 'Maybe he needs some distraction. Come on, hand over the goods.'

Karl got out of bed and slotted Graham into Martin's child-candelabra.

'You're a diamond,' said Karl. 'I don't know how I'm

going to manage Gray and Em without Claire, so a few hours extra kip will be the difference between enjoying the day and wanting to chop my own balls off with exhaustion. What I'm saying is cheers and thank you and goodnight.'

Fifteen minutes later, Graham was happily in his pen with a toy, and both twins and Em and Walt were seated in front of porridge and hot chocolate topped off with a flourish of squirty cream. They had literally *squawked* with delight at the cream, a sound so worth its weight in gold Martin had fired the canister again and again. Breakfast finished, Martin took all the children to the woods, fitting Graham into a little sling at his chest. He'd felt so happy surrounded by this small group of burgeoning minds and growing souls as he pointed out birds and trees and shared his local knowledge of the area, speculating on the buzzards flying overhead and the lost ship of Blue Bracken. It was a oneness he hadn't felt in a long time; as if his blood was flowing with the warmth of a soothing bath.

And so he was feeling much more positive when, two hours after all the children had woken, Karl heralded his arrival in the kitchen with a loud yawn, a pair of piped and striped PJs hanging off his neat, slightly jutting hips.

'Half a bottle of full fat cow's gold delivered safely to the little man, plus a few spoons of porridge with a dash of squirty cream to seal the deal!' said Martin.

Karl punched Martin gently on the arm and gave him a grateful smile.

Martin had laid out a second breakfast spread including marmalades, jams and cereals, warmed-up pastries and a pot of coffee primed to be plunged. While he didn't possess the knowledge to cure Annie, Martin was feeling extremely buoyed by his small contributions to the integrity of the group.

However, when Dex arrived in the kitchen, wearing the clothes he'd arrived in the previous day – a boxy, thick canvas peasant jacket and slightly too short trousers – that sense of warm stability began to waver.

'I've popped the twins *con Walt e Em*,' said Martin, adopting a faux Mediterranean accent in the hope it would keep the atmosphere light, 'outside where I can see them, on the front beach for a little play. In case you're wondering where your boys are.'

'No. Right. Yeah. Thanks. The bastard car's got a flat,' said Dex, voice hoarse with vape smoke. 'All I need. I was planning to get away like . . . ASAP. I've got calls to make later.'

Martin was so glad he'd stabbed Dex's tyre. Dex may not know it, but it was more important than ever that he stick around. The women would be in possession of life-changing knowledge by now and when they returned tomorrow they'd need their partners to support them.

'Could you have driven over a sharp stone?' said Martin, trying to keep a poker face.

'There's a bloody steak knife sticking out of the rubber.'

'Jesus!' exclaimed Martin, a word he never usually said but felt compelled to, as if laying the ground for himself as the opposite of someone who would consider trying to murder a tyre with a steak knife. He hadn't had the strength in his wrists to get the thing out again. 'Absolute tosser!' Martin added for good measure. 'What total madman did that?'

Dex turned around, his face unreadable at first. 'Maura, of course. Classic Maura. Maura being a dick. Classic dick-games-playing Maura. She likes to attack me and my property.

Sometimes with kitchen utensils.' Dex looked furious and was speaking with a candour that Martin found unsettling. Dex's rage seemed so unchecked and chaotic, Martin worried it would be thrown into a box to be used later in some sort of revenge crime against his wife.

But Martin didn't want Dex to take revenge on Maura when she'd done nothing wrong. 'Doubt it was her. Maybe a local nutter?'

'Bring back the days when we died at thirty,' said Dex. 'And didn't have to put up with another fifty years of living with and loathing the same person. There are so many unhappy couples around.' Perhaps not a revenge crime, then. Perhaps divorce? 'I don't know why people aren't OK with moving on.'

'Except you haven't.'

Martin had been aiming to convey a sense of support: that there was still something strong keeping the two of them together. And yet his tone had come out as sounding surprisingly confrontational which, judging by the look of distaste on Dex's face, was having the opposite effect.

Martin tried again. 'By which I mean, maybe you like the conflict?'

But Martin kicked himself again because what he'd meant was that perhaps they thrived on conflict, as if conflict was an expression of passion and how wonderful to have that in a marriage? He hadn't meant to make Dex sound like a sociopath who had a nose for a fight. Martin loathed himself in that moment: why did he get himself so tangled up in Dex's presence?

'Hey!' shouted Dex, with such force that Martin jumped out of his skin. Dex was looking outside to where Alfie stood on the front beach, one foot on Freddy, who was lying face down in the sand at the water's edge, while Em and Walt looked on. 'What the fuck do you think you're all doing?' Dex shouted, rushing to the open glass doors.

Freddy jumped up, his smiling face covered in sand. 'Wrestling.'

Martin breathed a sigh of relief that they were all still alive on his watch.

'Well, don't do it again!' snapped Dex. 'Not near the water. Or sand. Or anywhere. You'll bloody drown or suffocate your brother. And you two,' he snapped at Walt and Em, 'are just as bad, egging them on like that.'

'Hey,' said Martin gently, 'they're only two and four. They don't know it's dangerous.'

'Do you have an answer for absolutely everything?' snapped Dex.

Martin felt his stomach cave in a little, like he'd been kicked by an invisible foot. Was Dex referring to his previous shouting incident in the corridor when Martin had followed up with his magic toaster-trick? Did Dex think that Martin was using these tiny victories against him? That Martin had actual *power* over him?

If so, he was sorely mistaken because Martin felt nothing but empathy for exhausted parents who occasionally lost their shit.

'I'm just going to put Graham down for a nap,' said Karl quietly. He'd been busy nibbling on some watermelon slices, sipping his coffee and watching the whole thing play out as though he was watching the nine o'clock news.

Martin suspected Karl wanted to make a break for it and he didn't blame him.

'We're going to get the train,' Dex said stormily. 'I'll leave the car here and Maura can deal with the steak knife when she returns from her twenty-four-hour long massage.'

'Please don't go!' said Martin, panic and need threading through him, making his request come out as a squeak. 'There are bank holiday works on the track! Look!' He swiped at his phone to show Dex the page of red-boxed messages. 'I can change the tyre for you. It won't take long.'

'Can you?' said Dex, looking at him through narrowed eyes.

No, he could not.

'Absolutement,' said Martin, his jaw aching.

'OK, great, thanks, if you're sure? How long?'

'Soon as poss.'

'OK cool, perhaps I'll crack on with my calls then. Good man.'

Dex poured himself some coffee, grabbed a handful of pastries in the crook of his arm and wandered out onto the deck, while Martin breathed out at the prospect that he may have tamed the beast temporarily.

Martin started a little tidying around the kitchen, slotting plates into the dishwasher and stacking the toys into one accessible pile, all the while wondering where he was going to source a wrench, or whether indeed a wrench was what you even needed to change a tyre. While crouched at the mouth of the dishwasher, Alfie scuttled in and flung his arms round Martin's back. Before Martin had a chance to speak, Alfie grasped Martin's hand firmly and pulled him further down to the ground so Martin was cross-legged on the floor, facing the boy.

Alfie's eyes were haunted and wide with tears. 'Uncle Martin,' he said urgently.

'Everything all right, soldier? Were you worried out there?'

He nodded.

'It's OK. Your dad was just scared something might happen. You've got to be careful with the water, especially if you can't swim.'

'I want *you* to be my dad.'

Martin was both flattered and curious. The image of Dex's sneering lips as he caught hold of his son's sleeve had remained emblazoned on Martin's brain since he saw it: how he longed to hear more about Dex's personal failures as a father. But Martin could also feel the stony weight of his moral compass.

'You've got a dad,' he said. 'And your dad loves you.'

'He's too loud.'

'So what do you do when he . . .' Martin couldn't help it, he was only human, he didn't need to say it, but he did. 'Shouts that much? Shouts like a bloody train engine, eh?' He smiled.

Alfie smiled back shyly. 'I play in my Wendy house.'

'Aren't you a lucky boy then? Because this whole place is your Wendy house! Why don't I make you a snack and you can play away to your heart's content?'

Alfie ran off happily to join Freddy and Walt and Em and together they went on the move around the house, like a set of iron filings on a magnet.

'Hey, Martin,' said Karl, standing at the doorway, arms folded. Martin had no idea how long he'd been standing there. 'Dex seems to be the kind of person who . . . you know . . . cork up his arse. What I'm saying is, don't take it personally when he goes for you. He's given both his children the same name, after all.'

'What do you mean?'

'Alfie and Freddy? Both come from Alfred. It's fucking madness, is what it is. I've not the heart to tell him.' Karl winked and Martin smiled, grateful for the support. It gave him the boost of energy he needed to seal the deal on what his heart was already telling him: that he had it in him to go one better than making a good breakfast and fixing a tyre to ensure their integrity as a group.

Chapter 14

Annie

8 a.m. Saturday, 29 August
Blue Bracken Island

Annie was the first to wake the following morning from something that wasn't so much sleep as her consciousness running laps round itself before dipping beneath the surface into terror and dreaming. Her first thoughts on waking were of Suze and Claire and Maura singing in harmony on the boat, and of holding tightly on to each other as they watched the boat disappear. Then she remembered them laughing until they cried as they chased each other over the sand. And finally, of how the doubt had sunk into her bones as she rehearsed her speech to a sleeping Claire under the night sky.

Annie's eyes stung and her joints popped and ached as she stretched out on the sand and sat up. The sun was a smudged yellow-grey orb, its brightest light occluded by granite clouds, and the air was dull and close, smelling of damp wood and toffee, promising rain. The smell of mornings at home were her favourite thing. The fresh laundry-and-baby shampoo scented cuddles with Em when she first woke. Fresh coffee, nearly burnt toast and minted shower gel, all signalling hope for the start of a new day, the sense that anything was possible.

But what she felt when she looked at the thick mist boxing off the island like a surgical curtain, was the opposite. Her chest fluttered with panic. What exactly was their plan to get out of this place if it started raining? Tell the rain to stop using their worst swear words? British tourists that paid a premium to holiday in this beautiful conservation area wouldn't sail or swim in weather that was anything less than *clement* and *entirely safe*. They'd be making alternative wet-weather plans over coffee and toast right that minute: indoor tennis or soft play or driving to the nearest town to visit The Museum of Wool or The Museum of Goats. And without a windsurfer or a tourist on a boat, no amount of singing or swearing was going to get them the help they needed to get off the island. They were just too far from the mainland. None of them could swim that far.

She glanced over at her sleeping friends: Maura splayed out like a starfish, Suze lying on an outstretched arm and Claire, back still turned, almost completely unmoved from her sleeping position the previous night.

She was glad she'd made a first attempt at talking to Claire, even if it hadn't been heard. Just speaking the words out loud had helped. She'd treat it like a first draft: a chance to iron out the wrinkles and restructure things to sound more saleable and less panicked – less emphasis on the importance of vegetables, more on resilience and reassurance.

Annie's heart hammered against her chest as she felt her doubts resurface again. If not Claire, then who? Suze was about to travel again, a once-in-a-lifetime research post to Peru of all places. It was hardly Berkhamsted where things could be flexibly managed somehow. And Maura was in an irascible marriage, not to mention in the midst of her own psychological decluttering, at the stage where all hopes, fears, triggers and traumas had been tipped out from her mental wardrobes and onto the floor.

Claire, despite her mild weirdness with food, body image, new inclination toward melancholy and a bad piece of judgement vis à vis Dex, *had* to be the right choice.

Perhaps the best approach was to rip the plaster off and tell them, committee-style, that she'd chosen Claire, and then Claire would be obligated, in the glaring light of all their eyes, to do the right thing by never considering Dex again and look after her dying friend's child. Two birds with one stone.

Annie pulled her legs up and buried her face in her knees, feeling the thin cotton of her skirt dampen with tears. Of course she couldn't do that: it would amount to guilting and shaming Claire into the job, the very thing she didn't want any of her friends to feel, or for her daughter to learn. Most women she knew had guilt and shame running through them like the words on a stick of rock. She'd be a hypocrite for adding to that.

Besides, she wasn't sure she could face their collective intensity. She'd seen their facial expressions for every circumstance in the many years she'd known them: delighted surprise at pregnancy news, misery at break-up news, joy at seeing each other after a long period of travel, total excitement when their favourite songs came on the radio and through the speakers at weddings and in clubs. Concern, boredom, exhaustion, embarrassment.

How would they look when she told them she was dying?

She guessed at Claire's wide-eyed tears, the arched eyebrows of Maura's furious disbelief and Suze's mask of expressionless and weird, detached calm that would read as uninterest if you didn't know her, but was actually her taking a moment to assimilate and reframe in a way that meant she could metabolize it. And what else?

But why? One of them would ask with a pained expression. *How did you get it?* As if it was something she had caught and therefore could have avoided.

She'd have to field all the questions she'd never wanted to have asked of her. Questions she didn't have all the answers to but whose answers would be forced on her in the coming weeks, anyway.

Where was she supposed to begin? Symptoms? Tests? Diagnosis? Prognosis? The next few months? The next year? All the 'mights'? Like how to prepare for the moment Em might sit weeping at her kitchen table in ten years' time because her first period had arrived and her actual mum wasn't there to help her with period pants and possible pain and a story about when it first happened to *her*? Or how to hug her and what to do and say when she broke up with a girl or a boy or got involved in somebody else's relationship?

Annie wiped her eyes quickly as Maura woke, lifting herself up on one arm, eyes still half-closed.

'I swear someone called Flower is supposed to be massaging me in a bamboo shed near Bournemouth right now,' she groaned. 'And instead, I feel like a raccoon shat in proximity to me, and then in my mouth and then ran over me with a steam-roller. Why do people camp when there's plumbing and central heating and duvets?'

'It's nature, babe,' said Suze, rolling over and sitting up to scratch her head then pluck her hair as though she was shaping it with the morning's hair-wax. 'Communing with it, sleeping in it . . . it takes us back to our very essence. To who we once were.'

'My essence left caves and spears behind in the past, where they belong, and is at its happiest in a massive bubble bath with a pint of wine.'

Claire pushed herself up to sitting, managing to look both physically well rested yet emotionally weary. Annie wanted to hug away everything that was bothering her.

'Guess what?' said Annie, remembering something and feeling sparks of happiness that she was about to bring joy to a despairing situation: Martin's kintsugi gold in the form of doughnuts.

She reached back into her canvas tote and pulled out the crumpled pink paper bag. Inside, she felt the outline of the gritty buns with joy and relief. 'Slightly damp doughnuts but, wow, there are still three of them!'

'Three?' said Claire. 'Is that like one for Annie, one for Suze and one for Maura?'

'You last ate a doughnut in, like 1999,' said Maura matter-of-factly. 'You don't touch sugar or fried goods or cake or—'

'I'm stuck on a desert island, Maura!' Claire snapped. 'Of course I touch sugar and fried goods. I'd even eat your foot if it was better maintained. Do you *ever* cut your toenails?'

'Keep your hair on,' said Maura.

'You guys go ahead with your . . .' Claire looked stricken. 'Three. Three doughnuts.'

'Are you OK?' said Annie. 'They only came in bags of three and I bought them to eat on the car journey up here.'

'I'm fine,' she said. 'It's just that you don't always include me in everything. Do you?'

'What's she on about?' said Maura.

'Conversations. That kind of thing,' said Claire.

'We're not students anymore, babe? We don't all live in the

same space at the same time, so it's impossible to be sharing *everything*,' said Maura.

Annie wanted to ask more about what Claire meant but eating doughnuts felt more of a priority regarding their hunger pangs and primal need for survival, than who was including who in what conversations, which felt like it belonged back in the school playground.

'Can we please stop *talking* about the doughnuts and *eat* the doughnuts?' said Suze. 'Being hungry isn't going to help anyone make good decisions about getting off this island.'

'You were the one who suggested we get on this stupid island in the first place,' said Claire.

'Exactly!' exclaimed Suze. 'I had not eaten dinner and I had drunk far too much Aperol and I've lost track of how many times that's happened in my life without consequence, probably because on almost all those occasions it's been in Central London or some other place with a shitting Burger King round the corner. So this, right here, this zero-breakfast situation, has never been a problem.'

'Someone's sounding *han*-gry,' smiled Maura.

Annie felt their gazes bore into her as she tore up the doughnuts into awkward segments and shared them out as equally as possible.

'I need a drink,' said Maura.

'Of course you do, babe. You always need a drink,' said Suze.

'No, I need water.'

'So do I,' said Claire. 'We're going to die of dehydration, aren't we?'

'That's not the plan,' said Suze. 'Is it, Annie?'

'Absolutely not,' said Annie.

'So what is it? The plan?' said Claire.

'Yes,' said Annie. 'The plan!'

'The plan!' said Suze, exhaling with relief, like the adults had finally arrived. 'Tell us what it is!'

'Annie?' said Maura. But Annie was distracted by the thickening blanket of mist coming toward them.

'We flag down a windsurfer with good thighs, right, Annie?' said Maura.

'*Flag down a windsurfer?*' laughed Annie. 'What, like flagging a black cab on the Charing Cross Road?'

'We're not in the middle of the ocean,' said Suze. 'It's summertime, peak holiday season when people are out on the water. If the weather clears, we'll even be able to see Bournemouth.'

'If the weather clears . . .' said Annie, her insides twisting again. 'So while we wait for a cruise liner—'

'Even just an inflatable flamingo with a person on it,' said Maura, licking sugar off her lips.

'So while we wait,' continued Annie, trying to get her thoughts in order, 'we need to play to our strengths so we survive—'

'*Survive?*' exclaimed Claire.

'And leave,' reassured Annie.

'Exactly,' said Suze.

Annie pushed herself up to standing and put her hands on her hips. 'Maura, you can be in charge of making things. I'm sure I speak for everyone when I say that we really do appreciate last night's shelter. I'm only glad there was nothing much to shelter from. But today or tonight, when the weather comes in, might be different. What I'm saying is, please don't feel obliged to decorate anything with flowers, unless we have too much time on our hands.'

'Why are you saying *tonight*? Why are you saying *too much time*?' said Claire, on the verge of tears. 'Surely we'll be home for lunch?'

'There are some lovely shaped leaves over there,' began Maura.

'No, Maura,' said Annie. 'Just the functional, escape basics. Moving on . . .' Annie was starting to feel lighter as she applied structure to the mess. 'Obviously, I have the overview here.'

'The leadership role?' said Suze.

'Our *captain*,' said Maura.

'What qualifies Annie for *that* role?' said Claire.

'She's the only one who has actual medals?' said Suze. 'Swim team captain for her county, remember?'

'She was a child!' said Claire.

'OK good,' said Annie quickly. 'Suze, you can be in charge of morale?'

'Fine,' said Suze, sitting up in the sand and stretching her neck to each side like she was preparing for an aerobics class. 'Annie is the captain, Maura is the builder and I'll be in charge of entertainment, hobbies and pastimes aka morale. I'd also like to add navigational command to my job description because I'm not confident the rest of you have a grip on where north, south, east and west are.'

'So where does that leave me?' said Claire.

They all looked at her blankly.

'Organizational strategy?' said Suze.

'What exactly is that?' said Claire.

'The kind of role you give someone who ties up a boat with a bow,' said Maura.

'Stop it, Maura,' hissed Annie, not wanting any of them to exacerbate Claire's fragile state, least of all by falling out.

'Organizational strategy means nothing,' said Claire.

'You could . . .' Suze trailed off, distracted by a shell.

'You could, I don't know . . .' said Annie.

'What about . . .' said Maura.

'What?' said Claire expectantly.

'Sorry,' said Maura sheepishly, 'I've forgotten what I was going to say.'

'I know,' said Annie quickly. 'You could be *lookout*?'

'Lookout?' said Claire, her eyes filling with tears. 'I'm not *five*.'

'No, right. But it is an important role?' Although even as she said it, she knew that what they were all reaching for, but couldn't quite say, was that Claire, other than her understated fortitude and quiet sense of humour when she was in a better mood, did not present with an overriding personality *strength*.

'You could just, back us all up? Be an executive assistant?' said Annie.

Claire took one look at them all, her face a mask of hurt, 'Back you up?' And with that, she did something very unexpected: she jumped to her feet, turned and ran – away from them, in the direction of the water.

'Claire, stop!' Annie shouted after her. 'Where are you going?'

'I need some space. Leave me alone,' shouted Claire.

'When someone says, "give me some space", what they really mean is *come after me*,' said Suze.

'Yes, thank you, Suze. Of course I'm going to go after her.'

'She seems really annoyed with you.'

'No, she's not. She's tired and grumpy. And she's got a lot going on.'

'What's she got going on?' said Suze. 'She doesn't have that much going on.'

'You'd know better than the rest of us,' said Annie bluntly, remembering that Suze had been to visit Claire's new house. But Annie caught herself. She didn't want an argument. There was obviously a reason Suze hadn't told her about the visit and she wasn't ready to know. Besides, did she actually need to know?

'Maybe it's Karl,' Annie said breezily. 'Wouldn't you be grumpy if you lived with a man called Karl who'd uprooted you from everything you once knew and loved? What is she *doing*? Oh my God, why is she going into the . . .? Claire! Come back?'

But Claire was running straight into the waves.

'Looks like she's going for a swim,' said Suze casually.

'Yes, thank you very much, Suze,' said Annie, feeling as if her heart might stop right there and then. 'But people shouldn't swim or drive when they're upset.'

'She's definitely annoyed with you,' said Suze. 'She's going straight into the water because she knows it terrifies you.'

Annie had an awful feeling that Suze was right.

'Gah!' said Annie. 'How can she say she isn't five years old, and that she's too old for the lookout job when she does something as childish as that? Claire! Get out of the water,' she screamed. Then Annie started running after her, with Suze and Maura close behind.

As she ran toward the water, Annie remembered how the currents had pulled at her legs when she'd first got out of the rowboat, though then they had been close to shore. And from the safety of the boat she'd seen how fast the water sped past them, how quickly it changed direction, how the crests crashed into each other, how it swelled in strange and unknowable ways. Why couldn't everyone else see what she had known since she was nine years old? That water was designed to take lives.

'Claire, come back!' Annie screamed again, as her own legs gave way and she collapsed into the sand. She looked up from her crumpled vantage point, just in time to see Claire very much in the water, head bobbing as she attempted some sort of swimming stroke that took her away from land. And then Claire's head disappeared from view.

Chapter 15

Annie

8.30 a.m. Saturday, 29 August
Blue Bracken Island

'Claire!'

Annie scrambled back to her feet and darted toward the water's edge, feeling like she was about to be shoved off Niagara Falls without a life jacket. Claire had only just disappeared under the black waters and the wait for her to pop up again was interminable. The prospect of losing her was terrible, but the prospect of Em losing not one but two mums so intolerable that Annie took a deep breath and stepped into the water.

But as soon as the waves rose around her knees, her breath disappeared and she couldn't go any further. A thousand splintered thoughts raced through her in seconds. This was not a swimming pool with its tiled boundaries and water translucent enough to be seen in, then saved. These waters were deep and wide and unknowable and if Annie went under, opening her eyes to try to find Claire, she would be blindfolded by the darkness and stung by the salt and her fear would pin her to the silt bed then turn her in circles until she no longer knew which way was up.

Annie gasped, her breath returning in shorter bursts, her thoughts keeping time. If Claire drowned, and then Annie drowned and Suze was never there, that left Maura. Notebook. Cons: Claire, one page. Suze, two pages. Maura . . . three.

Come on, come on, she hissed to herself, like she was trying to revive herself from unconsciousness. *Do something. Get Claire back. Em needs her.* But she could no longer feel her feet, frozen solid in that cold, cold British water.

'Suze! Get in there and get her!' Annie tried to keep eyes on where Claire had disappeared while also trying to make herself heard.

Suze stepped forward but her foot slipped on the uneven sand, and as she crumpled into a pile, she screamed out in pain. 'My ankle!'

'Maura!' shouted Annie. 'Hurry up! Save her!'

'On it!'

At the very moment Maura clasped her hands together, bracing herself to collapse forward into a dive, Claire's head popped up, hair slicked back like a seal's. She righted herself to standing quite easily, and Annie was surprised when she did because her body, from the mid-ribs up was quite visible, suggesting that the water hadn't been that deep.

'Claire! What the actual fuck?' shouted Annie in the panicked and tearful manner of a mother who had lost, then found, her child in a shopping mall all within the space of five minutes, overcome with blind fury, horror, fear and relief at what might have happened but didn't. She clamped her hands to her temples in despair. 'We thought you'd *drowned*.'

Above them the sky rumbled like a heavy sofa rolling over

wooden floorboards. Annie looked up and groaned as the rain came, stippling the surface of the water.

Claire's expression changed from forehead-crinkling confusion to outrage. 'If you thought I'd drowned then why are you all still standing at the water's edge doing nothing? Suze is even *lying down*!'

'She slipped—'

'Never mind,' said Claire, wading through the water in the splashiest way possible and tripping her way back onto the beach, clothes clinging to her tiny frame, making her look like draped and polished marble, a Grecian statue on the move.

'Claire, wait,' said Annie, rain pixelating the water around her as she waded out and followed Claire back onto the beach. Maura and Suze hung back at the water's edge: best send the captain in for this one.

'No! What?' Claire snapped round to look at Annie. 'I want to sit down,' she said, continuing her furious stride up the beach.

'Maybe you should leave her for a bit?' called Suze. 'Whatever's going on, she needs to calm down.'

'Did you do that on purpose?' Annie shouted at Claire, adrenaline still rushing through her. 'To see if I'd save you?'

But Claire didn't reply and instead made her way to a mound of sand and plonked herself down. She twisted her hair into a rope and squeezed out the water as though she'd exited a beach on the Italian coast and was going to dry off on her towel. Then she looked up at the sky, eyes blinking with the rain and said, 'No, I, sometimes I think . . . Oh my God, why is it raining *so* hard?'

'What?' said Annie softly, seeing that Claire was upset and on the verge of something. 'What do you think? Is this to do with what happened on the beach before we left? Because if it is, you have to put that behind you. Bury it. I have. Mostly. It was a moment of madness—'

'What was a moment of madness?' said Maura, who'd just caught up behind them.

'Nothing,' said Annie. 'Nothing at all.'

Claire got up and walked off again, this time followed by Suze.

As Maura tried to towel herself down with the small red baby blanket, muttering something about *drama queen* and *cry wolf* and *the bloody British rain,* Annie watched Claire and Suze sit down at the edge of the woods together, their shoulders touching. Annie felt her heart ache with worry. Claire seemed to be travelling further and further away, just when she needed her close.

As the rain turned her hair into thin ropes, Annie watched Suze put her arm around Claire and Claire slump gratefully into the crook of Suze's neck. Soon, both of them were shuddering with laughter at a joke Annie couldn't hear. She felt a stab of jealousy: it had always been her who comforted Claire, not Suze. Those two had never been that close and had only ever seen each other when Maura or Annie were around. What had they been at Claire's house that they couldn't discuss in a group? And why hadn't they posted anything on the group WhatsApp like they always did when they saw each other in different formations, because everyone knew that side group-chats meant someone was being excluded, and hadn't they moved on from being twelve years old? Except . . . Maura *had* set up the *Karl Chose Those Curtains* WhatsApp group after she'd visited Claire's house for the first time. And it had excluded Claire.

Had Claire found out about it? Is that what she'd meant about being left out?

This sense of people she loved being so upset, this tangle of stuff that felt too hard to brush out, made her miss Em with an almost intolerable pain. Life with her friends used to be so straightforward, calm and happy. When did it become so messy? Would Em go through the same feelings of mess and exclusion when homed with her friends' children, whoever her new mum ended up being? Would she feel excluded from Alfie and Freddy's tight twin-bond? Excluded from the gang when Graham sucked all the attention out of the room, as babies do with their cute little feet and faces? Ignored entirely in Suze's house because the only other woman was always travelling and Martin and Walt shared a bubble of both DNA and gender. Would Em be able to *banter* like boys did? And even if she could, would she enjoy it? Annie never had.

There was no doubt in her mind: Em would be an island, whichever family she ended up with.

And then something far more painful occurred to her. What if Em was completely fine without her? Annie wanted her child to be happy, of course she did. But what if Em never remembered Annie's love, or their cuddles, or their breakfasts together, or the four stories they read together each night, or feeding the ducks with white breadcrumbs in the park, or when they'd first laughed together which was . . . when, she couldn't remember and she *needed* to remember, and her heart hurt so much that her eyes stung with tears.

Suze and Claire stood up together, with great purpose, as if they'd decided now was the time to inform everyone of a very important plan, and Annie watched them amble back on the beach to rejoin them.

'Look,' said Claire, visibly calmer, 'swimming conditions are bad.'

'Don't change the subject,' said Annie. 'Are you honestly saying that your display out there was just a field trip to assess the water?'

Suze glared at Annie as if to warn her off not destabilizing the good UN work she'd already done.

'I needed some space,' said Claire.

Perhaps this was a bigger problem than Annie thought. Perhaps Claire just didn't have the emotional space in her heart or family for someone else.

'I couldn't even get further than a few feet, the current was strong and kept pushing me back to shore.'

'Maybe that's because you haven't eaten for days, possibly months,' said Maura grumpily.

'I'm still strong,' said Claire, standing up straighter. 'I go to the gym and I lift weights.'

'Yes, but if you're not eating enough peanut butter then no amount of bench-pressing is going to help you. Having said that, I've not been to the gym since I was like fourteen . . . and that was only once.'

'What are you saying, Claire?' said Annie.

'Look at the weather!' exclaimed Claire. 'You said it yourself. No one's coming out in this. No one is coming for us. One of us has to swim.'

'But Maura wouldn't survive a second,' said Annie. 'And Suze can't swim.'

'No, I cannot,' said Suze.

'And I can't do it either,' said Annie, still bruised with fear from Claire's disappearance.

'You mean you *won't* do it,' said Maura.

'You really should see someone, a hypnotist or a shaman, maybe, about that,' said Suze.

'It's too far to the mainland for anyone to swim!' snapped Annie. 'Even people who lift weights or have an army of psychotherapists and shamans. It's a long bloody way back home! Just, give me a second OK, I'll come up with a plan.'

A few seconds turned into a few hours. The rain stopped and started but never for long enough for things to be anything less than dismal.

'This is what we're going to do,' she said at last, having gathered them together again. 'We're going to find some more food before we get so hungry we kill each other.'

'We should have had a spa lunch around now. Nibbles. Nice things,' said Suze ruefully.

'No one can swim without energy so a conversation about swimming home is like furnishing a house before we've even got the walls up. Let's do that and then the sun will come out, and then a ship will come and boom – it'll be home time before we know it.'

'I'd murder a bacon sandwich,' said Maura, interrupting Annie's thought process. 'Literally stab that thing in the side with my fork and cover it in ketchup then shove it down while I line up the next one. Stab, eat. Stab, eat. I'd go on and on until I couldn't take it any longer. I'd probably be sick but I'd still have eaten six bacon sandwiches.'

'Look at those fat seagulls over there.' Suze broke the circle and pointed over at the loud and gossiping group of gulls that Annie had spotted that morning but thought nothing of. 'A group of fat roast—'

'Wait,' said Annie. 'Why are they all together like that?'

'Maybe they're having an AA meeting,' said Suze.

'There's food under them,' said Annie jumping up. 'Haven't you seen any David Attenborough on TV? They are sitting on a *treasure trove* of fish. Right?'

'Riiight . . .' said Suze cautiously. 'Except what do we do? Catch them with our bare hands and cook them under the sun?'

'No, of course not!' said Maura brightly. 'You have to find a place, ideally above and slightly to the side of your target fish. That way, you're not casting a shadow and making them think there's a predator swimming above them. You wanna take them by surprise. Bang!'

All of them turned to look at Maura.

'Well, don't look at me like that,' she said. 'I do watch more than documentaries about Hollywood Housewives and yachts, you know.'

'She watches a lot of Bear Grylls,' said Suze. 'When I borrowed her—'

'I thought you weren't watching—' Annie began.

'Anyway!' said Maura, with far too much verve.

But Annie wasn't inclined to dig further into Maura's television habits, still wanting everyone to remain focused on hunting food, and only idly wondered whether Maura was being shady about it all because she was sleeping with alpha male TV personalities who specialized in survival.

'The point that our excellent Captain Annie was making,' said Maura, 'is there might be a load of fish down there, and there's seaweed on the shore which is basically YO! Sushi when you think about it.'

'That's the spirit!' said Annie, pumping her fist in the air, even though YO! Sushi was so far from their actual reality it was a ridiculous thing to say – though in a way it didn't matter because suddenly all four of them were running back up the beach with a spring in their steps.

Having skirted the edges of the wood for fallen branches they could use to spear the fish, the women returned to the shelter for Maura's *stick splitting*. First Maura tried bashing the sticks on the fallen log of their shelter to splinter them sufficiently to murder a fish, but it didn't work. Then she resorted to breaking the sticks across her thigh, which only ended up in a cut and several grazes.

'What now?' said Suze. 'You couldn't kill a beetle with these things.'

'Wait,' said Maura, as she prepared herself for business, hoiking up her skirt and tucking it into her knicker elastic and her T-shirt into her waistband, as though she was getting into a gym kit that would make her stronger and more mobile. Then she swept her hair over to one side, folded it into three twists of a hair-elastic and stamped down on the stick. There was a satisfying splinter and they all cheered as she raised a new spear in the air.

'Now *that* is strength,' she declared. And Claire scowled at her.

Once they all had splintered sticks in their hands they marched down to the water.

'Let's think about the movies,' said Annie.

'Personally, I just love *When Harry Met Sally*,' said Maura.

'I was thinking more of the Tom Hanks one when he gets stranded on an island. We need to look for signs of movement and then stab downwards? While also angling your shadow away, as Maura suggested.'

177

Annie stabbed downward. But it was no use because neither her responses nor the speed of the stick were faster than the seemingly incredible speed of the small fish moving beneath her. She knew it wasn't going to work and yet she couldn't afford to lose the positive team spirit gained by having a fish supper to look forward to.

'Come on, concentrate,' she cried. 'We can do this. We just need to focus inward.'

'I can't see any fish without my reading glasses and the rain's in my eyes,' said Claire. 'And I'm really, really cold.'

'So move your feet to warm up. And move the angle of your body to create more light and less shade,' said Annie. 'Stand more like this,' she said, adopting a fighting warrior pose. Then she stabbed downward again, into nothingness. 'Yah!' she cried. 'I nearly got one.'

'Did you?' said Maura, disbelievingly.

They talked less after that.

'If Dex was here he'd be every man for himself,' mused Maura, as if in conversation with herself. 'He'd stab a sea bass or whatever and eat the whole thing himself.' She paused to brush wet straggles of hair out of her eyes. 'Selfish bastard. He didn't know what he was getting into when he got married and had kids. Looking after a family is not compatible with his level of utter self-interest.'

'Yes, he's an absolute twat,' Annie chimed in, her mind on the ache and rumble of her stomach, the basics of survival, and as a result, caring much less about anything less important than that.

Maura spun round. 'What exactly have you got against him?'

Annie looked at her, amazed that Maura was even asking.

'The fact that he annoys *you* so much? The fact that you keep saying you *could have been someone* were it not for Dex standing in the way of your work as an artist because he's too lazy and selfish to help with the house and kids?'

'I can say that, but you can't. Maybe I'll change my mind about him one of these days and, when I do, I don't need your voice in my head saying he's a *twat and a knob and a lazy selfish bastard*. I'm married to him and therefore I'm stuck with him. I didn't go around saying The Canadian was an absolute twat.'

'Maybe you should have!' snapped Annie. 'Maybe if you'd told me your views sooner then I'd have been the one to leave him? Instead, he left me at a very vulnerable time, with no self-esteem, a crushed sense of my own identity and, crucially, no domestic help!'

'It wasn't my place to tell you whether he was a good person for you or not. Obviously he wasn't, he was obsessed with maple syrup and Crocs, but he seemed capable and nice enough. I hate that he hurt you, but honestly? None of us knows how we're going to react in an extreme situation like parenthood. Or marriage. And by then it's mostly too late to change your mind because you're bound by the shackles of obligation and history.'

'I agree,' said Suze. 'Most people wouldn't do it if they knew how hard it was.'

Annie felt hot fury rise in her chest. How could they take their role as parents for granted like that? Perhaps if *they* were faced with having it taken away they'd be saying something different. Annie stabbed and stabbed into the water to stop herself from saying something she'd regret.

'Anyway, The Canadian has left the building,' said Maura,

idly swishing her spear in the water. 'While Dex lingers on like a fart in a car. He's idle. Bone-idle and selfish.'

'I don't understand why you focus on all the negatives?' said Claire, as if she'd been thinking about it a while. 'Dex is smart and he has stuff to say and works in a field most people find interesting, and which pays the bills.'

'Don't get involved,' said Annie, shooting Claire a stern glare, willing her not to say anything about her flirtation on the beach. If her own hunger pangs were anything to go by, it would take extra encouragement and restraint to avoid all-out war on any flammable subject.

'No,' said Claire calmly, 'I think I will get involved.' Annie had heard Claire say the word 'no' more in the last half hour than she had done in their entire friendship. 'You see, I gave Dex to Maura.'

Annie's shoulders tensed involuntarily.

'You *gave* me my husband?' said Maura, her voice tainted with disgust.

'Yes,' said Claire. 'I was the first one to meet him at that party and then I handed him over, like a hairball out of a cat's gullet delivered to the feet of a human queen.'

'He's much better looking than a hairball,' protested Maura.

'You said you weren't interested because you didn't like the sound of his voice and didn't like the way he said *babe*. And then you listened to me say how interesting and funny he was, what a talented painter and how hot I thought he was, and *the very next day*, despite what you said, you took him off the shelf like I'd increased his price, like suddenly he'd evolved from being a Sainsbury's carrier bag to a Chanel Baguette.'

'*Fendi* Baguette,' said Maura.

'So, having whipped him off the shelf right before me, as I reached out, my hungry mouth open . . .'

'Oh gross, can you stop?' pleaded Suze. 'That image is sexual and not helpful? And also Dex is a living adult man. Dex had a choice?'

'And I'm confused,' said Maura. 'Did you give him to me or did I steal him from you? Either way it sounds like you thought you owned him. And anyway, why are you bringing this up now? It was years ago. My God,' she said slowly, 'are you regretting having *handed him over*? I wouldn't blame you. I'd feel the same if I was married to a man like Karl.'

Annie glanced at Claire and saw her face crumple into a wince.

'Karl's not exactly Fendi, is he?' Maura continued, fire in her eyes. 'More knock-off Michael Kors. He's about as interesting as a jar of mayonnaise, in fact. Whose idea was it for you to stop work, Claire? I thought you loved your job? And whose idea was it for you to wear athleisurewear every day because you're always on the move, signing your child up to the rugby club even though he's only just turned one, or exercising in a green field in the shadow of a fucking tree? Whose idea was it to wrap you in coloured fucking branded fucking Home Counties fucking cotton wool and tissue paper so you couldn't breathe? Karl's! Karl-bloody-Karl has stolen your bloody life, chucked it in the washing machine and folded it up all tight and neat on the great big polished oak shelf of the Home Counties.'

Claire glared at Maura, tight-lipped, eyes glazed cold. Annie ached with tension, her whole being primed to jump in and defend Claire against Maura's rudeness and lack of kindness. But then Claire took several wading steps toward Maura.

Annie went after her, standing in Claire's watery shadow because the last thing Annie wanted to happen was for Claire to hold Maura's head under the water and drown her. Unlikely, but hunger made people do the strangest things.

'If we're judging each other's lives . . .' Claire said close to Maura's face. 'No, wait . . . if we're judging marriages, the only reason I'm here is because Annie said yours was on the rocks.'

Maura looked at Annie, appalled. 'Why are you talking about my marriage being *on the rocks*?'

Annie felt her empty stomach swell like a wave. 'I'm not sure I used those exact words.'

'What exact words did you use, then?'

Annie's blood was racing, thick with residual anger from her friend's cavalier words about parenthood, anxiety about Claire blowing everything up with her 'dalliance', and the deep concern about her friendships splintering like the spears they held in their hands. Hunger, thirst, exhaustion and the cold coat of non-stop rain was twisting her body into pretzels of aching pain. She felt both focused and yet curiously out of her own head, not really looking when she stabbed her spear into the water with extra violence and firepower.

'FUCK!' screamed Claire. 'Ow!' She drew her leg up and held her knee, reaching for her foot.

'Oh God, I'm sorry!' said Annie, realizing immediately what had happened, and lifting up her spear quickly.

'What happened?' said Maura. 'Oh my God, Annie, have you *stabbed* Claire?'

'Her foot.'

'Same thing! Quick, Claire, get out, else the sharks will smell the blood. Remember what happened to Annie when she was nine. Quick, get out, get out, else they'll eat you!'

Claire's face balled up in pain as she turned and waded back to the shoreline.

'Claire, wait,' said Annie, following her. 'I'm so sorry.' Annie felt despair at the prospect she might have stabbed Em's best chance at a good mother to death; and yet at least it had stopped the argument with Maura from escalating. Swings and roundabouts.

Claire turned suddenly to face them all but addressing Annie. 'So you really don't think much of my marriage? You refer to my husband as *a man like Karl* behind my back? What, you think I've got no opinion, no say?'

But no one had a good answer because it didn't sound much like a question to any of them.

'Suze, is that really what you think of Karl?' said Claire.

'Why are you asking Suze's opinion?' said Annie.

'I mean, I guess I like mayonnaise,' said Suze. 'But it's more interesting when you add stuff to it like garlic or chilli, or even better if you make it yourself so it doesn't make everything taste the same. So . . .'

Claire glared at them then turned to take her final steps out of the water and onto the sand. She walked a few yards down the waterline before banging wet sand off her feet and rinsing them in the shallows so the fine trickle of blood ran clean.

'Claire, I'm sorry,' said Annie.

'Leave her to burn it off,' said Maura, grabbing hold of Annie's arm to stop her following Claire. 'Besides, I want to talk to you.' Then she nudged her gently. 'Tell me exactly what you said to Claire about my marriage?'

Annie pretended to be more interested in a streak of sand on her calf, struggling to find ways of washing it off at the water's edge without it sticking to her again. They both knew she was buying time, trying to think of what to say, feeling the regret burn poison like bleach through her veins.

'Look at me,' said Maura.

When Annie finally looked up it was enough for Maura to intuit the answer, to shoot her a dark look and turn on her heel, striding up the beach and striking out in the direction of the wood.

'Maura, wait,' Annie called after her.

But then Claire overtook Maura.

'Claire, wait,' cried Annie.

Chapter 16

Martin

12 p.m. Saturday, 29 August
Sandpiper Cottage

The weather was abysmal, sky the colour of a dirty city street with the rain coming down in graphite sheets – which managed to make the interior of the house feel damp and dark and almost as inhospitable as the outdoors.

Martin was trying really hard not to sink into melancholy. Poor weather of any kind made him worry about the present and the future, often also the past. But he had his plan to help everyone, and he couldn't afford to get side-tracked. He slapped himself on the side of the head and forced his focus back to optimism, making a start with snapping on the heating and every available side and ceiling light he could locate.

Karl and Dex were pushing pieces around a snakes and ladders board with zero energy or commitment to the game, the third cup of tea since breakfast having been cleared, a fourth going cold. The kids were building a wall of soft toys around baby Graham.

'Now the storm has decided to pay us a visit,' announced Martin, 'it somewhat limits our options so why don't you two just chill, and hand the kiddos over to me? I'll be *in loco parentis, Martin Poppins*, whatever you'd like to call me. I don't own a car so I won't take them to the local pork-pie museum, or whatever, and I think we'll give the water sports a miss because no one wants to find themselves responsible for small lives amidst the white-capped waves of a storm! But on the significant upside, there's a warm house, now, and piles of things to do from farmyard jigsaws to empty sketch books longing to be filled with stickmen. Not to mention a tyre to be fixed!'

It made abundant sense to Martin. Maura usually looked after the kids, Maura wasn't there, the kids were stressing Dex and making him want to go home and behave like an all-round grump, so why not remove the stress so Dex was more likely to stay and have fun? Karl had both a baby and Em to look after: although he'd seemed grateful that Martin had stepped up so readily for Em that he'd not really needed to lift a finger on that front. Martin didn't mind one bit. It took a village, after all.

'Par example,' said Martin. 'Dex, if I take the twins off then you can concentrate on being a creative genius?' Dex side-eyed him. 'I'm serious! Off you go!' he said jovially. 'Go paint some leaves and trees!'

'Leaves and trees?'

'Sure, whatever you like. Suze says your thing is *nature in neon*?'

Dex's face softened a little. 'No, sure. Well, actually I'm moving away from that . . . Anyway, thanks for your offer but while the tyre's being fixed I thought I'd try and hang with the little lads. When Maura gets back and finds me gone she'll be all like: *I knew you couldn't hack more than five minutes with the kids before you fucked off and handed them over to my mum.'*

'Right, right,' said Martin.

'Which I *will* do, once I've got through to her mum. But Maura can't be quite as smug if I manage to do some sort of activity with them.' He shrugged.

'Nope, sure, sounds good, room for it all,' said Martin. 'But did you finish those calls you had to make?'

'It's frustrating to finish a call here. Reception keeps dropping out.'

'So I can take them for a bit at least while you tie up the loose ends? I've got to find a wrench for your tyre anyway so the kids can help me do that. Spanner and a wrench . . . perhaps a nail or two?'

'Nails? To fix a tyre?'

'Nope,' said Martin hastily. 'Not nails . . .'

'Cool, OK, yeah sure, why not,' said Dex cautiously. 'I'll finish off with the gallery then I'll play a . . . play a jigsaw with them later or something.'

'No, sure, great. I'll get the kids started on something, put the lunch on and then get to it.'

Once he'd chucked some snacks out for the kids – mini biscuits and hulled strawberries in small bowls – and checked they were playing nicely with baby Graham, Martin set to work on lunch, splashing olive oil onto the skin of a large organic chicken and rubbing it in vigorously so the bird shone. But his hands quaked. He was worried that one bird wasn't going to be enough protein for the gang, estimating that Dex and Karl were the kind of men to eat half a chicken each.

'We're going to need a bigger boat,' he said to himself as he washed his hands with antibacterial soap, dried, unwrapped the packaging of a second chicken and tipped out the pale pink juices into the sink. Washed his hands again. Shone up a carcass all over again. Quaked a little more. This would be OK, wouldn't it? He could absorb himself in children's activities and cooking and before he knew it Suze would be home.

As he sprinkled the chicken skin with crystals of rock salt and a few really good grinds of black pepper, he recalled the words that had haunted him every day and night for the last three months. Suze had told him, over non-alcoholic mojitos, about her next round of funding: for a six-month trip to Peru to study tribal ayahuasca, a plant psychedelic that affected all the senses, altering a person's thinking, sense of time and emotions.

Right, he'd said.

Then she'd said: *But let's call it what it really is?*

And then he'd said, *Oh . . .*

He'd really hated how surprised he'd been to hear it. He shouldn't have been. They had a deal unlike any others.

So Martin had struck a sub-deal. Asked if she would stay longer, because surely you couldn't excise the family as easily as a boil? She had cried and said *of course not*. He'd asked her to stay until the end of the summer, just enough time to convince her of the power of the *village*, of how wonderful it was for friends and family to be able support each other in childcare and friendship, because once she was reminded of community it might make the whole business of raising a family more digestible and fun for her? So he'd been delighted when Annie had suggested a trip, a living chance to paint kintsugi gold into the cracks of his family, rounding it out and smoothing it into the perfect and precious nuclear shape.

Martin glanced over at Walt who was wandering about the kitchen with Em, dragging toy rabbits around by their legs as if they were small dead bodies, and found himself considering, not for the first time, what was best for his son. What would Walt want and need in his life, going forward? Karl was a successful entrepreneur. Dex made a living from being creative and, as such, both men were inspiring father figures to the twins and baby Graham – when Graham was awake long enough to witness his father in action! But what did Martin have to offer Walt other than a suitcase full of sleep medication that didn't work, a generous hand with chicken seasoning and a P45? He was a spineless jelly of a man, lying so flat on the road of life that men like Dex didn't even see him, let alone hear or feel him as they ran their carts rough-shod over his stupid body.

It was Walt he worried most about if Suze left, because Walt would not get enough inspiration in his life without Suze in the mix. Suze provided colour and vim with her slightly unreliable approach to everything. Doughnuts for dinner. Why not? She was a lovely mum. Affectionate, caring, chatty. Preoccupied with her work, sure, but who wouldn't be when looking into such interesting subjects as substances that removed you from reality. No, Suze was indispensable. And so, when he finally broke the news, Martin was fully expecting Walt to tell him what he already knew: which was that Martin was not enough. That Walt needed his mother. He dreaded that day and so he wouldn't even go near the subject, not while there was a chance he could still change

Suze's mind. And he was confident there was a chance. Especially if he nailed this weekend.

He heard footsteps, a chair scrape and more footsteps behind him, and forbade himself from any revealing display of emotion. He was prone to tears at the best of times. Smelling the musk-florals of Karl's aftershave and hearing the low guttural grunt of Dex clearing his throat, Martin turned and leant his back against the hob to face them both.

'We've completed a free play session which you can see is unfurling nicely on Graham's mat.' Martin motioned to the children stacking light plastic snack bowls on the baby's belly as Graham lay, bamboozled yet seemingly happy, on his mat. 'And now, the chickens are safely stashed in the oven,' he said, hammering all the joy he could muster into each syllable, 'I'll be able to roll out some organized fun for the children.'

'Ta muchly, mate,' said Karl, swooping Graham up and manoeuvring him into the highchair. 'Probably time for this little one to get some smashed apples into him. Come on then, Gray-Gray, let's get this lunchtime party started?' Karl looked up at Martin as Graham slammed his chubby legs against the side of highchair in anticipation. 'Christ, my palms are dripping. I'm nervous, you know? For if he doesn't eat?'

'Take it easy,' said Martin. 'Be yourself.'

'Okey-doke,' said Karl, taking a seat next to Graham and raising a plastic weaning spoon of apple puree in the air.

'Go on then,' said Martin encouragingly, not understanding why Karl was delaying.

'Not yet, Gray-Gray,' insisted Karl.

'What you waiting for, mate?' said Dex impatiently.

Then, as Graham was about to burst into tears, Karl put the spoon in his mouth.

Karl glanced up at Martin. 'Bing-Bloody-Go!' he said. 'Three in one: feeding; asserting my position in the hierarchy; and teaching him delayed gratification.' Karl looked really pleased with himself. 'Important lesson for all: if you want something, you've got to work for it.'

Did that rule really work for babies? 'Congratulations are in order then!' said Martin.

'It's all down to you, Martin-mate. It was you who told me to be myself.'

'Did you find that "delayed gratification" thing in a book, then?' Martin asked.

'No, I did not. I just knew it instinctively speaking as something I wanted to teach him, like I teach my staff and like my old man taught me. My old man was The Don. "ABC" is what he always said.'

'You what?' asked Dex.

'Always Be Closing.' He paused. 'The deal? Always be closing the deal?'

'Marvellous,' said Martin, confused. 'You're raising a baby and a businessman!'

'Speaking of always closing,' said Dex, 'any progress on my tyre?'

'That is item number three on the agenda,' said Martin, feeling a chill and a further pressure mount in the upper echelons of his rib cage. 'Prior to item number two, which is Martin's creche activity: an *objets trouvés* search, aka a found objects search on the beach. Weather be damned!'

'I don't think so,' said Dex. 'I've done my calls now so I'll do a quick game of snap or something with them, and then head off.'

'I don't want to play snap. I want to do an objet!' said Alfie, getting up from his position on the periphery of Graham's playmat.

'Simmer down. If you don't want to play snap then fine,' said Dex to Alfie. 'I'll take you out on the rowboat. There's one in the shed.'

'No,' said Alfie, 'I don't want to go on a boat. I want to find objets with Uncle Martin.'

Dex paused and then, through clamped teeth, said, 'Martin is not your uncle and we're going in the rowboat.'

'But I don't want to do that!' shouted Freddy. 'It's raining.'

'It must be time for Graham to have a nap,' said Karl. 'So I think I'll go for a run and put him down. Have fun trouvéing. I'll look forward to seeing what you picked up on the beach later. Hopefully not syphilis!'

'Come on you two,' said Dex to his kids.

'No,' said Alfie.

'Fuck,' snapped Dex.

'Loud,' said Freddy.

'Fine, go with him then,' Dex said belligerently, giving Martin a withering look.

'I'll just go and grab Em's jelly shoes then,' said Martin quietly.

When Martin had packed a trip bag with snacks and drinks and rain macs and small polythene bags for each child to fill with their *objets trouvés*, he returned to the kitchen, humming happily knowing that a little space and a little nature would help his melancholic panic.

'Avengers assemble!' he called out, expecting to see the kids but only finding silence. 'Dex?'

Dex was stretched out on the sofa reading his phone. 'Eh?'

'The kids? Where are they?'

Dex put his phone down on his lap. 'I don't know. I thought you'd taken them onto the beach in search of stuff. I popped out for a crap just after you left the room. Where's Karl?'

Karl wandered back into the kitchen.

'Martin wants to know where you've buried the kids, Karl?'

'Oh right, no idea. I put Graham down for a nap and sat with him for a bit to tell him where sand comes from aka how the world came to be,' he said, opening the fridge with a yank and surveying its contents with a frown. 'And then I had a piss and it's amazing, someone's been folding the end of the toilet paper into a triangle again?'

'Yes,' said Martin quickly. 'That's me. I like to do that wherever I use a toilet, you know, to give the next user the experience of being in a nice hotel. But this still leaves the unanswered and urgent question regarding the children's whereabouts?'

Dex looked up. 'They'll be here somewhere,' he said.

'Dex, how long does it take for you to have a crap anyway?' said Karl.

'Depends on what I'm reading.'

'So what were you reading? The Bible?'

'It was an article on—'

'No, no, not now,' said Martin, feeling the pressure of his anxiety rise into his throat. 'We need to find the kids.'

'But you said you were in charge of the kids?' said Dex.

'Sure, no,' said Martin, not sure at all, realizing he'd not made clear who was minding the kids while he went to the toilet, packed the day bag and tried to find a sodding wrench.

'And anyway, isn't the point, like, where the shitting hell are Em and Walt and the twins? That's someone else's kid we seem to have lost, as well as our own? I'm not throwing stones, Dex, but you could have taken them to the lav with you?'

'I can't have people watch me. It slows me down.'

'But it can't slow you down any more than your reading materials!' shouted Martin, the pressure reaching an agonizing ache in his chest. 'For *fuck's* sake!' he spat, his anger and suppressed anxiety exploding out of him like a bullet from a gun. 'Walt can't swim. And I don't expect Em can either.'

And they all glanced over at the open French windows that led onto the deck, down to the beach and out onto a calm and silent, seemingly endless body of water.

Chapter 17

Annie

4 p.m. Saturday, 29 August
Blue Bracken Island

After a second's hesitation, with only a look exchanged, the group split like a wishbone with Annie following Maura and Suze going after Claire.

When Maura stopped at the highest peak of a sandbank Annie held back and stopped, too. Annie deserved whatever was coming, she shouldn't have been so indiscreet nor should she have lied about the state of her friend's marriage, but if she engaged with Maura immediately she might as well douse herself in petrol and walk straight into a bonfire.

Annie sighed heavily and stepped forward, stubbing her toe painfully on something in the sand. She bent down and yanked at a piece of wood, brushing the sand away, pulling out a pallet, most of its wooden ribs in tact but for some breaks and splinters. Maybe they could use it as part of a shelter or as a table or chair? She glanced around for someone to discuss it with, for help carrying it to somewhere useful, but Suze was nowhere to be seen – doubtless having been told by Claire that she needed some space. Claire was at the water's edge, head bowed, kicking at shells and surf, getting that space, and Maura was still flumped at the top of the sandbank, head in her hands, looking like she might bite the head off anyone that stepped into her space.

So Annie picked up the edge of the pallet and heaved it to the edge of the woodland closest to the water, tripping on the sand, hands quaking, spiked and scratched with splintered wood, tears stinging her eyes. Unable to ask her friends for help because they were either absent or angry with her, was a pain she found intolerable, like holding her hand over a naked flame, the opposite of everything she hoped for, everything she needed and most importantly, everything Em needed.

All of this would have been so much easier to deal with at home. Sleep and food and space from each other, followed by a visit to the pub would have solved it. An hour's laughter and conversation would be enough to talk through a major mis-step, and to plaster over minor mis-steps and white lies – a final promise to forget any of it had ever happened even if, in the weeks and months that followed, that proved to be impossible. The point was that anything they couldn't get over was never dragged up again. It was kept firmly to themselves, which was how most relationships worked and that was absolutely, mostly, fine.

And yet, here they were, in sub-optimal circumstances, with their backs turned to each other. No crisps, no wine, no beer and frighteningly little good will left in the tanks.

Annie was concerned about what was going on with Claire but the issue felt like a scratchy throat she couldn't clear – annoying but also concerning enough that it might be the chronic symptom of something more serious. She felt bad about stabbing Claire's foot; it was a terrible thing to injure a friend, and though the injury didn't seem serious, she suspected it might be the straw that broke the camel's back for Claire and the prospect of her willingly fulfilling the role of Em's mum.

And so, with Suze still destined for worldwide travel, that left Maura as the prime candidate.

Annie looked up to find Maura a few feet away, and glaring at her.

'Mau,' said Annie, feeling her energy wane as she eased herself up to face her. But then Maura turned and stormed off in the opposite direction, somehow managing to create a stamping motion on the sand. Annie had to run to keep up with her, legs wobbling, chest straining with short breaths as she did so. It was as if they were in an adult game of chase – one that was much less fun than when they'd played it the previous night.

She'd almost caught up when Maura spun round without notice and confronted her at such close quarters that Annie could feel flecks of spit on her face as she spoke.

'Clearly you don't like Dex!'

'My God! What do you want from me?' said Annie, feeling her insides burn. 'Do you want me to be a supportive friend and just repeat your own words back to you? Or do you want the actual truth? Which is that *you* don't like Dex! You keep telling us all how selfish he is! How little art you make because he comes first, that he swings his big work dick and you're left looking after the kids and cleaning the fridge and paying the bills. You keep saying how you never get to watch TV anymore and TV was your absolute favourite thing!'

'Yes, thank you, I am married to him, I don't need reminding. But why are you lying to our friends? Telling them that we're breaking up? We're still *married*.' She said the word

197

with pointed exasperation in her voice. 'If I ever mention that he makes me feel so bad that I want to murder him, it's confidential, which, after twenty-one years of friendship, you should fucking well know by now.'

'Twenty-two,' said Annie. 'And I'm sorry. I don't know why I said it.'

'Don't give me that. You forget how long I've known you. Do you want me to break up with him? Why do you want me to break up with him? Are you in love with him?' She paused, her eyes widening and brightening, a hint of amusement, curiosity perhaps. 'My God! Are you in love with *me*?'

A spark lit in Annie's aching, exhausted stomach. 'Your ego!' she screamed. 'It's so big I'm surprised it fits on this island. *How* do you manage to make everything about you?'

'OK, OK,' said Maura, her shoulders and voice dropping. 'So tell me why you told Claire my marriage was failing.'

Annie studied Maura's flashing green eyes and the delicate lines that marked the areas under her lashes, as if a fine needle had been dragged gently across the wet clay of her skin. All the marks that held the history of her life to date: all the laughter and consternation, all the pain and question marks over everything. The idea of no longer being proximate to the circus that was Maura's mind and heart made Annie's stomach contract with a pain that felt as though she'd been winded. It was one thing to fall out with someone knowing that they still lived in the world. Quite another to leave them, never ever to return; to be so infinitely unconscious, so very extinct that they stopped living within you.

'Annie?' Maura said, both impatient and concerned.

'I needed to tell Clare *something* to get her to come this weekend.' Annie looked down at her feet submerged in soft wet sand, the rounded joints of her ankles swimming before her eyes.

'Couldn't you have said we're best friends so, like, *make a fucking effort*?'

'No,' said Annie, looking up. 'It wasn't enough.'

Maura looked at her, as if deciding what to say. 'If she didn't want to be here, she should have stayed at home.'

'She needed to be here.'

Maura craned her neck an inch. 'Why? Other than *it would be nice*, why? Why did she really need to be here?'

Annie looked down at her feet again, as if they'd give her the words that she struggled to find. 'Because we're friends. And friends turn up for each other.'

The words fell flat but seemed to be enough to soften the fury in Maura's eyes and erase the lines in her forehead.

'But she's an adult?' Maura expressed it as a question, but with the confidence of a fact. 'Maybe she doesn't want to spend time with us because she's got some better friends she'd rather hang out with now. And if that's the case then so be it. People change, Annie. And they possess *free will*. You can't just pick them up like a tantrumming toddler and carry them to wherever you want them to be.'

Annie turned her face toward the water so Maura couldn't see her eyes fill with tears. 'I get that. I understand that.'

'I am *so* annoyed with you right now.'

'I know.'

'You used my marriage as an excuse to *get the gang together*?'

And yet. Maura had used Annie as an excuse to take weekends off from her family. To do what? To spend time with a lover? To spend time with all those half-mast trouser-wearing coke-snorting North London primary school parents called things like Jude and Si, aka her *better friends*?

'But . . .' said Annie.

'But what?'

But Annie didn't want to know about the bigger cracks in her friendship. She didn't want to know if Maura was actually having an affair and the name of the man who might destroy her best friend's marriage. More than that, she didn't want to know that her adult *significant other* would rather be spending time with middle-aged primary school mums who wore fishermen's jackets because where would that leave her soul in its final months? She'd rather not know that she was less loved than she had once been.

'I think you're making some stupid decisions at the moment,' said Maura.

'I could say the same about you,' muttered Annie.

'Don't do that. We're talking about you, not me. It still bugs me you didn't ask Dex to look after Em. I'm her godmother.'

'So it's not really my decisions you're worried about so much as how my decisions make *you* feel? Dex isn't even her godfather. And if you're that bothered then . . .' She needed to test the ground, 'can you look after Em for a month?'

'A month? Why?'

'I'm really busy with work.'

'You've been busy with work for over a year now and you've managed.'

'I want you to get to know her. You should get to know her.'

'Get to know her? She's two. What's to know?'

'Everything! She's chatty and gobby and sweet and kind and smart and she bloody hates cats. I want you to know her.

She's my significant other. I don't have another one.' Annie could hear how barbed and sour and wounded she sounded. 'She's my best friend.'

Maura raised her eyebrows. 'I thought I was your best friend?' Then she tipped her head to the side as if waiting for what Annie had to say next. 'I'll take Em for a month if you tell me the truth about why you really need me to do that.'

Chapter 18

Annie

A year or so ago, and the months in between
London

Annie had been over the signs a thousand times. The uncontrolled tears in the months after Em had been born: easily explained by Ted The Canadian's abandonment and changes in hormones after the birth. The weakness in her legs and then arms: explained mostly by a lack of sleep and changes in hormones. The inappropriate and long bouts of laughter at poker nights several months after Em was born: partly explained by the giddy relief of having got out of the house after months of breastfeeding. And also changes in hormones.

But then, after many months of all that, Annie had fallen – hard, and face first, on the pavement just outside the Odeon on Holloway Road. She'd not thought the hospital was necessary until she found herself there, Em strapped in the pram, while a nurse stitched up skin over a fractured cheekbone as she asked questions about the fall and whether Annie could remember what had caused it. She couldn't. Then she had been handed an appointment letter for a few days later.

When she got back home from the hospital later that day Annie had called Maura, but Maura's phone had gone through to voicemail. Maura called her back the following afternoon, by which time the fall had become a clumsy trip, the fracture a bruise, the lengthy checks simply a quick visit to the minor injuries unit.

Annie had said something like: 'It was silly, I'm sure everything's fine.'

The next day, not feeling quite so confident that 'fine' was indeed fine, Annie had called Maura again and asked her to come to the follow-up appointment, keeping it breezy with 'just an investigation really, nothing much, covering the bases,' suggesting they could have dinner after the appointment and that she could stay over and hang out on the Saturday? Bring the twins?

'It's Mum's birthday so the whole family are coming for lunch, and Dex has taken the day off work to be there, which is fucking unbelievable, and the kids have come up with a dance routine which they've been working towards for ages, so what about patching me in on FaceTime?'

That was the kind of thing Maura had said though Annie found it hard to remember the exact details. But the idea of patching Maura into a medical appointment as she juggled salads and dance routines was too much, so Annie had gone to the follow-up appointment alone. The doctor asked her a lot of questions, and observed various things in Annie that Annie had thought were normal. Or at least, had got used to in the past months. More blood tests and scans and appointments were discussed and booked.

'What are you looking for?' Annie had asked the doctor that day.

203

She couldn't even remember their exact reply, only that there was nothing reassuring about it.

Annie had called Maura that night, with a sheaf of papers outlining different appointments and tests, laid in a neat pile on the kitchen table, including one for an MRI.

She told Maura about the MRI, saying something like, 'I thought they only gave you an MRI if they suspected cancer!' She said it like a joke, to reassure them both, but Maura hadn't even heard her because Annie had put the phone on mute by mistake when she'd dropped all her paperwork on the floor and spent ages trying to reassemble it in the right order.

Then Maura needed to take something out of the oven first.

When Annie finally turned off mute and got into the weeds of it, she said: 'The doctor's prescribed paracetamol but I already have a load of it. And so it can't be that serious.'

Then the rest was noise. A meltdown at the other end of the phone (both Maura and the kids) about burnt chips.

A deafening crash in the background as a dish fell out of the oven.

And once that commotion had calmed down, Annie was sure she'd told Maura that the tests were 'just to rule stuff out'. But Annie she wasn't sure whether Maura had heard that either because Maura said, 'I'll check back in soon because as you can probably hear, total fucking chaos because, having taken one day off, Dex has declared he will not be around to help for the next five nights to make up for lost time.'

Maura had probably then called Dex a selfish prick-twat, twice. And when the call ended Annie didn't much feel like bringing up the tests again other than to say, 'They're just keeping an eye on me; it's all fine, time of life and possible changes in hormones, blah blah blah.'

Maura didn't mention hanging out at the weekend, as Annie had suggested, nor any further dates, again, before she rang off.

And nor did she check back in – and so Annie had spent that weekend alone with Em, feeling preoccupied and tearful, googling and worrying, half-minded to march into the hospital and ask for more tests then and there so she wouldn't have to wait more days to find out what was really wrong with her.

More days passed with more inconclusive results – for what, she was still never told – and more time passed during which she found it harder and harder to pick up the phone to any of her friends. She felt like what was happening to her was becoming less amusing and less likely to be incorporated into a funny anecdote as the days wore on.

And then, in the two weeks that followed, as she waited for the results, it was Em's birthday and her mum's birthday and then her and Em were due to go away with some old school friends camping, and somehow the chance to call Maura again got swallowed up again and then morphed into the fact she would see her in Dorset in a few months, and what was the point in keeping her up-to-date with every beat and worrying her, too, when there was still an outside chance she could relay the whole thing as a temporary blip over orange cocktails on the beach?

But around the time of Easter bunnies and chocolate eggs, she knew.

Motor neurone disease.

No prevention.

No cure.

Early symptoms often missed, or misdiagnosed.

Fast moving.

Six to twelve months, someone said, but no one really knew because everyone was different.

Aren't they just.

Hope? Was there any?

They said she might defy it – there were exceptions to every rule, medicine was not an exact science. Then they looked at her and tipped their heads in a way that meant she shouldn't pin her hopes on that. Instead, she should make plans for the thing whose endgame was to outsmart her.

Chapter 19

Annie

4.15 p.m. Saturday, 29 August
Blue Bracken Island

In the close heat and rain, the non-stop bloody rain, Maura fixed Annie with a sharp glare. 'Well? Are you going to tell me why you want me to take Em, or what?'

Annie felt a sharp, shocked push of a feeling, like being shoved in the playground when you weren't expecting it, and retched up pearlescent bile on the sand, narrowly missing Maura's feet.

Maura put her hand on Annie's back and bent down to meet her gaze. 'Are you OK? What do you need?'

But Annie couldn't bring herself to tell Maura the truth, too afraid that seeing her friend's heart break might break her own.

'You know what?' Annie said instead. 'Maybe we're too old to have something as childish as a best friend. Maybe you should just go and spend time with all those school mums you talk about so much.'

Maura's eyes narrowed and darkened and she stepped back. 'Maybe I will. They're certainly more straightforward than you.'

'What do you mean by that?'

'We go out. We have a gin and slimline. Sometimes a bag of scampi fries. They don't ask about my past and I don't tell them. And I don't ask them about their pasts because, honestly, I'm not that interested in their trauma. We talk about the present. We talk about politics and Harry Styles and frosted lipstick and what's on Netflix and our children and mothering and the NHS.'

'Obviously you can't discuss any of those things with me,' said Annie mulishly.

Maura's eyes squeezed half-shut in annoyance. 'You can be so immature. Now, if you'll excuse me, one of us adults needs to focus on how we get off this island before we all die – or worse, kill each other.'

The words of the MRI radiologist popped into Annie's head.

You're very brave, she'd said when Annie had mentioned in passing how many tests she'd had already. But Annie felt the opposite of brave. She couldn't find a way to tell her best friend what she needed and, without her best friend, how was she supposed to fight? How was she going to make sure her daughter was protected?

'Maura, wait,' said Annie, as she strode off.

Maura turned around and they looked at each other for a few moments.

'Something's wrong with Claire,' Annie said. 'Though I don't know what. But I know she loves you. Go easy on her?'

Annie knew that Maura was waiting for her to say something more. But soon enough she nodded gently, and walked away.

Chapter 20

Martin

12 p.m. – 6 p.m. Saturday, 29 August
Sandpiper Cottage

They searched the bedrooms first. Under the beds, in the wardrobes and even inside the chests of drawers, tears pricking Martin's eyes as he imagined one of the children gasping for breath in the same small wooden coffin that held his Breton T-shirts.

But they found nothing.

Back in the kitchen he took a moment, placing his wrists under the powerful kitchen tap, feeling the water shoot out onto the front of his T-shirt in a bracing cold spurt. He glanced at his reflection in the shining steel of the fridge door, at his cod-white skin and his eyes, black with panic-induced dilation, then opened the cupboard below the sink to check there. When he found nothing, he turned to Dex and Karl who were darting around, lifting up curtains and checking behind the TV.

'They can't be outside, can they? It's raining like a power shower!' he said.

'Didn't you encourage them to go outside with your search for objects, "weather be damned"?' exclaimed Dex.

'Well of course we should check. No stone unturned,' Martin

said. 'My God, my heart is hammering like a washing machine at top spin cycle. I think I'm having a literal heart attack.'

He might have heard Dex say *If only you would*. But he didn't bloody care what Dex thought or whether his T-shirt was soaking or the floor spattered with water, not when life was being stripped back to its bare-boned essentials right in front of them, not when all that mattered was locating their children.

'Not funny now!' said Dex loudly, through gritted teeth. 'Hide-and-seek is officially over.'

'This is not good. This is really, really not good at all,' said Martin, his words stretched and squeaking. Then he clamped a hand over his mouth as if to stop the unsayable from pouring out. But inside he was riven with it. The funereal cold fear of losing Walt. Since the boy's birth he had run the gamut of fictional road accidents, illness and kidnapping scenarios so that when one of those things inevitably happened he'd be able to access internal plans and reserves to both change the situation, and psychologically manage it. He felt such a fool, knowing that now he was in the midst of it, all the preparation and energy had been a bullshit waste of time. Nothing could have prepared him for a pain as despairing and a vacuum as bottomless as his own helplessness in a world without his boy in it.

How had he gone from being within a hair's breadth of creating the family he wanted, to having the whole thing blown apart? How had he thought that the prospect of Suze leaving was the worst thing that could have befallen them? Suze would never forgive him if he lost Walt forever. She'd hate him. And he wouldn't blame her. He would hate himself.

'You should have been much, much clearer about what you were offering in the way of childcare,' snapped Dex, slamming a cupboard door so hard Martin's heart leapt. 'I don't understand it. Don't you schedule where students are supposed to go from class to class? Isn't that what you do? Isn't that the point of you?'

'The point of me?' said Martin, his voice starting to shake. 'Don't you mean the point of my job?'

'Hold on a minute,' said Karl. 'Sure, Martin might have been clearer but also we didn't ask for clarity. Let's be strategic instead of throwing stones. Let's identify the planks rather than where the gaps are so we can build a bridge toward effective collaboration?'

'Oh my God!' screamed Martin. 'The gaps between the planks in the jetty! The kids have slipped through them like sheets of A4!'

'Hold your horses,' said Karl, grabbing on to Martin's sleeve. 'Now we've covered the indoors we need a proper plan for the outdoors, else we'll never know where we've looked, and where we haven't, and we'll be going over old ground.'

Dex ignored him. 'I can't believe this! Maura's going to have a field day with this one. It's one thing not playing chess with the little buggers and quite a-fucking-nother to lose them.'

'They've only been gone seven minutes!' said Karl.

'Easy for you to say,' snapped Dex. 'Your child is safe in his cot where I expect he'll spend the rest of his life until retirement if you've got anything to do with it.'

'I know you're stressed but there's no need to be rude,' said Karl.

Martin's body quivered with trauma and pain and heartache, as if he'd already found Em's lifeless body. The potential for disaster just kept piling up in his head. Walt dying. Suze leaving. Em dying. And then what? Annie returning to find her daughter missing presumed dead – no! Confirmed dead! – having just told her friends about her own imminent death. A double death in the family? Was life really going to allow that to happen?

'Walt! Em! Alfie! Freddy!' Martin shouted, tears making his eyes sparkle like glass as he bolstered himself against the kitchen island.

Then he lay down on the floor in a series of quick and practised moves, sliding his legs up against the fridge, and beginning his breathing ritual.

'What the fuck are you *doing*?' yelled Dex. 'Get up! You can't lie down at a moment like this.'

'I'm lying down before my body does it for me! I'm trying to calm down so I can *think*. Where would they go, where would they go, where would they go,' he intoned.

'Let's *focus*,' said Karl. 'There is an expanse of wood on one side of this house and a depth of water on the other so I suggest we split tasks and then decide how to deal with that: I suggest *counter-laterally,* by which I mean we should go *across* the wood and *down* into the water.'

'That's not counter though, is it?' said Dex, looking confused. 'That's just working with the natural direction of land and sea. Do you mean we need to take a boat across the water? In which case there's a rowing boat in the shed. And then dig down into the ground? In which case, let's leave that to the police and fucking undertakers?'

'Call the police, now,' said Martin softly, hammering his temples with balled fists.

'Pull yourself together!' snapped Dex, which made Martin feel messy and ashamed and yet more on edge.

'Where would they go where would they go where would they go . . .' intoned Martin again but more quietly this time. 'If things are *loud* and distressing.'

'Distressing?' said Dex. 'Their day so far has been porridge and puzzles.'

'With their mothers, their very anchors, *gone?*' said Martin, amazed at Dex's singular lack of imagination and empathy. 'Take Em as an example! How must she feel? To be left alone with us brutes! And you can't deny there's been some shouting.' Martin hesitated from naming and shaming. He didn't need to, catching Dex in his peripheral vision cover his eyes with his hand. 'Where to go when it's loud loud LOUD? Oh my God!' he said, leaping for the patio doors. 'You'd go to a small space! I remember what Alfie said now.'

'What did Alfie say to you?' said Dex.

'The Wendy house. He said he went to the Wendy house at home when things got loud?'

'What?' said Dex.

'Is there a tree house here? There's no tree house . . . a small house . . . where's a small house? A bigger wardrobe, no . . . a cupboard . . . a car. A shed? The shed!'

When they arrived, Martin was so relieved at the scene in front of him that he collapsed into sobbing, ugly tears. There they were: Em, Alfie, Freddy and Walt all gathered in a circle on the floor with a hammer, a palette knife, an open tin of Ronseal and an unopened bottle of weed-killer, moving each item across the floor like members of a tea party.

'My *God*! *You* lot!' Dex jumped over to the Ronseal and slammed it shut with a punch of his closed fist.

Freddy gave a calm, ambivalent glance toward his father then shouted. 'Magic!' right at Martin, his face breaking out into a sunshine grin. Then he jumped up and clamped his arms tightly around Martin's calves.

'Walty!' called Martin, and Walt leapt up, throwing his arms round his dad, with Em and Alfie following suit so that within seconds Martin was an absolute maypole of children. 'The gang's back together! Everyone's a winner!'

'Where the fuck have you all been?' spat Dex, standing at a distance from them all, a lone oak to their glorious maypole. 'Who said you could even leave the house?'

'I did say stay in the house, guys,' said Martin, smiling. 'Bit *loud* was it?' He winked at Alfie.

Alfie nodded.

'What do you mean by that? You said it earlier,' said Dex. 'What is that secret handshake you've got going with my son? It's creepy. What did you mean by *loud*?'

Martin hesitated. He knew he could have clamped his hand over his mouth and said nothing, in an effort to keep the peace. But he was quivering with the energy of something far bigger. With the adrenaline of his hyper-focused aim of finding the kids, with the glorious relief of his mission's success, with the buzz of all his disastrous fears receding in one fell swoop, like a wave pulling back and leaving nothing but the beauty of glossy wet sand.

And so, instead, Martin said, '*Loud* refers to moments of loudness . . . When certain people, naming no names . . .' Martin hoped Dex would catch the inference because he was not interested in shaming him, shame never felt ideal, '. . . when certain people, people that he loves, raise their voice.'

'He said that? He's always full of stuff like that, Martin. He's emotional, like his mother. Bit of a show pony. Bit of an attention-seeker.'

'Well, of course,' said Martin, a bit amazed, if he was honest, by Dex's comment. 'He's a child. He needs and wants attention. His brain is designed and wired that way to ensure his survival. There are several papers I can . . .' Martin trailed off.

Dex glared at him and said, 'Come on, get yourself together, kids. We're going.' His response was so quick that he couldn't possibly have heard Martin's tip about research papers on children's brains.

'But I want to do the search. You said we could do the search?' said Alfie.

'And I've not fixed your tyre?' said Martin.

'I'll take my chances with the trains. I'd rather sit on a stationary train for twelve hours in a tropical storm with no water to drink than proceed with this chaotic shitshow for a moment longer.'

'I want to go on the shell search, too, though,' said Freddy, his face stretching in abject distress.

'I'm sorry to hear you're having such a gruesome time of it, Dex,' said Martin. 'But why not stay? Why not salvage it? You could tell Maura *you* did the *objets trouvés* search, thereby avoiding her wrath and encouraging her praise? Come on? Shells, chicken for lunch, tyre fix? What do you say? Chicken always calms a situation?'

All eyes were on Dex.

'Fine. We'll leave as soon as you're back from your walk,' Dex said more evenly.

* * *

An hour later Martin walked back into the house holding Alfie's hand tightly, Em and Walt and Freddy following close behind. He lined them all up opposite the coat hooks and piles of sandy trainers and flip-flops, empty shoppers and wine boxes – and held aloft a piece of pale blue sugar paper on a section of the blank wall space.

'Good work, everyone!' he said, pointing to a sketched diagram of the area, with red crosses and a big neon-green tick. 'Let's run it again! From now on, where are the no-go zones without an adult?'

'Water. Beach. Forest. Everywhere but the house!' the kids shouted in unison.

'And the meeting zone?' he said, pointing to the neon-green tick. 'In the event of an unplanned disaster?'

'The kitchen!'

Then they cheered and all held their palms open to reveal small chits of paper.

Martin checked them one by one. 'Excellent. Now stow those in your little pockets for safekeeping. Finally . . .'

The children all looked up at him, hanging on his every word. 'What is everyone? Everyone's a . . .'

'Winner!' They all cheered in unison.

He was hanging up their tiny rain macs and rearranging the shoppers when he caught a deep whiff of herbs and turned to see Dex standing at the door of his bedroom against a backdrop of pluming smoke. Dex's eyes were glazed and perhaps red-rimmed, though it was hard to tell in the afternoon light. He was flushed, ruffled, calm and angry – all in all, an completely stoned and deeply unsettling presence.

'Little bits of paper with a mobile number on in case they

get lost!' Martin said proudly, answering the question he assumed Dex was silently asking of him.

'Whose number?' said Dex bluntly.

'Mine? You said you'd rather clarity on who was looking after them, so . . .'

'Cross it out and put *mine* on for *my* sons.'

'No, sure, I can change that,' said Martin. 'Anyway. Did you have a nice "herbal" relax of it?'

Dex glared at Alfie and Freddy hanging round Martin's ankles. 'Happy at the university, are you?' he said. 'Happy with your work? Happy with the girlfriend? Happy with Suze?'

Martin's stomach contracted and he gave Dex an uneasy smile. 'Never been happier. Thank you.'

Dex's lip curled in an unkind smile. 'Goody-good.'

Karl walked into the corridor grasping an open packet of biscuits.

'Game of rounders?' said Dex, leaning to the side and picking up a rounders bat that had been left leaning against his door frame.

'I thought you didn't like sport or anything to do with balls?' said Martin.

'But I like using a rounders bat, you see,' said Dex, looking at Martin like he might eat him. 'I like the way it feels in my hand. Less of a sport. More of a feeling.'

'I love rounders!' said Alfie.

'Yes, my queen!' shouted Karl, punching the air. 'Bring it on!'

'I'll sit this one out if you've got Karl,' said Martin. 'Useless at competitive sports. I need to whip up some couscous for dinner anyway. It'll go well with the chickens.'

'Come on, rounders!' shouted Alfie.

'Come on, rounders!' repeated Walt, looking adoringly at Alfie and then hopefully at Martin.

'Looks like you haven't got a choice,' said Dex. 'And we all know you wouldn't want to disappoint your son.'

They all cheered and Karl led the kids outside.

Martin was about to follow them outside when Dex lurched forward with the bat in his hand, stopping suddenly, just inches from Martin's face. Martin flinched and then slightly hated himself for it.

'Only joking, mate,' Dex said, swinging the bat onto his left shoulder. 'Really love the way this feels. Keeps me sharp. See you on the pitch.'

Chapter 21

Annie

6 p.m. Saturday, 29 August
Blue Bracken Island

The light dulled as the air thickened with more rain and Annie decided that if she couldn't get the space she needed after an argument, as she normally might, then she'd just have to make it for herself. So she walked big loops round the island, along its waterline, avoiding everyone, reversing when she saw a flash of T-shirt or the bend of a leg: just wanting to imagine herself at home on the sofa watching *Friends* or making scrambled eggs or spending time with someone else, like her mum.

Finally tired of the looping, Annie made her way to the edge of the woodland with one of the biggest logs she could find so she could get on with making a raft. The rain was tapping so heavily on the canopy of leaves above her that she didn't hear Claire approach.

'Watch your arthritis doesn't flare up with all that lifting,' said Claire.

Annie turned and looked at her. 'Thanks,' she smiled. 'And also for dropping me in a barrel of shite over Maura's marriage.'

Claire dropped the branches she was holding. 'You can't be serious? You lied about their marriage, and then you lied to me?'

Annie sighed. 'I know. Thought I'd try my luck.'

Claire shrugged and smiled, so Annie continued. 'I shouldn't have used her marriage as an excuse. I was so tired and beleaguered with everything when I called you all those weeks ago to arrange this weekend—'

'What with the arthritis and everything?'

Annie looked up. 'I suppose so. And I felt like I needed to say something to make sure you'd come.'

'I wasn't going to come.' Claire took a seat at the edge of the log that Annie had carried to the woods.

'Obviously you're delighted you did,' said Annie quickly, not wanting to mull on what Claire had just said. Not after so many fractures had already branched through them. 'You're delighted because it's been a blast! The food has been fantastic, the company monumental—'

'And this . . .' Claire raised her eyebrows, holding up her right foot up to reveal the two-inch long incision, through the thin-skinned part of her foot beneath the toes, where a flip-flop might have fitted. 'This was the icing on the cake.'

'What total bitch did that?' said Annie, then they both laughed.

'Come on, sit down,' Annie said. 'And watch me build the boat that's going to get us out of this place while I apologize profusely for stabbing you.'

'There's a sentence I bet you thought you'd never say . . . It's OK, I know it was an accident. Besides . . .' she said, giving Annie an enigmatic smile, then glancing down at where her hands gripped the log she was sitting on. 'It

220

woke me up. Made me realize that I don't feel good about things.'

'Half the battle is admitting it to yourself,' said Annie, allowing the relief of finally making headway with Claire to wash over her like warm bathwater. 'You should see the doctor when you get back. Get him to put you on some antidepressants.'

'No. I mean I don't feel great.'

Annie examined Claire's face. She looked flushed and yet pale, like a raspberry ripple ice cream: but she was stranded and injured on an island so that would explain some of it. She glanced down at Claire's foot. 'Let's keep the injury clean with salt water and hopefully it'll be OK by the time we get home. Meantime, no morris dancing for you, young lady.'

'No, Annie. What I mean is that I don't feel great about what was said about Karl. That was my husband that you were all comparing to a jar of mayonnaise.'

Annie felt a mild flash of irritation about Karl taking up the airwaves when there were more important things to concentrate on. 'We can't all be good at everything which is probably why I asked Martin to help him out with looking after Em.'

'You did that? Why didn't you tell me?'

'Because I thought you'd be offended.'

'Why? I was offering him out because you don't have anyone else. He's not the world's most natural caregiver but he does try. It's good they'll be doing it together. I'm relieved, to be honest with you. He'll have enough going on with Graham. The fact remains that you obviously find him tepid and unremarkable. I've seen the dead-eyed way you look at him from across the room. How you cringe at his phrases and his long explanations about TV shows and things you already know about. You certainly don't light up when he speaks, or laugh at his jokes.'

'I barely see the guy!'

'Maybe you should make more of an effort then. But on the occasions that you do see him? You don't ever sit next to him, or go outside and have a cigarette with him when you've had too much to drink.'

'I don't smoke! And even when I've drunk enough to want to smoke I don't care who I'm doing it with as long as I'm with the cigarette. I've even smoked a cigarette outside with Dex, who we all know is an absolute prick.'

'Karl is good and interesting, though,' Claire continued. 'So why wouldn't you search him out to smoke with him? He manages like ninety people and several dark kitchens and new menus and he's cornered the market on the chickpea burger. He likes art, he goes to galleries, reads the paper, and is in the process of throwing out all his fleece jerkins. He really enjoyed decorating our house.'

'Yeah, your curtains are nice.' Annie remembered the *Karl Chose Those Curtains* WhatsApp group and felt anew how wrong it had been to get involved in a subgroup without Claire, mocking the choices that her husband had made.

Claire looked up at the sky. 'I've decided that it's my fault because I don't talk about his good side enough. And the reason is because Ted left you. And because Maura calls Dex a selfish fascist twat and because Suze rarely talks about Martin because he's such a limp dishcloth. And so, you see, in many ways I hold back about my remarkable husband because I don't want to seem smug.'

'You're many things but you're not smug. With the

exception of this very moment.' Annie sighed. 'Sorry. For not knowing your husband well enough.' And then Annie couldn't help herself. 'But why, if he's so wonderful, were you flirting with Dex on a beach?'

Claire's face crumpled in pain and she opened her mouth to speak.

'Actually, stop,' said Annie. 'I don't want to know. It'll just put me in a terrible position. I don't want to be party to your lie.' She winked. 'I learnt my lesson after lying to you about Maura. Sorry, again, for putting you in that position.' Annie breathed in like it was all settled. Like their chat had cleared away every last cobweb. 'So just put a stop to whatever's going on with Dex,' she said firmly. 'And stop goading Maura. Speak of the devil.'

Maura was walking toward them, head bowed, grasping a large-leafed plant, earth crumbling off fresh roots.

'But I'm fed up with her complaints,' hissed Claire quietly. 'All she *does* is complain about the bad stuff. And she puts me down like she thinks she's the best.'

Annie grasped Claire's hand, looking at her intently. 'Which she only ever does when she feels the worst. And she does it with you because she feels safe with you and knows you won't leave her.' Claire gave Annie a look that made her look away, like the light in her eyes. 'Please, put it all behind you and make up?' said Annie. 'She loves you.'

Maura stopped a few feet short of them both and looked at Claire, smiling, handing over the plant she was carrying.

'What's that? A bloody olive branch?' said Claire blankly.

'No, it's a massive leaf,' grumbled Maura. 'I'm sorry for being an idiot about Karl. Now can you get off your injured arse and help build the raft?'

'That's your apology? I suppose it's about three words longer than any I've had before, so . . .'

'Come on,' insisted Maura. 'I'd rather be with Dex than stranded here a moment longer without bacon and eggs.'

Claire took the plant and rolled it between her flattened palms as Maura whistled and shouted to Suze who was snoozing several feet away. 'Oi! Can you get big things, big sticks?'

Annie began easing herself up to help.

'Not you,' chided Maura. 'You've done enough damage for one day with your spears and your lies about my marriage. Besides, you puked so in the real world you'd be having a bit of a lie-down in front of *Friends*.'

Suze struck out for the other side of the island in search of raft materials, as Annie lay back on the sand like a starfish. She listened to Maura and Claire's conversation play out somewhere close by: part of her longing to sleep and the other part alert to any signs of a further rift between her friends. Maura had apologized but they all knew it was raw, tentative and fragile.

'How do you still look so gorgeous?' said Claire.

'Why, are you jealous of my beautiful physique?' replied Maura.

'Maybe I am now. But I wasn't when you were younger.'

'What, you weren't jealous of me when I was hot and beautiful and talented and everyone wanted a piece of this ass?'

'No,' said Claire and Annie was pleased to hear a smile nestled in the word. 'You were too . . . otherworldly. What's the point in envying something you're never going to have?'

'So, what, now I'm fatter,' said Maura.

'And more moany and things look harder for you . . .'

'And I'm less successful and trendy—'

'Yes, you're a bit like the rest of us, so it's easier to compare, and to envy.'

Annie sat up on her elbows, sensing they were moving too close to the cliff edge. 'Hey, Maura,' she said. 'Do you remember your first private view? When I ate so many bacon canapés I was sick?'

'Think that was the beer and margaritas, babe.'

'And the Russian artist who came on to you, Claire?'

'Yes,' giggled Claire. 'She was lovely.'

'We went to that pub in Leicester Square,' said Annie, speeding up, so that the warmth of the kintsugi golden glue filling the gaps between them didn't have time to cool. 'And, Claire, you raised a hundred toasts to Maura.'

'And we felt so immortal that we walked through traffic round Trafalgar Square,' said Claire. 'And that man in the lorry called out and thought Maura was Debbie Harry because of her bleached hair, and then she climbed in and travelled with him all the way down The Strand.'

'But that Russian artist?' said Annie. 'Those red lips and the black hair that fell in the shape of a V down her back?'

'She snogged me by the photocopier in the basement. I was so flattered,' said Claire, 'that someone so beautiful and famous and interesting was interested in me. Didn't that Russian artist want to work with you, Maura?'

Annie looked at Maura, daring her to tell the truth.

'It never happened,' sighed Maura, picking up a bundle of sticks. 'So let's just move on?'

'You should tell her why it never happened,' said Annie.

'We might die here and it would be a shame for her never to know.'

'Annie? For fuck's sake!' Maura breathed out. 'OK fine. Claire: the reason she didn't work with me was because when I caught her with her hands down your trousers in the print room, I thought she was assaulting you.'

'But she wasn't assaulting me,' said Claire.

'By the time I'd prised her off you,' said Maura, 'I'd been too aggressive and angry. I might even have lightly slapped her.'

'I don't remember any of that,' said Claire.

'Again with the margaritas,' said Maura. 'Anyway. She withdrew the offer of work the next day.'

'Oh. Well. Sorry and thanks, I guess?' said Claire, looking at Maura. 'I didn't think you'd go to the wall for me like that.'

'It's fine. My life has probably been better without the international stage and all that attention, to be honest with you.' She smiled. 'And anyway, it's not like you asked me to save you. Maybe somewhere deep in my subconscious I was jealous the Russian went for you, and not me.'

Claire laughed.

'I really miss you,' said Maura. 'Now you're not round the corner. I bet no one snogs female Russian artists in Market Crowbury.'

Annie lay back in the sand to the sound of their laughter.

'I love you both so much,' she said.

But they didn't hear.

Annie lay there for a few moments, feeling the conversation going on around her, and without her. She levered herself up on to her elbows and then her knees, tipping to the left as she stood, but righting herself before anyone noticed. Then she set out in the gloaming for the woods saying she was going to find Suze, but again they didn't seem to hear her, they were so engrossed in conversation. As soon as she was out of earshot, she sank back to the ground amongst the trees, legs weak again.

She should have been happy that Maura and Claire were friends again and yet all she could do was cry. Not for Em and the question marks that hung over her future, this time. But for herself. The idea of life going on without her was overwhelming: not just in death, but as her symptoms progressed. How was she ever meant to tell her friends that there would come a time in the near future – months, weeks perhaps – when she wouldn't be able to tell them she loved them because the muscles around her mouth and throat would weaken and her voice would warp until eventually it disappeared entirely? She would have to sit silently on the edges of conversation, unable to say anything.

What would they say when she told them that there would come a time in the near future – months, weeks perhaps – that she wouldn't be able to lift her arms to hug them? That levers, wheels, pumps and machines would help her get out of bed, go to the loo and hold her own child.

She'd be able to see and hear all the things that formed the heartbeats to her day – the phone ringing, eggs frying, bath running, chatter between Em and her friends – but she wouldn't be able to participate in any of it.

Annie knew then and there, in the silver half-light of the rain, that for a period, at least, she would be a ghost in her own life, living a half-death. A period in a transitionary waiting room made of glass where all her friends waited on the other side, close by, until she made the next part of her journey alone.

What would be worse: this half-death or the oblivion of a total death?

At least being dead she would never know the impact it had on others, whereas this half-death would mean having to bear witness to the brave faces and the tears without being able to reassure, hold, hug, talk or engage with any of it. She clasped a hand to her mouth as she imagined people telling her how much they loved and valued her even though she couldn't say it back. It would be like attending her own memorial service as they sat at her bedside and reminded her of times gone by. This holiday, that holiday. That time they got stuck on Blue Bracken Island. The times she helped them. All the positive and good stuff.

But she would want to remind them, too: *well hang on, I didn't behave that well on that occasion* and *please don't forget this memory* and *isn't that memory better* and *these are the memories I will always have of you*. Annie pressed a flattened palm to her heart, trying to push back the pain, as she realized just how many memories she had of them all. How would she know which one to choose when the final moment arrived? What would she say?

Annie was crying when she heard a panicked and pained shouting-scream coming from somewhere on the other side of the woods. At first, she thought the sounds came from an animal, like the sounds she heard at night in the allotments that backed on to her flat. Like an argument that turned, without warning, into an attack. But when she heard the scream from the woods again she knew it came from Suze.

Annie's body ran cold with dread. She leapt up, too quickly, nearly overbalanced again but righted herself, running onward, focused on getting to her friend, as fast as her still-living legs could carry her.

Chapter 22

Martin

The weather really had been on Dex's side when it came to creating the clement conditions needed for a game of rounders. The worst of the rain seemed to lift over their particular patch of land only, while all around the storm clouds continued to gather over the mainland, the water, and Blue Bracken Island. Martin's heart was on the floor. He'd rather put his head down a badger hole and risk his eyebrows being torn off than participate in team sports.

'Teams!' Dex shouted with a new, pulsing energy, so different from his usual brooding sluggishness, clearly brought on by getting high on his own supply.

Though he struggled to achieve it himself, Martin understood that competition was fuel for a man like Dex, a way of measuring how quickly he was continuing to overtake other people in the game of life. But Martin reasoned that if that was what Dex needed to feel like a better man and a better father, and therefore to stop being such a sourpuss, then so be it.

'We want to be on Martin's team!' shouted Alfie and

230

Freddy in unison, as they sat on the shale and pulled the Velcro of their sandals across their feet.

'Of course you bloody do!' roared Dex, waving the rounders bat round his head like a lasso. 'But who said you were included in the game?'

'That's a tad *playground*, Dexter,' said Karl, crossing his arms over his chest. 'What else are they going to do? They've played the shit out of every toy and puzzle we brought. At least this way they can learn to collaborate and—'

'How to lose,' said Dex bluntly. 'Fine. Adults vs. children then.'

'Really?' said Martin. 'But I doubt Em's even played rounders. She'll need some help. She's only two.'

'Start them young,' said Dex, thrusting forward in a deep lunge.

'Good, excellent,' said Martin, with a dash of sarcasm. 'I, for one, am not looking forward to humiliating myself because neither have I played rounders nor was I born with the correct physical attributes to play any sport effectively.'

'Which is probably why you get on with Alfie,' said Dex. 'What's Walt like as a sportsman? Does he take after his strong and lanky mum? Does he run away quickly, like she does?'

Martin felt the cogs grind uneasily inside him.

'Go orrrn, get ye to second post,' said Dex in a lascivious sailor's slur.

'You've got this,' whispered Karl, sensing Martin's unease. 'Literally plop yourself behind the post and I'll stand behind you in fielding position. All you have to do is catch the ball when it comes for you and try to get the batters out by slamming the post before they reach it. I've got your back. Don't you worry, pal.'

Martin nodded his gratitude back at Karl.

'I'll bowl,' said Dex.

'Hold on a minute, maybe Karl or I should bowl?' said Martin. 'Save your artist's wrists. And isn't that a . . . cricket ball?'

'Nice and heavy,' said Dex onerously. Martin did not relish the idea of Dex being in charge of a concrete-solid, conker-shiny missile.

'I'll stay fielder if you don't mind, mate,' said Karl. 'I'm an excellent catch. In all respects!'

'Let's kick off!' said Dex, speaking loudly over Karl's ensuing laughter at his own joke. 'Line up to bat, kids,' he said. 'Come on. Haven't got all day.'

Once Alfie, Freddy, Walt and Em had lined up he threw the bat at Freddy's feet for him to pick up. 'Hold it in both hands, mate! It's nearly as big as you!'

Freddy fixed his dad with a steely glare and whacked the ball as hard as any five-year-old could, which was not that hard, though it did make a nice shallow arc in the right direction.

Martin tried to catch it, but instead ended up creating a clumsy net with his bent arms and, to add insult to injury, as it fell through his elbows and back on to the shale, he then managed to kick it even further across the pitch with his poorly placed feet.

Meantime, Freddy made it all the way round the posts and pitch.

'One-nil to The Smalls,' said Karl.

'Yay!' shouted Martin. 'Everyone's a winner!'

'But they're bloody not, are they?' said Dex, looking as though he'd sucked a lemon. 'Get ready, Alfie,' he went on, tensing his jaw. Then his arm moved very suddenly, like a windmill on speed. Alfie jumped out of the way, the ball too fast for him to bat.

'Come on, mate, look alive!' said Dex, clearly annoyed.

'Hey, Alfie, does your dad play for England?' said Martin, half uncomfortable, half amused, limbering up for the next bowl.

Alfie hit the next ball.

'Run, you twit!' shouted Dex.

But Alfie stayed where he was and Dex threw the ball to Martin at second base. This time Martin caught the ball and held it high in the air.

'Get him out! Slam the post, Martin!' said Dex.

'I'm giving him a chance,' said Martin.

'Fuck sake, why?' demanded Dex, his face crumpling with fury. 'Those aren't the rules of the game!'

But still Alfie refused to move, so Martin went to him, took him by the hand and walked him gently all the way round the course to the finish so that Karl, for a second time, could declare a further point to the kids.

'You fucking what?' roared Dex. 'Play the point again! Come on! Now!'

And so Martin, to placate the rageful Dex, placed Alfie back in bat.

Alfie hit the ball again, and this time the ball landed close to Dex. This time Alfie ran because Martin had shown him what to do. This time Dex did not throw the ball to Martin and risk Martin either dropping it or holding onto it. Instead, Dex hurled the ball really, really hard in the direction of second post. It was unclear whether the throw was intended to hit the ground, or Martin, but either way Martin noted the nasty smile on Dex's face as the ball hit Alfie's upper arm.

Alfie wailed and clung on to Martin's legs tightly. Martin

was so shocked and appalled by Dex's actions, and his subsequent lack of any compulsion to check on his son, that all he could do was cling right back on to the boy.

Martin continued to look at Dex searchingly, to give him the chance to admit to what he'd done, apologize at the very least, but Dex's lips remained adamantly pressed together.

'Mate!' shouted Karl. To who exactly, Martin didn't know, but the words made a supportive sound.

'Hey, Alfie,' Martin said eventually. 'I think your dad didn't mean to do that. It was an accident and you got in the way of the ball. I think he'll apologize.'

'No, I won't,' said Dex. 'Why would I apologize when he should have moved faster to avoid the ball? That's the game. If you don't move fast enough, you get knocked out.'

This lack of culpability, this boyish sense of blaming something or someone else for his own palpable mistake at best, intention to hurt at worst, lit a smouldering fuel inside Martin that began to burn very brightly indeed.

Martin stood up as straight as he could. 'Why don't you take some responsibility, Dex? You hit your son with a ball and he's crying. He's already afraid of you. *Loud* is *you*. Loud is what he hides from.'

'In a Wendy house I built and paid for, which is more than can be said for where your own son can take cover.'

'My son doesn't need to *take cover*,' said Martin. 'Kids should never need to take cover unless they're in a war zone.'

'Stop it with your self-righteousness.' Dex waved the bat in the air, leaving his position and taking a few steps toward Martin. 'So, what, he just told you he didn't like me being loud out of the blue? No leading questions from you like *What do you think of your arsehole daddy?*'

'They weren't needed. Now, if you'll excuse me?'

Martin took a final look at Dex's face, at the whitened knuckles round his bat, and suspecting, in that moment, that he might have stoked the cannon with too much gunpowder, elected to turn away while he still had his legs.

But although Martin wanted to flee as quickly as he could he ambled, arms hanging loose by his side, to show that he was the one in control – though inside his own bubbling rage was pushing him to the verge of tears.

It was only when he stood on the cool tiles of the gritty bathroom floor with filthy feet, that he could no longer hold it in. He locked the door firmly behind him and leaning against it, slid slowly down its length until his backside reached the floor. He dropped his face into his open palms and cried hot, angry boy tears, for the fact that Alfie and Freddy felt exactly what he had felt his whole life. On the receiving end of bullies.

He tugged at a damp flannel that had been clinging to the side of the sink like a wound dressing and, paying no attention to the slick of toothpaste, the streak of dirt and its general mildewed odour, rammed the whole thing in his mouth and screamed.

When his heart had calmed, he removed the flannel from his mouth and used it to wipe the dust from his pale and downy calves.

Ready to face them again, he walked back onto the shale and what he saw was worse than any pain he'd left behind in that bathroom. The sight of Walt in floods of tears, face despairing and stretched, crying: 'What's happening to Mum? What's happening to Mum?' While Dex knelt just inches behind him, a devilish smile painted across his ugly face.

Chapter 23

Annie

6.30 p.m. Saturday, 29 August
Blue Bracken Island

The rain thundered down and the sand was damp and uneven underfoot – leading to calf-ache and tendon pain as the friends ran as fast as they could in the direction of Suze's cries. Annie's skin shivered like it was draped with a fine coat of electrical sparks from the adrenaline that drove her forward, powering her limbs like petrol and deadening any pain in her body to a dull throb.

'Why is she screaming like that?' said Claire, white and waxy with fear. The pathway through the wood had slowed them down and Maura was hauling Claire up by the armpits from when she'd stumbled into a shallow, root-tangled pit. 'It sounds like she's being mauled! What's happening to her?'

Annie didn't answer Claire, and instead took her by the hand, dragging her onwards, encouraging her to run faster, encouraging all of them to run faster as they hurdled more roots and fallen tree stumps, prickled pine needles jabbing at the soles of their feet.

When they arrived at the scene, they all gasped. Suze

236

was under a canopy of trees in a thick pool of quicksand, midway up her thighs. Her arms were held up in surrender, but the worst of it was her eyes, all swollen red and shiny with tears. Suze so rarely cried that the sight was shocking. Barely any light came through the canopy and the rain hit the leaves above like tribal drum beats. It was grim, funereal, sacrificial . . . and the sulphurous stench in the air made Annie gag.

'Oh, Suze,' said Claire. 'Are you stuck?'

Suze gave her a disbelieving look indicating that her question did not dignify a response. 'There's a pallet for the raft over there,' she said, pointing at the same kind of pallet Annie had found earlier. 'All I did was try and reach it. I stepped onto this, this ground, this shit underneath me that looked completely solid and before I knew it, I was stuck.' Her voice was quivering. 'I'm really cold. And I'm really . . . Can you get me out?'

Annie fixed her gaze on the tip of a wide-brimmed leaf behind Suze, and used it to track and confirm her suspicion that Suze was moving almost imperceptibly downwards every time she spoke.

'Just . . . try not to speak too much?' said Annie.

'And breathe deeply and slowly,' said Maura. 'Do not, I repeat, do not panic.'

Annie struggled to take a deep enough breath herself as she made contact with a terrible memory, feeling herself being pulled down by its tendrils.

'Have you tried to get out, babe?' said Maura.

'You what? No! I thought I'd just fucking stand here freezing my bones to ice like a hippo in a cryogenic tank on a spa break. Of *course* I've tried to get out.'

'OK, OK, don't get too upset,' said Maura. 'I think you move down a bit every time you talk. The upside is that you're tall, so—'

'What, so the length of my calves might give me twenty minutes to die rather than ten?'

'God, no, I mean, we can . . . like . . .' Claire sobbed between breaths. 'Can we get you a straw or something? For when your face is submerged?'

'Annie!' shouted Suze, her face full of rage. 'Can you stop these chumps from drawing up the palliative care plan and get me out of here? Annie?'

'Yes, yes, of course,' Annie said, snapping out of her shocked and muffled state. Annie had to save her. She couldn't let this happen again. She was thirty-nine and she was nine. She was on Blue Bracken Island and she was in a park in Bushey. Her friend was sinking down into the mud. Her friend was slipping under the ice.

'To be honest, I didn't think you'd hear me,' said Suze, and Annie's face crumpled into tears at her friend's sadness and confusion. 'And I don't know how you're going to get me out of here and if you don't . . .? I can't go now. I've got plans . . .'

'There's never a good time to die,' said Maura. 'Just like there's never a good time to have kids.'

'Different things, Maura!' snapped Claire.

Suze really believed she was about to die. It was all Annie could do not to leap off her piece of sanded grass and into that quicksand to throw her arms around her. They were sort of sitting in the same boat, waiting for death, weren't they? For a moment Annie allowed herself to feel horrified, afraid and a little less alone for it.

'Annie?' said Suze again. 'Tell me you're coming up with a plan?'

'You have to think positive, Suze,' said Maura. 'You've got a job you love, a gorgeous son and a man who . . . Oh my God. You look so miserable! You need to think of good things.'

'Bloody hell,' snapped Claire. 'This isn't Mary Poppins. Memories of sleepovers and poker games and cream buns aren't going to suck her out of the mud!' Claire's words shuddered and splintered into a pile at the end of her sentence.

Were these last minutes going to be Suze's living memorial? How could one person be there one minute and gone the next? One minute laughing on the ice. The next, floating under it, the heart arrested.

It had been freezing that day, unseasonal ice and snow, and Annie had been in the park with her friend. There were chains round the gate and a red warning sign. Inside, parents were drinking whisky and playing cards but their daughters had Mickey Mouse slippers to be tried on the ice, slippers that would surely slide like ice skates.

'Babe!' shouted Maura from the sidelines. 'Tip forward!'

'Wait! Don't!' screamed Annie, out of instinct and nothing more, back at Suze's side.

'Should she tip back then, like she's in a rip tide?' said Claire.

Annie had read about rip tides and other natural occurrences in the years following the accident, like she was arming herself with knowledge against the danger of wind and fire and snow and water. The kind of knowledge that might have saved her friend in Bushey Park if only she'd

239

known more. Fat lot of good that research had done her. Thirty-nine but here she was, still not knowing what to do.

Annie realized then that she really believed she should have been able to save her friend from the ice. It wasn't that she'd felt it was her fault. It wasn't even that skating on the ice in slippers had been her idea. It had been the way the girl's parents looked at her during the funeral. With anger in their eyes. As though they couldn't bear the fact that Annie had been the one to survive.

Had it been her fault? No one told her any different. And so, she had believed that it was.

'Annie doesn't know what to do!' said Maura. 'Tip forward!'

'No!' screamed Annie. 'She'll never get up again. She'll drown.'

'Obviously she should close her mouth,' said Maura, as if that was the issue. 'But I read if you tip forward that's how you get your feet unstuck.'

'You *read* it somewhere?' said Annie, coming back to the present.

'Yes? And where exactly does your info come from then? YouTube?'

'Which one should I do?' cried Suze. 'What if they both kill me?'

'Hard to answer that,' barked Maura angrily. 'Because you won't be here to blame the person who got it wrong.'

'Neither of us will have got it wrong,' said Annie, tears in her eyes. 'It will be neither of our faults because both of us will have been trying to save Suze in the best way we knew how.'

'Believe me, then,' insisted Maura. 'Lie forward and maybe

you'll live to fight another day! Either way you can't afford to wait.'

'I'm so cold and so afraid, why are you arguing with me?' asked Suze, bursting into tears.

'I'm not arguing with you, Suze,' said Maura more gently. 'I'm just telling you that I'm right.'

'Maura's right about one thing,' said Claire calmly, using the back of her hand to swipe against her forehead as if she was really hot. 'You can't sit on this like the other massive decision you need to make.'

'What other massive decision?' said Annie. Was this what they had been meeting to talk about? 'What decision? Is this really the time to be talking about life decisions?'

But no one said anything and the air hung onto those answers, too, along with the smell and the raining drumbeats and all their fear which felt like it would never leave them.

'I can't do this,' cried Suze. 'You're asking me to choose which friend I believe the most!'

'You're lucky to have a choice!' shouted Annie, loudly and angrily enough for them all to look at her in surprise. She took a deep breath. 'By which I mean that some people don't have any friends and how nice you're here with your three best friends who are all trying to get you out of the mud. The women you would trust with your happiness and your life. Maybe we're both right? Maybe we just bring different things to the same outcome? Right? I don't know.' Her voice wavered. 'Decisions are hard. How do you decide between your friends? But Claire and Maura are right. You need to make a choice. If you don't, you'll stay stuck. And you'll die anyway.'

'Maura is so confident,' said Suze. 'And yet also, Maura – I love you, but you can be so full of shit. Whereas when Annie speaks, I believe it. Mostly . . . before the lies she told about your marriage, Maura . . . but in general, history says she's trustworthy.'

'Tip forward now!' screamed Maura. 'You're nearly up to your fanny.'

'Lie back,' said Annie, her heart aching, eyes stinging. 'Do it now fucking do it now! Take my hand, Danielle!' Her heart was hammering and forehead sweating, falling in and out of the past and present as she leant over and grabbed hold of Suze's hand.

'Who in living hell is Danielle?' said Maura.

Suze stretched out her other hand for Claire to take it.

Suze looked around at all of them, as if for the last time, mouthing the words 'I love you,' before letting go of Claire's hand on one side and Annie's on the other, raising her arms above her and performing an odd and slow flop backwards.

'Shit,' hissed Maura.

'Yes,' said Annie, barely able to breathe.

'She chose you.'

Annie glanced sideways to check whether Maura meant that Suze had finally made a choice, or that the choice hadn't been her. It was hard to tell and not something she or anyone else wanted to untangle in that awful moment as they gawped at their friend lying back in the mud, her short blonde hair messed up tragically and onerously in the shape of an angel's halo. Seconds seemed like minutes seemed like an eternity and before she could stop it, a strange, loud laugh barked out of Annie.

Claire looked at her in pale disgust but it was useless trying to explain. Annie felt profound sadness, enough to want to cry endlessly, but all she could do was laugh, too loud and far too expressively – not because she was in touch with the fundamental pointless ridiculousness of life and what a joke it all was or because she was experiencing a moment of enlightenment, but because things weren't connecting properly in her brain.

'Why are you *laughing*?' said Maura.

'Shouldn't we see if she can hold her head up?' cackled Annie. 'Her ears are stuck under the sand and she won't be able to hear,' she said, breaking into more hysterical laughter.

'Stop it, Annie. Stop laughing! What is wrong with you?' shouted Claire. But it wasn't the moment to tell anyone about her malfunctioning nervous system.

And with that, Claire tapped Suze urgently on the head and Suze pulled her head easily out of the sand.

'God, are you OK?' said Claire.

'Do I look OK?' spat Suze, Dairy Milk coloured quicksand covering her hair.

'You look like you're mid spa treatment, not halfway to death. What's going on?'

'I don't know,' said Suze quietly, 'I was trying to give my feet a bit of time, moving them slowly to and fro, but I don't . . .'

'Great work, everyone!' said Maura angrily.

'Will you please keep your emotions under control?' said Annie.

'Annie, she's completely submerged apart from her upper body and face, the situation is so much worse and we obviously need RNLI apparatus.' The pitch of Maura's voice climbed higher and higher. 'We can't save you, babe!' she screamed, so loudly it hurt all their ears. 'Because we can't even save ourselves!'

The words rang out like funeral bells, ponderous and heavy, propelling their leaden vibrations into the heart of the whole group.

'Will you stop being so loud and dramatic!' snapped Suze, 'and let me concentrate?' Then she tipped backwards again. A few moments later, a knee emerged, Godzilla-like, from the sand.

'Hold up my head, Claire. Maura, get over here and get yourself dirty, come on.' She held her head up at an angle. 'My feet, I think they're moving up.'

Claire held Suze's head while Maura and Annie helped her wriggle her body further toward the surface, inch by tortuous inch, each woman straining and pulling, first softly, then more firmly, every second feeling like a lifetime. And then finally, Suze was free, slithering back over the shallower sand coming to rest between the other three women, splayed on their backs, looking up at the branches arching high above their heads, shaking with the cold.

'Oh my God, my God, you're safe,' said Annie, breathing quickly, tears tracking her cheeks. She was feeling so much grief for the little girl who had died under the ice, and grief for her younger self who had lived above the ice feeling like she'd had the power to kill people and drive people away, and so much relief that her friend got to live above the mud. Her body felt drained and spent, as though it had expelled the dragging dark cobwebs that had always lived in her peripheral vision, so that she could see new knowledge. That she was someone who had the power to save people, too.

She breathed out loudly, with a sort of joyous relief.

'You look like a doughnut,' said Claire to Suze, 'where the sand has stuck. Like, all over you? Like sprinkles?'

'I could murder a doughnut,' said Maura. 'Shall we eat her?' And they all barrelled on top of Suze in a pile of limbs, forgetting their hunger and how their hearts ached with fear, instead hugging her until their bodies hurt in the best possible way.

'Annie,' said Maura. 'Who's Danielle? Are you, like, really hungry or are you having a stroke?'

'She's got arthritis. Maybe it's that?' said Claire.

'It's OK,' said Annie thoughtfully. 'Danielle was the name of the shark that bit my toes. It's OK. It's OK.'

'Right,' said Suze, as the women rearranged themselves on the sandbank in various states of cross-leggedness and recline. 'Thank you all for being here.'

And they all cheered.

'But the pallet is still over there,' she said. 'And we're all still stuck on this island.'

'For God's sake,' said Maura. 'You could just have walked round here to get it?'

They watched Maura walk round the grassy border of solid earth and heft the pallet easily onto her shoulders, carrying it back to them.

'Great,' said Suze, smiling. 'I totally knew that. Seriously, Annie, your advice about lying back saved my life and what you said about being stuck made me realize something. You have to move either way else your body, or soul, dies. So I've made a decision about my job.'

Annie smiled, feeling happiness travel through each sinew as she joined the dots, making assumptions and drawing conclusions about trauma and tragedy and all the numerous pieces of anecdotal evidence that suggested people made new decisions about how to spend their days, and with whom, when their lives had been threatened. Suze had been gifted a second chance, and with it a solution to Annie's problem. Of course this was going to work out! All she'd had to do was let things take their natural path.

What a relief, not to have to fight decisions about Maura, or Claire, or *not* Maura, or *not* Claire. She could finally admit, now, that neither was the best solution. But Suze?

She was the right person now that she would be staying with the people that mattered. She was smart, she was solvent, she was interesting. She had a family and Martin was a kind man and Em would have an older brother.

'I'm going to resign,' said Suze, and Annie smiled.

Then Suze sat up straight and put a little distance between her and the rest of them. 'The thing is, it's not what I signed up for. It's exhausting. They don't pay me. I work all night. I get puked on, screamed at and it's stolen my freedom.'

'Why would you resign from your PhD? You fought for that,' said Maura.

'Not *that* job,' said Suze. 'Being a mum. I'm going to resign from being a mum. I don't want to do it anymore.'

Chapter 24

Martin

7 p.m. Saturday, 29 August
Sandpiper Cottage

Walt was crying as though he'd fallen on his knees and scraped the skin right back to the flesh. Only there wasn't a mark on him.

'What did he *say* to you?' said Martin, as he knelt and pressed Walt to his chest, feeling the small boy's wails send shockwaves through his own body.

'I told him the truth,' said Dex, standing up from his kneeling position and pinning his shoulders back.

'Mum's gone and she's not coming back!' howled Walt.

Martin triaged the situation at speed and stood up with the boy in his arms, pressing Walt's hot, tear-sodden cheek to his own, saying, 'It's OK, I'm here, little guy. Daddy's here.' Then he walked away from Dex.

Once Walt's grief-stricken full-body gasps had slowed, Martin knelt down on the cool tiles of the bathroom floor and grasped him by both clammy hands. Walt was wearing evidence of the day's adventures: hair ruffled, his face and knees streaked with grime. He was so like his mum.

'Look at me,' Martin said. 'Your mum loves you very much and she'll be back in the morning. Whatever that idiot said, everything is *OK*.'

There was a hard rap on the bathroom door and Martin braced himself, his body coursing with the kind of physiological petrol that primed a man to fight when his child had been threatened.

'Only me,' whispered Karl, pushing open a gap in the door, gently posting a slim box of chocolates into Martin's hands. 'Cheer-up supplies for the little chap. First thing that came to hand in the treat drawer.'

Martin looked at the glossy box of chocolates, decorated with a range of liqueur labels. Mostly whiskies, some gins.

'Thank you,' said Martin, smiling and shoving them under the sink. 'Very thoughtful.'

Martin took hold of Walt's hand and wiped his face down with the same wet flannel he'd used on himself earlier.

'Tell me exactly what he said?' said Martin. 'Tell me what that ffffff . . . said?'

Karl pushed the door open a little more and hissed through his teeth like he was slowly being burnt by an iron. 'Nasty bastard he was,' he said.

Walt looked up at Martin, his wide eyes shining with tears. 'He said that Mum's leaving us because you're a loser.'

Martin looked at Walt a beat, his face hardening into a mask, assimilating what he'd heard in the spaces behind it. But when Walt threw his arms around Martin's neck, holding on as tight as he would a life raft, Martin's face bent and contorted as the sobs pulsed up in a wave from his heart and pushed at the skin around his throat and mouth, fighting to get out.

'But I know that's not true, Dad,' sobbed Walt. 'Because *everyone's a winner.* Aren't they?'

Martin controlled his powerful wave of emotion, using it to embrace his child tighter still, as if his arms were a shield. He glanced up at Karl, who was looking down on the scene like a beatific Virgin Mary. 'Can I leave you with the little guy for a bit?'

'And some! I'll get the mini-gang all sorted with snacks and the idiot box while you do what you need to do.'

'Thanks, appreciate it.'

Karl took Walt by the hand and turned to go, before returning a few seconds later looking grave. 'Hey, Martin. I've got your back, mate. I *know* people. We'll take him down if needs be.'

'That won't be necessary,' said Martin, his face flushing with heat. 'But thank you for the support.'

Martin stepped into the corridor, kicked off his espadrilles and replaced them with a pair of foam sandals.

'Showtime,' he whispered under his breath, ripping the Velcro straps up and over his feet so tightly that flesh bulged in the gaps, feeling like a Roman centurion pulling on his hobnailed footwear to fight.

Out on the deck, Dex was sitting at the garden table with his feet up, regarding a line of three, small, empty French beer bottles – one hand shoved down his trousers and the other holding another small beer. He looked up, unmoved, as Martin stepped onto the deck. 'So bored and stoned I've taken to masturbating at every available opportunity,' he said.

Martin took a deep and silent breath. 'That's a bold move.

To jerk yourself off in a public area while the rest of us clean up the mess you've made.'

Dex's eyes flashed obsidian black. 'You mean the mess *you've* made? Why haven't you told your son the truth? Let me rephrase that: Why haven't you told your son about your lies?'

'I haven't lied to anyone.'

'Er, yes you have?'

Karl stepped onto the deck, hands hooked into his jeans, primed for tension. 'Anything I can do to assist here? Protein shake, anyone?'

Dex pointed his finger angrily at Martin. 'Number one lie. A job. You said you have one. But you don't, because you lost it weeks ago. Soon you won't be able to buy your son . . . *anything*? No Pokémon cards, no sliced bread.'

'How do you know about my job?' said Martin as calmly as if he was asking about whether they had an acquaintance in common.

'Because Maura told me,' said Dex baldly.

'But how does Maura know?'

'Oh, Marty Martin Martster! Suze told *her*!'

'I don't like the name Marty Martster. Don't call me that again. Did you know, Karl?'

'Oh yes. Sorry, mate.' Karl at least looked abashed. 'I've known for weeks. Suze sees Claire for coffee twice a week. But I couldn't care less about you losing your job, mate. It doesn't bother me. Not like it seems to bother Dex. Or you . . .'

'It's private info.'

'And yet,' said Dex, 'it is an incontrovertible fact of life that *women talk*. Like, all the time, and about everything from TV to periods to sex to thwarted dreams and a desire to bang the Defence Secretary. Surely you know that?'

Had they all been laughing behind his back? He felt tears well up from somewhere deep inside but he balled his fists to stop them. He had to focus.

'And what exactly did you say to Walt about his mum?'

'That she's fucking off and leaving you both because you're a . . .'

'Loser.'

'Quite.'

'She hasn't actually made up her mind yet.'

'Because you thought you could make her stay by roasting a few chickens? Because you thought that spatchcocking one of the fuckers might genuinely sway it?'

Martin did not respond, though inside his organs were really hurting, as though they were trying to escape his body and smash Dex to bits.

'The thing is,' said Dex, 'I don't really care that you're haemorrhaging life tokens: job, relationship, money, self-respect, fashion sense . . . Bleed away, son. What I care about is how you've rocked up with your stupid shorts and your Tupperware and criticized my fathering when you can't even hold together a family of your own: either with your capacity to provide, or your ability to make people love you enough to stick around.'

'Ouch, and double-ouch,' said Karl.

Martin felt his face tingle with heat and his chest tighten – yet his voice remained low and calm. 'You don't know anything about my relationship, or my job. Suze had some revisions of her own life plan to consider, and I've had a few issues with anxiety and low mood the last few months, so I've been put on some meds. I'm not ashamed of it. I had to take some time off to recalibrate and get the dose right and my absence coincided with a period when the university had to make some cuts. It's been bad timing all round.'

'Oh, mate,' said Karl, his voice laced with a warm and genuine concern that touched Martin, 'have you tried exercise, sleep and getting rid of the meds? I think if you read the evidence you'll find that the meds actually *make* you depressed?'

'I'm good, thanks,' said Martin, as Karl nipped back into the kitchen to deal with the children's cries coming from inside. 'Dex, how did you know that Suze was considering leaving?'

'I can't reveal my sources on that one. Only to say again that *women talk*.'

'Right. Excellent. So, are you finished?'

Dex looked up. 'For the meantime,' he said, before draining his fourth stubby beer.

'You see,' said Martin calmly, 'you can say what you want about me and my job, though I won't lie: your words certainly hurt. But what I can't stand. Where I draw a line. What makes me *really* angry, and I don't ever get angry, is when you involve the little people. Because children haven't had a chance to decide who they're going to be in the world. And yet, the way you are? You seem to be the kind of person that blots their horizons, rather than widen them. Every time you grab them by the sleeve to control them.'

'You were judging me then!'

'Or raise your voice to be heard. Or hit them with a ball to prove a point. And now this: violating my own son's sense of safety by telling him things that were not yours to tell. I don't like that at all. It upsets them and makes me want to grind your ugly fucking face into the gravel.'

'You what?' said Dex, like he'd been slapped hard around the chops.

Martin felt as though he was being pulled up by an invisible rope from the crown of his head. 'This weekend I've done nothing but support you. And cook for you. And offer to look after your kids. And pick up your jumpers and T-shirts and stubby beer bottles from all over the house. And make excuses for your behaviour: because you're an artist and you're busy and you're stressed with success and what you need is time and space to be a better person. And because you're good-looking and strong and you've walked the earth thus far believing that you own it, taking it all like you deserved it.'

Martin took two steps and shoved Dex with his outstretched palms. Dex cowered, then jumped out of his chair like he was escaping a wasp.

'But honestly?' continued Martin. 'All that time I was waiting for you to show just a glimmer of the better person you might be because I couldn't quite believe that such an *arsehole* could exist in the world.'

Dex stepped away from Martin toward the big-leafed plants and bushes at the edge of the deck. 'Don't know what you're talking about, mate,' he said, with a puff of bravado that belied the panicked look in his eyes.

'Look at you,' said Martin. 'You've got everything. You're good-looking, you make money from your talent, you're married to the woman everyone wants to be around and who is also interesting and beautiful and talented. And yet. You wear your life's riches on your face like a slapped cod. Yes,

Suze is probably leaving me . . .' Martin's voice wavered. 'So I'm facing life as a single dad without an income, but you don't see me walking around like a complete arsehole. Don't you know how lucky you are? What more do you want? More money? More adoration? More sex? I've got news for you: you can't handle what money and adoration and sex you do have, so maybe it's time to revise yourself.'

Martin continued. 'You were fifty per cent right about one thing, though. Women do talk. But so do men. I will not stoop to your level to say quite how much they discuss and possibly mock your forty-five-degree appendage, but let's just say the subject is firmly and regularly on the agenda.' And with that, Martin shoved him again.

'Get off me!' said Dex, pushing his arms out and shoving Martin away at the exact same time Karl stepped back onto the deck.

'Kids are— Don't you dare!' Karl said, as he saw Dex shove Martin. 'You get off him. The jig is up, Dex,' he shouted.

'No,' said Martin, turning to Karl. 'You don't need to do anything. It's OK. I've dealt—'

But Karl was in a reverie, and not listening. 'What a whiny Viking you are, Dex.'

'Why are *you* having a go at me as well?' cried Dex.

Then Karl shoved Dex, much harder than Martin had.

'No, stop!' said Martin, not quite loudly enough because a small part of him was prepared to admit that he might let Karl get on with it.

'You may have cool slides,' said Karl, eyes glinting, 'but that doesn't buy you anything other than a fleeting glance from the public. No one really cares about slides anymore. You may be successful, but I know what it is to be successful, too. At the top of your game. Sure, it's lonely at the top – with great power comes great responsibility. But to be an arsehole with it? There's no excuse, mate. To rag on a skinny little dude like Martin who has no job and no friends? Though he can certainly count on *me* as one,' he said, turning to Martin. 'You can, you know, Marty. I'd be happy to assist you in bulking out and amending your aftershave choices whenever you like.'

Karl turned his attention back to Dex and shoved him again. This time Dex had to bolster himself on his chair so he didn't fall over.

Martin pulled gently on the back of Karl's thick-knit ink-black polo shirt, his fourth clothes change of the day. 'Please, stop.'

'No. He needs to appreciate you and everything you do,' said Karl, tears in his eyes as he addressed his words half to Dex, half to Martin. 'You see, if I was to write your obituary—'

'You what?' Martin yelped, feeling worried.

'I'd say Martin was kind and nice. That he offered to help people when they were lacking skills or confidence. That he made kids happy by talking to them and asking them their opinions, which is a *talent*, in my books. He was like the Pied Piper of Hamelin, and I'd have had him run the company creche in a heartbeat if I'd made enough from the sale of the cauliflower patty recipe. He'd have made a great primary school teacher.'

Karl looked over at Martin as if he'd already died, tears welling in his eyes, and continued. 'And if I'd been lucky enough to have him teach me as a kid, I'd have said, "That guy moulded me into the man I am today." He taught me more about how to be a good dad in the twenty-four hours I knew him than my dad taught me in a lifetime. Forget slides and neon paint – *that's* what I call a legacy.'

'OK, thank you, Karl.' Martin blushed.

'Martin is the kind of guy who raises the good and interesting souls that are our hope of a better world. Not like you, Dex, you utter twat. You just bully people and make them sad and then you raise more people like Dex!' Karl roared. 'Gah! What a dick!'

Then Karl gave him a final shove and both Dex and the chair collapsed back into a bush.

'It was Martin who started it,' croaked Dex, lying on the ground with his hands over his chest, his trousers unzipped, boxers unbuttoned, eyes full of tears. 'Martin who threw the first punch.'

Karl swung round to face Martin, his face beaming. 'Was it?' he said, rubbing his palms together and righting his hair in alternate moves. 'Good for you, mate. Expected nothing less. To summarize, Dex: you're not funny, everyone hates you and you should never have had children.'

'All right, Karl, that's enough,' said Martin, suddenly exhausted.

'I really need to go home,' Dex wept. 'I really need my wife so we can just go home.'

Chapter 25

Annie

Of all the things Annie had expected Suze to say, it wasn't that.

'But you can't just stop being a mum?' said Maura, one side of her face smeared with mud from where she'd only just released herself from a grubby, relieved embrace with Suze. Her hair was a bird's nest of more mud and twigs and tangles. It was the absolute wildest she had ever looked.

'I think I can,' said Suze calmly. 'It's the twenty-first century in the UK. I've got some money. I have work. And I only have one life. Being stuck in that mud?' Her eyes filled with tears. 'None of us gets to choose how we die, do we? But we can choose how we spend our days. And I can't waste any more time. I've been sitting on the fence with this decision to leave for too long.'

'Exactly how long have you been perched on this fence?' said Annie, cold with shock.

Claire reached out and grasped Suze's hand, squeezing it supportively, which Annie and Maura both saw.

257

'Claire, how long have *you* known about this?' Annie cried. 'Is this what you've been discussing secretly at your coffee mornings? Resigning from being a mother is a *huge* thing. Why didn't you come to me?'

Annie could definitely have talked Suze round. What had Claire said, or not said, to encourage this rubbish?

'It's almost like Suze didn't want to be challenged,' said Maura.

'Hey,' said Claire, but Maura spoke over her quickly.

'This doesn't make sense,' she said. 'For every twenty times a child shouts at you, and shits on you, and throws a bowl of cheese at you, there might be, what, one time when they smile, hug you and tell you that you're their one true love? As far as positive feedback goes, being a mother is a desert. Every mother I know has one foot out the door, it's the nature of the job. The point is you don't step further than that. You crack on regardless.'

'I don't have one foot out the door,' said Claire.

And looking at Claire's face, suffused with deep emotion and intention, and the rumpled brow of not relating at all to what Maura had just said, Annie believed her.

'It's not one or the other!' said Annie. 'You can't just give up on the people you love, Suze!' She couldn't. Giving up on Martin and Walt was giving up on her, too. 'You just get through the hard stuff the best you can and you find ways of accommodating the rest. Should Martin *do* more?'

'Martin already does tonnes. He's a great dad. The point is I don't want to *crack on regardless*,' said Suze calmly. 'I don't want the sleepless nights when they're ill and all the responsibility of dealing with mental health and social media and the horror of leaving them to live on a dying planet. I don't want to have to make toast or lunch or endless snacks or spend a second more of my life matching socks into balls. I want to be able to take off for months at a time and to work through the night without having to ask permission because someone has to get up and make breakfast for Walt. I want to travel to Costa Rica, Iberia, France and the Andes. I want to do ayahuasca in Peru and take my time to come back from wherever I go. I want to do clowning classes and improv classes and go clubbing with my neighbours who are twenty years younger than me. And I want to do all of it without feeling guilty. And so, after my six-month research placement, I'm going to carry on my studies and travel to India, Nepal and Thailand in search of the indigenous cultures that can unlock the key to life and the fear of death and how to live a balanced life in between.'

'And how long are you going to do exactly *what you bloody well want*?' Maura demanded.

'Weeks, months, years? Forever? As long as I like. I'm not going to *crack on regardless* sublimating what I want just because our culture says that's what a mother should do, leaving their own dreams to fester until they're too old and creaky to do anything about them. History is littered with men who've found it too hard to parent and fucked off in pursuit of their own happiness without feeling a shred of guilt. Look at The Canadian! So I'm The Canadian in this situation but I am conducting my exit in an open, transparent, planned and controlled manner.'

'Is this because of Martin?' said Maura. 'Is this because he doesn't have enough *bite*.'

'Martin is great. He is kind and good and will make someone a really good boyfriend or husband one day and I stand by my decision that he's the best father for my child. He cares about kids. Understands them and wants to make their lives better. But Martin and I aren't a couple. We never were. We only slept together once. We're not a family. We're just good friends.'

'Aren't good friends the same thing as family?' said Annie, failing to keep the barbed panic out of her voice.

But Suze didn't reply. And what was worse, the others didn't either.

'So, er . . . how did you find yourself with child?' said Annie.

'Walt,' said Claire pointedly, looking up at her. 'The child is called Walt.'

'You know how Martin and I met,' said Suze. 'In a haze of fever during clinical trials for a flu vaccine. We got on really well. He was sweet and funny and really kind. We went out one night. I introduced him to mushrooms, we drank a bit and ended up in bed together. It was the only time, and soon after I found out I was pregnant. I was distraught, but he was so happy he cried because a child is all he's ever wanted. Then he suggested we consider raising it together. He said that the worst-case scenario was that it would be an experience. A *journey*. And you know how much I love a journey. But more than that – and he was right – he said that particular journey of motherhood might be my last one and that I might regret it if I didn't act on it. And then he said best-case scenario would be that I fall in love with it, and him, and the idea of the family. And somewhere in between those things was a unicorn moment: he said that if, after four years, I really didn't want to do it, then he would take over. Like a contract with a get-out clause.'

'Wow,' said Maura. 'Take the best bits, pull the ripcord when the going gets tough.'

'None of it was written down, and maybe he never thought it would come to this. Women find themselves drawn in by love—'

'Or obligation and guilt,' muttered Maura.

'But when I told him a few months ago that it was past Walt's fourth birthday and I was thinking of going, he couldn't quite accept it. He thought it was his fault. That he hadn't worked hard enough to show me that family and friendship were everything. Then when this weekend came up, he thought it would be a good chance to show me what "the village" is capable of. To remind me of that warm, fuzzy feeling of helping each other. But as much as I love you all – we lead different lives now. And much as I love Walt, motherhood . . . it just *isn't* me.'

How was Annie supposed to argue with what a best friend really wanted for their own life? She wasn't in Suze's head, she didn't live every day with her. She might know her. But did she really *know* her?

'So what was the tipping point?' said Annie.

'When I looked at all of you. At how tired Claire is and how stressed you are, Annie, like all the time? And how much children have messed up Maura's marriage? When I hear all the complaints and fears and grief I just think: why would I want that for myself?'

'That's us told,' said Maura bitterly.

'How is Walt going to feel when he finds out you're leaving? Have you told him?' asked Annie.

'Not yet. I was going to wait until after this weekend. To give Martin his chance. And anyway, sure, it'll be bumpy but Walt's going to be great. He's got an amazing dad who loves him and a mum who will come and see him when she's around and he'll grow up knowing that you don't have to feel obliged to stay in relationships – no, not even relationships, *arrangements* that make you unhappy. You can leave. You can go your own way. Isn't that an important lesson to teach a kid?'

'That's not what he'll think,' said Maura bluntly. 'He'll think you left him because he wasn't loveable enough for you to stay.'

Suze just shook her head.

Annie's eyes filled with sadness at how she was about to lose Suze, at how Em was about to lose Suze, at how Suze could treat this great bond, this gift, as something that could be returned to the shop.

'I don't understand!' said Annie. 'Why would you choose to leave someone you love when there are so many other ways people get separated without having a choice in the matter, like through war or death or—'

'This is *exactly* why I didn't come to you and Maura. You're judging me, Annie.'

'But you just judged all of us!' protested Maura.

'No, I didn't. I just said I didn't want what you have. There's a difference.'

Annie couldn't bear to hear it all put into words. Had Suze feared her judgement that much? Annie had never feared their judgement, had she? She told her friends everything, didn't she?

But of course, she hadn't. She'd told them the stuff she needed advice or a second opinion on, she'd told them the stuff that felt real enough for her to handle when it was out there. But the stuff she was afraid of? That she had never wanted to be real? She'd kept it to herself, hoping it would go away.

'What if you regret it?' said Annie.

'And what if I don't?' Suze said. 'Maybe it's a mistake. But if you're not making mistakes, you're not making decisions – and isn't that worse? It just means you're stuck and dying anyway. Remember? Remember what you said to me in the mud? You were right.'

'And Suze really does love Walt, don't you, Suze?' said Claire, turning to Suze.

'Yes, I adore him. I'll never stop loving him and I'll never stop telling him I love him. And I'll help Martin with the money he needs to raise him. I don't earn much but I'll pull my weight.'

'And you'll see him every time you're back in the country? She'll stay there. Each time she's back, won't you, Suze?' said Claire.

'Yes. I just won't be the one to raise him.'

Claire, who had been sitting on the sand, her arms wrapped protectively around herself the whole time, pressing her fingers into the top of her injured foot, pushed herself up to standing, and swayed a little. She looked white and waxy, and she was holding a bent leaf, shaped like a cup in her right hand.

'Annie and Maura, I agree with Suze that you two are very judgemental.' Claire's words sounded a little slurred but then they'd not eaten for a while, let alone drunk anything. Annie could almost feel her brain swelling against her skull with how much it needed feeding and watering.

'And you're narrow-minded,' Claire added. 'Dex thinks

Suze is very forward-looking for doing this and, though I wouldn't do the same, I would agree with him.'

Maura's head swung towards Claire. 'Dex?' she said. 'How does Dex know about this, when we don't?'

'I don't know.' Suze frowned at Claire. 'How does Dex know?'

'I told him.'

'You told Dex?'

Claire blinked and looked away from them.

'But when?' said Suze.

'Shall we all get on with building the raft?' Annie said quickly, fearing where all this was going.

'I dunno,' said Claire, pushing the hair out of her eyes and knocking back something from her leaf cup, like it was tequila. 'Friday night sometime?'

'That stuff was private, Claire, you knew that,' said Suze. 'What if he says something to Martin back at the house? He'll be a complete bastard about it.'

'Weird that you'd tell Dex,' said Maura, her gaze still fixed on Claire.

'Is it?' said Claire, swooning on the sand as she turned and faced the direction of the wood. 'I didn't find it weird at all. In fact, I rather liked it. I don't know about you, but I need another drink.' Then she looked into her leaf cup again, but found nothing.

Annie followed Claire, leaving the other two behind. 'Hey, what island bar are we going to? Can I join you for a drink? I think we should talk.'

'There,' Claire said, pointing at a brackish pool with a thin film of green. 'I got my drink from that.'

Why had Claire taken yet another stupid risk, this time

not with a man but drinking water that looked like a puddle on a London street in the middle of winter?

'Can someone please help me carry this pallet to the waterline so we can get on with building the raft and going home?' Annie said. She didn't add that they needed to get on with it before someone got injured again, or worse.

She looked up at the sky in confused desperation, anxiety pushing down on her sternum with the force of a boulder. And in the distance the birds circled and cawed.

Chapter 26

Annie

Annie woke up from the worst night's sleep of her life turning to find Claire lying listlessly a few feet away, her arms ramrod straight beside her like she was lying in a tomb. They'd all taken shelter at the edge of the forest as the rain came in again the previous night, and found the thickest layer of pressed bracken they could, hoping it might be like lying on a camping mat. But the cold had been unbearable. They'd all held on to each other where they could, but there was little warmth left of any kind between them.

Claire lifted herself up on her arms, slowly, weakly. She'd been the one to go without food the longest and was looking pale, and frail. 'How many days have I been asleep?'

'What?' said Annie, digging the back of her elbows into the damp grit of the woodland floor and lifting herself up to look at Claire properly. 'I don't know. Perhaps only a few hours. I think it's Sunday morning.'

'I feel really bad.'

'Things will be different today. I can feel it. The rain looks like it's stopping, and the men will be expecting us back in

266

a few hours which means something will happen to save us. Martin was keen on us getting back for brownies at eleven—'

'Please, Annie, don't mention brownies.'

'Though I can't remember how committed I was to the plan. I didn't know how much time we'd need—'

'Stop talking, please, I feel sick,' said Claire, agitation in her voice. But they had all become increasingly agitated and terse, like their batteries were running low, their water tanks were draining dry and their souls were gasping at the last dregs of positive energy.

Down on the beach in the near distance Annie could see Maura and Suze shifting pallets and wood around, still trying to find a workable solution to their most important problem.

'We should go help them with the raft,' Annie said finally. 'I think they've been up a while.'

Then, Annie glanced at Claire's foot which was gummed-up with blood and sand, pus and grit, the usually pale and elegant fan of her metatarsals pink and swollen instead. 'Can you walk?'

Claire got to her feet and swayed uneasily. 'My leg hurts. There's a pain all up my calf.' When she stood straight, with the slow and tentative energy of a frail old woman, Annie could see the swollen area, as though Claire had pulled a grotesque sweatband of extra flesh over her slim ankle. Her skin was stippled with pale red dots and goosebumps of cold.

'Lean on me,' said Annie, trying hard not to voice her concerns about infection, incipient sepsis, even. She was finding it harder, without any sustenance, to keep a lid on her ravaging anxiety about how the coming hours would play out, though there was still a pale, throbbing light left in her that said it wouldn't do to spread panic.

Claire used Annie as a crutch to stumble further down the beach to where Maura and Suze were sitting opposite each other, hair straggled, bird-nested and caked in mud, stooped in exhaustion, looking intently down at their work.

'Wow,' said Annie, as she approached, Claire breaking off to sit back down on the sand. 'That's a . . . that's a thing . . .'

'It's a raft, Annie,' said Maura sharply.

The raft, such that it was, constituted the two pallets they'd found, stacked on top of each other, and tied together with thick strands of twined grass. It looked blocklike and strong, yet very unfit for purpose: entirely unlikely to hold four grown women on a long journey across the water.

'Come on, guys,' said Maura quickly, almost feverishly. She threw a pile of thick grasses at their feet. 'Look at that,' she said, pulling a bunch of it taut between her hands. 'I could hang myself with that.'

'Stop it,' said Annie.

'Get plaiting then. Before we have to resort to jungle law.'

'How do you know about plaiting grass to make rope?' Annie said.

'I do read, you know. I was a big fan of *Swallows and Amazons* as a child.'

Suze grabbed Annie by the sleeve and whispered in her ear. 'She's watched every single episode of a Bear Grylls survival programme on Netflix, plus everything else he's ever made in the last two months. I saw it on her viewing history when I borrowed the iPad for Walt back at the house. Don't say anything. Just give her this moment in the sun? Premium Maura bullshit.'

Annie took a deep breath and felt her brow crumple, wondering why Maura kept lying about her TV habit. She supposed it was better than lying about a crack habit, but still. She parked the thought and concentrated on her work. The odd structure in front of her was the closest they'd got to a passport home since arriving, so she summoned all the enthusiasm she no longer had and all the self-control not to criticize their valiant efforts.

It turned out she couldn't summon very much.

'The four of us won't fit on that. It's far too small.'

'Don't hold back,' said Suze. 'I'm confident we can get all four of us on there . . . if Maura leaves her arse on the shore.'

Maura punched Suze in the arm.

'We need more pallets,' said Maura.

'Oh, shit, I forgot that we could search *Things to get me the fuck out of here* on Amazon.' Suze sounded uncharacteristically crabby. 'In other words, we've probably circled this island, like forty-five times? Therefore, I pinky-promise and swear to a God I don't believe in that there aren't any other pallets, boats, canoes, surfboards or millionaires' yachts to be unearthed. This is the best we're going to get.'

'Well, we need to try again,' said Annie.

Maura held up her hands. 'I don't know about you lot but I'm not looking for business-class comfort here. I just want to get home before we all perish. I'll happily pretzel my body for the whole journey if that's what it takes. Let's just cram on and see what happens.'

'How, though?' said Annie, feeling her legs drain of strength as they drained of hope, too. 'Your raft is lashed together with grass and look at the weather! It may have stopped raining but all it takes is some choppy waves and we'll all be in the water.'

Maura shrugged belligerently.

269

'OK,' said Suze. 'I've got it. Three squashed up on the raft. One in the water, kicking and holding onto us like we're one of those foam swimming lesson floats? Like, kicking really hard?'

'Aha, aha,' said Maura. 'I think I see where this is going. Can I ask who you have in mind for what role?'

'Captain, permission to speak?' Suze gave Annie a small bow and smile.

'You already are . . . but go on,' said Annie.

'On the raft,' said Suze in her best announcement voice, 'is me, because I cannot swim. And Annie who is too scared. And Claire, who is too weak to do anything else owing to the fact that she has not eaten for two days and is very thin. Annie and I will sit back to back with our feet in the water, Claire balanced over both our laps.'

'And?' said Maura.

'And, drum-roll please . . . The fourth woman, aka the swimming woman in the water, will be Maura, on account of her extra chub reserves giving her warmth and energy, and her basic, though not at all advanced, level of fitness which should be mitigated by her holding on to the raft.'

'A sort of middle-aged female outboard motor?' said Maura, narrowing her eyes.

'Exactly!' said Suze, clapping her hands together.

'Cool, cool, cool,' Maura said thoughtfully and calmly, her brow furrowing. 'That's definitely cool, really it is . . . Makes a lot of sense. Not something I've done before but I'm game, I really am. I guess I find myself asking: how can I be sure that any one of you won't, like, peel my fingers off the raft when the effort becomes too much to move us all in the water? You know, when we have to drop extra ballast? Because there's been a lot of swearing. Everyone's been annoyed with each other. Perhaps some of us still harbour some bad feeling. I don't know . . .'

'Let's give each other the benefit of the doubt?' said Annie.

But Maura didn't reply and turned quickly toward Claire, which set alarm bells ringing. Annie had noticed, with increasing frequency, that Maura tended to redirect the beam when she wanted it taking off her. 'And what do you think, Claire?' she said. 'Of the plans?'

'I think the plans are fine,' said Claire absently, wearily.

'So you don't have a view?'

'I don't mind. Do whatever you want. I don't feel very well.'

'You see, Suze,' said Maura. 'This is the key issue with Claire having been your sounding board for your life's biggest decision. She doesn't challenge anything.'

'OK, stop now,' said Suze. 'I've made my decision, Maura, and we've moved on. We have to focus on getting home. Claire doesn't look great and I might be about to kill someone.'

'Claire, seriously,' said Maura, completely ignoring Suze, 'I don't think you'd have ended up in the Home Counties with Karl if you'd just challenged him a bit more? You know, had an opinion about it. Or rather, an opinion about where you'd rather be. Like London?'

'Maura, what are you doing?' said Suze.

'I'd guess she's trying to distract us all from a plan where she has to get in the water,' said Annie.

'Don't patronize me!' snapped Maura. 'Claire needs to contribute once in a while! She has opinions. Surely you have opinions, Claire. Tell me, do you?'

'But . . .' Claire's face was stricken and pale.

'We don't all have to be a drama-tornado like you, Maura,' said Annie, feeling the frayed ends of her own tether. 'Some of us are just looking for a quiet life.'

'Sure,' said Maura. 'But sometimes it's important to say something that sets the world on fire, else everything is meh, just boring, and nothing, but nothing, changes.'

'Fine,' said Claire, her voice hoarse, her pale face flushing pink. 'I'll tell you something that'll set your world on fire. Dex and I snogged each other.'

'Hold on,' said Maura, holding up her hand, 'I didn't mean that kind of— I'm sorry, *what* did you say?'

Claire hobbled forward unsteadily and spoke a few inches from Maura's face. 'I said, Maura, that Dex and I—'

'Claire, shit,' said Annie. 'What are you doing? Please don't do this.'

A deafening crash of thunder came rolling through the skies, rinsing out the metal kinks in the clouds and bringing the heavy, driving rain of a shower on full power again.

'Oh, for God's sake, everybody! We should have left an hour ago when there was a break in the weather,' said Suze, as though they'd completely mis-timed the traffic.

'Friday night. On the beach,' said Claire.

Maura's eyes were granite and unreadable but her words were matter of fact. 'And how was it?'

'Terrific,' Claire replied, equally stony, her frailty seemingly forgotten.

'Anything more than a – a snog?' Maura sounded as if she was enquiring about something that had happened in the papers.

'No. But it was a good snog. A great snog, in fact.'

'OK,' said Annie. 'Let's move on. People do stupid things

when they're drunk. And people are attracted to each other and want to have sex with each other, like, all the time.'

'No, they don't,' said Suze quickly. 'I wouldn't sleep with Karl.'

'But you would sleep with Dex?' asked Maura, holding eye contact with Claire.

Suze hesitated. 'It depends on how fast other sex supplies were dwindling. He'd come somewhere between a low supply of both men and women.'

'Good to know,' said Maura, checking her fingernails, then looking up suddenly and pouncing on Claire in one swift move.

But Claire dodged out of the way just in time, stumbling on her bad foot. She righted herself as Maura got herself back together, then leapt in the direction of the raft, trying, ineffectually, to push Maura away with one hand and push the double-pallet lunk of a thing toward the water with the other.

'You want another one of my opinions? *I'll* take the raft!' said Claire, crying, persisting with pushing a raft that did not want to be moved, in the direction of the water.

'Oh no you don't, you thief!' said Maura, jumping on Claire's back as though she was about to get a piggyback.

'Don't let her take the raft!' shouted Suze.

Suze tried prising Claire's hands off the raft and Annie jumped in to try to prise Suze off Claire.

'Stop this!' shouted Annie. 'Stop this. Claire can't move a branch, let alone a raft.'

'Stop it, get off me!' yelled Claire feebly, stepping back and pushing Annie away, struggling to stay balanced. Claire's eyes filled with tears, turning from ice grey to black. Then, when everyone had stepped back, she redoubled her efforts and began pushing at the unstable, and largely immovable, raft again.

As they began wrestling again with struts and twine, things pinged and snapped and unravelled: Annie and Maura on one side and Suze and Claire on the other pulling the pallets apart, Annie trying to get Claire off the pallet, Maura off Claire, Suze off Maura off Claire. The already dry and bleached wood snapping and splintering.

'What have you done?' screamed Annie. 'You idiots!' she shouted, as they stepped back to survey the unlit bonfire of scrap wood and grass twine. In her hungry, dehydrated haze she found herself looking around for glue, kintsugi gold paint, for Martin's face, and words of reassurance that their raft, that their friendship group, could certainly be fixed to become stronger and more resilient than ever.

'Oh God,' said Suze, breaking down into tears. 'We're *never* going to get home.'

Annie felt a searing crack through her breastbone, enough to press her hand against it, like she needed to hold together the pieces of herself.

'Are you in love with him?' asked Maura, stepping back from group.

'I don't even *like* him!' Claire moaned. 'I was so, so *angry*, Maura. I was so—'

Maura held up her hand, her face frozen into an expressionless mask. 'It's OK,' she cut her off abruptly. 'I see it. And I feel sorry for you, Claire. It's all part of one big game. You do know that, don't you? He's just pushed it too far this time.'

'No, it's not that, Maura—'

'It *is*,' she said, aggression lacing her voice. 'You don't know Dex. You have no idea what he's capable of. You're just a tiny chess piece, babe, in a war that started nearly a year ago. That man has been on a mission to destroy me and my career and now, it seems, my friendships. This is nothing to do with you, and everything to do with me. You've no idea what came before this.'

'What exactly did come before this?' said Annie, speaking from the break inside her, the conversation with Dex on that moonlit beach just a few days before racing back in full technicolour. The silver moonlight casting the sand in indigo and the waters in navy and green, Dex's bright white face and the tickertape of receipts and tickets to museums thrown into the air with a flick of his Rolex-ed wrist. 'Because honestly,' she continued. 'You savage and you criticize Claire and yet, where are you in all of this?'

Maura crossed her arms and raised her eyebrows, primed for a fight.

'You've been lying to me, Maura,' said Annie, her voice shaking with the effort of not crying. 'And lying to Dex. What have you been doing, Maura? Are you having an affair?'

Chapter 27

Annie

A few moments later
Blue Bracken Island

Maura doubled over with laughter. 'An affair? An actual affair? I love the idea of it, and I'm not saying I haven't considered it, but if I was sneaking off to a hotel, I'd go on my own. I'd rather have the extra sleep.'

'What have you been doing at the weekends then?' said Annie coldly.

Maura's smile dropped and her eyes stilled. 'I was working.'

'You told Dex that you were with me. You don't lie to your husband about doing overtime. So where were you?'

'That's none of your business.'

'It is, though. I asked you to stay on a few of those weekends and you either ignored me or fobbed me off with an excuse about needing to look after the kids. But you weren't doing that. And you told Dex you were with me. So you lied to both of us.'

'Annie, this isn't a big deal.'

'Maura, are you having an affair or not?' said Suze. 'I'm so confused.'

'I'm not having an affair! If I was having an affair I'd probably be a million times happier.'

'Have you got a paper round or something?' asked Annie. Maura raised her eyebrows. 'Why would I get a paper round?'

'Because you said you were working, but you're not telling me what kind of work.'

'How does that lead to a paper round?' asked Claire.

'You stay out of this,' said Maura.

'Whatever it is, you're obviously ashamed of it,' said Annie. And she caught the flash of pain on Maura's face that told her she'd found something truthful. 'We're meant to be your friends. Whatever you've done, you can tell us.'

'I haven't done anything wrong. At least not in the way you're thinking.'

'You've lied to people,' said Claire. 'That's wrong.'

Annie glared at her. 'Claire, seriously, I will use the last of my strength to strangle you if you don't shut up.'

'Is it the job you're doing that you're ashamed of, or not?' said Annie. 'Are you a stripper in your spare time?'

'Maura doesn't need to be paid to take her clothes off,' said Claire.

Annie saw Suze discreetly take Maura's hand, and wondered whether it was a gesture of support or to prevent Maura from killing Claire. She was now more worried about Maura than angry with her. Maura looked defeated.

'What kind of work—'

'Bad work,' said Maura. 'Artwork. I've been trying to paint and draw my own stuff again.'

A long silence fell as they took in the news.

'Is that it?' said Suze. 'What an anti-climax.'

'No, it's amazing,' said Annie. 'But why didn't you tell us? I don't understand.'

Maura looked disconsolately at her feet and flumped down on the sand. Everyone else joined her. 'After the twins, I was depressed. Or maybe just low, anxious, or hormonal. All of those things, actually. And I never stopped feeling tired. Most mornings I'd wake up with the *cataclysmic* disappointment of not still being asleep. Like I couldn't quite face the day. Then it was into clearing up the kids' breakfast bowls, getting them to put their shoes on and dragging them kicking and screaming to school, then trying to make some money by moving monkeys and vines around my computer screen. And then it'd be time to pick up the kids again. There was nothing left of me. I kept telling myself I was going to be more than a shitty graphic designer and bad mother but it looked less and less likely every year.'

Maura blinked and looked at the sand, gathering herself for a moment. Suze put her arm around her and kissed her head.

'Me and Dex would have terrible rows where I'd scream at him about how unhappy I was because I'd lost my confidence, lost myself . . . and then he'd scream back saying only I was responsible for finding myself. But then one day he said that maybe a few hours on Saturday afternoons would give me a chance to think about what I wanted. I don't know. Maybe he felt sorry for me. Maybe he just wanted to end the argument so he could go back to his own work. But I said yes to it.'

Dex hadn't been lying. He really had tried to help her. Annie thought back to her conversation on the beach with

Dex and how he'd called Maura 'a damaging person'. Was this what he'd meant?

'I went and sat in a café and tried to draw. There was one idea I'd had that I'd thought about over and over, so I started drawing that and I didn't want to stop. But I didn't want to tell Dex what I'd done because I didn't want him to kill it.'

'What do you mean by that?' said Suze.

'With his opinion. I just wanted time to see if I could make something of it. So I told Dex I needed to take a break every weekend. I had a little bit of money left in my savings so I rented a shitty lock-up around the corner from us. I told him I was mostly hanging out with you, Annie. I'm sorry. It was easier than telling him the truth.'

'So all that stuff about the kitchen table and hummus in your keyboards and not having anywhere to work was bullshit?' said Claire.

'Let her talk,' said Annie.

'I'd had this image in my head of an angel with wings made of wire, with all the feathers punched out of them, leaving only their outline.' said Maura. 'I kept drawing this angel in different states of disrepair. But then Dex found one of my sketchbooks. I'd left it on the kitchen table. Stupid of me.'

'What did he say?' said Suze.

'That the image was too dark and twisted to be on a greetings card.'

'What did he say when you told him it wasn't a greetings card?' said Annie.

'I told him it was a private commission from a company client, and Dex said the client had awful taste. He said it looked like an album cover for a goth band that never charted.'

'What a bitch,' said Suze.

'Yeah, but he didn't know it was my idea.'

'But he knew it was your execution, your work,' said Annie.

Maura looked like she was about to cry.

'After that, I still went to the garage on the weekends, but I felt so flat that I just watched Bear Grylls on Netflix all day. I've watched a lot of television.'

'It was just Dex's opinion,' said Annie. 'He's probably wrong.'

'Yes, the successful artist is probably wrong about art,' said Claire.

Suze threw a shell at Claire's head.

'The thing is,' said Maura, 'even if he was wrong, I can't use it anymore.'

'What do you mean?' said Annie.

'A few weeks before his show, we were in the kitchen and I asked him about the timings for the first night of his exhibition, because I hadn't had an invite and Dex hadn't given me any details. Even *Fucking Beige Paul* got sent one. I know, because he wanged on about it on the family WhatsApp group. I needed to book a babysitter. But Dex was like, *I don't think you need to be there, you know what those things are like. They're boring.* And Alfie went and got something out of the drawer. *There you go, Mummy.* He handed me a card invitation, being helpful for the first time in his life. But I was nearly sick when I saw it.' Maura gazed into the distance like she was reliving the moment. 'It had one of Dex's pieces as the main graphic. And an angel with its wings punched out laid over the top.'

'Maura, what the fuck?!' Suze looked genuinely shocked.

'I ran up to his studio where all his canvases were, getting ready to be shipped off to the gallery . . . and all of them – every single one – was covered in my punched-out angels.'

'FUCKER,' shouted Suze, standing up, hands over her mouth.

'My *God*,' said Annie.

'I heard him running up the stairs after me, so I locked the door. And I was like: *You arsehole, when were you going to tell me?*' Maura was crying now. '*You told me my angel was boring and derivative and then you fucking stole it.* And he was screaming through the door saying I was mad. Then I smashed everything up. Broke the frames, kicked the canvases in and splattered them all in paint.'

'Hang on,' said Suze. 'The whole show was smashed-up canvases. I thought that was the point of it?'

'Yeah, he even took credit for that. He didn't say anything after I vandalized it all. Just left the house and came back ten days later with a van and picked up the pieces – what was left of them. I thought he'd cancel the exhibition, but he went ahead and put them on the walls like I'd left them. The only thing he changed was the title of the exhibition. He'd called it *The Bitch*.'

'I want to snap his neck,' said Suze.

The wind was blowing now, all of them shivering on the sand.

'I went to the opening night,' Maura said, 'and Dex gave me a glass of champagne like nothing had happened. Then I went round the room looking at it all, realizing that the angel was his now.'

'You could tell people the truth,' said Annie.

'Who would believe me? Dex would rather call me a liar

281

than admit he stole it off me. And he's the artist now. I'm a nobody.'

'We'd back you up.'

'He'd destroy me before he backed down. I don't want to put the kids through that.'

'You could still work on the idea though? Do it in your own way. Make it your own again?' said Annie.

'Then I'd just be Dex's talentless wife, ripping *him* off. Anyway, it's dead for me now. The whole thing.'

'He turned you upside down like a piggy bank and shook you empty,' said Suze. 'He just couldn't take it, babe. You were always *more* than him.'

'He didn't know, though, did he?' said Claire quietly. 'You didn't tell him it was your idea. You said it was a private client commission. He probably thought he was ripping them off, not you.'

'Claire, that's not helping,' said Suze.

'It's true though.'

'Dex didn't tell her what he was doing,' said Annie.

'Maybe he didn't think that he needed to tell her?' said Claire. 'He said it was a rubbish drawing and you let it stand. How was he meant to know it was actually something you'd created?'

'Don't be such a moron,' said Suze. 'He knew he'd ripped her off. That's why he didn't want her to see the exhibition.'

'I know we're all meant to be calling Dex a monster, but I don't think he did anything wrong,' said Claire. 'Did you even ask him about what he'd done, before you smashed up all his work?'

'No.'

'So I don't think it was his fault. I think it was yours.'

'Claire, fucking pick your moment!' Suze looked around for another shell to throw at her.

'I am. I'm picking my moment right now.'

Annie, Suze and Maura all turned to Claire.

Claire's face was cold when she spoke to Maura. 'It always has to be someone else's fault, doesn't it?' she said. 'You lied to him about where you were going and what you were doing. When he found your sketch, you lied to him again and told him it wasn't your idea. Then you smashed up his work without even talking to him about it. But somehow everything's still his fault.'

'She didn't show him her sketchbook. He opened it without asking her,' said Annie.

'And he was still ripping off work that she'd done, even if he thought it was for a client,' said Suze. 'That's not OK.'

'No, sorry, but I think you're full of shit, Maura. The only person who tells you the truth is Dex. He told you it was on you to change your life, which is true, and when you asked for time on the weekends he gave it to you. How is he the villain here?'

'How sweet that you're defending him,' said Maura, with a voice full of acid. 'You're so desperate for him to like you, it's pathetic.'

'What's pathetic is being married to someone you don't like and who doesn't like you either.'

'I'd rather be married to Dex than Karl. Agonizing over the scatter cushions and lawns. Fuck me, that'd be worse than anything Dex could manage.'

'Guys, this isn't helping,' said Annie.

'Oh, piss off, Annie!' Claire shouted.

'Claire, please. I know everything's hard because of the situation, but you have to remember we're best friends!'

'We're not.'

Annie felt like she'd been slapped.

'We haven't been real friends for a long time. I'm not even sure if we ever were.'

'Is this to do with Dex? Because people make mistakes,' said Annie.

'The kiss with Dex was a symptom. The illness is you lot. And you, Annie, you're the worst.'

Chapter 28

Martin

9 a.m. Sunday, 30 August
Sandpiper Cottage

After the rounders game, there was nothing communal
about Saturday night at Sandpiper Cottage, apart from the
children who sat snuggled up, side by side, in front of the
TV, eating mounds of chipolatas and ketchup. There were
no other shared meals, teas, drinks, board games or anything
else. Martin's chickens grew cold and greasy white on the
counter, picked at here and there by whoever was passing,
a white china bowl of wilted salad next to them that no one
touched. The couscous was forgotten about. Other than the
TV, the only sounds that poured through the house that night
were running water from the shallow baths and murmured
negotiations over pre-sleep Weetabix. Then bed for all, and
silence.

When everyone was up and awake on Sunday, and Dex
had still not emerged around the time that second coffees
were being drunk, Martin decided to check on him – an
uneasy knot at his chest, not knowing whether Dex had
departed for good, in anger and shame, got stoned and lost
himself in the woods, or worse.

Martin knocked hard on the door and opened it without waiting for an answer, finding a grey and swollen-faced Dex wrapped up like a burrito in his duvet.

'Come on,' said Martin, both relieved that Dex was not missing and irked that he wasn't pulling his weight yet again. 'The women will be back for elevenses in two hours. Time to get up and into the day. We seem to be in a good weather hotspot for once, so we're going to make hay. The kids need entertaining, we've a roast to prep and you'll want to gen-up on the rules for pétanque because that's this afternoon's activity.'

Dex peeked over the covers. 'I can't face anyone. Really I can't. And I can't play pétanque.'

Martin felt a flicker of compassion. 'I've got something you can crack on with. Hop to it. No need to pick an outfit. Just chuck on a T-shirt.'

'I should probably put some boxers on, too.'

'Fine. But hurry up.'

The kitchen smelt richly and reassuringly of ground coffee. Outside there were tentative rays of sun in their microclimate, though beyond them the storm clouds still hung over the water. Inside the house, everything was both clean and in its place – Martin had made extra sure of that in the early hours. He wanted the women to walk back into an oasis of harmony and calm so that they could focus on processing their feelings about Annie's news.

Karl held court at the kitchen table, handing out paper and pens to Alfie, Freddy, Em and Walt with Graham in his highchair, slamming his tray table with a full bottle of milk like a judge with a mallet.

'Come on, mate,' said Karl, returning the bottle to Graham, who'd batted it onto the floor for a third time. 'It's no good. He's not eaten a scrap. I think he wants to know when Mum's coming back.'

'Two hours and counting!' said Martin.

Karl laid his hands down on the table. 'That, I can handle. Now, chaps. The aim of hangman is to avoid getting strung up by the nuts.'

Walt's face stretched in horror. 'What's that mean?'

'Murdered.' Karl made a slashing action across his neck, as Walt's face stretched even further. 'So someone chooses a word and the other person guesses what it is. Every time you don't get a letter, you make another bit of your man with a stroke of the pen which will take you one step closer to death. But guess the word and you get to live. Good luck!'

And with that, Karl got up from his chair with a scrape – leaving the kids with their pens and paper and no further instructions – their young faces painted with either ambivalence or confusion because they'd not learnt how to spell, write or read properly, else a mask of terror because they were traumatized by Karl's description of the game.

'Yikes,' said Martin. 'We'll be untangling the horror of that game for nights to come.'

'What was it you wanted me to crack on with?' said Dex, his face hanging low and lifeless.

Martin gave him a serious look, as if he was peering over a pair of imaginary spectacles, and opened the counter drawer slowly to reveal a gleaming carving knife. He took it out, performatively slowly, and raised it to Dex, motioning for him to take the handle.

'Christ, mate,' said Karl under his breath. 'Seriously?'

Dex's eyes welled up with tears. 'Is that really what you think I should do?' He blinked. 'Wouldn't pills make less mess?'

Martin's face crumpled in mild disgust and he nodded at the colander. 'No, you idiot. Hull the strawberries, why don't you? And then slice them finely, please?'

'Good, excellent. Sure. It's just that the way you got the knife out of the drawer, so slowly by its handle and . . .'

'It's called *health and safety*, Dexter.' Martin noted a new grit in his own voice and he liked it. 'Have you ever made pancakes?'

'I don't eat breakfast.'

'You might not, but your kids do. So—' Martin waved his hand over the counter like a magician '—mix your dry ingredients. Instructions about weights and method are on that piece of paper.'

Dex looked down at the packets of flour and sugar and baking powder, the sifter and bowls and scales as though he was about to cry.

'Come on, mate, it's not hard,' Martin said gently.

'I'll be his assistant,' said Karl, nodding to Martin, opening up packets and passing them to Dex for weighing.

'You need to make a well, Dex,' said Martin. 'To chuck the wet ingredients in once you've mixed the dry ingredients. And then you need to stir until you've got a really nice and shiny batter that can sit for a while, during which time you can sizzle up that packet of bacon over there.'

Dex sniffed. 'Is this my punishment? Make me cook until I drop down dead?'

The men went to work in silence, pushing around packets and ingredients until the time came for Dex to fry the bacon.

When the oil looked hot enough Dex laid rashers down in a series of lines, like pan pipes. The oil spat in quick and tall jumps, one especially enormous spit landing on the back of his hand.

'Ouch! Fuck!' Dex jumped backwards, holding his hand to his chest like an injured bird.

Karl looked up from his work unloading the dishwasher while Martin shoved Dex's hand under a cold running tap, gathering up bandages and ointment from the drawer he'd crammed them in when they arrived.

Dex sniffed. He was attempting to staunch the tears running down his face with the back of his arm, to no great effect because one hand was under the tap while the other was held out as if he'd injured that, too.

Martin handed him a tissue.

'Raw bacon grease on that hand,' said Dex, holding up his spare hand.

So Martin blotted the tears gently from under Dex's eyes, then pushed the bacon grease hand under the tap for washing.

'Here, mate,' said Karl, lining up the bandage and ointments. 'When you're ready.'

'It must be nice,' said Dex, as Martin cut an appropriately sized bandage. 'To have people like you so much. People don't like me very much.'

Martin looked up. 'People would like you! If you were nicer to them.'

'Less of a dick,' said Karl helpfully.

'This is . . . who I am,' said Dex, his face collapsing inward in preparation for more tears. 'People don't change. Ask my wife.'

'Do you want to feel less lonely?' asked Martin.

'Why are you being nice to me?'

'That's what nice people do.'

'My life's a mess,' said Dex.

'That may be the case but you have good posture and your well-cut T-shirts give the impression of a controlled and interesting life so to the outside world, you're already winning. Now, come on, your bacon's ready. I'll bandage you up. Here, give me your hand.'

Dex held his hand out like a schoolboy, to be wrapped up and made better.

'Is your batter all done?' asked Martin, pleased with his work. 'Good. Now start the pancakes. Spoon on the batter in the same pan as the bacon. Just a few spoons, mind. Let it spread. Allow to cook a few minutes until it bubbles, then turn it over with the spatula and let it cook for about the same length of time. Right, now tilt it up and see if it's brown underneath. Yes, that's cooked, so now take it out. That's right. Well done.'

'You make everything – people, pancakes, children – look and sound easy,' said Dex, tipping the first pancake onto the plate Martin was holding out.

'It is easy. If you like those things.'

'I find it all so hard though. Does it mean I don't like those things?'

'Maybe you find it easier to just be yourself and not engage too much with other people.'

Dex looked at the ceiling as if that might be where he'd find the answer. 'I find being a dad and a husband really hard. Art is about making mistakes. You have to make mistakes to do something interesting. But raising a kid and having a relationship? Make a mistake and it's permanent. I get so annoyed with the kids, I just can't help it. And my marriage is a mess. She flirts with everyone. I don't know how many affairs she's having behind my back.'

'That's terrible,' said Karl. 'To break marital vows like that.'

'I think she's gone mad under the pressure of being a mother, a woman and an artist. She's really very mad.'

'Or unhappy?' said Martin.

'I try to support her work, to turn something destructive into something creative. I work so hard, all day and night to try and put food on the table but she's so unhinged and so ungrateful and so *envious*.' Dex's voice shook as he poured more oil into the pan, watching it bubble. 'A few months ago . . . actually . . . never mind.'

'No, go on, mate,' said Karl, putting his hand on Dex's arm. 'This is a safe space.'

Dex crossed his arms as Martin and Karl looked at him, urging him on to continue.

'She . . . well, she wanted some feedback on some sketches. There were only two of them in a little book. And so I gave her the truth. Said they weren't that good. A bit boring actually. But she didn't like hearing that.'

'The pan!' said Martin, tearing the smoking pancake pan away from the hob and shaking it a little to cool down before he added batter that bubbled up like a geezer. Then he handed Dex the pan and spatula. 'Over to you.'

'What would have been the point in lying and saying they're great? How's that going to help her? She drives me mad but I still want her to be a success. But she couldn't take the criticism. She was so angry with me, saying I wanted her to fail because I couldn't take the competition. Then she lost her temper and ran up to my studio and, and . . .'

'Take your time, mate,' said Karl.

'Well you need to keep an eye on those pancakes, too, please,' said Martin.

Dex re-engaged with the spatula. 'With just a fortnight to go she vandalized all my work for *The Bitch* exhibition. Covered the canvases in paint and kicked them in. I thought I was going to die when I finally got back into my studio. Worked through the nights just trying to fix it all.' Dex was silent as he lifted up the underside of the pancakes as he'd been taught. 'The exhibition had mixed reviews in the end. The reviewers loved some bits and thought others were . . . washed up. There were only a few sales.'

'So you're really worried?' said Karl quietly.

'About Maura,' said Martin.

'About my reputation,' said Dex at the same time. 'And yeah, sure,' he added quickly. 'Maura definitely needs help. Pills, probably. But she needs to do *The Work*, you know? It's one thing to find success in your twenties. Everyone loves a young person with talent. But hitting forty without an original thought in your head? It's messing with her.'

'I presume there's also the thorny question of how you pay the bills if no one wants your work,' said Martin.

Dex shifted uncomfortably. 'They'll want my work again. I'm just short on ideas at the moment.'

'Right,' said Martin, stacking a plate with pancake, bacon, butter and strawberries.

'That looks lovely,' said Dex.

'Well, go on then, you do the rest of them. It's your work.' And Martin pushed the stack of plates towards him.

Once Dex had arranged everyone's breakfast plate and handed them out, he returned to the hob and reflected. 'Even if I did tidy up my life I still don't think I'd be a nice person.'

'Maybe not,' said Martin. 'But in the meantime look at what you just did? You just made a bunch of kids really happy.'

And they were all happy. It was quiet, until Alfie looked up and said, 'Thanks, Dad. This is great.'

'That's all it is,' said Martin. 'Making someone a pancake once in a while.'

Karl passed Dex a tissue to mop under his eyes and Martin looked out of the kitchen window, then at his watch face. The women couldn't arrive soon enough.

Chapter 29

Annie

'Me? What have I done? Don't be silly, Claire. Friends don't just break up with each other.'

Annie willed her voice to remain steady as she had for most of their stay on the island and for most of their long, long friendship – but she couldn't manage it anymore. With every statement she made, her volume increased and her words became quicker and higher, like her panic might lift her into the clouds.

'Friends drift, they peter out and they grow apart until both sides are used to the distance. That's what people do!' Annie said, catching her breath. 'Or until one of them stops wondering what they did wrong in favour of saying they fell out of touch because *everyone leads such busy lives*!' She walked a few paces forward, then a few paces back. 'People don't end a lifelong friendship *just like that* unless someone's murdered or slept with someone they shouldn't have. And it was just a kiss, Claire. Big deal! We can all move on from that!'

'You don't understand,' said Claire, stony-faced. 'I don't

294

want anyone's forgiveness. I'm leaving you. Just as soon as I can get off this island.'

'*Off* this island? We all want to get off this island. We *need* to get off this island because I don't think anyone wants to die here. Where is the coast guard? I said we'd be back for elevenses. They probably think we're staying out. Having a sandwich. When will they miss us? In a few hours? Who knows? I can't take a few more hours! It's raining again! Why is it *still* raining? Maura! This is all *your* fault.'

Maura looked at her with disgust. 'I'm sorry, *what*? I know I'm shaped like a cloud, but I didn't cause the rain—'

'Oh, for God's sake! Claire's obviously leaving because she was left off the *Karl Chose Those Curtains* WhatsApp group.'

'What is *that*?' Claire's hair was almost vertical with tangles.

'Isn't that what you're talking about?' Annie clamped her hands to her hips, desperate for the missile of blame to land as far away from her as possible. 'If it's not that, then what is it?' The shards of their friendships kept breaking into smaller and smaller pieces, falling through the gaps in the crook of Annie's arms. Never mind a mother for Em, she wouldn't have any of her best friends left at the end of this.

'It doesn't matter anyway,' said Maura, waving her hand in the air.

'You used my husband's name in a WhatsApp group? Of course it matters,' said Claire.

'Tell her, Maura,' said Annie. 'You did it.'

'No. You opened that particular box of snakes. You tell her.'

'Oh, fucking hell,' said Suze. 'I'll tell her.'

Suze took Claire by both arms and looked at her intently.

295

'My friend, it was not intended to hurt you. It was a sub-chat set up by Maura after she visited your new house called *Karl Chose Those Curtains* because the interiors were not to her taste. The subtext, which to be honest was not always that *sub,* was despair at how you've been brainwashed by Mayonnaise Karl into moving outside the M25: away from your friends, to live in a home painted the colour of a camel.'

'Right,' said Claire, her eyes straining, her jaw tightening. 'I had no idea about that group and it's not the main reason I'm breaking up with you, though to be honest it should be.' She breathed deeply and tipped her head to the side, pushing her fingertips against her temples, as if the knowledge she held there was hurting her head. 'It's just *awful* that you'd slag off my life choices behind my back.'

'It was called *Karl* Chose Those Curtains, not *Claire* Chose Those Curtains, though?' Suze tried to pull Claire in for a hug, as though that was the end of it. But Claire stepped back as if she was nuclear.

'Why oh why oh why are we arguing about curtains?' shrieked Annie. 'I'm hallucinating about a tank of Buxton Spring water. I couldn't give a shit about chintz. Curtains just don't matter.'

'They do, though,' said Claire. 'Because I *did* choose those curtains – and all those other things,' she said. 'The pink *chintz* curtains, the beige carpets, the porridge-coloured handrails, all the brushed steel and the faux sepia prints of waterfalls and leaping deer.'

'Even the high-backed bamboo cane chairs?' said Maura.

'Even them!'

'Bit Seventies porn but that's cool, that's all cool.'

'I chose it *all*,' snapped Claire. 'Because those are my tastes. I *like* beige and light grey. I *like* playing the kind of classical music that's often played in lifts at a low volume while I make a lasagne. I *like* carpeted pubs, neat haircuts, Radio 4, John Lewis, soap on a rope and the missionary position.'

'So?' said Maura. 'No one's going to oust you for that. Much. We're not complete monsters.'

'No, but it was also my idea to move to the Home Counties. When I said it was Karl's idea, I lied to you. I said it was because of his work and him wanting more space for Graham. The truth is that it was for me. I wanted to live somewhere cleaner than London, with a low crime rate, a small Waitrose and Costa Coffee and with some space around me. It was *my* idea to leave *my* job forever and look after Graham. None of it was Karl's idea. I don't like loud people in finance, and Karl and I had made enough money between us for me to stop work and do what I love. Which is to be a mum. Which is something I also love doing with Karl because he is interesting and loving and kind and supportive. He is all those things. To me.' Her eyes filled with tears. 'My life is fucking fantastic. But you see, none of you ever let me say those things—'

'Well no,' said Maura. 'Because it sounds so smug.'

'*And* I didn't let myself say those things because you're all a hostile environment for someone like me. You don't like normal and standard and middle of the road and beige, you mock it and look down on it – even though you're all normal and standard and middle-of-the-road people just dressing up in costumes made of brighter colours.'

'Tell it like it is, why don't you,' said Suze, stepping away from Claire.

'So,' said Claire primly, 'you should call your next WhatsApp thread: *CLAIRE Chose To Snog Dex*.'

'Stop this!' screamed Annie, imagining the remaining shards of their friendship falling to the floor and being stepped over.

'What do you mean you chose to snog Dex?' said Maura, lunging at Claire again, just in time for Suze to grab Maura tightly by the back of her Ramones T-shirt and hold her back.

'No! Stop. Just stop,' shouted Annie.

'I'll kill her this time,' growled Maura.

'Why?' said Claire. 'I tried to tell you that it was my idea, not Dex's. But you didn't listen. It was not part of a game about you.' She spelt the words out slowly as if describing phonics to a schoolkid. 'He wouldn't have kissed me unless I'd instigated it. And I would have told you earlier except you spoke over me and then carried on spouting *your* opinions. You tell me I have no opinions of my own but that's because you drown them out with your constant talking.'

'Why would you do that?' said Maura, her eyes glossed with the arrival of tears. 'Why would you do that to me?'

Annie's body ached with sadness as she watched Maura cry, because Maura had not cried like this when she'd assumed that Dex had kissed Claire. It was Claire's betrayal that had truly broken Maura's heart.

'If you love your husband, why would you try and take mine?' said Maura.

'I was so *angry* with you. And him. And myself,' said Claire. 'Angry at you because you'd done nothing but snipe at me about the countryside and how boring it all was since I'd arrived. Then you sniped at Karl for saying *I just do what I'm told* with childcare. You were judging him, thinking he should be better and do more. Except that in our house he earns and I look after the baby. I tell him what to do with Graham because I'm just much better at it than he is. Not everyone has to share things out the way you think they should. And if it's not working for you, then you shouldn't be digging spears in other people's happiness.' Claire's eyes filled with tears and Maura looked to Annie for support.

Annie shrugged. 'Fine,' she said. 'You want to own your choices, Claire, and you're done with your friends judging them. Fine. Camel away. Beige it up. Go the fuck for it. I want to get home to my daughter now.'

Annie was glib, because she was tired, because she was hiding her pain, because she was still feeling anxious about why Claire wanted to walk away from her, of all people.

'I was angry with Karl, too,' said Claire, on a roll, but crying now.

'So much anger inside such a tiny body,' mused Maura.

'Oh, it was because of what you said, Maura! Down by the water on the first night, when you made some judgy comment about my village, Karl was like *yeah it's soooo boring* or whatever, and I know he doesn't think that. He loves our life too, but he said it to impress you. He betrayed himself and his choices and I was angry with him for it, and myself, for doing the same. And I thought, why do I feel like this? Why do I put myself in second place, why do I *defer* to them all the time? And I kept thinking about that time I handed over Dex—'

'You did *not* hand him over!' spat Maura.

'Because I was too underconfident to go for it then myself, so I thought fuck it, I'll rewrite the past. He's hot. I mean he's an awful person, but he's hot, and it'll punish Maura –

and more than that, I'll prove to myself I can be Alpha and take the Alpha stuff, too. I'll prove to myself that I am not someone who defers and demurs. I'll choose what I want: which is my life, with Karl.'

'That's just sad,' said Maura, crying.

'Karl was the first person I've felt *myself* with. When I met him, I realized how much I had bent to fit you all. And I don't want to do it anymore. And you, Annie, you're the worst.'

'Claire . . .' said Annie, her stomach churning. 'The worst? Why would you say that? I'm supposed to be the best. Your best friend.'

'No. You just downright broke my heart. You were the one who first unstuck me.'

Claire briefly glanced down at her filthy wound, now suppurating with pus, and glared at Annie again, no tears now, sticking out her jaw and folding her arms across her chest. 'I should have left you all years ago.'

'You couldn't. You signed a contract,' said Suze. 'We're blood sisters.'

'We are not,' said Claire coldly. 'I didn't prick my finger in the pub that day. And I certainly never shared my blood.'

'What?' said Suze, her face wide with distress. 'I don't understand. We all did it. There was loads of blood on that crisp packet? We used a penknife, for God's sake. Some of it dripped in my cider.'

'I only pretended to do it,' said Claire. 'I was afraid of getting a disease because Maura had shagged half of London.'

'Ouch,' said Maura.

'Besides, what did any of it mean?' said Claire. 'Best friends forever? I thought that meant honesty. But in the past year all anyone has done is talk about the bad stuff online, in sub groups, and behind each other's backs.' She stopped as her eyes filled with tears. 'Through thick and thin? Maura's been to visit once. Suze has visited me, but only because she needed to talk about herself. And Annie, *best friend*, where were you?'

'You said not to bother because car seats were a pain to fix,' said Annie.

'I didn't bloody mean it! You can barely even remember my child's name! Look at us! Maura was vandalizing, being plagiarized and watching Netflix for a living. But no one knew about that. Suze didn't speak to anyone apart from me about a U-turn on motherhood. And I've spent the entire year wondering how to separate from you all. I hoped that this weekend might bring us back together. I thought that if Maura's marriage was in trouble then maybe we'd bond over helping her.'

'Tell me what I did,' said Annie.

'That time at Maura's,' said Claire quietly.

'What time at Maura's? There have been a thousand times at Maura's.' Annie played for time, trying to locate the exact memory.

'The last time all four of us were properly together. Poker night. I was nine months pregnant, due any minute.' She paused. 'The night Maura sent her noodles back to the restaurant because she thought it was raw chicken but actually it was lychee. Then she made the guy at the restaurant a crisp sandwich to say sorry, then he asked her out and she said . . . oh come *on*, Annie. You must remember?'

'Yes, OK, I remember.'

'I heard what you said on the baby monitor. You forgot to hang up.' Claire looked at her now, knowing that Annie remembered everything. 'You said: *My God,*

Claire is so boring.' Her eyes filled with tears again. 'You said I was *boring.*'

Annie felt a lightning twinge through her abdomen and down her legs. She gulped. She knew something had been wrong with her body that night at Maura's. Even before she'd arrived, her skin had felt as though it was melting. After poker, she and Maura had left Claire down in the kitchen looking at takeaway menus while they did the kids bedtime together, and sang a duet of 'Like a Prayer' to the twins. It had lifted her spirits temporarily, reminding her that she was more than her circling anxious thoughts about how she was going to pay the bills, how she was going to be two parents-in-one and whether she was ever going to wake up in the morning without her body hurting. But then Dex had come down from his studio and Maura, warmed and happy on a few glasses of wine, had sung a Pink Floyd song to him with such soul and feeling – her voice gliding out and landing on him gracefully, like he was the moon – that Annie was sure she'd witnessed them fall in love with each other all over again.

But instead of feeling happy for them, all Annie could feel was envy. And disappointment in herself that with The Canadian she'd missed her chance to be someone's significant other. And she felt sad, and envious, like she was nothing but an audience member watching a scene from a Hollywood romance with all the impossibility of her life ever being like the plot. Then she'd thought of Claire downstairs and how beautiful and serene her pregnancy had made her, how secure in her marriage she was, with her money, plans to move into a new house and a longed-for baby on the way. Her friends seemed to be basking in a golden light, surrounded by significant others who weren't her. When she'd said Claire was boring, she'd plucked at straws for something, *anything*, to narrow the gap between her and Maura because every day she had felt her friends drift further and further away on their bubbles.

'You can't even deny it,' said Claire.

'I'm sorry, I didn't mean it,' said Annie. 'I'm really sorry.' But Annie knew from the way Claire was looking at her, with steel and shine in her eyes, that Annie's response was far from enough. 'People are boring sometimes. Myself included,' Annie tried.

'You know what the worst thing about it was?' Claire replied, as if dropping back into a conversation she'd started with herself a long time ago. 'For weeks after Graham was born I had this *I'm boring* on repeat in my head and I kept blaming myself for not being interesting enough for you all. For not being any good at glamour and confrontation and conflict like Maura or being tall and interesting like Suze or at being so *solid* and *themselves* like you.' She stopped to wipe under her eyes. 'I thought you loved me for who I was – unconditionally, without judgement. I thought I was safe with you. And when I heard you say that? It was the first time I became conscious of the opposite. It was the first time I began unsticking the truth of our friendship.'

'Claire,' said Annie, 'I said it because I was feeling bad and worried and alone. I was just being a kid in the playground again. Saying things to push away from some people and feel close to others. None of it was true. Can't we work through this?' said Annie desperately.

'Yeah, we definitely can,' said Maura. 'This is honestly about the most interesting thing you've said in months, Claire.'

303

'No,' Claire said bluntly. 'We can't. This weekend proved to me that when I'm with you, my radar gets cloudy. I got angry, and I'm not an angry person. I did things that undermined *my* relationship and *my* happiness. It's scared me how easily my radar can break.' She choked back sobs. 'It's made me see that this past year without you all, I've been fine in the Home Counties. Now I just want to go home to my family and start breastfeeding my child again, because honestly, I regret weaning him to spend time with you lot. Then I want to forget all of this ever happened.'

For a few seconds, Annie thought her heart had arrested. The pain in her chest was intense, the block to her breathing so strong.

'We won't say anything about what happened with Dex, Claire,' said Suze gently, as if that were part of tying up some loose ends on the end of their friendship. 'Will we? Karl will never find out.' She turned to the rest of them, and they nodded.

Claire looked up at them all, one by one. 'It could have been so much worse. If Annie hadn't turned up . . .'

And like slow marionettes, Suze and Maura turned to face Annie.

'You were there, Annie?' said Maura, her eyes full of sadness. 'You saw them together? You've known the whole time we've been here and you said *nothing*?'

Even though a friendship was broken, with its pieces on the floor, it seemed it could be ground further and further into sand. And sand could not be mended. It would simply disappear with the wind.

Chapter 30

Martin

4 p.m. Sunday, 30 August
Sandpiper Cottage

As Martin stacked the dishwasher with plates from lunch – hastily prepared sandwiches for all because the mums still weren't back and the squeeze of anxiety in his tummy had brought a stop to his joyful plan of chopping carrots for a roast – he'd found himself repeatedly glancing at the kitchen clock and questioning whether he'd misunderstood the arrangements for their return. He'd assumed an early check-out. He'd assumed that Annie would want to be back for Em as soon as possible. But perhaps they'd decided to amble back via Bournemouth for coffee and a pasty. Cream tea, at a stretch . . . He knew how much they had to talk about. Had he said they should meet for tea, rather than elevenses? Whatever was going on, the lack of communication on any front made him nauseous.

'Still no sign of the womenfolk?' said Karl, striding into the kitchen in his neon-piped black Lycra, sweating from a forest and beach run. He swiftly poured a short glass of water and chugged. 'Graham's still sparko from his lunchtime nap.'

'I must say it will have been a restorative break for little

Hannah Begbie

Graham, what with all that sleep,' said Martin, locking onto the distracting conversation to calm his skittish thoughts, finally deciding to brush crumbs off the kitchen table with the intensity of someone discovering life-changing text under a mossy gravestone.

Karl gathered up handfuls of cutlery from the dishwasher and flung them into their respective compartments with more force than was necessary. 'It's just that Claire had mentioned wanting to get back home today and she's not one to change a plan without an explanation. But they're only a few hours off schedule, right? Could be that the steak-knife plunger is on the loose and has slashed their taxi tyre!'

'Sure. No. Maybe. I just don't understand why none of them are on the grid. Unless we're in a comms blackout because the apocalypse is occurring outside in which case *duck and run.*'

'An extreme thought, compadre,' said Karl. 'But I get the gist.'

'Maura's still not picking up her phone,' said Dex, walking into the kitchen and scratching his head. 'That will be an entire weekend she's kept me in the deep freeze. A record, even for her.'

Alfie and Freddy ran over and thrust a piece of paper into Dex's hand. 'Where's Mum? We want to show her our picture.'

'Very nice,' said Dex. 'Why don't we turn these into welcome home cards and by the time they're finished, they'll probably be back?'

'Fab idea, Dex!' cried Martin and, gathering up a bag from under the sink, tipped a low hill of felt tips out onto the table. 'Nothing like a spot of art therapy to calm the mind.'

306

Dex gathered everyone round the table and for a while they all sat silently, drawing and listening to the tick of the kitchen clock.

'Anyone remember the name of the spa they went to?' said Karl. But either no one knew or no one apart from Martin heard the question and the silence that followed made his insides twist a little further.

'Oh, Walt, that's lovely,' said Martin, looking at the drawing of a tall and short person by a house. 'Who are they?'

'Walt and Dad.'

'Where's your mum?'

Walt shrugged. 'Gone.'

Martin's eyes filled with tears. 'I'm sorry,' he said, 'I get a bit teary without enough sleep.'

He got up from the kitchen table, turned away and leant on the back of the chair for support while he looked out toward the choppy waters, devoid of water sports for another day. Having lived with his dreams and fears tumble-drying inside his head, it was a shock to have them expressed so bluntly in a picture. His eyes stung with tears and he could feel the grief coming for him. Suze was his best friend and her loss was going to be intolerable: a cavernous, freezing gap in all their lives. The sobs continued to heave upward from somewhere terrible until Karl was by his side, grabbing him and holding him to his chest.

'I don't know what we're going to do without her, I really don't,' said Martin, glancing at thick black clouds still hanging heavy over Blue Bracken Island.

'You are going to live your lives,' said Karl. 'You will be fine,' said Karl. 'You're Martin.'

Dex looked at Walt. 'Hey, mate, you OK? You'll still

see your mum. And when you're older I bet she'll take you travelling with her.'

'She'll have to,' sniffed Martin. 'Because I won't be able to afford it.' He gulped. 'Don't know how I'll pay the rent. She'll help out but she won't have much money either.'

Dex turned to face Martin. 'You need a job, mate.'

'Yes,' said Karl.

'Primary school teacher,' said Dex. 'That's what you should do. I think Karl was the first to float it.'

'Thanks, mate. I did indeed float it,' said Karl, standing proud. 'What do you think, Martin?'

'I-I love it,' said Martin, blinking his tears away. 'Teacher,' he said, feeling how soft and delicious the word felt in his mouth. Even before Karl had mentioned it, the idea had whispered its promise of a different future on a few occasions throughout his life, most recently when he was collecting objects with the children on the beach, marvelling at the gorgeous curve of a shell or driftwood that looked like it had been torn from the deck of an ancient ship. But he'd never dreamt of speaking the word aloud, let alone inhabiting it. 'Yes,' he said, his heart swelling with pride. 'I really think I could do it.'

'You're going to have to do it,' said Karl. 'Else the picture of zero income and no consistent maternal presence for you both is grim. You and Walt don't want to find yourselves begging for money with a tin mug at Embankment Station.'

'Roger that. I need a plan.'

'You do. I thought of one last night if you'd like to hear it?'

'Fire away.'

'Give up your rental and use what money you do have

from your redundancy to pay for your daily costs and snacks. Then come and live with us and get a job in a school while you do your training. Claire might be up for taking Walt a bit while you work. And if she isn't then we'll find a way. No obligations or whatever. It's only a suggestion.'

Karl's cheeks flushed a confectionery pinky-red and Martin felt his own do the same. It was as if Karl was asking him out.

'It's just that we've a reinforced steel panic room with a self-locking door,' said Karl, 'that obviously we'd need to deactivate if you got caught in there without anyone knowing, but I don't see why we can't reconstitute it with throw-cushions and a couple of put-you-ups. And I'm sure we've got a spare cheese plant and a Monopoly board. Maybe Walt could babysit for Graham one night when we go out?' He winked.

'How thoughtful,' said Martin. 'I, well, actually . . . I mean, sure, I'd be delighted! Just while I get on my feet. To . . . *teach*?!'

Karl's face beamed with pride. 'It's all worth a shot. You gotta be in it to win it!'

'Guys,' Dex said, looking at his boys now. 'That's a lovely picture of Medusa there, all those snakes – what's she eating?'

'It's Mummy, eating you.'

'Excellent. Hey, shall we also put some nice words on the card like *Miss you, Mum*!'

When they'd finished writing Dex read out the words: '"Dear Mum, you smells nice and give us nice hugs and play games with us make nice puddings and helps us with our art."' His voice shook a bit as he went on. '"She's a nice mum. She does silly dances, too. She's funny and she makes people smile. And she's definitely not boring . . ." Shall we try calling them again?'

'I think we should,' said Martin.

'Hey, Dex,' said Karl, upbeat and high from his Martin goodwill. 'You said you were worried about your work. I'm sure there's room for you guys, too. A nice big hippy commune!'

'Haha no, thanks, we're cool.'

'Vis à vis work, we could always look at getting you involved with my new magazine? I'm looking to diversify our accessible healthy fast-food platform with it.' He moved closer to Dex. 'Extend our offering beyond *The Great Unwashed* to another class of gent. It's called *Feed Your Brain*. Still spitballing on the title. Printing it on thick paper. Distributing it in high-end health clubs, etcetera. You know, vegan recipes, exercises, break-beat playlists. Interviews with influencers and creatives. You know what I'm saying?'

Dex blushed. 'Thanks, but I dunno what it would be about? I suppose it could be an exploration of what's next?'

'What's next? Oh no, sure, but I was thinking about a job in magazine layout and perhaps some border design if my main guy isn't around?'

'No, sure, thanks so much, that could be cool . . .' Dex smiled, and Martin noticed that he looked a little tearful, though it was hard to tell whether that's because he was touched by the offer or because he'd realized how far he had fallen.

'Now come on, Gray,' said Karl, 'I'll make the card for you because I don't think you're old enough to draw as well as Dex yet!'

Then Karl put four pieces of paper together with Sellotape and drew an enormous heart in red pen, with two small hearts either side. Inside the heart he drew a big 'C 4 K.'

310

Martin saw the sadness in Dex's eyes again and recognized it for what it was: loneliness.

'What about you?' said Martin, putting his arm about little Em.

Em looked up at him with enormous eyes. 'I want my mum,' she said.

Her picture was of four stick figures: two standing vertical and two lying horizontal. He surveyed all the drawings and cards now spread out on the table. Had the women had an accident? Had they left for good? Were these nice words and sweet crayon images a visual eulogy for four friends?

Chapter 31

Annie

4 p.m. Sunday, 30 August
Blue Bracken Island

At some indefinable moment that day, the women lost their bearings on time. No one knew when, or if, they were moving through elevenses or tea time or the gloaming, or the start of another day entirely. The light was dim with dark clouds and more rain, and the women gazed into middle distances, speaking slowly, skipping thoughts and words and moving the wrong way through linear time: dehydration and hunger and exposure on their skin, under their skin and creeping into their organs.

The conversation they'd been having about Annie revealed as witness to Dex and Claire's indiscretions, had been violently interrupted by Claire pressing her hand to her stomach and claiming over and over that she was going to be sick, yet bringing nothing up. They'd been distracted, concerned at how she jumped and ran for the woods, hands still pressed to her stomach, returning each time saying that she still felt like she needed to be sick. Each time looking paler and greener than she had before.

'It'll be the emotion,' said Maura.

'The dehydration and exposure, you mean,' said Suze.

'The stress of not having answers or a way out, surely?' said Annie.

'What do we do now?' said Maura, waving her palm fronds disconsolately at the blank body of water in front of them.

But Annie had run out of answers.

The women sat together in silence and Annie tried to work out whether the sun was coming up or down, but unlike when she could use the tip of a background leaf to track which direction Suze was moving through quicksand, she had nothing. She had no tracking point for anything on the island, or in her life. She was turning in space.

She felt Maura's hand on hers and it anchored her, for a moment.

'Why didn't you tell me what you'd seen on the beach?' Maura said quietly.

Annie looked up, seeing the tight tangle of disappointment in the space between Maura's eyebrows, Suze's concerned beam of curiosity and a mess of resignation, vindication and nausea all swimming about in the darkness of Claire's eyes. With just a few words Annie would change all this. She let go of Maura's hand, stood up and stepped forward, collapsing onto the sand. She felt its soft ridges under her ribs, wanting so much to stay there and sleep, and let everything fade away.

'Annie?' said Suze, rushing to her side, easing her up to sitting. Maura sat down at her other side and Claire, spent, her face drained and yet a waxen green, sat opposite her.

'I'm OK. Just feeling faint.'

Maura took hold of Annie's hand again and looked at her intently, speaking as though she was calculating each step of a sum. 'You saw them together. You knew something was going on.' She paused. 'And you hate . . . no, you *dislike* Dex. A lot. You could have told me two days ago, and any time in between. You could have nailed that coffin shut. But you didn't.' She paused. 'You were never planning on telling me, were you?'

Annie shook her head. 'No.'

'You didn't want to see it. Like you didn't want to see what an idiot Ted was when you were pregnant and you just hoped he'd turn into a better person once Em was born. Like you ignored the pain in your boobs as you fed Em and hoped it would go away without antibiotics. Like you hoped Claire would go back to being Claire.'

Claire lifted up her bowed head. 'I was always Claire. Just not the Claire you wanted.'

Annie grasped onto Claire's hand urgently, as if she was about to hurtle off into space, too.

'Or you hoped that Dex would disappear in a puff of smoke,' continued Maura. 'You just *hope,* don't you, that the tangly, painful, difficult stuff in life that turns your stomach and keeps you awake at night with its incessant drumming on your thoughts will only go away if . . .' She brushed the sand off Annie's face. 'If you close your eyes tight enough and pretend it's not there.'

'Don't we all do that?' said Annie quietly.

'The question is why you did that, this time.'

Annie wiped at her face with the back of her hand. 'I didn't want that kiss to blow up two marriages, two families and all our friendships. Best friends stick together.' She squeezed Claire's hand harder.

'Annie?' said Claire. Then Annie followed Claire's gaze,

and Maura's gaze as they all looked down at her quaking hand. Annie laid her other hand over hers and Claire's, as though she could stop it, or hide it. But it was too late.

'Why do your hands keep shaking?' asked Maura.

'Your hands *do* keep shaking,' said Suze. 'I've noticed that too and I thought it was hunger, or cold or exhaustion.'

'Or arthritis,' said Claire quietly, her face paper white.

'Or the emotion of it all,' said Maura.

Then Maura laid her hand on top of Annie's, absorbing the tremor until it stopped.

'Your hands,' said Maura, looking up to face Annie. 'And your legs. The falling over. The doctor's appointments in the spring. The laughter when you should have been crying. The silences. The half stories, half sentences. Annie?'

Maura's eyes filled with tears.

'What's going on, what is it?' Suze pleaded with the desperation of a child wanting reassurance.

'I didn't want that kiss to kill us,' said Annie.

'You don't want it to kill *you*,' said Maura. 'What is it? What's wrong with you?'

Claire gripped Annie's hand tighter. Her grip felt cold and clammy but Annie was glad of it, glad to have them all close and in one place, listening. Then she felt Suze's arms loop round her neck in a hug that held her upright.

Annie felt calm in that moment. As though every single second, minute, hour and day that came before it was preparation.

'I've got motor neurone disease, I'm dying.'

Sitting on the sand, together, holding onto each other as they were, Annie heard the silence as screams and felt the low gasps as seismic tremors passing through them all. For a few

315

moments no one spoke, which was exactly how she'd been when the doctors first told her the news. In that short, dead silence Annie had been waiting for the doctors to tell her that it was all a mistake and only now did she accept that it was not.

'Annie?' said Suze. 'I've seen films about it. Are they sure that's what you've got? Will you be in a – a . . .'

'Yes, I'll be in a wheelchair. And yes, they know what it is. They did a lot of tests.'

'Are those the tests you wanted me around for a few months ago?' said Maura, looking horrified. 'You said they were just investigations? Nothing serious?'

'They *were* just investigations. Until I got the results. And then it was serious.'

'Why didn't you tell me at the time? Oh, God. You were hoping it was going to go away!'

'I'm going to lose the ability to walk, eat, talk . . . Looking after Em will be impossible soon. The next six to twelve months are going to be very hard.'

'Six to twelve months?' said Claire. 'And then what?'

Maura threw her arms around Annie's neck. 'I've got you, Annie. And I'm not going to let you go, OK?' Then Maura looked directly at her, tears blurring the pupils of her eyes, then falling down her cheeks slowly and thickly like acrylic paint. 'You're not going anywhere. You'll be at my fortieth birthday party. Do you hear? Annie? You'll be there.'

Annie nodded.

'Those doctors always have something up their sleeve,' said Maura. 'I'll come with you to every appointment and we will sit there until they tell us what clinical trials are available and then we'll fly you to America and we'll cure you and you will be a success story on the front pages.' Then her voice fell into tears. 'This is going to be all right.'

Annie nodded again, but she made Maura look at her. 'It's not going to be all right, Maura. It's not going to be all right.'

'It is,' said Suze, crying. 'It is, because it has to be.'

They grasped onto each other again as if finding something to hold on to before they fell over or drowned or toppled off a cliff. And they all cried whatever tears they had left in their dehydrated bodies. No one said they were sorry for her diagnosis, for which Annie was grateful because it was no one's fault. And no one said they were sorry for anything that had happened or anything that had been said on Blue Bracken Island, about what they felt, and who they were, and what they had decided, because it had all been the truth. And what good would there be in apologizing for the truth?

'Who's going to look after Em?' said Maura. 'Your mum can't do it and so it has to be one of us.'

Annie took her blue clothbound notebook out of her pocket and laid it on the sand. 'Notes I've taken on all of you. On me. On what Em needs. I definitely wanted one of you to be her mum . . . there, read it if you want.'

Claire was the one to pick up the book and leaf back and forth between the pages. 'Neurotic and overbearing,' she read, smiling. 'Sensitive: up to a point, but veers into narcissism after that. Cannot admit that anything is her fault. Completely unable to face her life head-on.' She shrugged. 'Vain.' She looked at Maura. 'Lovely.' She looked at Suze. 'More empathic than anyone else I know. Makes me laugh like a drain. Way more annoying when I'm hungry. Should I worry that there was a moment when I could have killed her for being so annoying? Should eat more. Not trustworthy regarding that subject. Disappointing, sometimes, but I still love her.'

The more Claire read, the more she laughed.

'Who's the neurotic one?' said Suze. 'Is the person who can't face her life head-on Maura?' She craned to look at the book but Claire snapped it shut and threw it back in Annie's direction where it landed in a spray of sand at her feet. Annie picked it up, cradling it to her chest.

'It doesn't really matter anymore, does it,' said Maura. 'It's not like any of that's a secret anymore. Annie . . .' Maura pressed her palm into Annie's knee. 'Obviously Dex and I have got stuff to sort out between us, but it goes without saying that, that . . .' Then she stuttered. 'Th-that you can, like, move in with us? And I'll look after you. And we can mind Em with the twins, and after that . . .'

'And there's loads of space at ours,' said Claire.

'Yes, and of course I'll cancel my, my thing. In Peru,' said Suze. 'I'm sure they can delay that sort of thing. I can call and find out?'

Annie blinked, feeling the warmth of friendship wrapping itself around her. All the good stuff that had always been there, just with more dimension, truth, light and shade. Why had she waited so long for this? Perhaps she had needed to know her friends for exactly who they were, and not just how they wanted to be seen. Perhaps she had needed to know all this before she died. Perhaps it had been the only way to make the right decision for Em.

'Thank you for that. All of you. I know your intentions are good and full of love but I also know a lot about how you all truly feel: about yourselves and the lives you want. And honestly? I don't think any of you wants, or is ready, to be Em's mum. You don't want this situation at all.'

'Of course we don't!' said Suze, crying. 'Because it means losing you.'

That night the four friends lay huddled together in the sand: Suze holding Maura, Maura holding Annie, Annie holding a shivering Claire. They held onto each other, cold and afraid, feeling the rise and fall of each other's breaths. And they waited.

Chapter 32

Martin

**10 p.m. Sunday, 30 August – 5 a.m. Monday, 31 August
Sandpiper Cottage**

By Sunday evening, and after some hastily prepared fishfingers and chips for the children, Martin knew in his bones that their holiday would not end with happy chatter on the veranda over the remainder of the weekend's wine as the sun went down. There would be no retreating for an early night because they all needed to be up the next morning to pack clothes and Tupperware and to wheel the recycling and rubbish bins down the driveway in preparation for a prompt departure the next morning.

The women were not there. They were gone.

After the kids had been put to bed, the adults speed-reading stories with rictus grins, promising double Weetabix in the morning when the mums were back, the men gathered in the kitchen.

'Part One of the Five-Point plan?' said Dex. And the other two nodded in agreement. 'Thunderbirds are Go.' And with that, he swept all the plates and oven pans, pens and scraps of paper into one corner of the kitchen table. Karl wiped the surface clean of fishfinger crumbs and Martin slid a pad of lined paper into the empty space, handing out a black Biro to each of them.

'Establishing the facts,' said Martin. 'We do not have the name or location of the spa they attended, but we do have the names of eight local spas, wellbeing and retreat centres to telephone and enquire about the whereabouts of the women. Please write any key notes on the paper provided and stop the clock when you've established any link. Go!'

After a tense half hour during which little was achieved and they hit various walls, Dex growled.

'Half these places won't answer, half don't have a record of our partners staying there and the other half won't tell me because they need to protect the privacy of their guests. I make that one-and-a-half *fools errands.*'

'Same,' said Karl in despair.

'Me too,' said Martin. 'Slightly different on the maths front regarding halves and thirds, but essentially the same result.'

'We'd better get on with Part Two of the plan ASAP,' said Dex.

For Part Two they had planned to drive round the immediate vicinity checking that the women hadn't got stranded or lost. The house was in a remote spot with winding paths and trails that led nowhere. It was a possibility.

But, as Martin and Dex stood out on the shale in the coffin-black darkness, observing Karl as he leant against the open door of his car, grunting as various switches let him down, Martin quickly accepted they would be moving on from this part of the plan as well.

Karl stepped back, took a wide swing of his leg and kicked the car door. 'Bloody electric cars!' he shouted. 'What is the point if you have to stop every ten minutes to charge them?' He lifted his kicking foot to rest on his calf like a sleeping bird, then bent down to rub it lovingly.

'I'd love to help, but . . .' said Dex, gesturing to his own car, the steak knife still stuck in its tyre.

'I really am sorry,' said Martin. 'I might as well tell you now that I had no intention of fixing your tyre. I know nothing about cars.' He inhaled deeply. 'And while we're here, I was the one that stabbed your car wheel with the steak knife.'

Dex turned and gave Martin a wide-eyed look. 'I guess one silver lining is that you stabbed the car and not me.'

'Indeed. I just didn't want you to leave. This weekend felt too important for me to allow it to simply disintegrate. Anyway, there we have it,' Martin said primly, as the mild yet thrilling electrical current of conflict rippled through him. 'So sue me.'

Dex smiled. 'Maybe I will once I've found my wife.'

Once it was established that Karl's car really was *hors de combat*, the exhaustion and stress seemed to amplify in all of them. Clouds thickened, smudging the moon beams, and they fell into a brief and tense silence.

'I think we should skip Part Three and move on to Part Four with immediate effect,' said Karl abruptly, plucking a stray oven chip from the table and chewing on it morosely. The men hadn't wanted to eat anything left in the fridge, which by now was a jumble of tiny dishes and jars with a variety of leftovers, from a few chipolatas to a vat of grey potato soup that had been pale yellow when Martin had shoved it in the fridge on Friday night.

Martin slid the brownie box in Karl's direction but Karl

only regarded it glumly and looked away. Dex craned over the kitchen table now littered with Ordnance Survey maps and half mugs of cold coffee, pencils and phones and chargers. The whole enterprise had the feel of a war room shot through with Blitz spirit, which Martin would have been ordinarily delighted by had he not been so concerned that Suze was lying at the bottom of a ditch.

'Come on, Dex, I think Karl's right,' said Martin. 'I think we need to get to Part Four ASAP.'

'If we're going to call the police at least let's give them some info by executing Part Three, first. Let's try the local taxi firms and work out which one collected them on Saturday morning? If we know where they were headed, then we might not even need the police.'

And so that's what they did. They split up the three local taxi firms between them and dispatched with the task in under three minutes.

'No record of a booking,' said Martin.

'No record of a booking,' said Karl.

'No answer,' said Dex. 'So one firm is still in play. Some idiot's probably turned off the phone to watch Pornhub. Maybe we should go there and ask them face to face?'

Dex tucked an unlit cigarette between his lips and let it hang there exhaustedly. 'Call it Part 3B of The Plan?'

'I'm a decent runner,' said Karl, as if they hadn't already been told this fact on several occasions. 'I can get to the village in under an hour at a decent clip. Then I can collar the Pornhub guy to drive me back in a cab. Sound like a decent plan?'

'Make sure you cite extreme urgency,' said Martin. 'Tell them we're a hair's breadth from calling the authorities.'

'Roger that,' said Karl, sprinting into the house to get changed.

'There must be a quicker way to get to the village,' said Dex.

'I think he was looking for the chance to have his fourth run of the day,' said Martin.

While they were still in the thick of night, and waiting for Karl, Dex and Martin sat in a charged, yet amiable silence as they waited for news. But as the first rays of light streaked the sky with the vivid reds and oranges of Monday morning, Martin said to Dex, 'I suppose I'm thinking . . .'

'Me too,' said Dex. 'Let's do it. Part Four here we come.'

'OK. This is going to be OK, Dex.'

Dex looked at him in a way that suggested quite the opposite and yet, unusually for Dex, said nothing to corroborate the worst of his obvious suspicions.

When it came to making the call Martin's fingertips slipped and slid all over the iPhone screen, his hands were so greased with worry.

Once he'd made contact, Martin put his hand over the receiver and consulted Dex. 'Which emergency service do we require?'

'Shit, I don't know. All three?' said Dex.

'Ambulance, police and fire?' said Martin. 'And maybe scramble a dredger, too? Just to cover all bases.'

Dex took the phone gently but decisively out of Martin's hand to speak. 'Please excuse my friend. He's worried. I appreciate how confusing it must be to mix up land and sea vehicles, but I think what he's saying is that we need the police. Our partners went to spend Saturday at a spa and haven't returned.' This time Dex consulted Martin. 'They're saying is anyone in danger?'

'We don't know!' said Martin in his high-pitched, panic voice. 'Aren't they supposed to tell us that?'

'They're asking if there's been any conflict?' said Dex.

Martin shrugged. Did arguments over nakedness and marriage and a game of rounders involving a hard ball to the arm constitute a police matter?

'No,' said Martin. 'Nothing illegal.'

'Damage to property?' said Dex.

Did a steak knife to a tyre count? And a broken vase? Flattened bushes?

'Nothing illegal there, either,' said Martin.

'Look,' interrupted Dex, speaking intently to the call handler, 'I think the whole thing can be simplified by calling it a missing persons' case. Four women are *missing* . . . What? They're all friends, yes. And they went on a planned trip. A sort of spa break nestled within a long weekend. Due back? They were due back this morning.' Dex paused, his brow furrowing. 'Really? Are you sure? Fuck-sticks. OK.' Dex scribbled a line of letters and numbers on the lined pad, and hung up.

'Well?' said Martin.

'Their behaviour doesn't constitute a missing person's case yet. Just a situation involving people who seem to be a bit late. That's our case number,' he said, sliding the pad toward Martin.

'Maybe we're just being anxious and they're on a bender, like the old days?'

Martin brewed a pot of tea and turned on a few more desk lamps to pour light over the maps. Several moments later the door swung open with force and the two men jumped out of their skins, cursing and splashing tea, only to find, in their shock and relief that it was Karl looking ruddy with exercise, streaked with sweat and mud.

'Everything OK?' said Karl, as he filled a pint glass of water. 'Tense in here!'

'I'd be worried if it wasn't!' said Martin.

'You'll be pleased to hear I've got some answers. I found the third cab company. There was just some scruffy bloke there, who'd accidentally put the phones on silent, but he was able to confirm that he *had* been booked by Annie and had waited for an hour for them to show at the end of the lane, unable to go further because the gate was locked and she wasn't answering her phone. After trying to get through again, and unable to get the motor through the gate without the combination code, he turned round and got on with his day.'

Karl was flushed with pride, but Martin and Dex looked at each other in alarm.

'But wait for the good bit!' said Karl. 'He was able to tell me which spa they were destined for so I rang them too – but they didn't arrive there either!'

The smile faded from Karl's face when he saw the panic in Martin and Dex.

'Think think think!' said Martin.

'Do that thing where you lie on your back with your legs up the fridge?' said Dex. 'Like you did when the kids went missing?'

'What? OK.' Martin lay on his back and stuck his feet on the fridge, which had the advantage of calming his anxiously beating heart.

'Think,' Martin said again. 'They were upset on Friday night. Maura especially. Claire, I think. Suze, perhaps so. Annie will have been shoring them all up. They went to the beach, walking. I heard Maura and Suze walking toward the jetty. I heard Claire in the forest near the back beach, laughing. When you're upset . . . *the Wendy house*.'

'They're not in the bloody Wendy house, mate!' said Karl. 'We've been in there a million times since Friday night.'

But Martin got to his feet regardless and sprinted to the shed with Karl and Dex in hot pursuit.

Martin swung open the door so hard it bounced on its hinges. He took a quick inventory. The pastel pink paddleboard and the mint green paddleboard were still sandwiched up together against the wall and there was still a muddle of sandy red and yellow buckets and spades that had been left, unwanted, by previous guests. The Ronseal that Dex had grabbed from Alfie sat on a long and empty shelf.

'The rowing boat!' Martin said. 'There was a rowing boat on that shelf on Friday afternoon. Walt and I visited it and I said someone should take that out for a little trip this weekend.'

'Haven't seen a rowboat in here all weekend,' said Karl. 'And I've often come in here to do lunges and squats. Probably six times a day.'

'Was it here when the kids were hiding?' said Martin.

'Are you saying they nicked it?' said Karl.

'No,' said Dex. 'I put the Ronseal there, on that shelf. Out of Alfie's hands.'

Martin looked at him. 'So the boat wasn't here then . . . Did anyone hear the women come back on Friday night?

I just assumed they'd come back late and then left early the next morning for the spa.'

'Are you saying they didn't come back from the woods, the beach . . .' Karl's words slowed down. '. . . from the jetty? But if they didn't come back then where are they?'

The three men filed out of the shed without a word, and followed each other down the path to the edge of the water on the front beach.

'Revert to a version of Part Two,' said Martin quietly. 'Search the surrounds for evidence they never made it back home on Friday night.'

But, after a swift move around the grounds, that part of the plan was dispatched with quickly, too.

'Part Two of the plan is aborted,' said Karl, tears in his eyes. 'There is no sign of the rowboat in the surrounding area and Claire did not take her hair elastics which . . .' Karl's voice broke. 'She takes everywhere with her.'

'Agreed,' said Martin. 'Suze has left her book, and Annie her important files and documents.'

'And Maura's left every single one of her eyeliners,' said Dex, all the energy drained from him.

'Time for Part Five, and the end of the plan, then,' said Martin, looking out at the black depths beyond. 'Call the coastguard.'

Chapter 33

Annie

4 a.m. – 6 a.m. Monday, 31 August
Blue Bracken Island

In the early hours of the morning, Claire sat bolt upright and vomited, her body lurching and emptying itself again and again of mustard yellow bile, blood and bubbling sputum. Then she turned to look at Annie, face greenly waxen, hair plastered in uneven strips across her forehead with a peculiar and unforgettable look of hurt, love and things unsaid. Then very quickly, violently, almost – as if she had been shot – Claire collapsed back onto the sand, eyes rolling back, head tipping sideways as if it had suddenly become too heavy for her body to support.

'Claire? Claire?' Suze shook Claire's lifeless body by the shoulders. 'Why isn't she waking up?' she said, her voice speeding up. 'What's happened to her? Is she asleep?' Suze looked up at Annie, pupils dilated in panic. 'Annie? What's happening to her?'

But Suze didn't wait for Annie's reply and instead grasped Claire's wrist. 'Where's her pulse? I can't feel a pulse. Claire? Where's your fucking pulse? Annie, she's hiding her pulse. Where do you measure a pulse?' Suze dropped Claire's hand

and pressed her thumb and forefinger into her own wrist. 'I can't even find my own. Where's my pulse? I can't find my pulse.'

Annie leant over Claire to listen for breathing as Suze sat back on bent knees, watching everything through her hands like she was shielding herself from the worst of a horror movie.

'She can't die!' roared Maura. 'We said some horrible things to each other. She can't die as well as you. We have to get out of here. We need help.'

'I know, Maura, I know,' said Annie sternly, 'but you have got to calm down. It's not like we haven't been trying and now it's dark again there isn't anybody around! I don't know, I just don't know . . .' Annie had an urge to vomit as she pushed back intolerable images of Claire's graveside: *mother of one, lived in the Home Counties, what a waste, how tragic.*

She took Claire's wrist from Suze. 'It's OK. I can feel a weak pulse,' she said, picking up a dull throb at the ends of her fingertips. She pressed her palm to Claire's forehead. 'She's clammy, and burning up.'

Aside from feeding and clothing Em and taking on the horrific task of potentially life-saving swimming lessons, Annie had also taken First Aid very seriously. A small kitchen fire hydrant, fire blanket and first aid box weren't a worthy replacement for the kind of supportive human partner you might need in an emergency, but they had been reassuring to own, alongside the research she'd done.

'We have to get her to a hospital,' Annie said. 'She needs antibiotics. Her foot looks really bad, swollen, infected perhaps, but I don't think it's caused this collapse. She drank some disgusting-looking water where Suze got stuck in the quicksand. I thought her bad stomach earlier was the dehydration but maybe it was infection from the water?'

'Oh God,' said Suze. 'That whole area was bog-land. Stagnant, dirty muddy stuff. It stank of illness. Of all the places . . .'

'Claire, wake up!' It was Annie's turn to shake Claire that time, but Claire remained unresponsive. 'I think she's in a coma.'

'A coma? For fuck's sake!' shouted Maura. 'We were all lucky enough to be born into an era of modern medicine and now two of you are going to die like we're still living in medieval times.'

'Not helpful!' chided Annie. 'She needs medical attention.'

Sensing the gravity of it all, the three of them gathered around Claire like a pride of lionesses, protecting her against what, they no longer knew. Her illness, the elements, the island, themselves . . .

Annie dug her hands in to the sand and closed her eyes, imagining gold grains running through her fingers. All she had to do was add water and it would be the kintsugi gold paint she needed to mend Claire, to save her from death. Annie opened her eyes, palms damp with sand, the deep red and gold of a new day coming over the horizon, knowing then exactly what she had to do.

'We have to swim,' she said. 'She needs medical help quickly, otherwise she'll die.'

'When you say *we*, you mean *who*, exactly?' Maura rested her hand protectively on Claire's calf. 'We've been through this already.'

'Obviously Claire can't, and Suze can't because she doesn't know how. Maura, I haven't seen you run up a flight of steps in the entire time I've known you, making you a liability. Which leaves me.'

'The one with the paralysing phobia of the water,' said Suze.

'Yeah, I'm terrified,' Annie said. 'But what choice do we have?'

'The one who hasn't swum since she was nine,' Maura said, as if Annie hadn't spoken.

'I've had a bit of practice. Maybe I'll be OK.'

'Maybe?' said Maura. 'That's not good enough.'

'What about your condition?' asked Suze.

'I'm not pregnant. I can still move. Come on, we have to get on with this,' said Annie.

'It's a really long way,' said Maura quietly. 'I don't think you're going to make it. It's the length of like, a hundred football pitches or something? You're not strong enough to do that. And if you don't make it and we're left here too long and then Claire dies, it'll just be me and Suze . . . Then what?'

'Seriously, stop,' Annie snapped, her voice like steel. 'Both of you, please stop. I can do this. I know I can do this.' Like Em learning to swim in a pool, like trying to speak to Claire on a boat. Like saving Claire's life. There were some things that trumped Annie's fears and Annie saw she only needed the strength to tell herself that, or die trying.

'This is what people do when they face unimaginable challenges,' said Annie. 'They get in the water and they swim.'

'But what about the . . .'

Annie watched Maura open her mouth to exclaim about the freezing water and the riptides and the distance and all her other fears, then close it again because she, like all of them, knew that the time for debate was over. They could no longer wait in a place where decisions were not made, in the frozen hinterland where souls go to die – and Blue Bracken Island would become exactly that if no action was taken.

'Are we all going to die?' said Maura.

'I don't know,' said Annie, standing up and walking to the water's edge.

She put her hands on her hips and her face to the sky, like Superwoman on a poster. Then she turned to face them.

'Always remember me this way,' she said, giving them her best smile. It was important, to her, that whether she died in the next half hour or the next few months that she be remembered as a woman who built herself and built a child. As a woman who ran and walked and jumped and laughed and had decided she was strong enough to swim against the odds, and save her friend's life.

Then she kicked off her shorts, and turned toward the water again.

'Wait,' Maura said, running after Annie and grabbing her by the hand. 'We need to say goodbye, don't we? I said some things, you said some things, but I love you, and none of the rest matters, right? Annie?' She gasped, tears choking the back of her throat. 'I've still got so much I want to talk to you about, and tell you, so don't go yet? I don't want you to go,' she sobbed. 'Please don't go. Don't leave us.'

Maura held Annie's hand so hard it hurt and Suze held on to Maura's back, like she was protecting her, beginning to pull her away.

'Please, Annie,' cried Maura. 'I don't know how to live my life without you. Don't go now. Suze, stop her.'

'She has to go, Maura,' Suze said through her tears. 'No

one is coming for us, so if Annie doesn't try now, Claire will die.'

Annie had to close her eyes then because she couldn't watch the moment Suze unclasped Maura's fingers, one by painful one, from hers. She couldn't watch her own death played back in the eyes of her best friend. Not then. She wasn't ready.

She let go of Maura's hand and walked to the water, then turned back to face them head-on. 'You're the loves of my life,' she said. 'Always have been. Always will be.'

'Who's going to look after Em? Annie? What about Em?' called out Suze.

But Annie didn't reply, and she didn't turn back.

There was so much noise at the water's edge. How waves could be so deafening just picking themselves up and falling down again. The screams of the fat seagulls and other birds whose names Annie had never learnt and never would. Her own screams, too: quieter, but distress signals nonetheless, as the iced dawn water lapped the backs of her feet, stroking them with sharpened fingers of iron, reminding her she could not step back this time: no boat or piece of land to escape to anymore.

Around her the blood red of the rising sun pooled over the black waters, turning them pinker, more bruised. She had left behind her two cheerleading friends, one unconscious friend and a battalion of trees. Beneath her the beige and brown of sharp-edged rocks and pebbles pressed painfully into her arches and under her toes, both holding her there and pushing her on.

There were times that weekend that Annie had needed

space from her friends – to absorb the hurt and the tears, to spend time thinking about what they'd said to each other, and what they'd done to themselves, and each other – without being blown around by hunger and thirst and the night's chill and the fear she'd never make it home again. And yet, none of that space mattered now. Here she was, swimming in stinking brackish water to save one of their lives, possibly all their lives, so she could have more time with them. So they could have more time with each other. With their children. And their partners. She was swimming for more time with the best parts of them and the worst parts of them.

Behind her she heard her friends cheer her on. She wanted to turn back, of course she did, as she felt the waves lapping at her thighs, her shoulders hunching forward protectively, toes gripping into wet sand beyond the beige rocks, skin rippling with shivers because there was no fuel left to burn inside her.

She was standing in the water but she might as well have been standing on the edge of the highest coastal cliff in ferocious winds. Had she ever been more afraid than this?

Her mind began sweeping up all the moments she could remember being scared. Giving birth. Being left by Em's dad. The first time her mum forgot who she was. Suze sinking in quicksand. Danielle slipping under the ice. The moments before diagnosis – that particular one, like being shoved at the top of the cliff but somehow managing not to fall. When she'd first stepped into that swimming pool after years of not swimming. And never more scared than in those island days before she'd told her friends what was really going on: like waiting to introduce them to a version of herself that not even she had wanted to know.

She'd survived it all so far, hadn't she?

The water stretched out and out and the light was not far enough up for her to see to the other side yet. But still, the water reached higher, gripping her round the chest with an iron cold, the ground beneath her feet turning silty and silky and uneven – Claire's pulse weakening for every moment she delayed.

She must survive again.

She reached back into the muscles of her memory bank, where the mastery of a nine-year-old swim team captain was stored, where the endurance of a mother lay and, sewn through the newest layers, where the new and remembered swimming skills from her recent lessons lived. With every shake of her legs and wrists and arms she summoned the memories, asking them to fill the spaces in her muscles, to rush into the gaps where they had begun to waste with illness and to flood them with knowledge, adrenaline, and magic – whatever she needed to stay alive.

She spluttered with the cold as the water continued to rise. Lifted her feet off the water bed and kicked, then fell under: submerged and blinded by the stinging salt water.

Death touched her. Or fear, that she would sink and instead of the skill and memory she needed, water would fill the spaces in her heart and muscles.

But she told herself: she was strong. She was not a coward. A coward would not be the way she thought of herself when there was so much evidence to the contrary, and it would not be the way other people remembered her.

She pushed her head above water – glancing up at the sky turning red, turning orange, shot through with bronze and gold. It was such a beautiful world.

Go now, she told herself, falling back down, legs pushing

her back up to the surface again and again, upwards and forwards, against the water. Soul facing forward. Forward in the direction of her dying mother, her living daughter, her life and the lives of her friends.

Her head filled with noise again, this time: *Come on! Keep moving!*

She kicked again and she was moving. Moving through that disgusting water with the sun starting rising in the sky. A taste of salt so strong, her tongue stung.

What a feeling! Like solving a maths sum, scoring a goal, winning a board game, getting a job, making a nappy stick and stay. Moments of total mastery. She was so happy to be swimming, so happy to be alive and moving that she opened her mouth and allowed the water to smash her face and crash into her, sending its salty shocks to the back of her throat where she coughed and choked and for a moment lost the confidence she'd gained.

But she kicked again.

She screamed at the top of her voice, craning her neck above the water: a full percentage point less of the coward than she believed she'd been. Still alive.

She took a stroke, and then another. Could see what was around her. A fine line of beach on one side of her. It was enough. It was there. She was still here. Eyes stinging, legs quivering, head quaking with cold. Still there.

Stable enough in the water, she allowed herself to remember.

She dived under the water, to get closer to something though she wasn't sure what. Her eyes stung with the salt and she could not see, though she tried. She imagined the silted sand beds rising up in clouds with the currents, plants flattening and rising, fishes swimming in opposite directions. Things moving and changing direction all the time. Life lived itself beneath those unknowable depths.

She didn't know what the ice-girl's parents had been thinking after their daughter's death, she didn't know whether the looks they gave her meant they'd rather Annie had died. She didn't even know what her own parents had thought. They'd moved on as quickly as they could by refusing to talk about it, the only acknowledgement of tragedy being Annie's ignored tenth birthday. Did they blame themselves for not keeping an eye on her? Did they blame Annie? Did they blame the weather? Did it stop them from living their lives in the decades that followed? No. It did not.

Most things were buried beneath the waterline. She would never know what went onto the chaotic bonfire of stories people made up to torture themselves, make themselves feel better, help them to move forward, or to stagnate.

She hadn't even known the truth behind her own best friends' smiles.

But now all the spaces between them had been exposed for what they were. Maura's fear of failure and the shame of her destruction. Suze's break for freedom from motherhood and her fear of judgement. Claire's unhappiness with them all, the parts of herself she'd hidden, so profound it had led to the desire to burn relationships to the ground.

However close they'd been as friends, a mirror was not something any of them had wanted, though Blue Bracken Island had given them exactly that.

And now they knew each other. They really knew each other.

Annie emerged at the water's surface and found she had
lost sight of the shore, but she kept swimming, crying as she
went.

All she could do was be honest about her own story.

She was dying.

And she had not wanted to be unwell, had not wanted
any of this.

And she had been afraid of what was coming for her.

She had wanted to be like her friends, living long and
happy and complicated lives with each other. She had wanted
to be a mum to Em and if that wasn't going to happen she
needed one of her best friends to be the next best thing.

Best-laid plans . . .

Which was all they were.

Annie's friends were all as unpredictable as the fishes and
the seaweed, swimming in whatever chaotic direction the tide
took them, else against it. It had been futile to try to keep
them all in amber. On land. To herd them on holiday, or into
boats, to keep them together for a moment in one place, and,
once there, to keep them from falling out and then falling
apart.

It was all a mess. A mess was all she had. She was lost in the
mess of the estuary, not knowing where she was going. And
yet, she loved that she was swimming again. With purpose.
And more than that, proving she could do it alone.

And the cold that had once been painful now felt beautiful.
It sharpened her mind and helped her to feel every limb, every
cell living inside her, shocking her heart back to life.

She flipped over and lay back, sculling gently. She could
still float with little movement. She didn't need to struggle.
She allowed the waves to cover her face, and then recede,

and for the water beneath to hold her as she looked up at the brightening sky: grey, yellow and blue. She saw the rays of a rising sun that would burn through the clouds, dispersing them in different directions. Then she glanced back, seeing where she came from, flipping onto her front and focusing on where she was going. There were figures on the beach: an adult and children playing a chasing game, gasping with joy. It was so beautiful.

She swam harder now, feeling her limbs weaken quickly. Water splashed into her mouth, and she choked and spat. She was in time for a different story, whose resolution she would never know. Life had been wonderful and her only wish was that it would be wonderful for Em. Then she called out a name.

Chapter 34

Martin

6 a.m. Monday, 31 August
Sandpiper Cottage

Em's cries splintered the early morning air, for no reason Martin could see other than she had firmly decided she needed her mother back like, *yesterday*. A tsunami of waking children had followed as the sky turned from cherry to copper and by six everyone was up and around, adding to a chaotic soundtrack: the twins hammering each other in front of Peppa Pig, Graham steadfastly sucking on breadsticks and refusing to take the bottle, and Walt repeatedly pressing the go button on his tractor toy that played a gratingly happy nursery rhyme on repeat.

None of the men had been to bed and were in a state of high alert. Ten minutes felt like a day when it came to waiting for the police and coastguard to arrive, and so it followed that the avalanche of dawn chaos soon tipped them into a collective place of *not-coping*. Karl's eyes brimmed with tears as the tempo on Walt's musical tractor increased, the volume of Dex's voice implied his patience was about to split suddenly and violently down the side like a sausage in a hot pan, and Martin could feel his heart hammering a fast

Scottish reel against his chest promising the imminent arrival of a panic attack.

Martin was gripped by the need to leave that chaotic zoo of a kitchen and get some air to his own worries, so shoving a packet of biscuits under his arm, he grasped Walt's hand, promising that yes, he could still take the singing tractor with him, and scooped up a sniffling wet-cheeked Em in his free arm, heading for the front beach.

Once he was on the sand, and the children were seated on a narrow incline, playing with a couple of shells, Martin allowed a complex set of emotions to engulf him. He was grateful for the reappearance of sunlight, the first since Friday, and also for the bellyful of bacon sandwich that Dex had cooked up in an effort to distract them all. He was heartened to have Walt and Em as company, and to have made one, if not one and a half, new and unlikely friends in the form of Karl and possibly Dex that weekend. He was deep in the raw pit of acceptance that Suze was leaving them, yet he also felt the exciting yet fizzing anxiety of something new around the corner. But he was deeply afraid that they were all unknowingly in the grips of a tragedy that had either already happened or was yet to unfold, the kind of tragedy that might upend everything he felt for a second, seismic time.

He broke down and sobbed.

But he'd only managed a few deep inhales before he was plucked violently out of his crying jag with the sound of something resembling a bird – possibly a bird in dire straits. When the sound came again, he thought it could be the cries of a tantrumming child riding the wind from a nearby beach.

But when the sound came a third time, there was something about the siren-pitched timbre that made him listen harder and finally compute that what he was hearing were adult cries of distress. When he searched for the source from somewhere in the water, he saw a foamed and chaotic struggle some five hundred metres away – the top of a head, the flash of flesh from a face, a raised arm, short moments of all those things disappearing beneath the water's surface – and his first instinct was to call Karl for help. Karl could run and no doubt swim, like the wind.

But Martin knew he must point at the struggling chaos and either follow it himself or not lose sight of that point at the end of his finger until help arrived; he'd done some extended reading after a rudimentary first aid and life-saving course some years ago.

When the limbs splashed and disappeared for what felt like an age, he scanned the water frantically, finally catching the flash of face stretched in wide dismay, the pitch of the cry louder, this time calling, 'Martin!'

It was Annie, and she was calling out for him.

At that precise moment the adrenaline tap slammed itself on full power and brought with it an uncontrolled gush of possibilities. Where were Suze and Claire and Maura? Where had Annie come from? And what would happen if Em heard her mother's voice and tried to jump into the water after her? One thing was for sure, he had no time to imagine the worst. There was nothing for it, but to dive right in.

So, while keeping his finger point on the splashing mess, he kicked off his espadrilles and shouted for help as loudly as he could, hoping the men would hear from inside the house.

Then he sprinted into the water, sharp flints digging into his heels and arches, though any real pain was numbed to

343

discomfort by the adrenaline. He dived forward at the first available opportunity, like he'd seen people do in the movies, to embark upon a bracing crawl. The tide was against him, water soaking his hair coldly, stinging his eyeballs, spattering its saltiness into his mouth. But he felt as strong as a muscular sea creature. He knew exactly where he was going and what he needed to do.

By the time he reached Annie, her cries had lessened but she was struggling more. He grasped her by the arm, to give her something to hold on to, but all too soon the weight she exerted on him threatened to drag them both under.

'It's OK, I've got you,' he said, when he'd lifted both their heads above water.

Her lips were pink-grey, like the inside of a conch shell, and her eyes were stretched and haunted but shining with life. He needed to get her out, and quickly because the shine in her eyes was the high glaze of someone on the wrong side of hypothermia: he'd read enough about the pitfalls of cold-water swimming as a mood booster, to know that. There was no time to waste, and so, he threw his arm around her neck and tipped onto his back so that she was lying on him like a mattress, keeping a firm grip across her breastbone with his forearm.

And then he turned in the direction of the shore, kicking his legs in a strong backward breaststroke, glad for a second time that he'd done a first aid and life-saving course. Granted those lessons had been easier in five feet of calm and warm chlorinated water, and he'd only ever tried out manoeuvres on a living and relaxed human being. Yet here he was, in the thick of it – dicing with life and the lemons it was lobbing in his direction.

'You can stop swimming now!' Martin shouted at Annie, because the splash of the water was loud and she was still struggling as if she was alone and swimming, making his job to keep them above water much harder.

'Safe, safe, safe,' she was saying and he could see from her profile that her face was stretched in pain, her gaze fixed at a point in the sky. He knew she was crying though the water concealed her tears. 'Safe, safe, safe.'

'You are safe,' said Martin, his voice calm and parental and firm. 'Nothing's going to harm you now. I've got you.'

And very suddenly she stopped struggling.

He felt the ripples of her throat beneath his forearm as she began to cry in bigger and heavier sobs. He didn't know if the pain in his own breastbone was due to the exertion of the task in hand or some other heartache of his own.

The water shallowed quickly and soon the waves seemed desperate to get them both out, spitting them powerfully onto the shore in a messy, spluttering heap. Martin felt the scrape of flint and rocks on his back this time as he was bumped backwards by the waves, but he wasted no time in righting himself, limbs shaking with the effort. Then he lifted an almost deadweight Annie upright so she wouldn't be washed over with more water.

And then Karl was there, effing and blinding, screaming Martin's name, Dex's name, Claire's name, running down to the water's edge to meet them with a towel held aloft, until together they were both helping Annie to dry land.

Once Annie was cradled in their dry jumpers and towel, both of the men leant over her, examining her face and limbs as if she'd been dropped from a spaceship.

Annie grasped hold of Martin's hand and looked at him

searchingly. Her eyes were a milky green, and her voice quiet but hoarse with the effort of speaking. 'They're on that island,' she said.

'Which island?' said Karl, voice quivering to contain the panic.

'Blue. Bracken. Opposite. Trees. Stuck. No boat. No food. No water. Claire unconscious. Needs help. Get help now.'

Karl began to cry. 'Claire! Oh God, Claire!' And in a moment, he was up and running toward the house as Dex was exiting with a tray of coffees, still caught in the hinterland of waiting for the authorities.

Martin held Annie's hand tight and pulled the towel around her head, not wanting any important heat to escape, rubbing his hands over her arms to get the circulation going in the way he did when Walt got out of a swimming pool. In the distance he could hear the urgent tones of Karl and Dex as information was relayed and plans were made.

'I'm sorry,' said Annie. 'I'm so sorry.'

Martin grasped her hand tightly. 'You don't need to be sorry for anything. It's OK,' he said. 'I'm here.'

She looked up at him. 'You're such a good person,' she said, and she reached for his other hand. 'Gold. You are gold.' And she smiled at him with such feeling in her eyes that Martin felt his heart swell with sadness and happiness all at once.

'Martin, I'm sick,' she said. 'I'm going to die soon.'

The words were so bald, so flint-sharp, so very unforgiving in their neon-brightness, that he blinked at them, his eyes filling with tears. And yet he swallowed hard because she needed him to be strong. It was not his place to feel grief in that moment, to anticipate the impact of her departure on the other women, on her daughter and the world, when what she needed was for him to be her brick.

'I know,' he said. 'I'm here for you.'

Annie smiled weakly and gratefully, with relief, perhaps, at not having to explain. And then she raised an arm which shook slightly as she squeezed his hand. She opened her mouth to speak but struggled to get the words out. 'I . . . I . . .'

'What, what do you need?' He couldn't hold back his tears, as all the weekend's thoughts and fears crashed into each other anew: Em too young to remember a mother who would die soon, Walt too young to remember a mother who might never come back once she was across the world, Graham too young to remember a mother who might already be dead. He wept. Children, adults: was anyone ever old enough and wise enough and strong enough to face what death took from them?

Annie squeezed his hand again. 'I . . .'

'What do you need? Anything? Tell me what you need?'

'Biscuit,' she said. 'Give me one of those biscuits over there.'

He smiled and tore open the biscuits, placing a tower of three and a bottle of water into her shaking hands.

And in the distance was a happier cry: Em, calling out for her mummy – laughing, running toward her, so happy to see her, not a blot on her horizon, saying, 'I love you I love you I love you,' throwing her arms around Annie's neck as though she would never let her go.

Epilogue

Em

8 a.m. 27 June
London, twenty years later

Em was woken that morning by a text message which made her smile because she knew exactly who it was from and that it should be read to the sound of jungle drum and bass.

I love you. Are you readyyy?

She hadn't been able to get back to sleep and instead listened to the dawn and its noisy silence, the birdsong and the hum of a fan cooling the overheated bedroom upstairs, the distant rumble of a snore and the bumble of the radio downstairs playing the shipping forecast to their neurotic dog who couldn't sleep without it. Soon there would be the smell of burnt toast and the erratic rise and fall of piano scales followed by a joyful but poorly executed rendition of Simon & Garfunkel's 'The Sound of Silence'. Bathroom doors would open and slam shut and there would be bickering and singing and shouting – all of it, the consequence of a baby, lack of sleep, two teenagers, hormones, teething, studying, the fact that no one liked the same food, ever, or had the energy to keep an eye on when the nappies ran out. She would miss it all painfully.

She climbed out of bed. Dressed and finished packing in two distinct piles: one for the rucksack and another for boxes that would be moved into a house she hadn't yet seen and probably wouldn't for many months.

She gazed into the bubbling turquoise fish tank and spoke to her clownfish. 'Barry, my friend, this is going to be a long day.'

She pulled on her musty-smelling, heavy robes and looked back at herself in the wardrobe mirror. She hated wearing black. It was not a colour. It was a feeling, the bleakest of feelings, and she needed all the positive energy she could muster. Later that morning she would be standing on a stage to accept her graduation certificate in front of thousands: that kind of attention was bad enough but what she dreaded more was the kind of attention she'd attract at the party they'd insisted having later that day.

Graduation was a *milestone*, so apparently that called for prosecco and 'saussie rolls' and a load of other people's bags and coats flung over her bed when that was the space she would need to retreat to. She would be surrounded by people she knew and loved, and she would have to smile and be grateful for them while also feeling like a part of her was missing. Along with every Christmas and birthday, she'd really rather it was over and done with so she could get on with her life.

She pinched at a flaking pile of fish food and sprinkled it into Barry's tank. She'd chosen Barry because of his bright orange colour. Em's walls were painted shocking pink, and her favourite clothes were grass green and fluorescent yellow. Much to Maura's delight, her hair was now also orange: the same shade, in fact, as Barry's.

'Wish you were here, Mum,' said Em, turning away from the tank and back to the mirror, playing the same game of visual bingo each time she missed Annie, ticking off features, one by one: the same sea-green eyes, the same voluminous hair that ballooned at the crown and tapered at the ends because it was perennially dry. The same curve to the shoulders and watchful gaze – so she'd been told a thousand times – and the same wide wrists she had observed in the many photographs she'd been shown.

And also, the differences: Em had a higher forehead, straighter teeth and a wider face – genes from an unknown relative in a past long forgotten. Certainly not features from her dad, whose picture she'd only seen once on Suze's phone, propping up the bar at a party. All the other pictures of him had been on Annie's phone and somehow, amidst the hell and sadness, the chaos and joy of the year that followed Annie's death, Maura, who was the most sentimental, who valued images from the past, had lost the charger to that brand of phone and vowed to replace it. Soon the phone, too, had got lost, along with the photos that could also never be replaced because Annie had never believed that something called *the cloud* was rock-solid enough to store anything.

Em had seen an email from her birth-dad that someone had printed out, thinking it might go in a memory box one day, but she'd never actually seen *him*, which was fine. She hadn't thought of a moment in her life when she had needed him.

She had a dad. A good dad.

Her phone beeped again:

I've changed my mind, burn the kaftan. Your mum hated anything that accentuated the waist and, worse, had no waist at all. Wish I still had her tartan trousers.

351

Em smiled at Maura's message because Maura had raised the issue of Em wearing her orange and pink kaftan at the party, the night before. She'd turned up, waving two bottles of wine in the air, and had then spoken for some time without drawing breath – flicking hair away from her shoulders to focus better, pinching a vape between fingers dashed with specks of rainbow paint. Her voice had grown huskier with age, and her laugh deeper, if that were possible. She was like an errant older sister who always wanted to stay up too late and was always ready to talk about anything that involved Annie *because we all know speaking about her makes us feel close to her.*

But last night Em had wanted Maura to go home after a few hours because sometimes, hearing other people's memories of her mum made her feel as if she couldn't breathe. She didn't always know why, but last night, when Maura had told her about their times at university and the row they'd had on Blue Bracken Island, laughing so hard it hurt her sides, Em realized it hurt her heart, too.

When Maura told her things like that it felt as though she was talking about a party which Em hadn't been invited to. And all that, on the eve of a party Annie wasn't coming to either. There was no symmetry to any of it, no comfort at all. Sometimes, the memories, though they were about her mum, felt like the opposite of home.

There were times it was easier to hear about Annie, though, and also necessary. Like the things she needed to ask Maura and Suze and Martin so that there weren't gaps in her history. Three was too young to remember anything much. Such as what happened that weekend on Blue Bracken Island when they got stranded. And how Claire had become very ill, then nearly died of sepsis that took three sets of IV antibiotics to tackle.

She must have heard Suze's words: *fearsome intense year* a thousand times, during which most of them put their plans on hold.

Em loved hearing about the moment Annie had proposed to Martin in a hospital bed during her recovery from the island adventure (profound dehydration and a mild case of Weil's disease from the water). It wasn't a marriage proposal, though it had looked like it, when she took him by the hand and thanked him for dragging her out of the water. Then she'd officially asked him to take on the mantle of 'Em's mother'.

He'd said *in sickness and in health, till death us do part.*

Finally, Annie had taken three pieces of gold ribbon and tied one on her wrist, one on Em's and the other on Martin's, using all the quivering strength she'd had left in her that day.

Then all of them, apart from Claire, who had been on the next ward, had held hands and cried as Martin explained that in the spirit of kintsugi, all breaks were treated as part of the history of an object which, once pieced back together in its new form, made it more precious than ever.

She heard how, when Claire had got out of hospital and they had all recovered their strength by eating and drinking and sleeping for a few weeks, everyone had rallied round Annie and Em. How Martin became the practical nexus at the centre of it all, keeping Em and Annie together as much as they were able to cope with, and jumping in when they weren't.

There were appointments and planning meetings, during which Suze enjoyed her Peru research trip and even a few weeks when Annie said she'd not had symptoms, where she believed that maybe the illness had gone away. Maura said she'd never know whether Annie had said that for their sakes, or her own *because that was the kind of woman your mother was.*

They'd made the most of their time together, mostly within the M25 and certainly nowhere near Dorset. Maura had jumped into The Serpentine for a bet, and they'd had picnics on Hampstead Heath where Suze had picked up a dog walker and ended up dating him for two weeks. Em was glad her mum had been happy, but she never stopped wishing that she'd been there to see her with them, especially when they told her about the Christmas lights at Kew Gardens with mulled wine and mince pies. Birthday cake in the snow in Regent's Park, using taxis and golf carts to transport Annie, and, toward the end, a private ambulance.

They made new plans for Maura's fortieth, changing bookings from a restaurant and Eighties club night to planning a bedside disco with just the four of them instead.

Toward the end it was easiest to move Annie and Em into the house with Claire, Karl, Graham, Martin and Walt, and look after her there. Maura visited every few days while juggling an office admin job and her own painting again, Dex looking after the kids.

And in the rallying, all the friends laughed. And cried. And they said what needed to be said even if, by the end, Annie couldn't say much back.

Sometimes the friends could tell Em what Annie had said in those last days and sometimes they couldn't, because all Annie had to communicate with in her last few weeks were her eyes and they were mostly filled with tears.

In her final days Annie's most effective communications were by nodding to various music tracks.

'Total Eclipse of the Heart', was all Maura could remember. And all she was able to say before breaking down.

Maura's birthday was cancelled and amidst the tears they transferred the playlist to Annie's funeral.

Em hated stories of the funeral more than anything.

Though people said they'd never been to a nicer one.

Maura sang 'Total Eclipse of the Heart'.

Suze's mum had looked after Em, but Em couldn't help but wish she'd been allowed to say goodbye, even if three was too young to remember it.

Em's phone beeped again: *I will not take no for an answer*, said the message.

And downstairs she heard a child cry, then a laugh and some more bickering. The bickering was caused by differences in how to raise the child, and it was annoying to hear, but she was confident they would move through this stage, and it would stop. The thing with Martin was that he was juggling a lot as an older dad with a twenty-year-old *and* a toddler and his work as a primary school teacher at the school round the corner.

Soon they would be moving from their South London cottage with a galley kitchen that they'd lived in since striking out from Claire and Karl's house to a smaller house in a different but more interesting neighbourhood, with affordable nursery care. It had been a good time for Em to move out, given she'd be travelling and then moving in with friends, probably with Walt if he could get his act together. Maura lived down the road from Martin's new place and planned to pop in and see him in between her teaching adult education classes, more painting and more office work and helping him out with his toddler. When her twins had moved out, she said the silence in the house was deafening and that she desperately missed having someone to look after.

Maura was the one who had introduced Martin to a friend of hers who would become his future wife, a Spanish ceramicist called Julianna who fell in love with Martin quickly. Martin had been shy, then ambivalent, then after briefly attempting to play hard to get, had soon given up and fallen in love, too – and within months they were gifted the child they never thought they'd have. The baby, now two, was named Carly.

Em pointed out that this name might be confusing given the existence of his friend Karl, but Martin said he could live with that because these similarities, like humour and goals and values, were what bonded a group of people – *the village*, as he liked to call it – just as much as blood and inherited genes.

As well as the happy times there had been a few arguments the year after Annie died, almost like everyone had been waiting for a respectful time to have them. The first was Maura's final argument with Dex. Their attempts to spend restorative time together fell apart, their marriage already spattered and made weak with the bullet holes of their past disagreements. There were no other parties involved and they cited irreconcilable differences. But when Suze spoke to Em about Maura and Dex's divorce, the story felt different. Suze once said there was rarely one thing that caused a divorce. Or one person. Often it was both. And time was always a factor: that if enough of it passed then one of you was likely to do or say something the other couldn't forget. Em hadn't pressed her on it further, deciding that perhaps she didn't want to know. And anyway, Suze said it wasn't her story to tell.

Besides, Maura still met Dex for coffee even though their children had both left home and the need for co-parenting was long gone. They bickered and argued, and Maura said that some things broke and were never meant to be mended. The upside was that, since breaking up with Dex, Maura had never painted, or enjoyed painting, as much as she did now.

Em liked Dex, though she never made much of it with Maura for fear of sounding disloyal. But she admired his single-mindedness – it was interesting – and she liked that he now made greetings cards which she used for birthdays and Christmases. He was a softie when you got to know him and, as a man of few words, it made him a good person to go to the cinema with when she, too, did not feel like speaking.

The second argument, after Maura's not-so-final argument with Dex, had been with Claire and the rest of the friends. It turned out that she had been stewing on why exactly Martin had been given sole responsibility for Em when she had the capacity, the resources and the motherly instinct. Claire's capacity for stewing, according to Maura, would have been better directed into a cooking course or something that stopped her from obsessing over soft furnishings, and Annie's decision not to ask her might have been something to do with the fact that she wanted to divorce them all and other indiscretions, *but hey.*

But, as Em would agree a thousand times over, Annie's decision to choose Martin had been the right one. Martin had come with a personal recommendation from Suze, which had been rubber-stamped by Karl and Dex when Annie had been told how valiantly he'd looked after everyone that weekend.

And anyway, Annie had been nursing her own instinct about him. She'd listened to how he'd talked about the people he loved, watched how much effort he put into helping them and had seen him with his own son – enough to know that he was a good man. And even better, a good father.

Maura held no ill-will herself about not being Em's official mum: she'd made it very clear to all of them that she hadn't the bandwidth for anything more than a disintegrating marriage at the time, alongside trying to get her own shit together and be a single mum to the twins in those years that followed. The idea of dealing with toddler sleepless nights alongside her own grief at having lost her best friend might have been too much – and then they'd all have been in a mess. Anyway, they could surely all agree that Em was much better served by Maura as she was now: annoying aunt, boozy older sister, cupid, cook and all-round fucking legend.

Likewise, Suze had held no ill-feeling, knowing that Annie wanted her to do the things that made her happy. And so, she had pressed on with her research and travels as she always said she would, coming into her own as Em's teacher and guide in the realm of international medicine and spiritualism when it was needed.

But Claire had failed to let go of her unique hurt which had proved her point that she had never felt secure in the group in the way the rest of them did. This was a conversation which Em often observed between the women, watching Maura raise her eyebrows and say there was complexity to all things. That you couldn't erase the mistakes of the past by thinking you could step into the role of being someone's mum. That none of them were going to get to the end of their lives without wishing there were some things they hadn't said and done, so . . . Slowly and quietly, over a few years, Claire drifted apart from them all – as she always said she would, though with less drama and violence than she'd first proposed on the island. No one said anything much about it other than Suze, who commented that just because you'd bought a seven-thousand-page book and had emotionally invested in 60 per cent of it, didn't mean you were hidebound to finish it.

There were other books Claire clearly wanted to read.

Em's phone buzzed with a message from someone else: *I'm so proud of you. You're the bomb.*

Em felt unlucky not to have known the mum that hated paper-bag waists and shapeless kaftans, that always liked to finish a job and could moonwalk and liked cooking crumbles because they were easy and delicious with custard, and hated being hemmed in by a sleeping bag and loathed cold winds and camping and loved laughing and cocktails more than wine, comedy more than drama. Who let Maura tell the stories, who cajoled and looked after and was looked up to. Who'd had the guts to use her last remaining physical strength to save them all.

But, as she listened to a piece of happy pop rising up from the piano and through the house, and her brother being told off for eating all the biscuits, again, she knew she was also beyond lucky to have her friends. Walt would call up and ask her if she wanted a coffee, soon. And later he would take her to the pub with the group of friends she would travel the world with for the next six months.

Ray, *I will not take no for answer,* who wanted her to have the window seat on the plane the next day because he was a kind person and he knew she loved to look at sunlight on clouds.

And Marnie, *I love you, are you readyyy*, who had planned the pub and karaoke so she could sing 'Total Eclipse of the Heart', knowing that these things would be both celebratory, cheering and cathartic for her best friend on such a milestone of a day.

And Ken, *I'm so proud of you, you're the bomb*, with his mad jokes.

And geeky, lovely, pretty Pete who she secretly thought she might fancy.

She breathed out when she was with them. They were funny and happy and sad and outrageous and quiet and interesting and dull and maddening and fiercely ambitious. They were wasters, wingmen and North Stars, and she loved them fiercely.

There was a knock at her bedroom door.

It was Martin, dressed in a gleaming white dress shirt, the collar unbuttoned, and his pyjama bottoms, all splatted with baby food, holding baby Carly in one arm.

He looked at her, unable to speak for emotion.

'Here,' he said, 'can you take Carly? I need to make the sandwiches for the picnic.'

Em smiled. 'You could always put her in the highchair? It's OK – I'm OK. I don't need a cuddle.' She smiled. 'But thanks for bringing her up. I'll cuddle her anyway.'

'OK, OK,' he said, hesitating. 'I love you,' he said.

'I know.' She did know, too. Because he told her every day.

'You can stay with us any time. There will always be a room for you.'

'I know,' she said. Because he'd told her that most days for the last six months.

He opened his mouth to speak, but then cried. 'The thing

is, I'm struggling to come up with a final piece of wisdom, like your mum might. Leaving home is a milestone and I know she'd have something to say about it. I know you're ready and all, to face the world. Look at you! You're amazing. The thing is that I don't think I'm done with being your mum and dad yet.'

They hugged each other, and cried. Because of how much they loved each other. And because of the grief that never went away for Em. And because of the new truth, and the new story, which was that he had a new family now and she was going out into the world to find her own way of living without him.

'I almost forgot,' he said, pulling a folded card out of his pyjama pocket. 'Maura left it on the hall table for you last night.'

It was a black-and-white postcard of James Dean in jeans and a T-shirt, Maura's looped and inked words scrawled on the back.

This is your reminder to pack a charged phone, water, snacks, flares, antibiotics and bandages, wherever you're going – and I don't just mean a mountain range or desert island, I mean the pub. Do not leave home without them, I repeat: do not leave home without them. Eat your greens. Be yourself. Know that your mum loved you then and that we love you now – and between us you will be loved every single day of your life. M x

Acknowledgements

Huge thanks to the tireless and talented team at HarperFiction: especially Martha Ashby – my forensic and endlessly creative editor who challenges me in the best possible way. Many thanks to Katelyn Wood, Martha's excellent editorial assistant, and for the extraordinary eagle eyes of copyeditor Kati Nicholl and proofreader Linda Joyce. Immense gratitude to the special talents that make this story visually arresting to the outside world: for Kate Styling's brilliant cover, Emily Langford's design and the keen production skills of Sophie Waeland. Big thanks to those that get this book onto the shelves: Holly Martin and Harriet Williams in Home Sales and Angela Thomson in International Sales, Liz Dawson and Elinor Fewster in PR and Sian Richefond in Marketing. And a big shout of appreciation for Fionnuala Barrett in Audio Production.

Everlasting thanks to my straight-talking, confidence-inspiring literary agent Veronique Baxter at David Higham Associates, and to my Film and TV guru and friend Emily Hayward-Whitlock at The Artists Partnership.

To my early readers Emma Barker, Emily Pedder and dear sister Louise; I appreciate your time, kind words, cheerleading and searing feedback. And to my later reader, Tom: thorough, unsparing, but always in the best interests of the work.

In the three years it took to write this book, there was death and love and illness and friendship and partnership and laughter: oftentimes so much of it that my heart was both broken and full all at once. Life often moved much faster than my ability to absorb and write about it, so in the end I had to settle for a moment in time rather than delay its delivery a moment longer. The story was not heavily reliant on factual research, though I could not have done without reference to the brilliant *Sea Fever* by Meg Clothier (any inaccuracies are my own), or Bear Grylls on Netflix. It was conversation with family and friends that mostly inspired the story. I feel like I've found the best conversationalists and the biggest hearts in the business. You know who you are, and you're probably looking for yourselves in the pages of this book. Any similarities are purely coincidental, but you are, and always will be, an endless source of fascination to me.

One friend in particular deserves special mention – Melissa, because she'd kill me if I didn't, and because we've lived in each other's top pocket for exactly forty years at the time of writing. There is so much plot to our real-life friendship, to date, that even the most seasoned Hollywood producer would struggle to find it credible. I call her now what I called her when I was seven. My best friend.

Thank you to Kate and John, my dear in-laws, for housing me for three consecutive summers as I tried to hit deadlines, each time during periods that coincided with seismic life events, when I would speak far too loudly on the telephone and emerge, ragged and covered in ink, as they lovingly fed the kids peanut butter sandwiches.

And a very special thanks to my mum and dad. Several drafts were written between hospital visits, home visits and saying goodbye. Nigel and Jenifer were, are, special parents and souls who loved words and art, each other and their children. I will always keep going, I will always reach for the stars and I will always, always love you.

And my boys. All three of you. My sons, Jack and Griffin. Sweet and kind and full of fire. If you're going to get in trouble for anything, may it always be for talking too much. Please, never stop. I love you so very much. Finally, my forever-thanks to Tom, who untangles my heart with the same elegant dexterity he uses to untangle my necklaces. Laughing with him clears every grey sky and makes sense of absolutely everything.

If you enjoyed *The Last Weekend*, turn the page for an extract from Hannah Begbie's gripping and emotional novel, *Mother* . . .

PROLOGUE

We were a normal family for exactly twenty-five days.

On the second day we brought her home from the hospital in a car seat. We put it down on the black-and-white weave of the living room rug and Dave said, 'I feel like I can breathe again.' Because for most of the pregnancy it was like we had held our breaths.

'Dave, come on. She's almost asleep.' My smile was fading but his was wide and bright like a row of circus bulbs and part of me thought, let him just enjoy it.

'BABY!'

His volume made me flinch. 'Dave, please stop.'

'What? Come on! Mia is here!'

Mia. Found on page 89 of *The Great Big Book of Baby Names* and circled like a bingo number. He kissed me on the forehead and I smiled for him. I kissed Mia and there we were, connected in a Russian doll of kisses. *What a lovely family*, someone looking on might have said.

'It's all right,' he whispered. 'Nothing's going to get us now.'

And I believed him. I really think I did.

*   *   *

It was the kind of summer where everyone knew it was going to be a good one, right from the first days of the end of spring. The week she was born, the doorbell rang twice a day with deliveries of fresh-baked muffins, wrapped packages of soft toys, and cards printed with storks, peppered with sequins.

Mum, my sister Caroline, Dave's mum. Our house seemed constantly full of people making the tea, padding in and out of the living room in their socks holding plates of cake, burbling their news. I would look up occasionally, to make a show of listening, but she was always there, cradled in my arms – a tiny person wrapped warm and safe in blankets, peacefully living out her first days in soft, new skin that shone like crushed diamonds.

I am *lucky*, I thought, in the mornings, as Mum emptied the dishwasher and waxed lyrical about the church pews being cleaned with an alternative furniture polish that had given Sarah-from-six-doors-down a terrible thigh rash.

I am so *fortunate*, I thought in the afternoons, as Dave and I walked – no, strolled – in the local park, gripping pram handle and coffee cup, like all the other parents.

A hood and a hat for the blinding sunlight.

Balled socks and folded babygros in neat stacks.

Floral fabric conditioner and frying onions lacing the air and warm, sweet milk everywhere. Bubbling away in me. Poured over the porridge that would feed me, so that I could make yet more milk to feed her. I never felt like an animal, not in the way of feeling hunted or preyed upon, but I also didn't feel any more complicated than an animal. It was hard to explain exactly. Grazing and feeding her. Sun up, sun down.

There were plenty of times when, despite how happy I was, how honestly happy I was, I would start to think about the past. But I could always stop myself, because the important thing was that she was here.

Dave and I had spent ten years together already, looking at each other – across kitchen and restaurant table. Staring and blinking and watching and glancing in bed, meeting rooms, waiting rooms and at parties. De-coding the hidden messages in each other's eyes. We knew every wrinkle, line and tic in each other: the single eyelash that ran counter to the rest. How the face contorted with laughter and tears.

The right time, then, to greet something new, a new version of ourselves with her barely there hair and tense red fists wrapped in a cellular blanket – cellular, like the mathematics paper marked with its complicated workings and rubbings out.

And there were other times, more than I care to remember, when Mia writhed and bobbed and made her warning siren sounds with a rounded mouth. And I worried. Like any mother would. I would pull her away from a feed, the sweat that had once sealed us now escaping, tickling and itching, all the while thinking: She is in pain. Something is hurting her.

'She needs a new nappy, that's all,' Dave would say. 'You're just worried about things going wrong.' That smile again.

Didn't he know that after ten years together you can tell a genuine smile from a fake smile?

Why didn't he say what he meant? *Don't spoil this for us, Cath.*

On the early evening of the twenty-fifth day I drew the curtains against the setting sun and answered a phone call.

'Is this the mother of Baby Freeland?'

Her mother. Hers.

Yes, I belonged to her.

'Mia Freeland is her name now.'

I wanted her tone to change, to lilt into a floral excla-mation of how *lovely* a name, but she was hesitant. She told me that her name was Kirsty and she was a health visitor, based at our local GP practice in Terrence Avenue.

'There were some results from the blood test, the heel-prick test,' she said.

I got hold of a flap of skin on the edge of my thumb-nail and sucked through my teeth as it tore. *Test.* My four-letter word. Dave and I had failed so many tests already, each time more stinging than the last. But Mia was here now. Our final pass.

'Are you still there?' said Kirsty.

The heel-prick test, yes. They had taken a spot of blood

from Mia's heel when she was only a few days old, like they did with every newborn in the country. I had flinched when the thing like a staple gun had punctured her snow-white skin, so much worse than if it were piercing my own. A card was pressed to this tiny new wound and then lifted away to reveal a roundel of red. Now there were results. They hadn't told me to expect results.

'Yes, I'm here. Do you phone everyone with their results?'

'Not unless there's something, you know, *definite* to say. In Mia's case they are *inconclusive*, which means we need to do more tests. Can you come to Atherton General tomorrow morning at eleven?'

'The hospital?'

'Yes, Atherton General, a bit past Clyde Hill . . . Fourth floor, paediatric outpatients' reception. They'll know to expect you.'

'But what are the tests for?' My stomach twisted and complained.

'Her levels look a bit abnormal.' There was a pause and paper shuffle. 'For cystic fibrosis. I'm putting you on hold for a moment.'

The soft thump of blood drummed its quick new tune in my ears as I googled:

Cystic fibrosis – A genetic disease in which the lungs and digestive system become clogged with thick and sticky mucus . . .

Stomach pain . . .

Trouble breathing . . .

Must be managed with a time-consuming, daily regimen of medication and physiotherapy . . .

Over the years, the lungs become increasingly damaged and eventually stop working properly . . .

Debbie Carfax, twenty-three, was diagnosed with cystic fibrosis at the age of two and has been told she has less than . . .

Catching the common cold could kill this young man with cystic fibrosis as he waits for a life-saving lung transplant . . .

End-stage cystic fibrosis and how to manage the final days . . .

One in every 2,500 babies born in the UK has cystic fibrosis . . .

Average age of death . . .

Like drowning . . .

Just breathe.

A piece of hold music droned on, vanilla and classical, chosen to calm interminable situations.

I could feel the adrenalin rise inside me. Everything sharpening, narrowing, ready for flight as I stared at that single question.

Her levels looked abnormal.

I understood that there was a level to everything.

Under the right level, you drowned.

Above the right level, you overflowed.

Finally, a new crackle as the hold music was killed.

'Yvonne says it'll be something called a sweat test. You'll need to bring lots of blankets for the baby to make her sweat. Do remember that. Blankets. And maybe some snacks and mags to pass the time?' I had no time to reply before she said, 'And make sure that your husband is with you. Have you got the address? Paediatric outpatients . . .'

'Yes. Thank you.'

'Best of luck.' And with that, Kirsty was gone.

I hung up, the appointment details scribbled on the back of a tea-bag box with a free T-shirt promotion.

Make sure your husband is with you is the same thing as saying: *Are you sitting down?* It's what a person says before they give you the news that will knock you to the floor and turn out the lights.

The consultant with a blunt fringe took a deep breath before she said, 'I am sorry to have to tell you . . .'

The hospital, God, just the smell of the place – the mashed potatoes and disinfectant and newly opened bandages – the only way to have kept that air from crawling into my cells would have been to stop breathing altogether.

I threw up when she told us, but I made it to the sink. Still holding Mia, there was no time to pass her to anyone.

Everything emptied.